BEYOND THE
DEAD FOREST

Amazing and sometimes spooky tale of two kids and their adventure to a mysterious land where every decision has life-changing ramifications. The author has created a unique fantasy world that is a framework for the Truth the children learn - and that the reader can learn along with them. This one kept me up past my bedtime on multiple occasions.

—Dave Pedersen - youth leader, Sunday school teacher, camp counselor, father and lifelong sci-fi & fantasy fan

The partners' adventure captures one's imagination and never lets go. Steve Groll has a fascinating ability to write suspenseful stories that emphasize Biblical wisdom and spiritual principles in a most entertaining way. Beyond the Dead Forest is riveting to the terrifying end.

—Susan Cook

I have never been a fan of fantasy literature, but I have to admit that I found Beyond the Dead Forest captivating, exciting, and just a lot of fun. I enjoyed how the excitement grew with each new chapter. Children and adults of all ages will enjoy the wild ride and hate to see it end. I have read it twice and plan to read it again.

—Polly Hart–singer, teacher, mother

BEYOND THE
DEAD FOREST

BEYOND THE DEAD FOREST

THE BIZARRE ADVENTURES OF CARTER AND KAT

STEVE GROLL

TATE PUBLISHING & *Enterprises*

Published by Tate Publishing & Enterprises, LLC
127 E. Trade Center Terrace | Mustang, Oklahoma 73064 USA
1.888.361.9473 | www.tatepublishing.com

Tate Publishing is committed to excellence in the publishing industry. The company reflects the philosophy established by the founders, based on Psalm 68:11,
"The Lord gave the word and great was the company of those who published it."

Book design copyright © 2009 by Tate Publishing, LLC. All rights reserved.
Cover design by Kellie Southerland
Interior design by Blake Brasor

Published in the United States of America

ISBN: 978-1-61566-436-8
1. Fiction, Fantasy, General
2. Fiction, Christian, Fantasy
10.1.27

DEDICATION

To my best friend and biggest fan, my wife, Paulette. Without whose support, encouragement, and love, I would be lost.

To my mother, Joycelyn, who sacrificed so much for her children and who served God at home and in foreign lands. I wish I had told her how proud I am of her.

To my father, Billy, who showed me that I could be creative, I wish I had thanked him for one of the best things he ever did for me.

To my sister, Stephanie, who put up with so much growing up with me.

To my son, Bill, and my daughter, Juliet, who put up with so much growing up with me.

Know that you are all loved.

TABLE OF CONTENTS

FOREWORD

I sat mesmerized watching all the kids sitting mesmerized as they listened to Steve Groll weave his captivating stories. I've had the privilege of witnessing this at camps for children and young teens since the early 1990s. For more than 20 years, I have traveled the country as a full-time speaker/musician. When I am asked for a recommendation for a children's event, Steve Groll always comes to mind first. His humble, gentle manner makes his storytelling that much more enthralling. On top of that, he has even unselfishly shown me how to do several of his illusions!

I love to read fiction, as my bookshelves can testify. I believe there is an intellectual art to telling or writing stories as well as a gift with which one is born. Steve Groll has both of these. As I have read just about everything CS Lewis has ever written, I have observed another dimension to his fictional writings—they can be read at face value for their fascinating and captivating storylines but even beyond that, most recognize deeper levels of meaning and allegories that give wisdom and insight well beyond the surface story. Steve Groll has mastered this art as well.

As I was growing up, I remember reading a series of books about some young investigators who solved crimes and mysteries. Even though I enjoyed them very much, at some point I made a conscious decision to stop reading them because there was not much of positive value that would ultimately help improve my quality of life or result in making this world a better place (unless I decided to become a private detective or a CSI like everyone else these days!). There was nothing bad about these books, but there also was not much that would fulfill or enrich my life.

As I think back on those days, it would have been so wonderful to have a book like "Beyond the Dead Forest" to read. Not only does it have the suspense, mystery, and intrigue leading to that "what's going to happen next" fascination, but it is also filled with valuable insight and wisdom that can help us all in making wise decisions to enhance our lives and those we love. To quote the character called "The Guardian" in the book, "The kind of foundation you build your life on, determines how well you will survive against the challenges of life." In a very unassuming and natural, yet action-packed way, the book shares principles that can help us clearly see the difference between right and wrong in this world of ambiguity, as well as the thrilling consequences when we choose correctly!

I love to use humor when communicating to a group (though you'd never know it from reading this foreword). I kind of have a Mary Poppins style…just a spoon full of humor helps the message go down. Steve employs a similar style by using suspense and mystery to captivate a reader and then before you realize it, you have just absorbed a powerful life-changing truth that may bring a tear to your eye or result in making this world a better place in which to live. He paints word pictures through experiences and not lofty abstract ideals that tend to land somewhere over our heads. I was amazed to see how this "other-worldly" fictional adventure even dealt with such relevant topics as greed, deceit, self-esteem, peer pressure, and even drugs!

As I read this book, I could hear Steve's voice reflecting his genuine down to earth storytelling manner. Since I have heard him tell some of the stories in this book "live," let me suggest using it as a springboard for discussion within a small or large group of people. Many of the chapters could serve as standalone short stories that would be excellent discussion starters for various groups.

And then again, maybe life is weighing you down these days and you just need to escape ... to forget about responsibilities and decisions. I welcome you to travel Beyond the Dead Forest. You just might find yourself mesmerized and seeing life through the eyes of another dimension.

Larry Bubb–International Speaker, Recording Artist, Homiletical Humorist, CEO & Founder of Larry Bubb Ministries, Former TV Show Host (not to be confused with Former Child TV Star)

THE DEAD FOREST

When Catherine Hamsted saw Carter coming for her, she jumped off the porch and ran to meet him. As she approached, Carter could see her heart shaped face lined with annoyance. She was having troubles at her house too.

"It's about time you got here; I've been waiting for fifteen minutes," Kat scolded.

Her tone irritated Carter, but he decided to try to avoid starting their day on the wrong foot.

"Your mom on your back again?" Carter asked. Kat's home situation was not any better than Carter's. Her father left when Kat was only five. Mrs. Hamsted was bitter and would often rant about how Kat's father abandoned her in the middle of nowhere. She tended to take her unhappiness out on her daughter.

"Yes, does it show?" Kat answered with a half smile, her lightly freckled features softened.

"Let's just say I know the feeling. My parents were getting a fight started when I left my house."

"Let me guess," Kat said. "Your mom is getting on your dad again for spending too much time on his computer when he should be spending it with you."

Carter snorted and said, "How'd you guess?"

Tobias Carter and Catherine Hamsted were both twelve years old. Carter's parents called him Toby, but he preferred Carter. Catherine Hamsted preferred to be called Kat. And whenever anyone asked why she did not spell her nickname C a t, she was quick to say, "Because I am not a cat." She preferred to spell her nickname with a K, and liked it when people called her on it. Carter and Kat were the only children who lived (and grew up together) in a little cluster of houses in a sparsely populated part of Texas. The area consisted mostly of oak speckled hills and a river.

The closest town was four miles away, and truth be told, it was not really a town. It was just a convenience store, a gas station, and a café. The convenience store specialized in selling live bait to fishermen who came to fish in the river that passed near where the children lived.

Because of their life circumstances, how they grew up, and because they had similar interests, the children were more than best friends, more than brother and sister.

Of course, there were the usual childish squabbles. Kat took a fiendish delight in the knowledge that she was exactly one month older than Carter. Carter, on the other hand, took consolation in the fact that he was a boy. Even though Kat could do almost everything as well as Carter, and some things even better, Carter was convinced that being a boy gave him an advantage. However, he could not say exactly what the advantage was other than to be able to say, "Well, I'm a boy."

To make matters even more uncomfortable for the male half of the duo, Kat was an inch taller. Carter insisted that the way she wore her hair just made it seem like she was taller, but since she usually wore her hair pulled back into a ponytail, not even Carter believed that one.

Despite the usual boy-girl tension, they liked each other very much. Since they shared similar interests, they decided to refer to their relationship as a partnership in the business of adventure.

"Well let's not let our parents spoil the day. I've been looking forward to getting back to the Dead Forest all week," Kat said as they headed out. "I feel drawn to it even though it's the most frightening place I've ever been."

Carter glanced at Kat as he walked next to her and flashed a disapproving smirk at her attire. She was wearing her favorite lavender tee shirt, blue jeans, and high-top tennis shoes.

Kat met the boy's eyes and knew what he was thinking. He had tried many times before to impress upon her that she needed to wear clothes that were a bit more rugged for exploring. Wanting to ward off a lecture and deciding to have a bit of fun at Carter's expense, she said, "I see you're dressed in some serious exploring clothes there, Toby. All you need now is a wide brimmed hat, and you would look like a forest ranger," she teased with a mischievous twinkle in her green eyes.

Carter frowned as he looked down at his clothes. He was wearing khaki pants, lace-up tan leather boots, and a light brown short-sleeve shirt. "What's wrong with it? I got these for exploring the Dead Forest. At least I don't look like I'm dressed for a sleepover."

Catherine found it amusing that most people expected her to have a hot temper to go with her red hair. Even though, like most of us, she could raise a temper, the blond haired boy was more likely to let his temper get away from him. Kat had a little too much fun with Carter and his tendency to become annoyed. She usually bested him when it came to teasing and poking fun.

"Now I know what to get you for your birthday." Kat grinned. "I'm going to get you one of those hats that Smoky Bear wears."

Annoyance filled the boy's handsome round face and his blue eyes flashed. "I got a better idea," snarled Carter. "Get me some earplugs so I don't have to listen to you."

After a bit of cooling down, Carter changed the subject with, "Did the pictures we took last week come out this time?"

"No, and I don't understand it. My pictures always come out. Even if the lighting isn't right, you can still see what the picture is. And the ones you took were the same as mine: blank."

"Do you think you might have gotten hold of some bad film?"

"No, I took pictures on three different rolls of film, and I had taken pictures of things other than the Dead Forest on all of them. Every shot I took on the three rolls came out perfect except the ones in the dead area."

"It doesn't make sense. We can't get any pictures, everyone we ask has never heard of the place, and when I finally get my dad to go with us to see it, we can't find it. It's like the place doesn't really exist."

"It doesn't seem to exist for anyone but us," said Kat as she looked over at her partner to see his reaction. The boy met her gaze and nodded thoughtfully. For a time the two walked in silence lost in their own thoughts.

Over the past several weeks, the partners had been exploring and studying a mysterious forest that they recently discovered near their homes. The place fascinated them unlike anything had before. They called the strange place the Dead Forest because every tree was dead, and there was nothing alive in it. There were no small animals, no insects, not even the wild grass that grew everywhere else could be found anywhere near it.

The Dead Forest was an uncomfortable place to be. For one thing, the trees were so twisted, gnarled, and deformed that one could call them monstrosities. The bizarre shapes and eerie shadows they cast made it appear that gruesome creatures and nightmare phantoms were sneaking up on you. But when you turned toward them, there was nothing there but another odd shaped stump or twisted branch peeking out of a shadow. The sole natural sound heard in the forest was a chilling ghostly moan made by the wind when it blew through the trees. One other thing that added to the discomfort of the forest was that it had a strong odor of smoke and very ripe garbage. It took a great deal of courage just to walk through the place.

Another curious thing about the forest was that there were seven small, abandoned, one-room cabins near its center. The cabins were little more than wooden boxes. Each one was about the size of a large adult bedroom. Carter planned to focus this day's research on two specific cabins.

Carter broke the silence and said, "Maybe I'm crazy, but when I'm there, it's like...I don't know. It feels like there's someone else there watching us. I'm not talking about the times we see things out of the corner of our eyes that are not there. I mean that it feels like another person is nearby watching. Do you know what I mean?"

"You're right," Kat agreed.

Encouraged by her response, Carter asked, "You too?"

"Yes, I've always thought you might be crazy," she said with a smirk.

"Come on, Kat, I'm trying to be serious here. Don't you feel it sometimes?"

Catherine sighed, nodded, and said, "I have to admit that I feel like there's some sort of presence or power or something. I don't know either, but yes, I do feel it."

They were headed in a northwesterly direction. The thinly forested hills that surrounded the general area were rounded and not very high. As the partners drew closer to their destination, the ground leveled out and the natural living forest grew thinner until the Dead Forest came into view. From a distance, it looked like a strange island made up of weather blackened and rotting trees totally devoid of foliage. Wood chips and fallen branches in every stage of decay covered the ground. On their extensive exploratory adventures of the area where they lived, they had never seen such an eerie place before. They agreed that up until a month prior, the Dead Forest had never existed. It was as they were traveling through the location on one of several visits to a rock formation (that they suspected might be manmade) that they discovered the foreboding place.

On previous expeditions to the Dead Forest, the partners spent most of their time walking through it in order to get an idea of what was there and how big it was. They estimated that the total area of dead trees was about one square mile and the shape of the forest was circular.

Now, they wanted to know who built and lived in the seven small cabins, and why they lived in such a desolate and frightening place. They also wanted to know what happened to the people and what killed the forest.

Since there was nothing in the cabins except dirt, bits of rotten wood, and dust that blew in through the doorways and window spaces, Carter decided to see if he could gain insight by learning some specifics about the individual cabins. On this, the last fact-finding mission that they would ever make to the forest, Carter made a crucial discovery that was so important their lives would depend on it. The discovery concerned the only two cabins that were close enough together that they could be seen at the same time. The children called these two structures the twins.

The twins were about the distance of a football field apart, and while that was not very close, the other five cabins were much farther apart. Carter had not been more than ten minutes into his examination of the first twin when he muttered, "That's interesting."

THE ADVERSARY

Kat stopped measuring the cabin's window spaces and asked, "What's interesting?"

"This cabin is built directly on top of the ground."

"Hmm, that is strange. It should be built hovering over the ground," she said in a mock-serious tone.

Carter, looking annoyed, said, "No, genius. What I mean is that there is no foundation; it's not anchored in the ground. It just sits on top of the dirt."

"Do you suppose all the cabins are built like that?"

"I don't know; let's check the other twin," Carter said, and he headed for the other cabin. He was so absorbed in his investigation that he did not even wait to see if Kat was following.

On first inspection, it appeared that both dwellings were built on top of the dirt with no foundation. However, after moving the ground cover around with his foot, Carter knelt down and began brushing the rotting debris and dirt aside with his hand. "Kat," he said excitedly. "There is solid rock here. Go around to the back and see if the same flat rock is under the dirt on that side," he commanded.

"Yes, sir; right away, sir, would you like me to shine your shoes too, sir?" Kat said as she stood at attention and saluted like an army private. That was her way of telling Carter that she did not appreciate being ordered around like a hired hand.

"Well excuse me all over the place," Carter said as he looked up at her. Kat was still standing at attention. "Will you please, with sugar and chocolate syrup on top, check out the back area?"

Kat smiled and said, "You bet. I'd do almost anything for chocolate syrup." She saluted again and ran off to her appointed task.

"*Girls*," Carter exclaimed through gritted teeth.

After a brief wait, he heard Kat yell, "There's rock back here too!" When she returned to the front of the cabin, she found Carter standing in the doorway looking into the center of the structure with his arms crossed.

"I bet if we cut through that wood floor we would find solid rock there as well. Just like I know that if we cut into the wood floor of the twin, over there, we would find nothing but loose dirt."

"So, what? What difference does it make? Is it important?"

Before Carter could respond, the sky and everything around them suddenly turned dark. It was almost as if someone turned a dimmer switch down to darken a room. It was so quick and dramatic that it caused both of them to yelp as if they had been jabbed in the ribs. They looked at the sky to see if the sun had gone out. There was no sign of it. There were only clouds so dark that it looked almost like a night sky without stars.

So frightening was the weird event that the two, out of sheer panic, ran as fast as they could, trying to get out of the Dead Forest. In their haste, Kat tripped and fell. She fell so hard that even though Carter was a couple of steps in front of her, he could hear the thud of her body. He stopped and turned to help her.

"Are you okay? Can you run?" he asked as he pulled her up.

"I am afraid you are both in considerable danger," said a male voice.

The two looked in the direction of the voice and saw a clean-shaven man of average height step out from behind a dead tree. He had gray eyes, a handsome, strong face, and wore a white robe. His hands were crossed and tucked in the opposite sleeves. The robe had a hood, but it was not covering the man's head. His most shocking feature was his hair: it was so brilliantly white that it looked quite unnatural.

"Who are you? What's going on here?" Carter demanded.

"There is no time for that now; you must hurry," said the man just as a huge bolt of lightening filled the sky. The following thunderclap was so loud that it shook the ground. The robed man pointed to the nearest cabin and said, "You must take shelter now." Due to the partner's panic-driven run, the closest cabin was the first one they had examined, the one built on top of the dirt.

"Come on, Carter; he's right. This storm is going to be dangerous, and we need to get inside. It's close, Carter; it's only a few more steps—*hurry*!" The frightened girl pulled on the boy's arm.

Carter took a step toward the nearest cabin and then stopped.

"No, not that one!" he yelled. He had to yell now because the sound of a mighty wind arose, and it was almost too loud to talk over. With every passing moment, it blew harder and louder. Even though the wind was blowing in the direction of the nearest shelter, Carter insisted, "We must get to the other cabin." To make things worse, a heavy rain started to fall.

"You do not have time for that; it is too far away," said the man. Though the partners had to yell to be heard over the wind and rain, they could easily understand the robed man as he spoke in a normal conversational tone.

Kat was still pulling on Carter's arm as she screamed, "Please, Carter, hurry!"

Carter grabbed the girl by her upper arms, looked in her eyes, and shouted, "Trust me, Hamsted."

She stopped struggling, met the boy's eyes, and nodded.

Kat let Carter lead her back toward the cabin built on the rock.

"*No!* You will not make it in time if you go to that cabin," the white-haired man said. His voice was still easy to hear over the storm. It had a sharp edge of authority to it and something else . . . Was it contempt?

23

The determined boy spared a glance over his shoulder at the stranger. What he saw frightened him more than the storm. Just as he looked back, a flash of lightening lit up the man's face, and it was no longer handsome. It was hard and cruel, full of anger and hatred. It was like nothing he had ever seen on any face before. Despite the chaos of the storm raging all about, this strange man looked like he was standing in total calm. His robe was not moving in the wind. His hair was perfectly still, and he was completely dry.

Carter turned all his energy to getting Kat to the shelter built on the rock foundation. He needed to focus because he was trying to move against the powerful wind and pelting rain. The storm was so fierce that he started to doubt if they were going to make it. Lightning was flashing all around them. Suddenly, a huge bolt of white-hot electricity hit a dead tree only a few feet away, and it exploded into a thousand pieces, showering them with chunks of dead wood.

Kat screamed, "We aren't going to make it. I shouldn't have listened to you. We're going to die!"

That was the push Carter needed. "We're going to make it. Now run. *Run for your life!*" he yelled at her. He tightened his grip on her arm and almost dragged her the last few yards to the cabin.

Just as they stepped through the doorway, they heard what sounded like a wild animal shrieking in pain. They turned and looked back to where the strange man stood. As the lightning flashed, they could see him looking up and pulling his hair with both his hands. The shrieking was coming from him; it was the sound of angry defeat.

The storm continued to rage long after they entered the shelter. For a time it worsened to the point that it drowned out the sounds coming from the creature, or man, or whatever he was.

Kat reached out and threw her arms around Carter; she had never done anything like that before. Rather than protest, Carter put his arm around her. They stood in the dark cabin, trembling with fear. They never imagined that they would ever experience anything as terrifying as this.

Though Carter could no longer hear the thing outside screaming over the sounds of the storm, he was, however, able to see him with each lightning flash. The sight of him sent a constant stream of fear through the boy. Then suddenly, he saw that the man-thing had stopped screaming. He was looking at Carter and Kat with eyes bulging and face contorted in rage to such a point that it was obvious that nothing human could look so hideous. It caused Carter to take a step back. Then with a last flash of lightning, Carter saw the creature actually ride the lightning bolt back into the sky.

After he disappeared, the storm died down quickly. The wind slowed, the rain stopped, and the clouds began to break up.

The partners cautiously emerged from their shelter. "Look," Kat said and pointed to where the cabin built on the loose dirt once stood. "It's totally destroyed." Carter looked and saw that there was nothing left of the foundationless building. "Oh, Carter, you were right. If we had gone into that other cabin, we would have been killed."

Carter usually took every opportunity to say I told you so. However, this felt like a time just to be glad that they were still alive. So instead, he smiled and just said, "Yeah, I know."

THE GUARDIAN

"Let's get out of here before anything else happens," said Carter.

Kat was about to agree when something caught her eye. She pointed off to her left and asked, "What's that behind the clump of trees over there?"

"It looks like fire," Carter said thoughtfully. "I don't like it. This whole thing has been too weird, and I think we should get out of here as quick as we can." The odd thing was that as he was speaking, Carter was walking toward the fire.

"Where're you going?"

"I'm going to check it out."

"I thought you said we should get out of here," Kat protested as she stood watching her partner.

"Yeah, we should."

"I don't like this. I don't like this at all. Besides, it's getting late. The sun's setting, and my mom is going to get onto me if I'm not home by dark," Kat said to herself, running to catch up with Carter.

As they drew near the clump of dead trees, it became clear that what they saw was a campfire. A man was sitting by it and looking directly at the children. As soon as the two saw him, they stopped short. At first, they thought it was the man from the storm. He was wearing the same type of white robe, and he had white hair. Before they could say or do anything, the man smiled and called out, "Come and join me. It is safe now; the danger has passed. Come, get warm, and dry off."

The partners could tell by his voice that it was a different man.

Carter whispered to Kat, "What do you think?"

Kat shrugged and shook her head.

"Come on, Carter, Kat; it is okay. I am here to help," the man said as he waved them over.

"He knows our names," Carter whispered, his eyes wide.

"That is not all I know; I know why you are here and what is happening to you."

"He can hear us even though we're whispering," Carter whispered to Kat again, his eyes even wider.

"So why are you still whispering?" Kat asked aloud. Before he could respond, she grabbed his wrist and headed for the campfire. Carter went along without protest.

As they approached the fire, the man in white stood and pointed to a log across the fire from him. "Welcome, welcome. Please have a seat."

Their host was short; he was only a little taller than Kat. He had the face of an old man. His eyes were blue, bright, and full of kindness. After the children sat down, the old man resumed his seat.

"There now; that is better," their host said with a satisfied smile. "First, let me tell you that I am the Guardian. You may call me Guard for short." The Guardian chuckled as if he had just made a little joke. "Second, I want you to know that you do not have to be concerned that your parents are worrying about you. This place exists outside your time and space. You could stay here a hundred years, and when you return, it will be as if you had been gone for only a few short hours." After a moment of silence, Guard continued. "I see that you do not believe me."

The children had doubtful looks on their faces. "Why should we believe you? We don't know you. We don't know what's going on here; we don't know anything," Carter said, his voice full of emotion.

The Guardian sighed and looked at the children with eyes full of compassion. After a moment he said, "I know, and I am sorry if I seem to take your concerns lightly. Sometimes I forget what fragile creatures you are. I really am here to help you, and even though you do not know me, I invite you to trust me. Perhaps after we get to know each other a little better, you will come to realize that I am telling you the truth."

Unexpectedly, the old man gasped as though he had just remembered something important. "Oh, dear me, you must be getting hungry. Would you like some food and drink?" the Guardian asked as he pointed toward the flame.

Kat and Carter glanced at the fire, and there, for the first time, the children saw two game birds on a spit, roasting. "I don't remember seeing those before," said Kat. "Do you?" she asked Carter.

"No," Carter answered with a look of wonder.

"As you can see, the birds are roasted to perfection. That takes time, does it not?" Guard had a sly smile on his face that seemed to say, *You have not seen anything yet.* "How about we just enjoy this wonderful food?" Guard reached around behind him, brought out some metal plates, and handed them to the children. He reached around again and said, "Here are some drinks for you to start on while I dish up the food." The partners each received a full metal cup.

While their host was putting pieces of the roasted meat on the children's plates, Carter said, "Hey, this is grape juice—my favorite."

"I don't believe it," said Kat.

"What's that?" Carter asked as he looked over at his friend.

"This is chocolate milk—my favorite."

"I am glad you both got what you like."

"You don't expect us to believe it's just a coincidence that we got our favorite drinks, do you?" Kat challenged.

The Guardian continued serving the children, smiled slyly, and said, "I told you I knew a lot more than just your names, did I not?"

Carter piped up, "Yes, but it isn't just what you know, it's what you do. We didn't see the birds roasting on the fire when we first got here. We didn't even smell the meat cooking, and where did the drinks come from?"

"Not only that," Kat said thoughtfully. "What about the fire? Everything was drenched from the storm, yet the moment we stepped out of the cabin, we saw the fire burning as though it had been going for a long time."

"Children, I appreciate your curiosity about these little mysteries, but these are not the questions you should be asking. Why not rest a bit, eat your food, and consider what you would really like to ask me."

The partners sat looking at the plates of food resting in their laps. Then, after a time of silence, broken only by the sound of the campfire snapping and popping, the children began to pick at their food and sip from their cups. As they ate, the fullness of night fell. It felt to Carter like the whole world had disappeared and nothing existed outside the glow of the fire.

"That is good, do you not agree?" Guard asked.

The partners did not see Guard get food for himself, but when they looked at him, he had a plate of meat in his hand, and there was a metal cup of milk on his log next to him.

The children were not hungry. They were still too shaken, scared, and confused about all that was happening to care about eating. After a few minutes of picking at their food, Kat finally asked, "Who was the man we saw in the storm—the one who tried to get us to go into the cabin that was destroyed?"

The Guardian smiled and nodded approvingly as he answered, "That was an adversary. You must beware of him and his kind. The one you met in the storm is a particularly determined adversary that will try to lead you astray at every opportunity. He is deceitful, cunning, and a liar."

"I don't understand."

"What don't you understand, Carter?" asked the Guardian.

"This … This whole thing; why is this happening to us? Why

are we the only ones who know about this place? Why is this adversary trying to destroy us? Who is behind all this? Is it you? Who are you anyway? *I don't understand!*"

Kat could tell that Carter's temper was rising. It did not take much to get Carter angry if he was frustrated or confused. She put her hand on his shoulder to comfort and calm him, but he shrugged it off and accidentally spilled his cup of grape juice into his lap. Embarrassment along with his frustration made his anger flair. He stood up and threw the cup into the fire. Looking at the Guardian he defiantly challenged him with, "Well, what about it? You said you knew everything. What's going on here?"

The Guardian calmly put his plate down, folded his hands, and placed them in his lap. With a firm voice, he said, "Carter, please sit down. I believe Kat has the same concerns you do about your situation."

Looking down at Kat, she nodded and patted the log where he had been sitting. Once Carter was seated, they turned back to Guard, but he was gone.

THE BEDROOM

"Where did he go?" Carter asked. He stood up and looked around quickly. "Guardian," he shouted. "Where are you? Oh, this is great. Now what are we supposed to do? It's dark everywhere but here at the campfire, and we don't have a flashlight."

Kat cleared her throat and said, "We could stay here by the fire for the night and then head home in the morning."

"I guess we don't have much choice. I really hate the idea of spending the night in this place. It's obviously haunted or enchanted or something that isn't normal. At least we're dry now, and it isn't cold." The boy sat back down next to Kat. "I guess we can sleep here on the ground by the fire. We could scoop some of this wood dust and chips into a pile, and it should be soft enough to sleep on for the night."

Kat sighed and said, "I don't know if I can sleep, but at least we can make the pile and try to get comfortable."

"I don't get it," Carter said as he got up and began making a pile. "Why did the Guardian leave? I thought he was going to explain all this to us."

Kat got up to help Carter. "I don't know. The way things are going, I don't think we can trust anyone or anything here. One thing is for sure: once we get out of here, I'm never coming back."

Carter thought, *If we ever do get out.* But he kept that thought to himself.

When the partners finished organizing their sleeping arrangements, Kat made herself comfortable on the pile and stretched out in front of the fire. Carter decided he would just sit on the ground and lean back against the log where they had been sitting.

The children still had their plates of food, and Kat had her chocolate milk. The partners were more comfortable now and beginning to relax. As they stared at the fire, they began to feel hungry, and finished their food. Kat offered Carter some of her drink, but he declined, saying, "It's my own fault I don't have anything to drink." Then he added, "Maybe if I hadn't lost my temper, Guard would still be here."

Kat did not respond; she was too tired. In fact, she was having a hard time keeping her eyes open. She decided to close them just for a moment, and she fell fast asleep.

Suddenly, a loud *boom* woke Kat. She sat up like a shot; her heart was pounding, and she was wide-awake. She could not see a thing. Catherine Hamsted was in total darkness. She could feel that she was in a bed with covers and sheets. That caused her to think, *I must be home in my bed. Maybe everything that happened at the Dead Forest with Carter and me was just a dream.* Beginning to feel relieved, she smiled to herself and thought, *Wait 'til I tell Carter about my dream, what a crazy nightmare.*

Catherine's moment of relief was short lived because a bright flash of lightning, visible through a single window, lit up the room. What she saw in that brief moment of illumination made no sense. It was true that she was in a bedroom, but it was not her bedroom. She had never seen it before; she had no idea where she was.

Kat jumped again as the loud thunderclap, which follows a lightning flash, made the walls shake. Obviously, there was a storm raging outside. She could hear the wind howling and the rain beating on the roof.

Where am I? What's going on here? She was screaming to herself. She was too afraid to make a noise that might give her presence away to whomever or whatever might be in this unfamiliar house with her.

The fact that she was in another storm made Kat think that, perhaps, the memories she had of what happened at the Dead Forest were not from a dream after all. Her fears grew stronger as she began to consider that there might be some connection with this room and the Dead Forest. As a second flash of lightning lit the bedroom, she saw that the room was similar in size to the cabins in the Dead Forest.

Ready for a third lightning flash, Kat glanced about to get a better idea of what exactly was in the room. She could see that the bed was the only piece of furniture, and it was located in the center of the room. There was more than enough space on all sides to walk easily around the bed without touching the walls. The walls were bare and unpainted. In that third moment of illumination, the trembling girl also noticed that there was a door on each of the four walls.

When the thunderclap from the latest lightning bolt shook the structure, Kat let out a loud yelp. She quickly slapped her hands over her mouth and listened intently for any indication that she had been heard. For over a minute, she held her breath and trembled with fear. Hearing nothing suspicious, she decided it was safe to breathe again.

The girl remembered from her scan of the room that there was a door to the outside on the wall to her right. She knew the door would take her outside because of the window next to it. Kat decided her best course of action was to go outside and try to get an idea of where she was. The storm did not seem as strong and destructive as the one the children survived earlier that day. She thought that if she was still in the Dead Forest, maybe she would be able to find Carter or see the campfire if it was still lit. If she was not in the forest, she figured that she might see houses, roads, or other landmarks that would give her a clue as to her location. Since there were no obstacles to block her way, Kat was confident that the door would be easy to find in the darkness.

Sliding out of bed, she noticed that she was wearing what felt like her favorite pajamas. She also had stockings on her feet. The girl was a little concerned that it might not be wise to go out in the storm while wearing such skimpy clothes. But it soon became clear that there was no need to worry about how she was dressed because the door was locked and so was the window.

Kat decided to try the other three doors. Feeling her way along the walls, she found the door that was directly across from the foot of the bed. She put her ear to the door; hearing nothing, she turned the doorknob and pushed it open just enough to see that there was nothing to see. It was as dark behind the door as the bedroom. Deciding not to risk entering the dark place, unless there was no other choice, she quietly shut it.

Catherine moved on to the third door. Again, hearing nothing, except her heart pounding in her ears, she slowly pushed it open. This time there was some illumination. Though she could not see the source of the dim light, it revealed a room about half the size of the bedroom. The room was empty and had no windows or any other doors. Again, she decided that there was no reason to explore this room until she checked out the last of the four doors. She left the third door open because the light allowed her to see the outline of the bed and the fourth door located behind the bed.

This time when she put her ear to the door, she thought that she could hear voices. The sound was so faint that she was not sure if she was hearing something, or it was her imagination. She stood for a long time listening, but she just could not be sure.

There had been no more thunder and lightning since Kat got out of bed. The wind was still blowing, and the rain was pounding on the roof. That made it difficult to determine if there were any sounds coming from behind the door. She finally turned the doorknob and pushed the door open. What she saw was unexpected; she found herself looking down a flight of stairs leading to a basement. There was a light coming from below, but it did not appear to be from a light bulb or a fire. Rather, it looked exactly like the sort of flickering that came from a television.

Cautiously, Kat began to descend the stairs. She left the door open so that she could make a quick retreat, if necessary. After she had gone down enough steps to be clear of the doorway, the door *slammed* shut with such force that the wind it generated hit Kat in the back and almost caused her to fall the rest of the way down the steps. Catherine shrieked in fear, ran up to the door, and found it locked. She started beating on it and screaming, "Let me out! Let me out!"

She kept at it until she finally collapsed on the steps, exhausted. She continued to repeat, in a weak voice, "Let me out. I want to go home." After a time, she quieted. Then, coming from the bottom of the stairs, a woman's voice called, "Catherine ... Catherine Hamsted, please come down here. I want to talk with you."

Kat looked back over her shoulder down the stairs and trembled. She was afraid that the owner of the voice might appear at the bottom of the steps and come up after her.

"Come down, Catherine, or would you prefer that I call you, Kat? I cannot hurt you. I cannot even touch you. Come and see for yourself." The terrified girl did not move. "You might as well come down. The door is locked; you cannot open it. The only way out is down the steps."

After a few more moments of contemplating her situation, Kat finally descended the stairs. When she reached the bottom, she found herself looking into what appeared to be a family room. Rows and rows of books on shelves covered the walls. In the middle of the room, there was an ugly, faded green couch. A beat up coffee table was located in front of the couch. On the coffee table, an old portable black and white television set was the source of the flickering light. There was static on the screen, and no sound was coming from the set. Kat felt somewhat comforted by the feel of the room; it was warm and cozy. She liked to read, and she liked TV. These familiar things made her feel a little less like she was in some horrible nightmare.

Kat stared at the flickering screen and saw a shape begin to form in the static. As the picture cleared, an image of a beautiful woman standing on an empty, white set came into focus. The woman was looking straight ahead. *No,* Catherine thought. *Not looking straight ahead—she's looking at me.*

The woman smiled warmly and said, "Yes, Kat, I can see you. Now you know why I cannot hurt you. I am here on the screen; I am not in the room with you. Come over to the couch and sit down; make yourself comfortable. I know that you have been upset."

The woman on the TV sounded so caring and concerned that Kat did what she told her to do. The fact that the woman was talking to her from a TV would normally have Kat full of questions and concerns. However, she had been through so much in such a short time that the whys and wherefores just did not seem that important at this point.

"I suppose you would like to get out of here?"

Kat nodded with her mouth half open, as though she was in a bit of a stupor.

"Actually, it is a very simple matter. Do you see that little wooden box to your right on the edge of the coffee table?" The image on the TV turned in the direction of the box and pointed at it.

Catherine looked and saw a plain pine box that was about five inches square and three inches deep. "Yes," she said in a weak, faraway voice.

"Good. Now pick it up and lift off the lid."

With a small, trembling hand, Catherine obeyed. After opening the box, she could see that it contained some very cheap costume and toy jewelry. Some of it was made of colored plastic, which a child would use for dress up play.

"Very good; you're almost there. Do you see a ring with a blue plastic jewel?"

The girl searched through the junky ornaments until she found a gold colored toy ring with a blue plastic jewel that was cracked through the middle.

"Ah, very good; that is the one. All you have to do is slip the ring into your pajama pocket to take with you when you leave."

Kat asked, "Is it yours to give?"

"Never mind that; it is not important. Just do as I say, and you will be out of here in no time at all."

"I'm sorry," Kat persisted. "I don't want to be difficult, and I'm grateful for your help, but if this isn't your ring, and I know it isn't mine, I cannot take it."

"Wonderful. Oh, it is so refreshing to find a young person who is honest. I know how frightened you are and how much you wish to go home, and here you are, concerned with this little piece of junk that is not worth three cents. You really are a special little girl. Rest assured, Kat, no one is going to miss that ring or even care that it is gone. It is simply a worthless piece of broken plastic. Now trust me; do as I say, and you will be on your way in a jiffy."

Kat stared at the ring, trying to decide what she should do. Finally, she looked up at the TV and asked, "What if I don't take it?"

"Well, you see, the ring is like a key. By taking it, you are opening a way out of here. Look, it does not matter to me one way or another. I am just trying to help you, but it is your decision."

Kat had never taken something that was not hers; she never had a reason to. She tried to find a way to make taking the ring okay. She figured that if ever there was a justifiable reason to take something that was not hers, this was surely it. Besides, the woman was right: this ring is just a piece of junk. Taking it would be like snitching a French fry out of a friend's box of fries when he was not looking. *I've done that before*, she silently confessed. *Yes, I need to get out of here. And what harm would it do to snitch this little thing that's not even worth a French fry?*

Kat, feeling good about her decision, pocketed the ring, looked up at the TV, and said, "It's done; how do I get out of here?"

"Very good; you have done the right thing. Look over at the wall of bookshelves to your left." Kat obeyed and saw the middle section of bookshelves swing out like a door to a secret passage. "That is your way out. Step through there, and walk straight ahead."

For the first time since she had awakened in the upstairs bed, Kat began to feel like she was going to be okay. She had a way out, and all she had to do was take it. She stood up and looked back at the TV to ask the woman where the passage leads, but there was only static.

Oh well, Kat thought, *I'll just have to find out where it leads on my own. It has to be better than being locked up in here.*

She walked over to the opening of the passage and peered through the doorway. She saw nothing but darkness. Kat stepped into the passage. She reached out with both arms supposing she might feel a wall to follow, but she found nothing. After taking a few steps, she glanced back to see if she was still lined up with the doorway. To her disappointment, there was nothing but darkness behind her now. *I'll just keep going the way my feet are pointed, and I'll come out somewhere,* she promised herself. Yet, after walking for a very long time, there was still nothing. There were no walls or doors; there was only darkness. It was so dark that Kat could not even see movement when she waved her hand in front of her eyes.

It was getting hard to keep panic from taking hold of her. She began to walk faster, and as each moment passed that she could not find anything in the endless dark, she walked faster and faster until she was running, waving her hands around in front of her, and trying desperately to find something, anything, other than this empty, silent, odorless dark.

Eventually, the girl tripped over her own feet and fell hard. The sound of cruel laughter filled the void. It was a man's laugh. Kat lifted her head and looked around, but still, there was only darkness. The laughter continued, and the panic-stricken girl exclaimed, "Who are you? Why are you laughing? Why can't I find my way out of here?" The laughter grew in intensity and she shouted, "Stop laughing!"

The laughter quieted down until it was just an evil chuckle, and then the male voice said, "I am laughing because it is all very funny. You wanted out, and now you are out. What is the matter? Can you not make up your mind?"

"I don't understand," sobbed Kat. "I did what the woman on TV told me. I took the ring that was supposed to be a key out of the basement and to my home."

The male voice was the voice of the Adversary, and it was gleeful and gloating as it said, "I never told you that taking the ring would get you home. I told you that it would provide a way out. Now you are out; you are in the darkness."

"When did you tell me that the ring would provide a way out? The woman on TV told me that, not you."

"You are not very bright, are you, Catherine? I was the woman on TV. I can appear in any form I wish. I can even appear as an angel if it suits my purposes."

"Why do you do it?" Kat asked, bewildered.

"I am the Adversary. I am the enemy, the one who opposes you and everyone. I have you exactly where I want you. You chose to come here. Everyone has a choice. I never make anyone choose wrong."

"But how am I going to get out of here? How am I going to get home?" Kat pleaded.

"That is not my concern. I have won, and it was far too easy. I cannot believe that the Guardian thought that you might be one of the youths of the prophecy. You are pathetic!" mocked the Adversary and then laughed his cruel laugh. The laugh faded away until there was silence again. Kat just sat where she had fallen. There was obviously nowhere to go. Anywhere she might walk would be just the same as where she was. As she thought about her situation, she muttered to herself, "What am I going to do? What can I do?"

She reached into her pocket and felt for the toy ring. She pulled it out, and even though she could not see it, she felt it and remembered what it looked like. She said aloud, "It *was* my choice. The Adversary was right about that. But it was the wrong choice. I'm sorry that I took the ring; I would put it back if I could."

Immediately, Kat saw a vertical line of light appear directly in front of her. It gradually grew wider until it became clear that it was the doorway that led back into the basement room with the books, the TV, and, most importantly, the wooden box. Kat sprang up, ran through the doorway, picked up the wooden box, and promptly replaced the ring. She closed it and put it back on the table. The secret door swung shut, and as it closed, Kat heard the same terrible scream of defeat coming from the darkness that the Adversary made when the partners chose the cabin built on stone to weather the storm.

No sooner had the secret door closed when Kat felt a wave of fatigue come over her so intense that she had to lie down on the couch. She closed her eyes and fell asleep.

THE WILDERNESS

Carter sat staring at the campfire. His stomach was full, and even though he was thirsty, he was starting to feel relaxed and a bit sleepy. He closed his eyes just to give them a rest.

Immediately, he felt something hot and bright on his face. He opened his eyes and quickly closed them and covered them with his hands. He stood up and peeked through his fingers only to find that the source of the heat and light was the sun. The sun was fully up and shining in a clear blue sky. Looking about, Carter discovered that he was no longer in the Dead Forest; he was in a wilderness. All he could see were rocks, sand, and a scattering of scrubby, little wild plants.

He called out for Kat, but getting no reply, he decided to explore his immediate surroundings to get a better understanding of his situation. There were no other footprints around but his own, and these he had made since he awoke. Carter was delighted to find a canteen behind a rock just a few feet in front of where he had been sitting.

When he picked it up, he was disappointed to find that it was much lighter than expected. He had hoped that it would be full because his thirst was very strong; nevertheless, the canteen was only about a quarter full. He took a taste to see if the water was safe to drink and was relieved to find it cool and refreshing. He drank about half, and even though he could easily have drunk it all, he stopped himself. He decided to save some for later in case he did not find more soon. He also thought that if he found Kat, she would need a drink.

Eventually, he came across a narrow walking path. Since the existence of a path suggested that others had passed this way headed somewhere, he decided to walk it in hopes of finding his way back to the Dead Forest or at least finding some water.

The path had footprints all headed in the same direction. Carter slung the canteen over his shoulder and headed in the direction everyone else had traveled. There was no breeze, and it was very hot. The boy was worried that he would have to drink more of his water soon or face dehydration. He tried to keep his mind off his thirst by taking in his surroundings. He noticed that there was some wildlife about. He saw lizards darting among the rocks, some blackbirds, and crows flying overhead. Sometimes a snake would slither across the path, and he would stop to give it plenty of room.

After he had been traveling for about an hour, Carter sat down on a rock to rest. He sipped enough water to moisten his mouth, which was so dry that his tongue was sticking to the roof, and his lips were sticking to his teeth. So far, there was no change of scenery. Everywhere he looked, there was just more wilderness.

Carter was starting to get worried. He was sweating heavily. If he did not find water soon, he was going to be in big trouble. To make matters worse, his face, neck, and arms were already sunburned.

Reluctantly, he started walking again. The dehydration was taking its toll. His head was pounding, his legs were cramping, and his nose was so dry that it was starting to bleed.

He was only able to go another half-hour before he had to rest again. This time he took a full swallow of water, leaving only a couple swallows for later. He realized that if he did not find water and shelter soon, he was done for. His skin was starting to blister, and his lips were cracking and bleeding.

With great effort, he continued his journey. He was wobbly and weak, but he kept putting one foot in front of the other. After he had traveled another hundred feet, he saw something up ahead on the path. At first, he assumed that his eyes were playing tricks on him. Heat waves shimmered off the rocky ground, making it hard to see into the distance.

Shielding his eyes with his hand and squinting to see if he could make out what he was seeing, he realized that it was a person looking down at a body. This concerned Carter greatly; what if the person standing had robbed or murdered the one on the ground?

Carter stopped, focused on the scene ahead, and tried to decide what to do. He could not go back, and he certainly could not waste precious time waiting for the person to leave. Then he saw that the individual was waving him over.

The boy decided that he had no other choice. He needed water, now. If the stranger had water then maybe Carter would survive a little longer. If the person was dangerous, there was not much to lose as Carter was near his end anyway. He took a deep breath and continued walking. As he drew closer, he could see that the stranger was a young man. He was thin, sunburned, and had about three days' worth of facial hair growth. He was wearing sandals, dirty, torn blue jeans, and a dirty, white tee shirt.

Carter called out, "Do you have any water?"

The young man shrugged and yelled back, "I only have about half a canteen; just barely enough for me."

The boy was near collapse when he reached the stranger. "I only have about two swallows left. Do you suppose you could spare a little of yours?"

"I am sorry, no. I said I only have half of a canteen left." The stranger looked at the body on the ground and said, "I am afraid this poor fellow is almost gone."

Carter, with a look of surprise, asked, "You mean he's still alive? Can't you give him a little of your water? You can't just let him die."

"What good would it do? He is going to die anyway. At least I have a chance to survive if I conserve my water and save it for myself. If I give him some of my water, I will be wasting what could be the last few drops I need to make it. I suggest that you save what little you have. You might get lucky. Well, I must be off." The man turned and walked away.

The boy was shocked. He could not understand why the stranger would not share a little of his water with a man that was obviously near death. *I would give him some water if I had a half-full canteen, but how can I give him what I have left?* Carter thought. *If I do, we will both die. It would be better for both of us if I just let him die in peace without waking him just to tell him I don't have any more water. Who knows? I might be able to find water before it's too late for me.*

I need to get going, Carter told himself. But he felt guilty about leaving the man. *What if that was Kat laying there? Would I just go on and let her die?* "Oh, I can't think like that," moaned Carter aloud. *And yet, I don't think I can just walk away and live with the knowledge that I let a person die to save myself.* Carter continued to struggle with himself. *The guy with the half-full canteen just walked away. I bet he isn't struggling with feelings of guilt. He just made up his mind and then acted on it. That's what I need to do; that's the smart thing to do.*

Finally, Carter knelt down and turned the man over on his back. He positioned himself so that his body shielded the man's face from the sun.

The dying man was middle-aged. He had brown skin, black hair, and a thin, scraggly, black beard with gray along the edges. He was wearing dirty, tattered, beige pants, black boots, and a faded blue short-sleeved shirt.

Carter opened the man's mouth and poured a little water into it. He swallowed the water as though by reflex. His eyes fluttered open, focused on Carter's face, and he gave the boy a weak smile.

"Here, let me give you a little more."

The man swallowed and then said, with a whispery voice, "Thank you; you saved my life."

44

Carter frowned as he told the man, "I'm afraid that isn't true. I don't have any more water, and I fear that by reviving you, I have doomed us both. I'm sorry."

The man closed his eyes and said, "No, no, no."

Carter realized that reviving the man only to tell him that there was no more water had upset him terribly. "I'm sorry. I shouldn't have revived you. I don't know what I was thinking. Don't be upset. Please forgive me."

The man opened his eyes and said, "You do not understand, my young friend. Your unselfish act of kindness has saved both our lives." Talking was difficult for the man, but he continued, "I collapsed here before I could reach the pool of fresh water."

Carter understood that the man was delirious from exposure and dehydration. He decided that he had done enough damage by reviving him with no way to help, so he played along. "Oh, I see … well … You just rest now, and you'll be fine."

The man shook his head and said, "No, you do not understand. Behind that pile of large rocks," he pointed at a formation made up of several large boulders, "there is a waterhole. I know this wilderness. I was on my way to the water when I was overcome with exposure. There is no other water for several miles in any direction. If you had not revived me, there is no way you or anyone could survive the walk out of here, unless you had a full canteen of water. Now you must *hurry*. Take your canteen, and fill it."

Carter hurried as best he could around the pile of boulders. The pile was not very large. Still, in his weakened condition the walk around to the back of the formation seemed much longer and more difficult than it would normally have been for the boy. When he finally made it around to the back of the rocks, he saw a pond full of clear, clean water.

Carter let out a whoop of excitement that came out of his dry throat sounding like the call of an old crow. The thirsty boy shoved his canteen under the water, and while it was filling, he stuck his face into the water and took a few big gulps. He came up for air, put the lid on the canteen, and hurried back to share the water with the man on the road.

When he returned to the path, he called out, "I found it! I found the water!" But there was no longer anyone on the trail to hear his good news. Carter looked up and down the path as he called out, "Mister, mister, I've got the water! Where are you?"

Carter scratched his head and muttered to himself, "I hate when that happens."

THE GUARDIAN
RETURNS

"Catherine, Carter, wake up, children." The Guardian was back in his place by the campfire watching the children sleep. It was still dark, and the fire was burning. "I have breakfast for you; I made waffles. Come on now. It is time to talk."

To Kat it sounded as if Guard was calling her from far away. At first, she did knot know if it was real or if she was dreaming. As she became more alert, she realized that it was real. Her body was stiff from sleeping on the pile of wood chips; they did little to soften the ground.

Carter could hear Guard calling, and as he grew more awake he grabbed his neck and rubbed it. Sleeping on the ground had left him with a serious case of muscle cramps in his neck and upper back.

"Ah, that is better. It is good to see you again, children."

The partners looked around with bleary eyes and confused expressions. "What happened? I was in a wilderness and almost died of thirst," Carter said, still rubbing his sore neck and shoulders as he moved to sit down on the log.

"I was in a strange house, and I got lost in a secret passage behind a door that looked like a bookshelf." Kat stood up and stretched before she sat down beside Carter.

"Yes, I know all about it, and you both did very well. I am proud of you." Guard handed each child a metal plate with a stack of waffles covered with butter and syrup. "Eat up. I also have cold milk for you." He reached around behind him and brought out two metal cups of milk.

The children were grateful for the food. They felt as if they had not eaten for a long time.

After taking a few bites and a long drink of the cold milk, Carter looked at the Guardian and asked, "Were we dreaming? I don't know about Kat, but everything that happened to me in the wilderness seemed very real. It wasn't like when you're dreaming and you don't know it's a dream until you wake up. It felt real when I was there, and it still feels real, just as real as here and now."

"It was the same for me," said Kat. "I was really there. I felt in control of my actions and decisions. It wasn't like a dream where you watch everything that happens and you aren't actually in control of what you do."

While his partner was talking, Carter's foot bumped into something on the ground. He reached down and picked up the canteen he had used in the wilderness, and it was still full of water. "It was real!" Carter stood up holding out the canteen for Kat and Guard to see. "I found this canteen in the wilderness, and just before I woke up, I filled it full of water, and it's still full!"

The Guardian said, "Be sure and hold on to that. You are going to need it."

The Guardian's statement seemed to push all other questions and concerns to the back of the children's minds. "What for?" asked Kat.

It was as though Carter had lost the strength to stand; he flopped back down on the log with a thud. "Now, children, do not look so troubled. You are going on an exciting adventure full of challenges, mysteries, and treasure. It is right up your alley. Is that not what you love to do? Did you not come to this dead forest looking for adventure, for answers, and perhaps the possibility of treasure? I would think that you would be thrilled to find out that this place is much more than just a bunch of dead trees and a few rotting cabins."

Kat put her plate down, and answered, "Yes, that's true, but since we've been here, we have been in constant danger. What treasure could possibly be worth more of the same?"

"Ah, what *treasure* indeed could be worth so much, and more?" For the first time since the partners had met the Guardian, he seemed to take on an attitude of reverence. Until now, he seemed to be carefree and jovial, but as he talked of the *treasure*, he spoke with authority and a seriousness that gave the children a chill down their spines. "The treasure you will be questing for is one that is worth more than all the gold and jewels in the world. It is a treasure that comes through facing danger and taking risks. So great is the value of what you seek that there was a time in history when kings and queens went on long journeys to seek it out."

"What is the treasure?" asked Carter, his eyes wide with wonder. "What could be more valuable than gold and jewels? If we find it, can we keep it?"

Guard's expression softened a little and he said, "Yes, absolutely you can keep it. It is meant for you, and it will enrich your life, but I am not going to tell you what it is. You must figure that out for yourselves."

Kat was a bit flustered as she said, "How will we know where to look if we don't know what we're looking for? That makes no sense."

"There will be clues everywhere. The path you take will lead you to it. Everyone who faithfully seeks it finds it. On the other hand, the foolish never value it nor profit by it. From what I have seen thus far, you two are not foolish. I believe that you are up to the challenge. I am confident that you will do well. Now, finish eating, and you can be on your way."

"When I was in the place of darkness," Kat said. "The Adversary mentioned something about a prophecy."

The Guardian shrugged and said casually, "There are many prophecies floating around the universe. Who knows what strange and exciting things you will accomplish on this adventure."

The children had questioning looks on their faces. "Trust me," Guard encouraged them. "You will be okay. Just use the tools, weapons, and resources that you have at your disposal."

"What resources are you talking about?" asked Carter. "We have a canteen, the clothes on our backs, and ... our health," he added sarcastically.

"Well, you have me," Guard said with his arms open wide and wearing a big smile. He was obviously trying to lighten the mood. "You have much more than you realize. For example, Carter, why did you give your last few drops of water to the man dying on the path? Did you know that if you revived him, he would tell you where there would be more water?"

"No, I had no idea things would turn out the way they did."

"I believe you. If you had tried to save yourself as the fellow with the half-full canteen did, you would have ended up like him. You would not have made it out of the wilderness alive. You survived due to a little known principle of life that goes something like this: To save your life, lose it. Somehow, Carter, you knew that. You felt it in your heart and your conscience. You knew that if you saved your life and let another person die, your life as you know it now would have been over even if you survived. Your conscience saved you; a healthy conscience is a powerful tool.

"Catherine, what do you suppose it was that brought you out of the dark place in which you found yourself after you took the toy ring?"

Kat shrugged and looked down at her feet. She was embarrassed and a little ashamed for Carter to find out that she had taken something that was not hers. "Well, I wouldn't have taken the ring if I hadn't been so scared. The Adversary tricked me. He told me if I took the ring, I would be able to get free of the house. I took it. I got out, but it was worse where I ended up than where I had been."

Carter, with a look of shock on his face, asked his friend, "You mean that you trusted the Adversary after what we learned about him? Wow, Hamsted, you surprise me. Why would you do that?"

Kat's embarrassment turned into tempter, and she answered, "For one thing, Carter, the Adversary didn't look the way he appeared during the storm. He was in the form of a beautiful woman on a TV, and she talked to me with kindness. I was afraid, and what I did didn't seem very bad at the time. I didn't know what else to do. I did the best I could." She glared at the boy, daring him to say something else.

Showing wisdom, Carter did not comment further on the matter. The Guardian, however, did have a few things to say. "The Adversary is very clever, deceitful, and dangerous. He will do whatever he can to hinder your quest and lead you astray. Appearing beautiful, harmless, helpful, or as a trustworthy individual are just a few of his tricks.

"Kat, I know that you do not understand why it was so wrong to take the little, broken toy ring. It was not as though you stole a diamond bracelet, was it?"

"That's right. It wasn't very bad. After all, it was broken and worthless."

The Guardian said patiently, "Kat, I want you to understand just how deceitful the Adversary is, so I will tell you why he wanted you to take that specific ring. You might assume that the reason he wanted you to take that particular ring was to make it easier to convince you that it would be okay. On the surface, it seems such a worthless thing. The problem with that thinking is that it was a thing of great value to someone.

"It was the most precious possession of a four-year-old little girl named Trisha. You see, Trisha had a fourteen-year-old brother who was the most special person in her life. He was her best friend, her protector, her hero, her *big* brother. That little plastic ring was the last thing he gave her on the same day a car hit and killed him. Whenever she misses him so much that it makes her hurt all over, she gets that ring, kisses it, and puts it on. She cannot wear it for long because it is too big for her little fingers, and she does not want to lose it. When she is done with it, she puts it back in the box, and says bye-bye to it."

Hearing this made Kat feel dreadful. The thought that she could have added to the pain of that already brokenhearted little girl was almost more that she could bear.

Guard continued, "I can see that you understand more clearly the evil of the one with whom you contend. By talking you into stealing that ring, he was bringing torment to more than one person. Not only did he lead you into the darkness by turning you away from the right thing to do, he almost succeeded in making you an instrument of suffering. That is usually what happens when people do wrong. They hurt themselves, and at the same time, they become the means to hurt innocent people. However, you thwarted his plan. You used a powerful weapon against him. Your weapon was restitution. You recognized that what you had done was wrong, you admitted it, and you were willing to make it right by putting the ring back."

Guard turned to Carter and asked, "Carter, if you have no resources to help you survive the quest, how is it that you knew to weather the storm in the cabin on the rock? Most people would have run into the closest shelter. On the other hand, you insisted on heading for the cabin on the rock, even though it was far enough away to make it seem a risky, if not a foolish, choice."

Carter considered for a minute and then answered, "It was nothing really. It's just that when Kat and I were investigating the twins, I noticed the first cabin we examined was built on top of the ground, and it reminded me of a story my mom told me about two men who wanted to build houses on the beach. One was lazy and just wanted to do as little as possible so he could enjoy the surf. He decided to build on the sand. The other man built his house anchored to a big flat rock. It was farther from the water and took a lot of hard work to prepare the foundation, but it paid off. One day, a hurricane hit the beach and destroyed everything except the house anchored to the rock. "By the time the storm hit us, we had determined that the other twin was built on rock. Since I had already been thinking about the story, it occurred to me that the cabin on the rock foundation might have a better chance of surviving a serious storm." Carter smiled to himself, and said thoughtfully, "I never thought a simple story like that would save my life. When my mom told it to me, I remember thinking that it wasn't much of a story, but it came in handy."

The Guardian laughed and said, "That is a great story! It means so much more than just what type of building construction will best stand against a storm. It actually teaches that the kind of foundation you build your life on determines how well you will survive against the challenges of living. If you build your life on selfishness, only doing what you want and taking the easy way, it is like building on the sand without a foundation. On the other hand, if you seek out and live by wisdom, your life will be solid, strong, and rich.

"Stories are a great resource. Obviously, you already have some good stories and words of wisdom that you can rely on as you go on your quest. And, who knows, maybe the story about you and your adventures will be a source of wisdom for others some day," Guard said with a knowing smile.

That last statement caused the partners to share confused looks. Curious about what he meant, they turned back to ask him his meaning, but once again Guard had vanished.

THE QUEST BEGINS

"Now what?" Kat asked.

Carter sighed and answered, "I guess we go on a quest. Hey, what's that?"

Kat turned to look at her partner. "What's what?"

"That—over there on the log where Guard was sitting." Carter pointed at what looked like a piece of brown paper. He stepped over and picked it up. "It's a folded brown paper lunch bag, and it has a note written on it. It says, 'Head east into the sun and find the adobe.'"

"Well that's something. I guess Guard is a resource. He's given us a clue, and I have a feeling that it won't be the last one he sends us," Kat said.

Carter nodded and said thoughtfully, "Come to think of it, Guard has given us a lot of clues. It seemed to me that what he said was his way of telling us what we're supposed to be looking for."

"What do you suppose it is?"

"I don't know yet. It's just that I have the feeling he was trying to tell us what the treasure is." Carter shrugged and looked up into the dark sky and said, "Some clue, huh? Walk east into the sun. There's no sun. Do you suppose it's some kind of riddle?"

"No, I believe it's supposed to be taken literally. We just need to wait until the sun rises." Even as Kat was talking, the horizon began to grow lighter.

"We ought to start now while the sun is still below the horizon. Once it's up, we're going to have it directly in our eyes."

Kat disagreed. "I think we should finish our breakfast first. Who knows when we'll get anything to eat again?"

The children sat back down and consumed every bit of their waffles and milk. When they finished, the sun was just about to peek over the horizon.

Carter got up and kicked dirt over the campfire.

Looking around, Kat asked, "Where's the paper bag with the clue written on it?"

"I tossed it somewhere. We don't need it. We already know which way to head and what to look for."

"I know, but it might come in handy. Maybe there's a reason the clue was left on a paper bag rather than on a piece of paper."

"I doubt it."

"There it is." She found it on the ground just a few feet from where Carter had discovered it. She picked it up and stuffed it into her back pocket.

"I suppose that's one of our assets. Is it a tool, a weapon, or a resource? Hey, I know, let's take the plates and the cups too," Carter said, trying to bait his friend.

"That's not a bad idea," Kat said seriously and looked down for the plates and cups only to find that they, like the Guardian, had vanished.

"Oh, come on, Kat. You can't be serious. I don't want to be dragging a lot of junk with us. Let's just get going and leave the plates."

"It doesn't matter; they're gone like the Guardian. Let's get out of here before we vanish too."

Carter shouldered the canteen and turned toward the rising sun. The children had taken only a few dozen steps when they found a dirt road heading straight into the fully risen sun.

Now that they were beyond the Dead Forest, they found themselves in an area thinly forested with oak trees. Green shrubs of various sizes were scattered about, and brown wild grass covered the ground. It was very similar to the terrain they were used to exploring. In fact, the children were encouraged by the familiar feel of the place.

The more distance the children put between themselves and the Dead Forest, the better they felt. It was a beautiful day. The sky was blue, and a gentle breeze from the east blew into their faces. It was the first time since the killer storm that things seemed normal again. The children traveled in silence for the first couple of miles. Carter seemed to be deep in thought. Kat finally broke the silence and said, "A penny for your thoughts."

"Wow, I haven't heard that one since my grandmother died." Carter sighed and answered, "I'm not sure what to make of all this, but I believe we're in for the adventure of a lifetime. I also think that we should try to go with the flow. If we accept the fact that we're a part of something mysterious and beyond our understanding, then we don't have to be overwhelmed with fear. We should take things as they come and deal with them the way we always have. Guard was right, you know; this is right up our alley. It's what we love to do, and I'm looking forward to what's out there. I'm also excited at the prospect of finding treasure. How about you, what do you think?"

Catherine turned her thoughts inward and began to contemplate the danger of their situation. In spite of the Guardian's confident, even jovial demeanor, Kat was naturally skeptical of his motives. It is true that she, like Carter, loved to explore and venture out to see new things, but most of their wanderings were close to home and very natural. This, on the other hand, was something much bigger than anything they had ever imagined. She knew that this was going to be dangerous. They had already come close to death in their first few hours of being in the Dead Forest, but she did not want Carter to know how afraid she was. She smirked and said, "Okay, but if I get killed, I'm never gong to speak to you again."

Carter smiled at her and said, "Cool, that's another good reason to go on the quest."

Kat yelled in mock rage and punched her friend on the shoulder.

"*Ouch!* That's going to leave a mark."

"Good. It'll serve as a reminder that there's more out here for you to fear than just the Adversary."

It was approaching noon, the children had walked about eight miles, and though the road wound through gently rolling hills, the general direction was still east. The landscape had not changed, and except for a few blackbirds, some ground squirrels, and a jackrabbit or two, there was not much to look at. Besides getting a little bored, the partners were feeling hungry and tired.

"Tell me something, Carter. What is an adobe?"

"An adobe is a building made out of sun-dried mud bricks. It's built in dry areas that have little rainfall. If you didn't know what we were looking for, why didn't you ask me earlier?"

"I was hoping that you would say something about it and I could figure out what it was without having to ask. But, since you haven't, I figured I would just go ahead and ask, hoping you wouldn't make a big deal out of it."

"Oh, come on now, when have I ever made a big deal out of the fact that I knew something you didn't? I would never do that." Carter smiled smugly.

"Okay, here it comes. Let me have it, and get it over with." Kat was resigned to the fact that Carter was going to give her the "business."

"No, Hamsted, you did the right thing. We need to work together on this."

"I can't believe it, Carter; you're actually being mature about it. I have to say, I'm finding a new respect for you."

Carter was about to change the subject when he was interrupted by Kat, who yelled, "Hey, look at that! I think those are blueberry bushes." Kat pointed straight ahead at a large clump of bushes growing along the side of the road.

Carter ran toward the bushes as he shouted, "You're right! I see berries! I love blueberries."

The children wasted no time getting started picking and eating large handfuls of the sweet fruit. After they had eaten their fill, they sat down under a large oak tree for a much-needed rest.

Sitting in the shade with their heads resting against the trunk of the tree, Carter rubbed his full stomach and let out with a long belch. It was so loud that it startled some blackbirds sitting in the top of the tree, and it caused them to fly off as they squawked their protest at being disturbed.

Carter expected his partner to verbalize her disgust at his rudeness, but was delighted and quite impressed when Kat exhibited her own belching prowess with an equally loud, though not quite as long, burp of her own. She quickly clamped a hand over her mouth and began to giggle.

"Wow, that was impressive."

Kat's giggles turned into a laugh, and then the laugh turned into snorting.

When his partner started snorting, Carter started laughing too. This went on for some time because when Carter started laughing, Kat snorted even more. Every time the girl snorted, the boy laughed harder, and so it went.

After the children regained their composure, they decided it was time to continue their journey. Kat suggested that they fill their paper sack with berries for later.

Carter responded, "Good idea. I'm glad I didn't throw that sack away."

"What do you mean? I was the one who ..." Kat flared and then stopped as she saw the mischievous grin on her partner's face that said, *Gotcha.* She grinned at herself as she started filling the sack.

Continuing their walk, they shared their stories of what happened to them when they fell asleep at the campfire. After that, things were rather dull the rest of the afternoon as they continued their search for the adobe.

Carter did find a way to have a little fun by periodically belching. Every time he did, it started the two laughing all over again. The children did not know it, but it would be the last bit of fun that they would enjoy for a long time. It was going to be night soon, and with the night would come new terrors for them to face.

THE INCONVENIENCE STORE

About five miles beyond the berry bushes, the dirt road gave way to a paved road with a broken white line painted down the middle. Shortly after they came to the blacktop, the entire landscape changed. The rolling hills, the oak trees, and the brown wild grass gave way to fields of ripe sunflowers. The plants were taller than the children, and as they traveled, the fields grew thicker. Eventually, they became so thick that it was impossible to see through them.

Things got even more worrisome once the sun started to dip below the sunflowers. As the shadows grew long, it occurred to Carter that they had no flashlight, no matches, nothing to see by when it got dark. He decided not to mention this to his partner just yet. He hoped that the road might lead to a café or gas station where they could purchase what they needed before it got too dark.

Breaking into Carter's thoughts, Kat asked, "Don't you think it's strange that we've been walking all day, and we haven't seen a car, a house, not even a sign? And where's the adobe?"

"We could be on a private road, and if we are, there wouldn't necessarily be any signs."

"It seems to me that this is a bit long for a private road. Oh, what am I saying? Nothing is as it should be in this place. Wherever we are, it's all part of the same existence as the Dead Forest."

Carter nodded. "I believe so. That's what I meant earlier when I said we're a part of something mysterious, and we need to go with the flow. I wasn't going to mention this just yet, but it's going to be dark soon, and we don't have a flashlight or matches. I hope that since this place has paved roads that it also has convenience stores; we need to buy a few things."

"I'm glad you brought some money. I didn't bring any. I didn't think we would need it."

Carter stopped abruptly, smacked his forehead with the palm of his hand, and said, "I must be losing it. Money. We need money. I don't have any either."

"I guess we'll just have to go with the flow," Kat said mockingly.

"Okay, wise guy, do you have any brilliant ideas?"

"Let's check our pockets and see if we have anything we can trade or sell," Kat said, pleased with herself for getting a rise out of her partner.

Carter, wanting to get a little payback, said, "That's actually a good idea. I'm surprised."

Kat knew Carter was baiting her, but she was ready for him and said, "I'm surprised too. I thought boys were supposed to be smarter than girls."

Carter opened his mouth, wanting very badly to say something clever, but nothing came to mind. Giving a snort of contempt, he searched his pockets.

Kat grinned triumphantly as she reached into her left back pocket. Feeling a folded piece of paper that turned out to be a ten-dollar bill, she started to report her find when Carter cried, "Hey, look at this. I found ten bucks."

Catherine responded to Carter's good news by holding up her discovered money. "You know what this means, don't you? It means there's probably a place to spend this nearby."

The partners only traveled another quarter-mile when they came to an intersection. There was barely enough light now to see that their road came to a dead-end about twenty paces beyond where the roads crossed.

They stepped out into the middle of the intersection and Carter blurted out, "Look there!" He pointed to his right down the south-bound road. Kat looked and saw an old two-pump gas station. Behind the pumps, there was a rundown shack with a few patches of white paint still clinging to the front wall. A single large incandescent light bulb at the top of a weathered wooden pole provided the only outside illumination. The pole was located a few feet to the right of the front door, and a wooden bench was positioned between the pole and the door. Above the bench was a sign that read "For Customers Only." This was the only sign displayed anywhere around the station. There were no ads, posters, not even a brand name or logo on the faded green gas pumps.

The bright light attracted swarms of flying insects. The shadows cast by the large moths that circled the bulb added to the surreal feeling of the lonely place. The only sound heard was a loud electrical hum coming from nowhere in particular.

Approaching the station, the children saw that a light was on in the shop, but they did not see anyone through the doorway or the small window next to the doorway. Stepping up the single wooden step and into the store, the first thing they noticed was the overwhelming smell of body odor and car oil. Dirty wooden shelves covered with cans of car oil, old car parts, and greasy tools lined the walls.

In the middle of the store's wooden floor, there were a few racks containing bags of potato chips, beef jerky, corn chips, candy, and other familiar snack foods.

There was a sales counter to the left of the doorway. The surface, like everything else that made up the building, was dirty and worn. An old-fashioned manual cash register sat on the counter next to the doorway. On the shelves along the front of the counter were things like candy bars, chewing gum, and small packs of cookies.

Unexpectedly, a man in a dirty beige uniform stood up from behind the counter and slammed his hands on it so hard that it made the partners jump. He leaned forward, glaring at the children with his bloodshot, gray eyes. He had a brown, bushy mustache, a deep cleft in his chin, a bulbous nose, and sun-browned skin with deep acne scars all over his face. He looked to be in his mid-fifties and wore a very unfriendly expression. The name patch over his left pocket simply said, "Owner."

"What are you kids doing in my station?" the man demanded with a harsh, angry voice.

Carter stepped up to the counter wearing a big, friendly smile and said, "We've been walking all day, and we saw your station. We want to buy a few things and eat them on the bench out front."

The man stared at Carter for an uncomfortable length of time. Carter stared back, still wearing his friendly smile; he was determined not to look down or away. "Do you have any money?" the owner growled.

"Yes; we both have money."

"Hurry it up then, get what you want and be on your way."

Carter nodded to the owner and said in a low voice, "Come on, Kat; let's stay together." Their footsteps made loud clomping noises as they walked on the wooden floor. Since there were no shopping carts or baskets available, the children had to place their items on the counter as they shopped. They selected a variety of snack foods and were lucky enough to find a very old soft drink cooler in a back corner that contained glass bottles of cola. The cooler was the type that lay horizontally and had a door that lifted.

At one point during their shopping, Kat saw a dead rat on the floor that had been there for so long that a thick layer of dust covered it over. The sight of it made her shudder. She whispered to her partner, "Carter, let's hurry up. This place is disgusting."

"I want to check out that rack across from the cooler. I think it has flashlights." Carter was right about the flashlights. It also had batteries and box matches. It had something else too: black widow spiders crawling through webs that covered the merchandise. "Nice product display. Did we keep the paper bag after we finished the blueberries?"

Kat reached into her back pocket and handed the empty bag to Carter. He put his hand in it and used it like a glove to reach in and get a flashlight, some batteries, and a couple boxes of matches.

"I think that about does it. Let's pay for this stuff," Carter said with disgust.

Kat was glad when their shopping was finished because the place was revolting, and the owner stared at them the entire time. After they paid for everything, they only had a couple of nickels left.

Before they left the store, Kat got up enough courage to ask the owner, "Pardon me, sir, do you know if there is an adobe anywhere around here?"

"No. There is no adobe around here. But I warn you, do not go into the old stone house. Do you hear me? *Stay out of the old stone house!*" the man shouted, spraying the partners with spittle as he raged through blackened teeth. "Now take your stuff and get out of my shop."

The two travelers gathered their goods into a single shopping bag and headed for the exit.

Once outside, Carter sat down on the bench with the shopping bag in his lap. Kat stood, looking at her partner, and asked, "What are you doing? I don't want to eat here. This place gives me the creeps, and the bugs around this light are terrible."

Carter looked at her and said, "I'm tired. We paid for this stuff, and as customers, we can sit on this bench. Now, you can stand there and watch me eat, or you can sit down and join me." The determined boy reached into the sack and pulled out a bag of potato chips, a cola, and a packet of beef jerky.

It was clear to Kat that Carter was in his stubborn mode, so she sighed in resignation and sat down beside him. "You know, *Toby*, you can be a real pain sometimes." Kat called Carter Toby when she wanted to annoy him. Since Carter was already annoyed with the station owner and the way he had treated them, he just ignored her.

Carter was already chewing on a piece of beef jerky by the time Kat got her cola out and opened. She said in a low voice as she opened a small bag of cookies, "I don't like it here. That man is watching us; he keeps peeking around the door and scowling at us."

Carter shrugged and said loud enough for the man to hear, "I don't care. I'm not going to leave until I'm done eating." Then he took a big gulp of cola and belched defiantly.

"How can you relax and enjoy your food like this? I want to get out of here as soon as possible," Kat whined, and then she glanced over her shoulder to see if the man was still looking at them. She saw him leaning over the counter and peering out the door. Then he casually moved back out of sight.

As Carter ate his junk-food meal in stoic silence and Kat ate hers in fearful silence, a car drove up to the gas pumps and parked.

ENTER MR STEWBORN

As expected, the driver turned off the engine and headlights. The car was dark blue with tinted windows. It was a large luxury model that looked very expensive. The children could not see if there was more than one person in the car, and for several seconds no one emerged from the vehicle. When the owner failed to move out and offer service, the driver began honking his horn. After several loud blasts, the owner stepped into the shop's doorway. For a time, he just stood looking at the car.

When it appeared that the station owner was not going to tend to his customer, the driver got out of his car and yelled, "What do I have to do to get some service around here?" The driver was a man in his mid-thirties, wearing a dark business suit. He was tall, balding, had a pointed nose, and small, narrow eyes. His face was pale and stern.

For a few more long seconds, the owner stared at the customer. The partners were watching with interest to see what would happen next. Then, they saw something that put a chill down their spines. The station owner smiled a full tooth grin that reminded Carter of a wild beast showing its teeth to its prey before it pounced. It scared Kat so much that she scooted closer to Carter.

The grinning man moved toward his customer.

"Fill it up, and wash the windows," the driver ordered.

The owner, still grinning, said in a low, cold voice, "Yes, sir, anything you say." He took the gas nozzle from the pump and began filling the car.

The children could see that the owner was making the customer uncomfortable. The driver's attitude seemed more subdued as he introduced himself and tried to be cordial. "My name is Stewborn. I am sorry about being so abrupt. I guess I am a little tired from my business trip. I have been up all day, and I have been on the road two hours heading for home. I am lucky I saw your station. I was almost out of gas, and I have not seen anything except lots of nothing for over an hour now. I still have an eight-hour drive ahead of me. Can you tell me, if I stay on this road heading south, will it take me to Highway 21?"

"No."

Mr. Stewborn was obviously getting annoyed again as he asked, "What do you mean *no*? Do you mean no, you cannot tell me, or no, it will not take me to Highway 21?"

The owner walked over to a bucket of water that was sitting between the two pumps and pulled out a wet sponge. He began washing the windshield and said, "Head south half a mile, turn east at the first stop sign. The road heading east goes to Highway 21."

"I see. Thank you for the information," Mr. Stewborn said, trying with great difficulty to sound polite.

The owner smiled his disturbing smile again as he reached into his back pocket and pulled out a dirty, greasy rag. He began drying off the windshield with it, leaving dirty streaks on the glass. "If I were you," he said in a mocking tone, "I would turn back and hit the main freeway. It has rest stops, gas stations, and restaurants. If you continue traveling on these country roads, you will never make it home."

The children did not know if it was the attitude of the owner, the dirty streaks he was making on Stewborn's windshield, the suggestion that Stewborn head back and take the main freeway, or all three that broke down the businessman's effort to be civil. "Just do your job, and let me worry about which way I go. Look at what you are doing to my windshield. Stop it! You are streaking it up."

The owner made a strange pulsing hiss that sounded like it might have been a chuckle. He returned the rag to his back pocket as he stepped over to the gas nozzle. He removed the nozzle and deliberately slopped gas down the side of the car before he hung it back on the side of the pump.

Stewborn took out a white handkerchief and tried to wipe some of the greasy streaks off the driver's side of the windshield. He talked to himself, loud enough for everyone to hear, the whole time he worked on the streaks. "I do not know why people cannot keep their noses out of my business. Everybody knows what I should do, but they certainly do not know what they should do."

"I will tell you something else you should do, and if I were you, I would listen to this piece of advice," said the owner.

"Keep it to yourself. I do not want to hear it. I just want to pay for my gas and get out of this insane asylum."

"*Stay out of the old stone house!*" The owner screamed at the top of his lungs.

It was so unexpected and so intense that it took Stewborn totally by surprise. The blood drained from his face. "Yes, yes I will do that. I will avoid the stone house. Thank you for the information," Stewborn said in a shaky voice. With a trembling hand, he reached for his wallet to pay for the gas.

Carter looked over at Kat and said, "Maybe we can get a ride with that Stewborn fellow. It looks like he's going to be heading east, and I don't want to be stuck out here in the middle of nowhere all night."

"Sounds good, but he doesn't seem like the type who would pick up two strange kids and give them a ride."

"Maybe not, but it won't hurt to ask. Why don't you stand next to me and look pathetic or something." Carter looked at Kat and said, "Yeah, like that; that's good. You look like a whipped puppy."

"I'm not trying to look pathetic yet," Kat said indignantly. "I just look the way I feel."

"Oh," Carter said. "Well, keep it up."

Kat wanted to say something snotty, but Carter was already headed toward Stewborn. She hurried to catch up.

Stewborn was handing some bills to the owner as the children approached. "Excuse me, sir, but we couldn't help overhearing that you are going the same direction we are. We were wondering if you would give us a ride to Highway 21."

Stewborn had not noticed the children until now, and he did not know what to make of their unexpected appearance. "What ... who are you?" he asked as he put his wallet back into his pocket. "What are you kids doing out here? Where are your parents? I do not have time to be bothered. I have to get going."

"That is right, Stewborn. These children are none of your concern," the owner said in a belligerent tone. "It is best if you leave them alone and be on your way."

The owner's comments surprised and worried the partners. It made them feel uneasy because it seemed as if he did not want them to leave. They began to suspect that he might have plans for them once Stewborn was gone. This thought caused their appeal to have a sense of urgency to it. "Please, sir, we're stuck out here, and we need to get home. Can you please help us?" Kat pleaded, looking even more weak and desperate than before.

"Are these your children?" Stewborn asked the owner.

"No, I have never seen them before, but they are not yours either, are they? Now get in your car, leave, and forget you ever saw them."

"Please, sir, don't leave us here. We really do need a ride, and I doubt we will be seeing another car out here anytime soon." Carter had enough genuine fear and urgency in his voice to convince most caring people that their need was genuine. Nevertheless, people's pain or need of help was not what moved Stewborn. His arrogance and pride were the things that motivated him. He was not about to let some dirty backwoods gas station worker tell him what he could and could not do.

"Very well, go get in the backseat, and be sure you buckle your seatbelts," said Stewborn as he shot a defiant look at the owner.

"Thank you, sir. Thank you very much," the partners said as they hurried into the car.

"Suit yourself," the station owner said with a look of satisfaction on his face. That look annoyed Stewborn because it gave him the feeling that he had just been manipulated.

Stewborn got into his car and slammed the door. He started the engine and revved it as he gripped the steering wheel so tight that his hands where white as bones.

Stewborn was reaching for the gearshift when there was a knock at his side window. He looked and saw the station owner bent over, peering in at him. The driver rolled his window down about two inches and snarled, "What?"

"Stay out of the old stone house," the owner ordered. Then, looking at the children in the backseat, he yelled, "Do you hear me? *Stay out of the old stone house!*" The man's eyes were bulging, and he had little bits of foam in the corners of his mouth. He looked and sounded quite mad.

"You *are crazy!*" Stewborn yelled as he sped out of the station. The children turned and looked out the rear window. They saw the owner standing in a cloud of dust, pointing at them, and yelling, "*Stay out of the old stone house!*"

HITCHING WITH MR STEWBORN

For the next several minutes, Stewborn ranted about the station owner and the terrible service he received. "I have never been treated with such disrespect and outright rudeness as I was by that gas man. Lucky for him I was in a hurry, or I would have given him a piece of my mind. I cannot believe the arrogance of that bumpkin. How dare he tell a man like me what I should and should not do. And that terrible service he gave me. He put streaks all over my windshield, and he splashed gas on the side of my car. And what was all that nonsense about some old stone house?"

"He said that we should not go into the old stone house," Kat offered.

Stewborn turned and looked into the backseat with a questioning look. It was as though he had forgotten that he had a pair of travelers with him. He seemed to remember his circumstance and turned back to watch the road as he said, "Well, I have no intention of going into any house, stone or otherwise, until I get home." He seemed to calm down a little, and for a time, the three travelers rode in silence.

There was not much to see because it was dark. The glow of the dashboard instruments gave an eerie green cast to everything in the car. Though it had long since lost its new car smell, the interior was so clean that it looked like it had just been driven off the showroom floor. The leather seats were dark brown, and the carpeting was black. The interior trim and dashboard were made of hardwood.

It occurred to Carter that most people who had just picked up two strange children in the middle of nowhere would be concerned about the details of their situation. Yet, as Stewborn began to carry on again, it became clear that he was not even curious about them. He was a completely self-obsessed individual full of inner turmoil.

With a snort of contempt, Stewborn started a new rant. "I called my wife just before I checked out of my hotel to let her know that I was on my way home, and she starts in on me, 'Why not stay the night and get a fresh start in the morning?' I let her have it. I said, 'How dare you suggest that I stay another night in this flea trap of a hotel.' I told her that if she liked being away from me so much that she could just move out. Then she starts to cry and says she was just concerned for my safety. She said that she worries about me driving at night. Well, I do not believe that for one minute. She must think I am a total idiot. I know what she is up too. She is not kidding anybody, especially me."

The children did not understand what he was trying to say, but they were not going to ask. At this point, they decided to say as little as possible.

"Then," Stewborn continued, "as I am checking out of the 'Flea Trap Inn' (That is what they should have named it.), I ask the manager the best way to get to Highway 21. He starts in with, 'You would be better off taking the main freeway because of the rest stops and conveniences.' Then he goes on and on about how the roads to Highway 21 are country roads, and there are not many places to get gas, and if I breakdown I will have a hard time getting help, and blah, blah, blah. Believe me. I gave him a piece of my mind. I told him to mind his own business and just tell me what I wanted to know or else I would report him to the company that owns this flea infested hole-in-the-wall. He finally told me what I wanted to know, but he got me so frustrated that I forgot to gas up before I left town. After two hours, I was just about out of gas when I finally saw that station where I picked up you kids."

Carter was nervous about asking the man anything, but his curiosity got the better of him. "Mr. Stewborn, I hope you don't mind me asking, but why is Highway 21 better than the main freeway?"

Stewborn seemed almost normal as he answered, "No, I do not mind. You are a young boy, and the only way you are going to learn is by asking the right people questions. The reason I am taking this route is that it is thirty miles closer to my hometown than the main freeway, and I am in a hurry to get home. It has been a long, tiring trip, and I just want to get back to the comforts of my own place."

Encouraged by Stewborn's attitude, Carter continued to probe. "I don't mean to sound stupid, but it seems to me that since you can drive faster on the freeway than on these two lane country roads, you should be able to make better time taking the main freeway, even though it's a little longer."

The driver's attitude became cold, and his tone condescending as he answered, "It seems to me that someone your age should be able to grasp the simple concept that if one way is shorter than another, then there is less distance to travel."

Carter just wrinkled his brow and looked at Kat to see her reaction. She returned his look and shrugged. Then, with a slight shake of her head, she signaled him to say no more.

"Well, what do we have here?" Stewborn said as he looked into his rearview mirror.

The children turned to look out the back window and saw a pair of bright headlights off in the distance.

"That is the first vehicle I have seen in over an hour, and it is moving up fast," Stewborn observed.

The partners continued watching the lights as they drew rapidly closer. Finally, the lights were so close that the brightness hurt their eyes. When the vehicle was close enough to pull around and pass Stewborn, it just kept inching closer and closer to his car.

Stewborn was becoming agitated again. The vehicle was so close and the lights were so bright that he was having a hard time seeing. "Why does he not dim those lights and go around? Is this whole area filled with lunatics?" Stewborn honked his horn, rolled down his window, and motioned with his arm for the car to pass. "Come on, you nut; pass," he growled.

Kat and Carter ducked down below the window. They were becoming increasingly fearful as the bright lights inched closer. "Do something, Carter," Kat pleaded.

"What do you expect me to do? We're moving too fast to jump out, and Mr. Stewborn doesn't seem to be the type of person to take suggestions."

Before the boy could say more, their car started slowing down. They sat up and Kat asked, "Are we stopping?"

Stewborn ignored her question, yet it was obvious that he was slowing the car. "Come on...go around...go around!" Stewborn was saying through gritted teeth as he continued slowing. Yet, no matter how much he slowed, the lights stayed the same few inches from the rear of his car.

Finally, Stewborn pulled off the road and turned off the engine. The vehicle behind him came to a stop, but it did not pull off the road. It just sat, idling in the right lane to the rear of Stewborn's car.

For a time, the two vehicles stayed in this position. "What is this maniac doing? Why will he not go around? Well, that does it. I am going to see what he wants," Stewborn growled as he reached for the door handle.

"No!" Kat squealed. "Please don't go out there and leave us alone. He might want you to get out of the car so he can run you down. As long as you stay in the car, you're safe."

"I do not care," Stewborn bellowed. "I have had enough of this whole trip!"

He pulled the handle, and just as the car door opened, Carter yelled, "Wait, he's moving again."

Stewborn closed the door, looked over his shoulder, and saw that the headlights were moving very slowly. As the vehicle pulled along side of the luxury car, it became clear that the bright headlights belonged to an old, black pickup truck. The cab was dark until it pulled alongside the car.

As the passengers of the parked car strained to see who was driving the pickup, the truck's cabin light came on and revealed the owner of the gas station sitting behind the wheel. He reached over and rolled down his window.

Stewborn was furious, and he was ready to let the owner have it with "both barrels." However, before he could get his first word out, something stopped him.

The owner let out with a blood-chilling scream that sent a stab of terror through all three passengers in the car. They froze, gasping in shock. The scream went on for several seconds, and then it abruptly stopped. The station owner lifted a trembling bony hand and pointed at Stewborn as he said, "Do not go into the old stone house." After a brief pause, he started to chant, "Do not go into the old stone house. Do not go into the old stone house." Each time he said it, he said it louder and faster. It was a truly frightening spectacle. As he continued, he seemed to become more maniacal.

Kat put her hands over her ears and yelled, "Stop it! Stop it!"

Carter put a trembling arm around her shoulders and tried to calm her.

Finally, the chanting grew into a hideous laugh full of insanity that continued as the station owner turned the old pickup around and sped off back the way he came.

Kat lost her battle with holding back her tears and sobbed. "What are we doing in this place? I should be home in my bed. I don't know if I can take any more of this."

Carter patted her back and tried to reassure her that they were going to be okay.

Stewborn ignored the children and just sat for a few moments trying to calm himself. When he finally tried to restart the car, nothing happened. The engine did not turnover, and the dash lights remained dark. The car was dead. "Oh, this is *great*! I am stuck out in the middle of nowhere with a raving lunatic running around loose and a couple of blubbering kids in the back seat of my car. This is just peachy. I cannot wait to see what happens next."

THE OLD STONE HOUSE

Kat finally got a hold of herself, and Carter stopped shaking by the time Stewborn tried to restart the car, but when it failed to start, their anxiety flared up again. "What's the matter with the car? Why won't it start? Do something! We have to get out of here *now*! The owner may come back, and who knows what he'll do," Kat said on the verge of hysterics.

"Yes, can't you do something?" Carter asked in a shaky voice.

It was so dark in the car that the three could only see shadowy outlines of each other. Stewborn turned toward the backseat and said, "And what, exactly, do you suppose I can do? I do not know anything about cars. I do not have any tools, and I do not have a flashlight."

Before Carter could tell Stewborn that he had a flashlight, Kat said, "We're parked in front of a house; look." She pointed to a dimly moonlit outline of a small building about thirty feet from her side of the car. "Maybe there's someone home who can help us. Perhaps they have a phone."

Carter and Stewborn strained to see the building. "I see it," said Carter.

"Yes, I see it too," said Stewborn. "It is so dark that I cannot make out very much. I wish I had a flashlight."

"I have a flashlight," Carter said. "I also have some matches."

Stewborn looked at the dark outline of the boy and said, "Why did you not say so before? Never mind. We need to go see if anyone is home."

Carter took out his flashlight and offered it to Stewborn, but the man said, "No, you keep it. We are all going to go up to the door."

Carter was concerned about Kat because he knew she was still afraid. He did not want to admit it, but he was shaken up as well. "I think Kat and I should stay in the car. You can use the flashlight and see if anyone's home."

"If there is someone home, they will feel much better about helping us if they see I have children with me. No one wants to open his or her door to a strange man at night."

"He's right, Kat; we better go too. Do you think you can handle it?" Carter asked with genuine concern in his voice.

The question cut right to the girl's pride. The realization that she was the only one crying and that she was being treated like a weak, emotional girl made her embarrassed and angry. "Of course I can. If you can do it, I can do it," she said peevishly. "Come on; let's stop wasting time and check this place out."

As soon as the partners exited the car, Carter turned on his flashlight and took a quick scan of their surroundings. Stewborn was out of the car by the time Carter focused the light on the building. A cold chill ran down his spine as he saw that the building was a stone house. "Oh no, we can't go in there; it's a stone house."

Stewborn stepped around the car, stood by the children, and said, "So what? I am not going to let that crazy lunatic from the gas station dictate to me what I can and cannot do. Besides, who says we have to go inside? We will just go to the door, knock, and see if someone is home." Stewborn looked at Carter and said, "You go first so we can see our way."

Carter headed up the gravel path to the house; Kat was at his side. Stewborn walked behind the children, looking over their heads. As they drew closer, it became clear to the partners that the building was abandoned. There was no door in the doorway, and the large window to the left of the doorway was broken, with only a few pieces of glass clinging to the frame.

Standing on the porch, Carter shined the light into the house. All they could see were pieces of wood, broken glass, lumber from the door, and abandoned furniture in various stages of decay.

It suddenly occurred to Carter that Stewborn was not saying anything. That seemed odd considering the man had a complaining attitude. The boy expected him to rant about his bad luck at not being able to get help because the house was in ruins. Carter turned toward Stewborn and was surprised at the look on the man's face. His eyes focused on the doorway in such a way that it seemed as if he were looking at a door that was not there.

"Well, I guess there's nobody home," Kat said sarcastically.

"How do you know? You have not even knocked yet. What are you waiting for anyway? Go ahead, and make it good and loud. If there is anyone home they are probably asleep," said Stewborn in his typical stern tone.

"You can't be serious. It's obvious that no one has lived in this house for a long time," Carter responded.

"Do I have to do everything? Get out of my way. I will take care of this," Stewborn snarled as he shoved his way roughly in front of the children. He began knocking on a door that, apparently, only he could see.

Carter and Kat shared perplexed looks as the man started shouting, "Is anyone home? My car is broken down, and I have children with me. We need a phone or some help. Please, is anyone home?" Stewborn stopped the knocking motion, leaned his ear toward the imaginary door, and listened for a response to his plea. Apparently hearing nothing, he began knocking and shouting again. After a few moments, he stopped and listened as before. "I believe you are right.

I do not think anyone is home. I am going to try the door and see if it is unlocked."

"Oookay," Carter responded, as he was beginning to wonder who was crazier: the station owner or Stewborn.

Kat drew close to Carter and whispered in his ear, "He's as crazy as—"

"I know," Carter cut her off as he whispered back. "Just wait for now, but be ready for anything."

Stewborn reached out, took hold of an invisible doorknob, and made a turning motion. He looked back at the kids and said, "It is unlocked. Shine the light inside once I get it opened."

Carter decided that it was best to play along with the man—for now. He waited for Stewborn to open his imagined door and then flashed the light around just as he did when they first stepped up to the doorway. "There's nothing but broken glass, debris, and old pieces of broken, rotting furniture," observed Carter.

"What do you mean? The house is neat as a pin. It is true that the furniture is simple, but it appears to be sturdy. The carpeting is adequate, and I see no broken glass. You need to get your eyes checked, son. A young fellow like you should be able to see better than a man of my age. Now, I think we should go in and see if we can find a phone. I am sure that whoever lives here would not mind. After all, it is an emergency. Come with me," he said as he motioned to the children to follow him.

Kat decided it was time to speak up and said, "We're not going in there. I don't know why you can't see that this place is abandoned and in a state of decay. Not only is it a waste of time going in there, it's not safe either."

Carter backed up his partner with, "I agree, sir. There is nothing in there that is going to help us, and it would be hazardous to wander around in the place."

Stewborn folded his arms and scowled at the children. "It is that crazy station owner, right? He has you two spooked. That is why you do not want to go into the house, and you are making excuses with all this nonsense about broken glass and hazardous debris. Well fine, you stay here, and I will go in by myself. Give me some matches."

Carter tried offering Stewborn the flashlight, but he refused it, saying, "I do not need that. Just give me a box of matches."

Carter gave the man what he wanted.

"Shine the light into the front room. It will be enough light for me to find what I am looking for."

Carter angled the beam toward the ceiling. The ceiling was white, and the light reflecting off it was enough to illuminate the entire room.

Stewborn stepped inside and navigated the debris as easily as if he were seeing the room the same as the children did. "There is a hallway up ahead leading into the back of the house. Keep the light pointed where you have it. I am going to use the matches as I move down the hall."

Straining, the partners could make out the dark opening of the hallway. Stewborn took a few more steps toward and into the hallway and then stopped. He lit a match, held it up, and almost immediately let out a gasp of surprise and dropped it.

"What is it? What'd you see?" Kat called out anxiously.

"I saw someone in a back room looking at me." Stewborn took a few more steps down the hall as he said, "Excuse me, I am sorry to barge in like this, but we have found ourselves in a bit of a fix." By the time he had finished this last statement, Stewborn had traveled to the end of the hall, and he had a second match lit.

From the doorway, the children were having a hard time seeing the businessman. Carter pointed the flashlight in the direction of the hallway. They saw a dim outline of his back, and then they saw the light of the second match flare as he held it up. The children expected him to say something else to the person in the room, but they did not hear any more conversation.

Kat was about to call out to Stewborn and ask if he was all right when flames suddenly flared up where he had dropped the first match. Everyone had assumed that the match went out when it hit the floor. Obviously, the match smoldered and finally ignited the rubbish on the floor. Once the flames caught, they moved rapidly throughout the structure, catching the wood paneling on fire. It happened so fast that a wall of flame almost immediately blocked the opening to the hall.

The partners shouted, "*Fire*! Get out now! The whole place is going up in flames!"

Stewborn yelled back, "I am *trapped*! There are no windows or doors to the outside, and the fire has filled the hallway. I cannot get out. *Help me! Please help me!*"

The children were frantic. The horrific situation was beyond imagining. Carter started to enter the house to help Stewborn, but Kat threw her arms around him and shouted, "*You can't go in there; you'll be killed too!*" Carter struggled to get loose of her grip, but then there was a terrible crash. The wooden ceiling and the rotten support beams collapsed in on the back of the building. Mercifully, there were no longer any shouts or screams coming from Stewborn.

The partners backed away from the house as the fire moved toward the front of the building. For a long time the two stood close to each other, trembling as they watched the fire gut the old stone building.

Carter eventually suggested that they return to the car and wait until morning. Kat nodded agreement, and the two climbed into the backseat. Neither of them said anything for a long time. As the fire began to burn low, the children started to feel the fatigue of their traumatic adventures. Once Kat fell asleep, Carter moved to the front seat and fell asleep.

Carter was the first to wake. The sun was up, and it was late in the morning. He sat up, rubbed the sleep out of his eyes, yawned, and stretched. He checked on his still-sleeping friend and then looked at what was left of the stone building. The outer walls were still standing, but the roof, along with all wooden supports, had collapsed into piles of black smoldering ash. Carter continued to gaze at the remains, when suddenly his heart jumped into his throat. Someone was walking around inside the ruin.

No Such Thing as Mistakes

Carter's first thought was that Stewborn was still alive. He quickly dismissed that notion, and thought, *Maybe it's the station owner.* As he pondered the possibilities, a soft moan came from his partner. He looked at Kat and saw that she was stretching awake.

"Carter," she said sleepily. "You're awake." She sat up and asked, "What's wrong? You look worried."

"There's someone walking around in the burned out stone building."

"What?" she said and turned quickly to see for herself. "Who is it? Is it Mr. Stewborn?"

"I don't know, but I think we better check it out."

"Why don't we wait a few minutes and see if he comes out? Whoever it is will probably come to the car, eventually. There isn't anywhere else to go; there aren't any other cars or buildings out here. I don't want to go near that place again, anyway," Kat said with a shudder.

"Whoever it is, he's waving us over."

"What?"

"I think we should go."

"I have a funny feeling about this."

"Come on; we'll be careful," said Carter as he opened his door.

With a sigh of surrender, Kat stepped out too. "Leave the door open in case we have to run back."

The two had not taken more than three steps when they saw the Guardian walk out of the building. He flashed them a warm smile and called out, "There are my two adventurers. Come over here. I want to show you something."

Upon seeing Guard, the children did not know whether to be relieved or annoyed. Truth be told, they felt a little of both. The two quickened their pace as Carter called out, "Guard, do you have any idea what we've been through and what happened here last night?"

"Indeed I do, and let me say you handled yourselves very well. You made good decisions, and here you are, still alive and ready to continue your adventures."

"Two people died here last night, and all you can say is congratulations you're still alive?" Kat said with reproach in her voice.

"Yes, yes, it is a tragedy," Guard said with convincing somberness. "But, do you know why he died?"

"It was a terrible accident. When Mr. Stewborn lit a match inside the house, he saw someone, and it startled him. He dropped the match, and it set fire to the place. Everything went up so fast. Stewborn and the person he saw couldn't get out, and they were burned alive," the girl said with emotion.

The Guardian reached out and gently touched the girl's shoulder. It looked to Carter like a gesture of comfort and reassurance, but Kat felt a genuine sense of loving warmth and inner strength fill her whole being. Kat took a deep breath and let it out slowly. She stood more erect, and then she smiled.

"Are you all right, Kat?" her partner asked. "You look like you're feeling better."

Kat nodded and said, "I am. I feel much better, thank you."

"Come, you two. I want to show you something." Guard turned and headed for the stone house.

The children did not move and Carter said, "I don't think we should go in there. The owner of the gas station was very adamant that we keep out of that place."

Turning to the children, the Guardian said, "It is all right now; the danger has passed. There is nothing more to fear in there unless you fear the truth."

Kat looked at Carter and said, "I believe we can trust Guard; he won't hurt us."

Carter smiled crookedly and asked, "Are you sure you're all right? I think something might have happened to you when he touched you."

Kat said thoughtfully, "Maybe something did happen to me. All I know is that I feel better, and I feel that we can trust Guard."

Carter sighed, rubbed the back of his neck, and said, "Okay, but if you've been turned into a pod person under Guard's control and you two are trying to trick me into that building so you can eat my face or something, I'm going to tell your mom on you."

"If we wanted to eat your face, we wouldn't have to trick you into the house first. Besides, you haven't washed your face lately, and I could never eat a dirty face," Kat said with a grin then headed toward the house.

Carter said to himself as he followed her, "That's the same old Kat."

Once the three were inside, the smell of smoke was almost too much for the children. It burned their eyes and caused them to cough. The Guardian, however, seemed unaffected. "Try not to stir up the ash as you walk. It will make it harder for you to breath," said Guard.

The Guardian led the children directly back to the hallway. As they approached the place where Stewborn fell, they saw a mound of ash. At the head of the mound, there was a white gravestone. "This is what I wanted you to see. Read the engraving on the stone."

Carter read aloud, "Here rests Mr. Stubborn." Carter looked at Guard and said, "I think whoever left this here misspelled Mr. Stewborn's name."

"No," Guard responded. "Mr. Stewborn's name is spelled Stubborn. He just pronounced it Stewborn. His name was Stubborn, and he was a stubborn man. That, more than anything else, is what got him killed. You see, some would say that there is no such thing as an accident, just bad choices that lead to what some like to call accidents. Stubborn was an accident waiting to happen. He walked right into harms way because he only listened to his own arrogant pride. You, on the other hand, were wise enough to avoid Stubborn's fate."

Kat asked, "What happened to the person that startled Mr. Stewborn and caused him to drop the match?"

"There was no one else here last night. Come, and I will show you what Stubborn saw." Guard led the children to the room at the end of the hall, and he pointed to the remains of a full-length mirror. "That mirror was positioned so that Stubborn saw his own reflection and mistook it for another person."

"What about Mr. Stewborn's wife? How will she learn of her husband's death?" asked Kat.

"You do not need to concern yourself with that. I suggest that you continue traveling until you find the adobe. Go get what is left of your food; have a little breakfast, and then keep heading east."

At Guard's prodding, the children headed back to the car. When they reached the car, Kat turned to ask Guard to join them for breakfast, but the Guardian was gone.

"I don't know about you," Carter said as he reached into the car for the sack of snacks, "but I'm not hungry. I'd rather head out now, and when we take a break, we can have a little something to eat."

Kat nodded and said, "Sounds good. I want to get out of here."

The partners found that the sunflower fields had given way to adobe soil peppered with stones and clusters of cactus plants. After walking for about an hour, they came to a large pine tree along the side of the road. It was the first tree they had seen since the oak trees from the day before. They decided to take a breakfast break on the nice bed of pine needles under the tree.

"What's left of our food supplies?" Kat asked as she and Carter sat down.

Carter poured the contents of the bag onto the ground between them. The children were not surprised to find that there was still quite a bit of food left. So much had happened right after they bought their supplies that they did not have an opportunity to relax and eat until now.

Kat reached for a chocolate bar and said, "This'll taste good, but I would rather have a nice plate of bacon and eggs with toast."

"I'd like to have a big plate of waffles and sausage," Carter said as he picked up a bag of salted peanuts.

The partners ate a good portion of their supplies that morning while they chatted about what they would like for dinner and other trivial subjects. They knew that they were avoiding talking about their situation and the events of the night before, but they did not care. It was good to take a break and enjoy being two friends eating junk together for a while.

The young friends finished off their meal with two swallows of water from the canteen, which was still about half-full. "We have enough food left for a light lunch. After that, we'll need to find something else to eat," Carter reported.

Continuing their journey, Kat commented, "This time I really do hope we get something better than snack food. I'm feeling a little funky from too much junk."

"Let's keep our eyes peeled. So far, we've been provided for. I feel sure that when we need something like water, food, or equipment it will be made available," Carter stated with confidence.

Kat looked over at Carter and smiled.

The boy noticed the look and said, "What?"

"You're enjoying all this, aren't you?"

Carter looked down at his feet for a moment, and then he looked back at the girl. "Yes, I am. It's the kind of thing that people only read about in novels or see in a movie, but we are actually living an adventure. And it's not like some old road trip type of adventure where you just see new places and faces. It's downright mysterious, bizarre, and even terrifying. It's something that if we told people about, they wouldn't believe it."

"The trick is that it doesn't change us by driving us crazy or getting us killed," Kat offered. "But, you know something, Carter? Back at the stone house when the Guardian touched me, I felt something happen inside me. I felt courage, and I got a sense that no matter what happens we'll be able to deal with it. I know that I'll be scared again before this is over, but it's okay. I'm going to handle it."

"To be honest with you, Hamsted, I think you've done really well considering what we've been through." Carter gave his partner an encouraging look.

Kat knew that Carter was being serious, and it made her feel a little uncomfortable. To lighten things a bit, she said, "Now, if only we could get you to stop blubbering like a baby every time a screaming lunatic chases us, we might be able to find some of that treasure Guard mentioned."

"Yeah, I'll have to work on that," her partner said with a chuckle. He knew what Kat was doing, and he played along to let her know that he meant what he said about her.

"It looks like we're moving into a forest area." Carter changed the subject. "The pine trees are getting thicker, and the road up ahead is unpaved again. That's odd. I thought this road was supposed to empty onto a highway."

"Right, I think it was Highway 21, wasn't it?" Kat asked.

"That's right; it was highway 21. What do you suppose it means that it isn't here?"

"Does it mean that it never existed?"

"Maybe it did exist until…"

"Until what?" Carter asked.

"Maybe until Stewborn died, or until the situation changed and it was no longer needed. I don't know. If you haven't noticed, this place isn't like home." Kat sounded a bit uneasy.

Carter sighed. "Yeah, you got that right."

As Carter had predicted, the travelers moved into a thickly forested area, and the terrain gradually became mountainous. "It doesn't look like we're going to find any convenience stores out here. I wonder if we could have made a mistake somewhere. We're supposed to be looking for an adobe structure. We traveled through a region covered with adobe type soil, but we didn't see any adobe buildings. Now, we're moving into a forest area where it's very unlikely that we will find anything made of adobe."

"I'm beginning to wonder if it really matters which way we go. Still, if it does, I believe we're going in the right direction. We've been heading east. There haven't been any turnoffs or intersecting roads, so there is no way we could have taken a wrong turn," noted Kat.

For the rest of the day, the partners traveled deeper into the dense forest. Their rest stops became more frequent as the road continued over hills that grew steeper. Their food and all but a few swallows of water were now exhausted. With the sun dipping below the mountains, the children were relieved to see that the road took them to the front door of an inn.

PEOPLE RULE INN

The name on the sign in front of the inn was People Rule Inn. The children's relief quickly turned to apprehension as they realized that the building did not fit in a forest setting. It was made of solid black interlocking shingles. There was no trim because it had no windows. Shaped like a large shoebox, it looked to be two stories high. A narrow porch ran along the front of the building with an ominous looking iron door located in the center.

"This place looks like some sort of giant lockbox," Kat said with a shiver. "And where's the parking lot? There aren't any cars around here. Besides that, the road leading up to the inn is too narrow for car traffic anyway. And the place looks abandoned. You can't see any lights. What kind of inn has no windows? There is something seriously wrong with this place. And if there are people staying here, I'm not sure I want to meet them."

"The building is just a simple design; that's all. It might be an experimental structure using less energy or something. It's true it doesn't look like the type of place you would find in a forest, but what difference does it make? We need food, water, and a place to sleep. We should at least check it out," Carter said, trying to sound optimistic. "I don't know about the cars and parking lot. Maybe people who stay here hike in like we did. It's probably like getting away from everything and roughing it."

"What about money? I checked my pockets again, and I'm still broke after shopping at the gas station," Kat reported.

"Yeah, me too, but maybe we can work out something where we can do chores for what we need. Besides, we're a couple of kids in a forest at night. Nobody would just turn us away."

"That's true. It certainly won't hurt to try. But I still have to say, the look of this place makes me nervous. If we knock and Dracula answers, I'm out of here," said Kat with a shudder.

The partners stepped onto the porch, and they found themselves transported inside the inn. "Wow, what was that?" asked Carter.

"I don't know. I stepped onto the porch, wondering whether we should just walk in or knock, and then I felt dizzy. Everything went black for a second, and here we are. I assume we're inside the inn. There's the registration desk in front of us."

"Right, but there is no one to register us," observed Carter.

"Welcome to People Rule Inn," said a man who popped up from behind the counter. "I am the manager, and since I have no staff, it will be my pleasure to register you." The manager was average size and height, wearing a dark business suit. He was peering over wire-rimmed glasses that rested halfway down his nose. He was balding, had a little black mustache, and had a pale, round face. "Step up to the desk, and you can sign the book."

Moving to the front desk, Carter said, "We would like to spend the night here, but we have no money. We need food, water, and a place to sleep. We were hoping that we could do some chores to pay our way."

"There is no need to worry about that. Everyone who comes to People Rule Inn gets food, drink, and lodging."

Kat responded with, "That's very generous, but we do want to pay our way."

Carter nodded his agreement.

"Just your being here is all the payment that is required," said the manager, holding a pen out to the children. "Sign the book, and I will show you to your rooms."

The partners looked at each other with expressions that said, *This does not smell right.* Carter reached for the pen as he said, "I don't mean to sound ungrateful, but I don't understand. What do you mean just us being here is all the payment that is required?"

"It is just what I said. The inn would not exist without patrons. The inn needs you as much as you need it. Please sign in so I can show you to your rooms. Dinner is about to be served in the dining area."

Carter shrugged, signed his name in the registration book, and then handed the pen to Kat. She took it, shrugged, and signed her name.

"Excellent. Everything is official now. You are the newest *permanent* residents of People Rule Inn. Follow me, and I will take you to your rooms."

"Wait a minute. What do you mean *permanent* residents? We're just here for the night. We'll be leaving in the morning," Carter said in a firm voice.

"I do not think so, uh …" the manager looked in the registration book for the boy's name. "Mr. Carter. You and, uh, Miss Hamsted will never leave the inn."

"*What?*" the partners exclaimed at the same time. "What do you mean?" Carter asked in a louder-than-normal voice.

The manager's tone was no longer friendly as he answered, "Once a person enters the inn, they never leave. Oh, it is possible to leave, but so far no one has ever solved the riddle."

"What riddle?" asked Kat.

"The riddle of the inn that goes like this: If your freedom you would win, answer the riddle of People Rule Inn. That is it. In order to leave the inn alive, all you have to do is answer the riddle. However, as I said before, no one has ever solved it. Furthermore, I doubt that the two of you will be able to succeed where others, more intelligent, clever, and brave than you, have failed. I warn you, if you exit the inn without solving the riddle, the moment your foot hits the ground outside, you will instantly perish."

"What do you mean *brave*? What does bravery have to do with solving a riddle?" asked Kat.

"I am surprised that you picked up on that," said the manager with a condescending tone. "You will find that the inn is not a very friendly place. It has a way of making a person's stay, shall we say, unpleasant. Many who might be able to solve the riddle simply cannot take the torments of the inn long enough to solve it, so they choose death instead. That is why it takes intelligence as well as bravery to leave the inn alive. Now, I will show you to your rooms."

The manager turned and headed for an arch located to the right of the registration desk. The children followed in silence. Once through the arch, the manager pointed to a large room off to the right. "That is the dining room. You will meet the other residents there when you take the evening meal." Then he took them up a flight of stairs.

"Why is everything so dark in here?" Kat asked with a shudder.

The manager looked back at the partners. Wearing an evil grin, he answered, "You will find that this is a place of darkness in many ways."

Kat also wondered what made the inn stink so badly. She decided to keep her questions to herself. The manager seemed only to be interested in taking pleasure in the discomfort of two frightened children.

When they reached the top of the stairs, the manager turned left down a long dark hallway. There were numbered doors on either side of the hall. He stopped at door number four on his right, opened it, and said, "Mr. Carter, this is your room. Miss Hamsted, the next room down, room number five, is yours. There are no locks on the doors, so you will not need keys. There is a single bathroom at the end of the hall. Dinner will be served in twenty minutes. If you are late to meals, you will go without. This is the last time I will tell you the time of a meal. After tonight, it is up to you to figure out when it is time to eat. Though breakfast, lunch, and dinner are always served at the same time, there are no clocks or windows in the inn, thus, making it difficult to keep track of the time."

"Let me guess," Carter said sarcastically. "The lack of clocks and windows is part of the inn's unpleasantness."

With an annoying snort, the man replied, "Yes it is; however, you will find that it is a very minor unpleasantness in comparison to what awaits you." The manager turned abruptly and headed back downstairs.

Alone now, in front of Carter's room, the boy said, "Let's go into my room and close the door so we can talk." The two entered a small, plain room. The walls and ceiling were the color and texture of pea soup. The only furnishings were a single bed, a nightstand with one drawer, and a lamp resting on top of the stand. The room was so small that there was barely enough space to walk along one side of the bed to reach the stand.

Once inside, they sat on the foot of the bed, and Carter asked, "What do you think?"

Kat frowned, wrinkled her nose, and said, "What do I think? I think we're in big trouble. I think that if solving the riddle of the inn is the only way out of here, then we had better get it solved. I think…" Kat stopped in mid-rant as loud banging started. It sounded like someone from Kat's room was pounding on the wall that separated their rooms. It was so loud and forceful that the wall vibrated from the force of the blows.

The partners jumped to their feet, and the pounding stopped. When it appeared that nothing else was going to happen, Kat asked, in a soft, shaky voice, "What was that?"

"I don't know; let's go take a look in your room."

"Okay, but you go first."

Carter nodded, opened his door, and stepped into the dark hall. The partners moved to Kat's door. Carter rested his hand on the knob for a few moments as he tried to find the courage to open it. Finally, he turned the knob, but before he could push the door open, it flew open and pulled him forward with such force that he fell on his face.

"Carter!" Kat shrieked and rushed to his side. "Are you all right?"

The boy groaned as he turned over on his back. He saw Kat's frantic look of concern, and said, "I'm okay; I'm just bruised up a little."

Kat helped Carter up, and he sat down on the foot of the bed. The girl sat beside him, looking him over to see if there were any signs of injury. Seeing nothing other than some nasty carpet burns on his forehead and arms, she glanced around the room for evidence of what might have caused the disturbance.

The room was an exact duplicate of Carter's. "I don't see anything that could have caused the pounding or the door being flung open," Kat said.

All of a sudden, the open door slammed closed with such force that the whole room shook. The children jumped, and after a few moments of silence, Carter looked at Kat and said, "And so it begins."

DINING AT THE INN

"The inn isn't wasting any time starting its torments. You're right about us figuring out the riddle as soon as we can. If we don't get out of here soon, our nerves will be shot, and our anxiety will be so intense that we won't be able to think straight. I suggest that we go down for dinner, meet the other residents, and then get to work on solving this thing."

Kat frowned and responded with, "Are you out of your mind? How can you think of food now? I couldn't eat a thing after that. I say we solve the riddle now and get out of here tonight."

"I know how you feel, but I don't think solving the riddle is going to be easy. We need food to keep up our strength. We need to learn everything we can from those who have been here for a while. And we need to get out of these rooms for now. At least I do. It should be about dinner time; let's go downstairs."

Kat sighed and nodded her agreement. When they arrived at the dining area, they found three others already seated at a large wooden table, which could have accommodated twenty.

"Well, well, two new victims. Welcome to your first feast at People Rule Inn," said a man sitting at the head of the table. He looked to be in his early twenties. He had a couple days of stubble on his gaunt face. His light brown hair was uncombed, and he looked like he had slept in his clothes for several nights. His eyes were sunken, possibly from lack of sleep, and his skin was pale from lack of sunlight. "Sit anywhere you like. My name is Sidney; you may call me Sid."

"Nice to meet you, Sid," said Carter as he and Kat sat in the two places to the right of Sid, with Carter closest to the young man. "My name is Carter, and this is my friend, Kat."

"You will not be glad for long to meet Sid," said an attractive blond seated at the foot of the table. "Sid takes pride in being as cruel as the inn."

"Oh, come now, Summer. I am not cruel to you," Sid said with a wink and a smile.

Summer was a little older than Sid. She was dressed in a long black dress. A silver necklace with a single white pearl hung about her long neck. She was pale, and though she had beautiful, large, blue eyes, they were marred by anxiety. She had a shapely figure and looked like she could be a model.

"You have spared me only because you think that by doing so I will be interested in you romantically. Well, I would not have anything to do with you even if you did not have a black heart."

"Ouch!" Sid said in mock pain. "I do not have a black heart, do I Margaret?" he asked, looking with a sneer at the girl seated across from the partners. She was about fifteen, slightly overweight with straight brown hair and thick glasses. She was wearing a light blue bathrobe. She sat slumped over in her chair gazing down at the table. When Sid's attention shifted to her, she glanced up at him with her eyes only. It was obvious to the partners that Sid intimidated the teen. She said nothing, turned her eyes to the partners, and then looked down again.

"Leave her alone!" Summer shouted. "I think you need to step outside for a breath of fresh air and take a walk, Sid."

"Ha, ha, you are very funny. You seem a little tense, my dear; perhaps *you* should go out for a little walk."

"That is what I am going to do right after dinner."

Sid stared at the beauty for a moment and then said, "You are kidding of course."

"No, I have solved the riddle, and I am going to leave tonight."

"Ridiculous. You may be beautiful, Summer, but you are no genius. I seriously doubt that you have solved the riddle; you are going to die if you step outside."

"I do not care. I cannot take this place or you anymore. I am leaving one way or another," the young woman said as tears welled up in her eyes.

Before anyone could say more, the manager walked in pushing a serving cart. "I see that you all made it in time for dinner. I trust that you will find tonight's meal a rare treat," he said with a sneer.

"I do not know what is worse: this same garbage you serve us at every meal or that lame joke you make every time about it being a rare treat," Sid spat.

The manager said nothing more as he served each diner a bowl filled to the top with a green substance that had the consistency of pudding.

Carter looked in his bowl and asked, "What is this stuff? It's the same color as the walls in my room."

Kat sniffed the contents of her bowl. "Oh, I can't eat this; it *stinks*! The smell makes me gag." She pushed it away.

Carter stuck his finger into the green pudding and tasted it. "Nasty! This stuff tastes as bad as it smells. Nobody can eat this."

The boy was wrong about that. He looked around the table, and the three residents he had just met were shoveling the green substance into their mouths using their fingers. There were no eating utensils, and worse, there were no beverages to wash the nasty stuff down.

The partners grew sick as they watched their fellow inmates eat. Sid was getting the green slop matted in his stubble. Margaret was dribbling large clumps down her chin. Summer was licking her fingers with loud smacking sounds. The combination of the stench, the repulsive look of the food, and the sight of the three diners eating the slop in such a disgusting manner was more than the partners could take. Kat was the first to run for the bathroom. Carter was only seconds behind her. They could hear Sid laughing as they ran up the stairs. "When you get hungry enough, you will be sucking this stuff down like it was ambrosia," he called after them. Luckily, the children made it to the washroom in time to empty their stomachs into the toilet.

The partners sat back on the floor and wiped their mouths with the back of their hands. "Is the canteen in your room?" Kat asked.

Carter nodded. "There isn't much water left, but there's enough for a couple of swallows each."

When they arrived at the boy's room, they found the door open. Sid was inside drinking the last of their water. When he was done, he rubbed his stomach and smiled. "That was refreshing. I have not had fresh water since I have been here. I came looking for you to see if you were all right. I did not see you, but I did see the canteen. I figured you would not mind if I helped myself."

"What gave you the idea that we wouldn't mind if you drank the last of our water?" Carter asked angrily as he snatched the canteen out of Sid's hand.

Sid just smiled (a very annoying smile) and shrugged uncaringly. "The others are done eating, and Summer is about to commit suicide. Are you going to watch the show?" he asked as he headed into the hall.

"Let's go. I want to hear if she has solved the riddle and what actually happens either way," said Carter.

Kat was about to protest and then realized that if they were going to survive this place, they needed to learn all they could, even if it did end up with seeing someone else die. She did not feel good about it. She had already witnessed Mr. Stewborn's death, but it suddenly occurred to her that there might be many more deaths to witness before they were finished with their adventures. The fact that she or Carter could die was something that Kat was beginning to accept as a real possibility.

When they reached the bottom of the stairs, they met the other two residents coming out of the dining room. Sid, Carter, and Kat fell in behind them as they walked down the corridor that led to double doors. Above the doors was a sign that read "Egress." Carter asked, "What does egress mean?"

For the first time, the children heard Margaret speak. "It means exit." The partners were surprised that the teen had more than a hint of contempt in her voice.

"You will have to excuse Margaret," said Summer. "She is disgusted by ignorance. She believes that if you do not know something that she knows, you are worthy of contempt."

"Just get on with it already," Sid demanded. He wore an annoying grin and was dry washing his hands. Then he said, "Here, let me get the doors for you, Summer." He stepped forward and pulled the doors open.

"Thank you. You are too kind," Summer said sarcastically.

Still grinning, Sid said, "Not a problem."

With the doors open, the partners could feel the cool night air rush in with the strong sent of pine trees. A nearly full moon provided enough light to see a dirt path that cut straight through dense forest. The inn floor was even with the path. All Summer had to do was step from the indoor carpet onto the path, and she would be out of the inn.

"It is time, Summer. Solve the riddle, and be on your way," Sid prompted.

Sid was standing to the left of the doorway. Summer stepped up to the center of the doorway and looked out into the night. She attempted to wet her dry lips with a tongue that was just as dry. She looked at Margaret, who was standing just behind her, and then at the partners that were standing together behind Sid. "The name of the inn is the riddle: People Rule Inn. The word *rule* is a kind of slang that means the best, the greatest, and the most awesome. Everyone knows that the beautiful people are most valued in civil society. Beautiful people like me rule in the world. That is the solution of the riddle," Summer finished with an air of superiority.

"That is your answer? Beautiful people rule. Summer, you little stuck-up snob, if you go out there with that stupid answer, you are dead for sure," Sid said with a snort, shaking his head.

Sticking her nose in the air haughtily, Summer replied, "We shall see." She turned, took a deep breath, and stepped out of the inn. The instant her foot touched the dirt path she turned to dust and blew away into the night.

Kat gasped, and with her mouth agape, she put her hands on her cheeks.

"Wow!" Sid exclaimed. "That is the third time I have seen that, and each time it gives me a rush."

Carter was so shocked at what he had just witnessed that he stood frozen until Sid spoke. Sid's heartless comment shook him out of his daze. "Is that how you get your thrills, seeing people die?" He stepped in front of Sid and looked up into the man's face. With rage and disgust in his voice, the boy said, "What kind of a person are you anyway? I've had enough of your smart remarks and that lame smirk you wear."

Sid gazed down into the boy's angry face as he continued to grin annoyingly. "Is that so? Perhaps you would be happier with Summer." Without warning, Sid grabbed Carter by his upper arms, lifted him off his feet, and threw him out the door into the night.

WHERE DID HE GO?

"*No!*" Kat screamed as she witnessed the unthinkable act. What she saw next was not what she expected. She expected to see her partner disappear in a cloud of dust just as Summer had. Instead, she saw her partner fly back inside the inn as if he had bounced off a solid wall. He fell face down onto the carpeted floor and lay stunned.

Kat rushed to his side while Sid laughingly said, "He will be all right. The inn will not allow anyone to leave unless it is of his own free will; you can only leave once you decide to."

"Are you all right?" Kat asked with a trembling voice.

"I think so. Just let me lay here for a minute."

Kat looked up at Sid and said, "You really are a cruel person, aren't you? I don't understand it. This place is horrible enough as it is without you making it worse. If we worked together, maybe we could find a way out of here."

"Fat chance, little girl, and what makes you think I would help you escape the inn? Let me make something perfectly clear. When I figure out the riddle—and I will figure it out—I am not going to reveal the solution to anyone. I am not even going to announce when I leave. One day you will just find me gone, and you will know that I have escaped and left you all to your fates." With that said, Sid went to his room.

Margaret stood by and watched as Kat helped Carter to his feet. "What about you, Margaret? Would you work with us? Maybe we can help each other."

"I have been here for over three weeks now. You two have been here a couple of hours. Do you really expect me to just give you information I have accumulated?" she said with a snort.

"That isn't what I meant; we don't want a free ride. We want to work together with you and share thoughts, ideas, and observations. We want to help you as much as we want help from you."

"I do not need any help from a couple of little kids. You will just get in my way, and I do not need the distraction," Margaret said arrogantly. "But I will give you some advice. Watch out for Sid. He believes that by being as cruel as the inn that the inn will go easier on him. I think he just likes being mean. Sometimes, I actually think he enjoys it here, and I wonder if he has any intention of leaving. As for me, I will not bother you as long as you stay out of my way." Margaret turned abruptly and left.

"Let's get you to your room so you can lie down," Kat said. She put her arm around Carter's back for support.

"I'm okay, Kat. I can walk on my own," Carter said, and he gently pushed her helping arm away. The two walked up the stairs and stopped at Carter's door. He said, "Let's talk in my room." They left the door open and sat on the foot of the bed. "As I see it, we have two options tonight. Either we get some sleep and start exploring the inn after we are rested, or we can start now."

"I think I know why you want to explore the inn, but you tell me what you're thinking."

"We can't afford to overlook any possible source of information. Exploring the inn may lead to the discovery of some important clues. Our other resource is our new companions. Even though they seem reluctant to share what they know, we have already learned a few things just by being around them. I say we spend as much time around our fellow inmates as we can and see what else we can learn."

Kat yawned, stretched, and then said, "I'm getting tired. I say we get some sleep, and whoever wakes up first come and get the other. That way we can get a fresh start exploring every nook and cranny of this place."

"That sounds good to me. I'm getting tired too. Let's leave our doors open, and if you have any trouble just call out for me."

"Will do, but I'm going to the bathroom to clean up a little first." Kat stood up and looked at her partner, smiling.

"What?"

"Do I have to say it?"

"I don't know what you mean."

Kat sighed and said, "You could stand a little washing up yourself."

"Carter sniffed his armpits, frowned, and said, "I guess you're right. Let me know when you're done."

"You can count on it." When Catherine entered the dirty washroom that reeked of human waste, she wondered if it would be possible to get clean in such a filthy space. She turned the water faucet on over a sink brown with rust stains. The water that flowed out of the faucet was brown and smelled of rotten eggs. She let the water run for a few minutes in the hope that it would clear. When it became obvious that the water quality was as good as it was going to get, she decided to wash with it and hoped that she would not smell of rotten eggs.

There were no towels, soap, or tissue in the room. Everything was old, stained, and had not been cleaned for a very long time—if ever. The girl did the best she could to make use of the facilities. She was careful not to touch anything that she did not absolutely have to. When she was finished, she was not sure that she was any cleaner.

While his partner was getting ready for bed, Carter sat and pondered their dilemma. He could not seem to shake feelings of guilt. He felt responsible for getting Kat involved in their dangerous situation. This was not the first time he and Kat had risked their lives in pursuit of adventure. In all the years they had known each other, they had done many things together, and some of those things were downright life threatening. Carter still struggled with feelings of guilt over the time Kat broke her leg. To be honest, he felt guilty about more than just the broken leg.

It had happened during summer vacation when they were nine years old. Carter talked Kat into a late-night adventure that almost got her killed. The partners were bored; there was not much to do in their little community. Kat was having the worst time of it. Her mother had been riding her more than usual, so she was feeling rebellious as well as bored. One day, while the partners were relaxing under their favorite shade tree down by the river, Kat said, "You know something, Carter, this place really stinks. There's nothing to do, it's hot, and my mother is so miserable that she wants to make sure I'm just as miserable as she is. I swear if we don't think of something exciting to do, I'm going to run and scream until I pass out."

Carter said, grinning, "Now that might be worth seeing. Maybe I won't tell you what I've been planning just to see you blow a gasket and act like a maniac."

"What? What have you been planning?" Kat perked up.

"You aren't going to like it." Carter wore a mischievous expression that he knew Kat could not resist.

The girl got upon her knees, and with her face as red as her hair, she glared at Carter and said, "Tell me what you're planning, Toby, or so help me, I'll—"

"Okay, okay." Carter snickered as he lowered his voice to a conspiratorial whisper and said, "It has to do with the old Wilson barn."

Kat's face drained of blood until she was as white as a ghost. She sat back on the grass and said, in a voice tight with fear, "My mom told me never to go to the Wilson barn."

"Why? Because she knows it's haunted?" asked Carter.

Kat wrinkled her nose and said, with a hint of irritation, "No, my mom doesn't believe in those stories. She said the place is old and unsafe."

"You know what I heard? I heard that several years ago this family named Wilson had a son named Jimmy. One night he went crazy and set his house on fire while his parents were asleep. Then he went out to the barn and hung himself in the hayloft."

"I know the story, Carter. Who do you think told it to you? I told you that story last Halloween. I told you Jimmy's ghost is supposed to haunt the barn."

A little embarrassed, Carter mumbled, "Oh yeah. But what you didn't say was that if you go to the barn after midnight you can hear Jimmy Wilson's ghost up in the hayloft, kicking and banging around at the end of the rope."

Kat had told him that part of the story too, but decided that she did not want to argue with him about it. She just said, "Well, I think it's just a bunch of nonsense."

Carter challenged, "Oh really? Why don't we find out for ourselves?"

Irritated, Kat said, "I can't. I told you my mom won't let me go near the place."

Carter knew exactly what to say to make Kat give in and go along. "Hey, Kat, if you're too scared to go, just say so. You were the one looking for some excitement. I was thinking we could sneak out of our houses tonight around eleven thirty, meet here, and be at the barn by midnight. But I can see that you're too chicken—"

"Chicken!" Kat squealed. Rising to her feet, she glared down at her friend with her fists planted firmly on her hips. "Who are you calling chicken? Listen here. I'll be right under this tree with my bike tonight at eleven thirty *sharp*. You had better be here, Toby. We'll just see who the chicken is."

Later that night, the partners snuck out of their bedrooms. Kat arrived at the meeting place first. She had just gotten off her bike when she saw a light from Carter's flashlight headed toward her.

The moon was to be full, but it had not risen above the trees yet. Fortunately, the old Wilson barn was only a half-mile down the dirt road and then another quarter-mile off on a side path. Both children had flashlights, and by the time Carter reached Kat, she was already back on her bike. "Well," Carter said, "I bet you aren't bored now." The two chuckled, and Kat had to admit that she was excited.

It was rough going riding at night on dirt roads with only flashlights to light their way, but eventually they saw the outline of the old barn take shape out of the darkness as they drew near. They stopped about fifty feet from the barn. It all seemed like an exciting adventure at first, but now that they were actually there, the partners were both having second thoughts. It was so dark, and the huge barn opening, where the doors had long since fallen off, looked like a giant open mouth, hungry for them.

Suddenly, Carter's flashlight went out. "That's just great. My batteries are dead," he whispered. "You know what I think?" he said in a tone that hinted he was going to quit the adventure.

That made Kat angry all over again. She forgot her fear, and before Carter could finish his suggestion, she interrupted. "Oh, no you don't. You got me out here by calling me chicken, and now you're going to chicken out on me? Don't even *think* about it, Carter," she whispered back so forcefully it was almost as if she were shouting.

Carter thought better of sharing his original suggestion, and instead he said, "I was going to say, we better hurry before your light goes out too."

Kat calmed down a little, but the truth of the matter was that she was scared too. And being angry with Carter helped her feel a little less scared. She responded with, "Whatever. Let's go."

With only one flashlight between them, they huddled close together and moved cautiously toward the huge doorway. The closer they got, the slower they went and the more fearful they became. When they reached the doorway, they stopped. Kat pointed the light around to see what was in the barn. It was big and empty, and it was obvious that they would not be able to see much unless they moved in farther. Kat said, in a rather shaky voice, "Do you hear anything?"

"No, I don't. There's nothing here; let's go home."

Kat, feeling a little more confident now, said, "No, not yet. Let's go in a bit farther." Without waiting for Carter to object, Kat started walking again. Carter was pulling on her arm, trying to slow her down; suddenly, behind them and off to one side, they heard a scratching sound along the wall to their left. Kat shined the light in the direction of the noise, and they saw something move. But it was only a mouse scampering through a crack in the wall. Relieved, though a little shaken, they laughed nervously. Their laughter must have disturbed something bigger because high up in the hayloft they heard a loud *boom, boom, thump, thump, thump.* They jumped and let out with a yelp of surprise.

Shaking with terror, they stood waiting to see what would happen. When nothing did happen, Kat whispered, "I'm going to climb up to the hayloft and take a look."

Carter felt that he should be the one to go because he was the boy, but Kat was already on the ladder that was affixed to the loft. Since she had the only working light, he could do little more than be ready to render help if needed. At least that is what he told himself.

The ladder was old and rotten. Some of the rungs were broken or missing, but Kat was determined to climb it. She carefully made her way up the rickety thing. She was half way to the top when one of the rungs broke under her foot. It made a terrible cracking noise, and she almost fell. Luckily, she had a firm grip on the sides of the ladder. Seeing Kat almost fall caused Carter to call out, "Come on, Kat! That's enough. I'm sorry I called you chicken. You're very brave; now let's get out of here." All the noise and commotion stirred up whatever was in the loft, and again there was a loud *boom, bang, bang, bang.*

Kat froze, and it looked to Carter like she might not be able to move. Actually, she was just waiting for things to quiet down. Carter began pleading with her to come down and leave with him.

Kat called down, "Be quiet." Then she resumed her climb. Eventually, Kat's head came even with the bottom of the hayloft. One more step and she would be able to see what was there. She swallowed hard and slowly moved the final step up the ladder.

As her head came up to a point where she could see into the loft, she brought the flashlight up and screamed! She lost her grip on the ladder, fell, and hit the ground. Kat's left leg broke with a loud snap. She hit her head on something hard and lost consciousness. The flashlight broke, and the barn was plunged into darkness.

Carter turned and ran out of the barn. He was so terrified that he could not think about anything except getting out and back to safety. He did not know that Kat was hurt. To his shame, he did not care. He just knew that he had to get out of the barn and back home. Once outside, he saw that the full moon was well above the tree line. Able to see the road clearly, he got on his bike and rode home as fast as he could. He jumped off his bike, climbed back into his room, jumped into bed, and pulled the covers over his head. Carter told himself that Kat had jumped off the ladder, she was right behind him, and that she made it home too.

When Kat first regained consciousness, she did not know where she was. Her eyes were blurry, her head and leg hurt. She moaned in pain, and then it happened again. Somewhere above her, she heard *boom, boom, bang, bang, flap, bang.*

Then she remembered where she was. Worst of all, she remembered what she had seen up in the loft: two big, glowing eyes looking right at her. She shook in fear, and then she remembered Carter. She did not know that he had run off. She called out in a loud whisper, "Carter, where are you? Are you okay?" But there was no answer. She called again a bit louder and then louder still. Then she heard it again: *bang, bang, boom, boom, boom.*

Kat squealed and then fell silent. She could not imagine what had happened to Carter. *Where is he,* she wondered. *We have to get out of here. That thing, whatever it is, is going to come down here any minute now and do who knows what!*

Try as she could, she could not stand. Her leg was badly hurt. Her eyes cleared, and there was enough light from the moon coming into the barn through the doorway that she could see that Carter was gone. She realized that she was alone with that horrible thing in the loft.

She could not run. No one knew where she was except Carter, and she did not know what had happened to her friend. She was terrified. *Oh, why didn't I listen to my mom*, she thought to herself. *She told me this was a dangerous place. If I ever get out of here, I'll…*

Before she could finish her thought, she heard a car drive up and park. She could see the headlights shining in through the doorway. She heard car doors open and slam shut and people calling, "Kat!" It was her mother and Mr. Carter. "I'm in here!" she yelled. "I'm hurt: I think my leg is broken. We have to get out of here. The ghost of Jimmy Wilson is up there. Please hurry!"

Her mother ran to Kat. Concern filled her face. "Kat," her mom cried, hugging her. "What were you kids thinking coming out here? Look at you; we've got to get you to the hospital."

Then it happened. Up in the hayloft, a strange eerie noise cried out, along with a loud *thump, flap, flap.* Kat's mom and Mr. Carter looked up at the hayloft. Kat screamed, "It's the ghost of Jimmy Wilson!" Out of the loft and over their heads flew a barn owl. Its eyes glowed yellow in the car headlights as it soared into the night.

Kat was still screaming hysterically, "It's Jimmy Wilson. It's Jimmy Wilson!" Her mom hugged her and tried to calm her.

Mr. Carter said, "Kat, it's just an old barn owl that lives in the loft."

Then it all made sense to her. The noises they heard came from the owl flapping his wings and hitting the wall in the loft. The glowing eyes were the owl's eyes reflecting her flashlight. She was so relieved that she started to laugh but not for long. Laughing hurt her head and her leg. Then she remembered Carter. "Where's Carter? Is he all right?"

"Yes, my brave son is home in bed." Mr. Carter helped Kat into the car as he explained, "We heard Toby sneaking into his room, and we caught him hiding under the covers fully dressed. After he told us what happened, we called your mom to make sure you made it home safely. When your mom found your bed empty, she came by and picked me up to help her look for you. That's how we found you. Now, young lady, we have to get you to the hospital."

It took Carter a few days before he got up enough nerve to face Kat. He visited her after she got home from the hospital. When he saw her in bed with her leg in a cast, he started to cry. He felt such shame and guilt that he did not know what to say. After a few minutes, Kat said, "It's okay, Carter. I'm okay. Please don't cry." Kat had never seen her friend cry before this. "Just tell me, after I fell off the ladder, what happened to you?"

"Kat, I'm so sorry. I was scared. I thought you were right behind me. I ran to my bike, and I thought you did too. I don't know. I was so scared I just wasn't thinking straight. If I had known that you were still there alone and hurt, I would have gone back for you. Kat, I swear I will never leave you like that again."

"I believe you. I don't buy that you thought I was right behind you, but I believe that you won't leave me again. Besides, I probably would have done the same thing. I was scared too. I know what it feels like to be so scared that you're not thinking clearly. Please don't feel bad. It's okay."

Even though his partner had forgiven him, Carter could not help feeling guilty. He felt responsible for the fact that Kat seemed to be more timid ever since she suffered the trauma of that night. Carter changed too, after what happened. For one thing, he never called Kat chicken again. He also became more protective of her; he was determined never to let her down again.

Kat poked her head into Carter's room and broke into his thoughts. "It's all yours, and you can have it with my regrets. The washroom was disgusting before I used it, so don't blame me for the smell and filth."

Kat could see that her friend had been deep in thought, and whatever he was thinking about was troubling him. "I've seen that look before. This isn't your fault, you know. And if you're feeling guilty again, I'm going to be upset with you."

Carter smiled sheepishly, stood up, and said, "I don't believe you about the washroom. I hear girls are worse than boys when it comes to making a mess."

Kat slapped the boy's arm playfully and responded with, "If you tell anyone I'm responsible for that disgusting mess, I'm going to hurt you. Now go and get ready for bed. I'm almost asleep on my feet."

Carter obediently trotted off to the washroom. The condition of the facility disgusted him as much as it did his partner. Even though he had been in the room earlier, when he was sick from the dinner, he did not remember it being this bad.

By the time Carter finished getting ready for bed, Kat was already asleep. He wondered if Kat felt any cleaner after washing with the brown, stinking water. Even though he looked cleaner, he did not feel cleaner.

He was very thirsty, but the water was too disgusting to drink. The boy was so tired that he figured he would be able to fall asleep in spite of his thirst.

Before he went to bed, he checked his right front pocket for his flashlight. Luckily, the light was small enough to fit in his pocket if he angled it right, and after catching Sid in his room, he was glad he had put it there. He knew the light would come in handy when he and Kat explored the inn. He decided to put the flashlight and box of matches under his pillow while he slept.

Carter did not know how long he had been asleep when a piercing shriek from Kat's room woke him. He sat bolt upright and was temporally disoriented. Screams of sheer terror ripped through the night.

SECRETS OF THE INN

"Kat, I'm coming! I'm coming! What's wrong?" He threw his blankets off, leapt out of bed, and ran to Kat's room. When he got to her doorway, he turned the light-switch just inside the door that turned on her lamp, but nothing happened. It was so dark that he could not see anything in the room.

"Carter, *help me*! I can't breathe!" Kat said as she made choking and gagging noises. "They're in my mouth and nose!" It sounded like she was trying to speak with her mouth full and her nose pinched at the same time.

Carter gave up on her light switch and ran back to his room for the flashlight. He was gone only seconds, but by the time he got back to Kat's door, she was no longer screaming or calling out. He heard only muffled sounds of distress that could no longer escape her mouth.

Carter turned on the flashlight. The batteries were fresh, and the light was new, so it was bright. What he saw made him gasp. He had never seen anything like it before, except maybe in a horror movie. Cockroaches covered the girl's bed. In the middle of the bed, a figure was sitting up. Roaches covered it so completely that the only way Carter could tell it was a person was by the shape. Kat was digging at her face and mouth trying to dislodge the roaches so she could breathe.

This vision lasted only a second because the moment Carter turned on the flashlight, the cockroaches rushed to the floor and through cracks along the baseboards of the walls. In an instant, they were gone.

Kat was hysterical. She was crying, screaming, and still trying to shake off and spit out roaches even though they were gone. "It's okay, Kat. They're gone now," Carter said in a soothing voice. "The light—they're afraid of the light. They won't come back. It's all right now; calm down."

As she calmed, her flailing stopped, and her screaming turned into sobs. Carter was not good at comforting others, partly because he was a boy and mostly because he had no practice at it. Yet, he was so upset at seeing his best friend this vulnerable and broken that he could not help putting his arm around her shoulders.

"Ah, look how sweet," Sid gushed with phony saccharin sweetness.

The screams aroused the other two tenants. Sid and Margaret stood in the hall in front of Kat's door to see what was happening. Carter tried to ignore them.

When Sid noticed several dead cockroaches scattered over the bed and floor, he surmised what had happened. He said, "Like I was saying to Summer the other day, this place can really *bug* you." Then he laughed as if it was the funniest thing ever said.

Carter became furious; he rushed to the door with fire in his eyes. Sid stopped laughing, crossed his arms, and said, "Back off, boy. We have been through this before. Do not make me hurt you for real."

Carter slammed the door in Sid's face. Outside he could hear him laughing again, and then he called thorough the door, "Hey, Carter, that is a nice flashlight. You better keep a close eye on it; you would not want to lose it." Then he laughed again as he returned to his room.

Carter turned back to Kat and found her looking at him. She was shivering, but she had stopped crying. "It's going to be all right. I'm not going to leave you alone again. We can take turns standing watch over each other."

Kat blinked, took a deep breath, and said, "If this had happened before the Guardian touched me, I wouldn't be able to continue. But I'll be okay." After a pause, she added, "Carter, we have to get out of here."

"I agree. I had no idea it could get this bad. What happened to you was beyond frightening, and I'm sorry I let it happen."

"Carter, you didn't let anything happen. You saved me. If it hadn't been for you, I would have suffocated."

The boy shook his head thoughtfully and said, "I don't think the inn would do anything to kill us. It wants to shake us up; it wants to rattle us so much that we won't be able to solve the riddle. It wants us to act hastily or make us so miserable that we'll just give up. It doesn't want us to solve the riddle, but I don't think it would kill to keep us from solving it."

Kat nodded and said, "Yes, you're right. I sense that. It's as if it wouldn't be sporting to kill us. It's a contest, and so far the inn, or whoever is behind it, has never lost."

"Kat, you're brilliant!"

"I know that, but what do you mean?"

Carter snorted and said, "You said whoever is behind this. This is a contest, and it has to be the Adversary who is behind it. I wouldn't be surprised if the manager was the Adversary in disguise."

"Makes sense, but how does knowing this help us?"

"I don't know. Maybe it just helps us to understand what we're dealing with."

Kat nodded thoughtfully. "Well, I know that I'm not going to be able to sleep anymore tonight. Maybe we should get busy exploring this place."

"Are you sure you're up to it? We can sit and talk a little more, or we can just rest."

"I'm all right, really. The sooner we get busy, the sooner we can get out of here."

"Well, if you're sure you're up to it, we can start by searching the unoccupied rooms down this hall."

"Do you think we should search Sid's and Margaret's rooms when they're out eating breakfast or something?"

Carter considered the question, and then he answered, "I would like to, but I don't know. Let me think about that for a bit. What we can do is search Summer's room first."

"What do you want to bet that Sid has already searched it?"

"Oh, I'm sure of it. That character doesn't miss a step. Let's check it out. I believe she was in three."

"Yes, she was. Margaret's in two and Sid's in one."

Carter stopped in front of his room and said, "Hold on a second. I'm going to get the matches." He checked under his pillow and discovered that they were gone. Returning to his partner, he said, "I was afraid of that. Sid paid me another visit while I was in your room. I had the matches under my pillow, and now they're gone. It's a good thing I took the flashlight before he checked under the pillow."

"We better be sparing with the batteries. We didn't get an extra set, did we?"

"No, but the batteries in this thing are alkaline. They'll last us awhile. You're right, though. We don't know how long we're going to be here, and we may need it to fight off more roach attacks. We've got to make them last."

"Make sure you keep it with you at all times," Kat said.

"Don't worry, I will."

The light was on in room number three. The bed covers were tossed back, the mattress had been turned over, and the nightstand drawer was pulled out. "Looks like one or both of our neighbors did a thorough job of it."

"If there was anything here worth taking, it's gone now," Kat said. "Let's go."

"Hold on," Carter called to his partner. "Let's consider this for a minute. Summer was here longer than we have been here. She had more time to deal with Sid, Margaret, and the inn. If she had anything to hide, she would have learned, as we're beginning to, hiding something under a pillow or a mattress won't keep it out of Sid's hands. Think. Where else might a person hide something important in a room like this?"

"I don't know. There really aren't a lot of places to hide things in here," Kat said as she glanced around the room.

"Maybe she hid something under a loose baseboard or under the carpet."

"Hmm, okay, but we'll need the flashlight for that kind of search."

The partners got down on their hands and knees with the flashlight and worked their way around the base of the walls. When they came to the nightstand, they moved it away from the wall. "What's this?" Carter asked as he reached for a tiny corner of yellowed paper sticking out from under the baseboard. "I can't get it; my fingernails are too short."

"Let me try." Kat used her longer nails to grab the corner.

"Be careful. Don't tear it, or we may never get the rest of it out."

"Got it! It looks like an old fortune cookie fortune. It has something written on it. It says, 'Seekers find.' What do you make of that?" Kat asked, looking at her partner quizzically.

Carter shrugged. "I don't know. What do seekers find? What do they seek? How did this piece of paper get under the baseboard? Do you think Summer put it there, or has it been there for a long time? If she did put it there, why did she? It raises more questions than it answers."

"Boy, are you over thinking this thing or what," Kat said, amused.

Carter smiled at himself and said, "You're right. It is what it is. It's a message for anyone who finds it. We're seekers, and if we keep seeking, we're going to find what we are looking for: the way out of here."

"Now you're talking. Our success depends on our determination. I suspect that people fail to survive leaving the inn because they aren't willing to put out the effort it takes to discover the real answer to the riddle."

"That's it!" Carter exclaimed.

"That's what?"

"You said, *discover the answer*, you didn't say, *solve the riddle*," Carter said thoughtfully. "I think that's what this piece of paper is trying to tell us. It's a clue that means if we seek, then we will discover the answer to the riddle. That means the answer to the riddle isn't a matter of cleverness like the manager said. It's just a matter of finding it. The answer is here in the inn. Maybe it's somewhere specific, or maybe it's scattered about in bits and pieces, but it's here for anyone who's willing to seek it out."

"That makes sense, but why couldn't someone clever and smart enough figure it out eventually?" Kat wondered.

"If it was just a matter of being able to figure it out like a common riddle, someone should have been able to do it by now. My guess is that the answer is something that goes against human logic or maybe even human nature. The answer might be something people would consider ridiculous, so it wouldn't occur to them."

"That makes sense. Do you think we should finish searching the rooms?"

"Maybe later. First, I want to satisfy my curiosity about something. I want to search the kitchen."

Kat turned pale at the suggestion, and said, "The kitchen? Why would you want to do that? Just the thought of that food turns my stomach."

"Come on, and I'll explain," said Carter as he headed out into the hall. "I'm getting hungry, and I want to find out what that green stuff is. If I knew what it was, maybe I could overlook the smell and sight of it and eat it. After all, we can't go forever without food. I also want to see if there's water in there that doesn't stink like rotten eggs. The water in the bathroom was almost as disgusting as the green food."

"I like the water idea, but what if we find out that the food is something so totally disgusting that we would never be able to eat it no matter how hungry we got. Sometimes it's better not to know."

Carter ignored his partner and said, "Let me grab the canteen before we go to the kitchen."

As expected, the kitchen was behind the door the manager used to bring food out to the diners. The children found themselves in a clean, large room lit by a single dim bulb in the ceiling. The floor was concrete, painted yellow. Around the walls were stainless steel kitchen appliances, sinks, and counters. In the center was a large food preparation island with a white marble top.

"It's clean, and it doesn't stink. It smells like fresh vegetables in here," Kat observed.

"Here's why," Carter said as he pulled a handful of Brussels sprouts out of an open box. There were several boxes stacked on the preparation island. "And there are boxes of broccoli, lima beans, spinach, and just about every other green vegetable kids hate. It looks like the smelly green pudding is just a lot of boiled down green vegetables. It's good for you and will keep you going even if it is nasty."

"Yeah, but knowing that it isn't something like sheep guts or cockroach pudding makes it not even seem to smell so bad. I'm almost looking forward to breakfast now that I know it's at least edible," Kat said.

"Okay, now we're getting somewhere. Let's check the water." The boy turned on the water, let some run into his cupped hand, and then smelled it. "Smells like fresh water." He took a sip and smiled. "It tastes fresh too. Good thing I brought the canteen," he said as he stuck it under the running faucet. After filling it, he drank his fill and offered it to Kat, who also drank. Carter refilled the canteen and shouldered it.

"You know, I'm not crazy about any of these vegetables, but I'm hungry enough to eat a few clumps of broccoli," Kat said and reached for one of the boxes.

A loud bang from the door stopped her cold. The two jumped and looked toward the sound only to see the manager standing in the doorway. He had a nasty snarl of anger on his face. "What are you doing in here?" he raged.

Carter shrugged and responded, "We were curious about what was going to be served for breakfast."

"You do not belong in here! Get out now, and do not let me ever catch you in here again!" The manager's face was so red it looked like it might explode.

"Come on, Kat. I think our host wants to get breakfast started," Carter said with a self-satisfied grin. They left the kitchen and headed down the corridor that led to the egress.

Once Carter was sure they were out of earshot, he asked, "What do you make of that?"

"I believe he was angry that we were in the kitchen."

"No, he wasn't just mad we were in the kitchen. He was outraged because we discovered an important secret. It reminds me of a bumper sticker I saw once."

Kat was starting to get annoyed. "A bumper sticker? Carter, you're not making any sense. I think this place is starting to get to you."

"The bumper sticker said, 'The truth will set you free.' That's why the manager was so angry. Now that we know what the green pudding is, we'll be free to eat it without it freaking us out. Part of what makes this place so terrifying is the unknown; the unknown adds to our fears. The manager was angry because the more we learn about the inn, the less of a hold it will have on us. It's the truth that's setting us free."

"Do you think that's the solution of the riddle: the truth will set us free?"

"I think it's another clue, not necessarily the actual solution."

Kat nodded thoughtfully and then said, "Okay, I say we wait for breakfast and then continue our search. I'm so hungry I could actually eat some of that green stuff, especially now that I know what it is. I want to be sure we don't miss it."

"I suspect that the manager came to the kitchen to begin breakfast. I'm no expert, but I'm guessing that it will take about an hour and a half to prepare the food. I have a place I want to check out. Let's plan to be back here in an hour."

Kat's stomach let out with a hungry growl loud enough for Carter to hear. "Good. I am glad you agree. Let's be off," Carter said with a mischievous smile.

Kat blushed, put her hand on her stomach, and said, "Very funny. Where are we going?"

THE SOLUTION

"There's a door down this corridor next to the dining room. I want to see what's behind it."

"You have good eyes, Carter. I didn't see that."

"Let's just hope it isn't locked," he said as he reached for the doorknob. Luckily, it swung open easily. It was dark behind the door, so Carter pulled out his flashlight. The light illuminated a narrow passageway about thirty feet long. The partners stepped into the passage single file, with Kat bringing up the rear. "There's another door up ahead." Carter walked up to the second door, tried it, and said, "It's locked."

"Now what?" Kat asked.

Carter said, half jokingly, "Knock I guess." Then he did just that. To their surprise, they heard someone turn the lock, and the door swung open. They found themselves facing a kindly looking, elderly, black woman. She had gray hair, deep wrinkles, bright, friendly eyes, and a smile that would make anyone feel welcome.

"How wonderful, I have visitors! Come in children, and visit with me a spell." The woman opened the door wide to let the partners into a warm, comfortable room. In the center of the room, there was a small, round coffee table. Directly behind the table was a yellow couch with a variety of colorful throw pillows. On the right side of the room was a wooden rocking chair, which appeared well used. "Please, make yourselves comfortable on the couch," the woman said as she closed the door, locked it, and then sat down in the rocking chair. You must be Carter and Kat. Do not ask me how I know that. It is not important. Please join me for some tea and cookies," she motioned to the coffee table.

The children had just settled down on the couch when they looked at the table and noticed that there was a plate of three cookies in front of each of them. A cup of strong, hot tea sat next to each plate.

Remembering how the Guardian had a habit of making food appear, Kat turned to the woman and said, "That food was not on the table when we walked in here. Are you the Guardian?" Before the woman answered, Kat's stomach growled loudly in anticipation of the cookies and tea. She blushed and said, "Excuse me. We haven't had anything to eat for a while, and I'm afraid my stomach is protesting."

"Help yourselves to the cookies. They are very tasty and filling," the woman said as she reached for a cookie. She sat back, watched the children, and smiled warmly.

Both children bit into a cookie. "Wow, this is one of the best cookies I've ever tasted," Carter said and stuffed the rest of it in his mouth.

Kat agreed, and told the woman that the tea was very refreshing too.

The old woman rocked in her chair and seemed happy that the partners were enjoying themselves.

After a moment, Carter said, "Excuse me, but you didn't answer Kat's question. Are you the Guardian?"

The woman stopped rocking and responded, "I am a guardian, but I would not say that I am *the* Guardian. Now let me ask you a question. Why did you knock on my door? I have heard people try to open my door with brute force. I have heard them try to pick the lock. I have heard them yell through the door, demanding that if there is anyone inside that I had better open up, but you are the first to knock."

"Are you saying that we are the first visitors you have entertained here?" Kat asked, her head cocked to the side.

"Yes, you are the first ones to knock, and you have not answered my question. What caused you to knock on my door?"

Carter swallowed what was left of another cookie. "I assume you know what's going on here in the inn. We entered the inn and learned that we couldn't leave (and live) unless we solved the riddle of the inn. We decided to search and see if we could discover the solution. We discovered a piece of paper that had *Seekers find* written on it. From that clue we assumed that if we hunted for the solution we would find it. Everyone else seems to be trying to figure out the answer, and so far, nobody has been successful. That's why we thought that maybe we could *find* it rather than figure it out. It was while we were searching for the answer that we saw your door. Since it was locked, I knocked. It just seemed like the right thing to do."

"Indeed it was the right thing to do," the woman said. She sat her teacup down, leaned forward, and told them, "The piece of paper you found that says *Seekers find* is the first of three steps to discovering the answer to the riddle. The second is *Knock, and it will open*. Somewhere in your past, you may have heard the three steps to discovery, and subconsciously, you acted on the second one. Do you remember the third step?"

Carter sat back and looked up thoughtfully. He muttered to himself, "Seekers find. Knock, and it opens. And . . ." The boy shook his head in frustration. "I don't know. How about you, Kat, do you know anything about the three steps?"

"I just figured we were going to ask anyone we found if they knew the answer." She looked at the old woman and asked, "Do you know the answer to the riddle?"

The woman nodded and said, "I am the guardian of the riddle."

"Will you tell us the answer?" Kat asked.

"Of course I will. I have been waiting a long time for someone to find me and ask that question. That is the third step to discovery: *Ask, and it shall be revealed.* Since you have sought and found, knocked and asked, you shall have the answer. The people rule is the rule people live by if they wish to be at peace with themselves and their fellow man. Do you know this rule?"

Carter shrugged and said, "Live and let live?"

The old woman frowned sadly and shook her head. "Can you not think of something that would challenge you to be a better person and could warm the cold heart?"

After a moment of meditative thought Kat said, "A passive rule that tells us to just stay out of each other's way would never change us or others. Instead of just leaving people alone in their struggles or their behavior that hurts others, we need to be actively seeking to do for others what is needed."

The old woman broke into a beautiful smile of triumph. "Yes. Go on, child."

"It is true that we ought to avoid doing things that would harm our fellow man, but it has to be taken farther. We ought to do the things needed to *help* our fellow man, this is what I would want done for me, so it is what I must do for others. I see that now."

"Yes. I sense that you do. Let your last statement be your guide. *What I would want done for me, is what I must do for others.* With this understanding, you are free to leave this place anytime you wish. How about you, my boy, do you understand the people rule like your friend does?"

Carter nodded and said, "I believe I do. It's quite a challenge, isn't it? It will be difficult to apply to every person that comes into my life, but it's a worthy goal and a powerful principle that could change the world."

"If you understand that, then you also understand the solution to the riddle." Now, it is almost time for breakfast. You will want to eat more before you leave the inn. The cookies are good, but the green pudding is good for you. Before you leave me, I must tell you that your quest is vital. The fact that you are the first to discover the meaning of the people rule and will exit the inn is a very good sign."

The partners did not know how to respond to this, so they just smiled and nodded politely. Then Carter spoke up and said, "Before we go, I have another question. Can we tell the others the solution to the riddle?"

"Why are you asking me? What do you suppose the people rule would dictate that you do?"

"I would want them to tell me the solution if they knew it, so I should do for them what I believe would help them."

"There is your answer," said the guardian of the rule. She got up from her chair and unlocked her door. "Hurry along now, or you will miss breakfast."

Even though the children had just finished eating cookies, they still looked forward to breakfast. They were not necessarily eager to eat the green pudding, but they were eager to share the solution to the riddle with the others.

As the partners headed back to the dining room, Carter wondered if Margaret and Sid would believe them when they revealed the solution. He decided that when they saw him and Kat survive the egress, they would have the proof they needed to be able to leave too. On the other hand, is it enough just to know the solution? Neither Sid nor Margaret seemed to be the type who would accept the concept as a way of life, even if they did understand what the people rule meant. Carter had no affection for those two, but he did not want to see them die.

The partners were the first to arrive at the dining room. They sat in the same places they had the night before. Once seated, Kat turned to Carter and asked, "Do you think Sid and Margaret will believe us?"

"I was just thinking about that. Even if they see us exit safely, will they accept the concept? If they don't, I fear they'll die when they step out."

"Are you saying we should just keep it to ourselves and leave? Because I think, I feel like you. They don't seem to be the type that would accept the idea of living your life treating others the way you want to be treated."

"I think we have to try. We have to try to convince them that it's the right thing. The proof of what we say will be when we successfully exit the inn."

"You're right. When we survive the egress, they'll have to believe us. Okay, I feel better now." Kat sighed, sat back in her chair, and looked relieved.

The partners did not have to wait long for the others to arrive. Sid and Margaret sat in their same chairs as the night before. "I am surprised to see you here, Kat. I thought you would be full from all the cockroaches you pigged out on last night," said Sid, then he laughed a very nasty laugh. Even Margaret snorted and wore a smirk.

Before either of the partners could respond, the manager came into the dining room with four bowls of the green vegetable pudding. As the manager served them, Margaret said, "I am surprised to see you here too. It usually takes at least four or five days of going hungry before anyone can stand eating this green barf they call food around here."

Sid reached for his bowl and said, "If you guys are going to hurl again, please leave now before you start getting sick."

The manager shot looks of pure hatred at the partners as he served bowls of food to them. The attitude of the man toward the partners did not escape Sid's notice. After the manager left the dining room, Sid asked, "What have the two of you been up to? I have never seen the manager so angry before."

Carter reached for his bowl, scooped out some food using his two fingers, and put it in his mouth. "It's not bad really, especially when you know what it is. Go ahead, Kat. We are going to need all the nourishment we can get. Who knows when we'll find our next meal."

Kat reached for her bowl, took a mouthful of food, and said, "This really isn't bad. It even smells better once you know what it is. And you're right; it could be awhile before we find food again on the outside."

"What are you two talking about? You cannot seriously be thinking of leaving so soon. You have been here only one night, and you think that you (a couple of little kids) have solved the riddle of the inn?" Sid ranted.

Carter smiled at Sid and said, "What do you care? I thought you got a kick out of seeing people turned to dust and die?"

"He does, but he was looking forward to tormenting you for a while before you killed yourselves," Margaret said sarcastically. "I hate to admit it, but Sid is right. You have been here one night, and there is no way you could have figured out the riddle. Do not be stupid; you can never leave the inn."

"Should I tell them, or do you want to do the honors?" Kat asked her partner.

"You tell them. You've earned it after what you went through last night," Carter said with his mouth full of food.

Kat leaned back in her chair and began, "We didn't solve the riddle; we found the solution."

Margaret furrowed her brow and asked, "What do you mean you found the solution?"

Kat proceeded to tell Sid and Margaret the entire story from the time they found the clue in Summer's room, to the examination of the kitchen, to their visit with the guardian of the rule.

When she was through with her story, Sid shook his head. "You kids are such chumps. The inn is playing with your minds. I guarantee you that if you go through the egress with that answer, you are dust." With a contemptuous snort he continued. "Only a couple of little kids like you would fall for that do-unto-others-as-you-would-have-others-to-do-unto-you line. The inn is laughing at you and hoping you fall for it."

Margaret nodded and said, "The inn is trying to get you to go through the egress by appealing to your immature concepts of human nature. What the old woman said to you just does not make sense. Do you really believe that if you treat someone like Sid with the same decency that you want to be treated with that it would change him and make him human?"

Carter jumped in with, "I don't really know about that, but that isn't the point, is it? If I treat people with the same kind of courtesy and kindness I would like to be treated with, it may change some people, but the person it changes most is me."

Suddenly, a loud moaning sound came from everywhere at once. It was followed by a loud explosion that rattled every loose item in the inn. All four diners jumped up off their seats. "What was that?" Margaret asked with a trembling voice.

"You have been here long enough, genius, to know that it is just the inn trying to shake us up," Sid spat.

"No, I do not think so. I feel fear coming from the inn. Do you not feel it?"

Kat was rubbing her shoulders with her arms crossed in front of her chest. She looked terrified. "I feel fear. Not just my own—a mood of fear is coming from all around me. I think you're right, Margaret. I think the inn is afraid."

"Do not be ridiculous. Do you think the inn is afraid that it is going to lose its first victims? That is absurd," challenged Sid.

"Hamsted, I think it's time that we continue our journey. Do you have everything out of your room?" Carter asked in his most serious voice.

"Yes, I'm ready to go. You?"

"Let's do it," Carter said as he put his arm around his partner's shoulders and encouraged her toward the egress.

Sid and Margaret were close behind the two as Margaret called out, "Why not give it a day or two to think it over. If you do, you will see that you are on the wrong track."

"What do you care, Marge, old girl. The inn is going to get them eventually anyway. Do not ruin the fun. Three dustings in two days must be some sort of record."

"Please do not go and leave me alone in the inn with this creep," Margaret begged.

Carter and Kat could not help but feel compassion for the teen. They were leaving her in a lonely situation. "It's going to be okay. All you have to do is watch us step through the egress, and then you'll know that what we have discovered is the true solution to the riddle. This will be the day that you leave too."

"You really do believe that. You believe it with all your hearts. I can see it in your faces. But it is not true. You are going to die and leave me here alone."

"Just watch and you guys will know the truth; you will be set free too," Kat assured them as she stood next to Carter. The doors to the egress were open. The eager children stood looking out of the doorway at the beautiful forest as the morning sun came streaming through the trees. Then the partners did something they never did before: they reached out and took each other's hands.

Sid and Margaret stood behind them. Margaret was ringing her hands, and Sid had his arms crossed and wore an arrogant smirk on his face. The partners looked back once, then at each other, and then out into the sunlit forest. Together, they stepped over the threshold just as a blood-curdling scream ripped the air from behind the four. Sid and Margaret immediately looked back over their shoulders to see the manager screaming and running down the corridor to the egress.

Even though Carter and Kat heard the scream, they were already in midstep and were intent on exiting. The scream did not deter them from leaving. As soon as their feet touched the dirt path, they vanished. They did not turn to dust and vanish; they just vanished.

The manager suddenly stopped screaming and stood looking past Sid and Margaret out the door. The two remaining guests followed the manager's look outside. They saw nothing of the partners. Because the manager distracted them, they did not see that the children vanished without turning to dust. Of course, they assumed that they were dead like all the rest.

THE WITCH AND THE SCARECROWS

The partners expected that they would just walk out into the forest and continue down the path. Instead, they had the same sensation of falling into darkness that they experienced when they were transported into the inn by stepping on the porch. When the darkness cleared and the sensation of falling stopped, they realized that they were still standing on a dirt road facing east. However, they were no longer looking at a forest.

"Wow! What do you make of this?" Kat asked as she scanned her new surroundings. The partners were stunned to find themselves standing in the midst of row upon row of scarecrows. Each one was different, but they were similar in that they all appeared to be handmade out of old clothes, stuffed with straw and rags. They were each impaled upon single poles that ran from their lower back up through the back of their heads. Their faces were drawn with charcoal onto stuffed burlap or cotton flour bags. The sun had risen to such an angle that it cast long shadows of the scarecrows over the flat ground making the scene look like something painted by a madman.

"There must be thousands of them. What are they doing here? I thought farmers put scarecrows in grain fields to scare away crows. There's nothing around here but yellow sand and gray rock. I don't even see any wild plants."

"Where are Sid and Margaret?" Kat asked with concern in her voice. "They should have come through right behind us."

"I don't know. I heard a scream as we stepped out of the inn. Maybe something happened and they weren't able to follow. Besides, even if they did make it, maybe theirs is a different path. I don't think we'll be seeing them again."

Turning back to the odd sight that surrounded them, Kat observed, "If these are scarecrows, they aren't very good ones. There's a crow perched on top of each of their heads."

"Oh, this is creepy; the crows are all looking right at us," Carter pointed out.

"They are waiting to see which god you are going to pay tribute to," said a high-pitched, scratchy voice directly behind them. The partners turned startled looks toward the voice and saw an old woman that looked like a witch right out of a fairy tale. She was stooped over, had wild, white hair, a large nose with a hairy wart on it, and several missing teeth. Her clothes were dirty, tattered, and too big for her.

"Who are you?" Carter demanded.

"I am no one you need to be concerned about as long as you pay tribute to one of the gods," she said.

"What gods are you talking about? All I see are a bunch of scarecrows," said Carter.

The old woman's face fell into an angry frown; she stood up straight, and said, "These are not scarecrows. Since when do you see crows sitting on scarecrows as if they are at home? These crows are the protectors of the gods. I suggest that you not anger them or me."

The woman settled back into her stooped posture. "Now, there is no need for anyone to get upset." The old woman reached inside her loose clothing and pulled out a strange-looking knife with a curved blade and a wooden handle. "All you need to do is chose one of the gods, kneel down before it, and each of you let out ten drops of blood onto the ground. Once you have done that, you may continue on your way."

"And what if we don't?" Kat asked with her arms crossed in a defiant pose.

Suddenly, a rustling of wind arose, and when it passed, Carter exclaimed, "Kat, look at the scarecrows!"

When the girl turned to see what Carter was concerned about, she gasped in shock and fear. All the scarecrows, like the crows, were now facing the children. The terrifying sight caused Kat's knees to buckle. Carter had to catch her to keep her from falling to the ground.

The old woman cackled, and sounded just like you would expect a fairytale witch to sound. "If you fail to pay tribute, the gods will watch as the protectors rise up and pluck the flesh off your bones while you scream in agony."

Carter had not noticed until now that even though the scarecrow faces were drawn in a variety of expressions: smiling, frowning, angry, frightened, laughing, they all looked somehow sinister.

"We need a few minutes to talk this over," Carter said. He took Kat by the arm and stepped out of the old woman's earshot. Facing away from the witch, Carter told Kat, "We can't do this; it isn't right. This place is evil. I feel it, and I don't want to do anything that will play into the hands of the Adversary."

"I agree, but what are we going to do? There are thousands of crows all around us; we can't outrun them."

Carter thought for a minute and then said, "Let's stall as long as we can. We can say that we need time to consider which one of the gods we feel we are to honor. We head east down the road as we examine the scarecrows. We pretend to be discussing them. When we have gone as far as we can get away with, we'll make a run for it."

Kat turned toward the witch and said, "We've decided that this is something that should not be taken lightly. We want to continue down the road and see if we can sense which of the gods we should pay tribute to."

"That is a wise decision. I am glad to see that you are taking your responsibility seriously. You may have some time to consider this matter, but let me warn you: do not try anything foolish."

The children turned and headed down the road. Carter whispered to Kat, "We need a backup plan. I doubt that she is going to let us get very far before she figures out what we're doing."

For almost a quarter-mile, the partners pretended to consider certain of the scarecrows closest to the road. They stopped from time to time as they pretended to talk and point at a possible candidate. After a moment, one or the other of the children would shake their head and encourage their partner to continue looking.

"If you think I do not know what you are doing, you are mistaken," the crone said. "Hurry up and make your decision, or I will set the protectors on you."

The partners nodded and then continued down the road. "What now? I don't see an end to these things, and if we try to run for it we're not going to make it," Kat whispered.

"Don't turn your head, but when we stop to check out the next scarecrow, scan with your eyes to the left a little. There is a cabin a couple hundred feet out," Carter whispered as he continued walking along the right side of the road. After they passed a few more scarecrows, Carter said aloud, "Let's check this one out." The boy turned to a scarecrow made out of blue overalls, a green-checkered shirt, and a frowning face drawn on a white bag stuffed with straw. It was wearing a red ball cap with the visor pointing back.

Carter peeked around and saw that the witch was in the middle of the road about fifteen steps behind them. She was paying close attention to every move they made. "Do you see the cabin?" whispered Carter.

"I see it, but we cannot make it there before the crows are all over us. What we need is a diversion. Maybe if we set fire to one of these things it will cause enough confusion that we might make it."

Carter said aloud, "I don't know about this one. The ball cap and frowning face doesn't feel right." Then he whispered to Kat, "That might work, but Sid stole all our matches back at the inn."

"I see one over there that might be what we've been looking for," Kat said aloud as she pointed to a scarecrow in the general direction of the cabin. Heading toward the next scarecrow, the girl whispered, "I have some matches."

"You do? Where'd you get them? I didn't give you any of the ones I bought."

"There was a box of free matchbooks on the counter at the gas station. I just picked one up and put it in my pocket when you were paying for our stuff. I forgot about it," she said with a shrug.

While the children stood pretending to examine the current scarecrow, Carter whispered, "Okay, here's what we'll do. We will pick one more scarecrow a few feet closer to the cabin. While I examine the front, you walk around to the back of the scarecrow and set fire to it. Be careful that the witch doesn't see what you are doing, and be quick about it. As soon as the protecting crow sees you light the match, it'll go berserk."

"That one there is the right one," Kat said as she pointed to a scarecrow made out of black cotton pants, a faded red shirt, and a hideous smiling face drawn (unlike the others) with orange paint on a burlap bag. Pieces of straw sticking out of holes in the top of the bag made it look wildly insane. The partners were able to move another ten paces closer to the cabin with this final selection.

"This better be your selection. I am out of patience with you two. It matters not which one you pick. What matters is that you perform the sacrifice and that you do it now," the old woman growled.

As Kat moved casually around to the back of the final pick, Carter stood with his hands behind his head looking up at the face of the scarecrow. "Yes, I believe you're right; this is the one. Are you ready to begin, Kat?"

"I have already begun, Carter." Suddenly, several things happened at once. The crow sitting on the scarecrow's head spread its wings, opened its beak, and screeched (a hideous call) as it lifted off its perch. Smoke and flames began to shoot up over the head of the scarecrow so fast that the crow's tail caught fire before it was clear of the flames. Carter and Kat began to run as fast as they could toward the cabin. The witch shrieked as if she were in mortal pain.

As they ran, the children could hear a sound like a roaring wind, but there was no breeze. Looking up, they could see that, as one, all of the crows lifted into the sky. The children realized that what they were hearing was the sound of thousands of birds taking flight. The witch's shrieking was lost in the sound of thousands of cawing crows.

Adrenalin rushed through the partners' bodies, and they ran faster than they ever thought possible. As they drew nearer the cabin, they kept imagining thousands of angry crows ripping and tearing at their skin with sharp beaks and claws, but the attack never came.

When it became clear to the children that they were going to make it to the cabin, Carter glanced over his shoulder to see what was happening. To his surprise, he saw not one but hundreds of scarecrows on fire. There was chaos in the sky; most of the crows were on fire as well. In their panic, they were flying into each other, which caused the fire to spread from one crow to another. The dying crows instinctively returned to the scarecrows that they protected, and the fire spread from the burning crows to the scarecrows. Eventually, the fire would cleanse the entire area of the so-called gods and their protectors.

The birds were not interested in the children, so the partners slowed to a fast walk.

Focusing on the cabin, they noticed that it was the same size as the cabins they had discovered in the Dead Forest. Unexpectedly, the cabin door opened. Standing in the doorway was a tall, thin man with a thick, black beard. He was dressed in blue overalls, a red shirt, and heavy, black boots. His head was bald, and he had an angry, red scar that began on the left side of his forehead and extended down across the bridge of his nose to below his right eye.

"Hurry!" he shouted as he beckoned the children with his hand.

The partners stopped and looked at the man with uncertainty on their faces.

"What are you waiting for? Hurry up, and get in here. I saw what you did, and the witch will want her revenge for destroying her precious scarecrow gods."

Just then the children heard the witch screaming from behind, "You little monsters; you will pay dearly for this!"

Carter and Kat looked back over their shoulders and saw the old woman running toward them with fiery anger and hatred on her face. "I think we better get inside," Carter said.

The man standing at the door said, "Yes, you better be quick about it. The old crone moves fast. She is almost upon you, and I am going to close this door. Now hurry!"

The partners jumped up the single step and in the door just as the man started to close it. The door slammed shut with the witch only three steps behind. The man lifted a heavy crossbeam in place so the door would not open from the outside.

"Why are you helping those little retches, Dark Beard? You and I have nothing to do with each other. I have no grudge against you. Now give me the brats, and I will trouble you no more!" the old crone yelled through the door.

"And what will you do if I do not give them to you, dear woman?"

"I will do whatever it takes to get my hands on them. You saw what they did. They destroyed the gods and killed the protectors. They are all gone now because of them. I will have my revenge!"

"I am going to ponder this for a time. I rather like what they did. Those things were such an eyesore. Now I will be able to enjoy the beauty of the wilderness," Dark Beard responded in a pleasant tone, which he knew would further enrage the witch. "By the way, how is it that if those things were gods that they could be so easily destroyed by two children?" he added to further provoke the hag.

"Do not play with me, Dark Beard. You are in as much danger as those brats you are protecting. I am willing to leave you in peace if you turn them over to me by sunrise tomorrow. If you do not, I will burn your cabin down, and I will show no pity. I will leave now and mourn my loss. Tomorrow, I will have my revenge on all who defy me."

Dark Beard turned away from the door and looked at the children. "I have been waiting for you. Welcome, my little friends. Please sit and make yourselves at home." The tall man motioned to a square wooden table that stood on an old brown rug in the center of the floor with four wooden chairs placed around it. Everything in the cabin looked old and well used. The crudely constructed one-room structure was made out of bare weathered wood, dried mud sealer, and a sheet metal roof. A stone fireplace, used for cooking and heat, took up most of the back wall. Shelves of supplies, tools, and personal items covered the rest of the walls. Each of these walls had one small window space equipped with a wooden shutter.

The room was warm, comfortable, and smelled of freshly baked bread and beef stew. Two loaves of bread sat on the hearth, and a black pot of boiling beef stew hung over a gentle fire.

The partners shared a look and Carter said, "We don't understand. What do you mean you've been waiting for us?"

Dark Beard reached for three wooden bowls as he encouraged the children, "There is plenty of time for talk. Please make yourselves comfortable. Lunch will be ready soon. He set the table and the partners seated themselves. "I doubt that you feel much like eating just yet. You have been through quite a stressful experience, but after you have rested and we have talked, perhaps then you will feel like eating."

"Everything smells so good," said Kat.

"Do we call you Dark Beard?" asked Carter.

The big man nodded and said, "You may call me Dark Beard, and what do I call you?"

"I'm Carter, and this is my friend, Kat. What's the story with the witch and the scarecrows?"

"Let me ask you something first. Did either of you allow yourselves to be cut so that blood fell on the ground before one of the scarecrows?"

Carter shook his head and answered, "No, we stalled until we saw your cabin. Then we set one of the scarecrows on fire to distract the crows long enough to make a run for it. We didn't intend to destroy everything and kill all the crows. What will the witch do to us?"

"She will kill you if she gets her hands on you, but I will do all I can to protect you."

"Why did you ask if we let ourselves be cut?" Kat questioned.

"Because, the witch is not alone. She has a pack of vicious wolves that roam the wilderness looking for food. The blood on the ground is just the first step in a complete ritual of sacrifice to her idol gods. Once you let your blood fall to the ground, the wolves come at night and get your scent from it. When they have your scent, they will hunt you down and feed on you. If you had gone through with her blood ritual, it would have been almost impossible for you to get out of this wilderness alive. But, since you were wise enough to refuse, you have a good chance of making it—with my help."

"Why are you helping us?" Kat wanted to know. "You're putting yourself in danger; you're risking your home and your life. Why don't you just turn us over to her and save yourself?"

"Like I said before, I have been waiting for you. I am supposed to assist you and give you two gifts. Once I fulfill my responsibility, it will no longer be necessary for me to stay here."

"How long have you been here?" Carter asked.

Dark Beard looked up and ran his fingers through his beard; he appeared to be considering an answer. "That is strange; I do not know. I have no memory of being here before you knocked on the door," he said with a confused look on his face. With a shrug, he continued. "While we wait for the stew to finish cooking, I will give you your first gift: a story.

DARK BEARD'S FIRST GIFT

Dark Beard folded his hands, leaned forward on the table, and began his tale.

One day, a mighty king of a faraway land wanted to inspire his people. He called his wisest advisor to his side and said, "I want you to go on a quest."

"What sort of quest, Sire?"

"I want you to search for the greatest, most valuable man in my kingdom so that I may reward and honor him before the people. He will stand as an example and a champion. He will be a role model to the children and an inspiration to the adults."

"I see. That is a worthy quest, Sire. Perhaps you already have someone in mind?"

"I do. There are rumors of a self-made man who lives in the southern region of the kingdom. I hear that he has many servants, a large house, and is fabulously wealthy. Perhaps you will find your quest shortened if you start with him."

"Very good, Sire. I will leave immediately."

Before the counselor could take his leave of the king, the king added, "Take my royal carriage and four guards. When you find the person I am seeking, I want him brought to my court in the style befitting the people's champion."

The wise man bowed deeply and said, "It shall be done as you have commanded, Majesty."

The man that the king had heard of was indeed very wealthy. He began with almost no money, and as his wealth grew, he took every opportunity to make himself richer and more powerful. It was also true that he had many servants. He had house servants to clean and cook, field servants to work his land, and he had one other servant that he kept for his amusement.

In all honesty, the rich man was selfish, cruel, and petty. One day, a few years before the king's quest began, a man with a wooden leg came to the rich man's home. He was poor and desperate. "I have tried everywhere, and I cannot find work. You are my last hope. I beg of you, sir, please give me a chance, and I will not disappoint you."

The rich man was curious about Goodman's wooden leg, and he asked, "How did you lose your limb?"

"I was in town one day when I saw a runaway horse and carriage headed for a little orphan girl who was playing in the mud in the middle of the road. I ran to grab her and take her to safety. I was fortunate enough to move her out of danger, but my right leg got caught in the wheels, and it was broken so badly that it had to be removed. Yet, even though I find it very hard to find work with a missing leg, I would do it again."

The rich man shook his head and said, "What a fool. I do not know if I want someone as stupid as you working for me, even if you had two good legs."

"I am sorry, sir, but why do you call me a fool?"

"Anyone stupid enough to risk his life to save a worthless street orphan is too stupid to work for me. Look what it has gotten you. You are crippled, and you cannot find work. I do not have any use for a man like you."

"Thank you for your time," the poor man said and turned to walk away.

Then the rich man got an idea. He thought that because this man was so stupid he might provide some amusement. He called out, "Wait a minute, Goodman."

"Yes?"

"I tell you what I will do. I will hire you at half of what I pay my other servants. You will do anything I tell you to do regardless of how dirty or difficult the job. I will let you stay in the barn with the animals instead of in the servant's quarters. You can have anything to wear or eat that I throw out. I will give you one day a week off. If you accept my terms, you are hired."

"I have little choice, sir. I must accept your terms."

From that day on, the rich man did everything he could to break the spirit of the poor man. He made him work from sun up to sun down, cleaning up after the horses, chopping wood, digging holes (even when there was no need of the holes) in the hot sun. Moreover, Goodman worked harder than any of the rich man's other servants, and he did so without complaining. He was respectful and kind to everyone. He always sought to encourage the other servants and make them feel proud of doing a good job. The servants respected him and treated him with affection. They shared their food with him and saw to it that he had warm blankets at night. The more the servants showed their love for the man, the more jealous the rich man became. The more jealous he became, the more he hated Goodman and the nastier he treated him.

It was on one very hot, sunny day that the king's royal coach pulled up in front of the rich man's home. The rich man greeted his royal visitor with, "Welcome, welcome to my humble home. I am honored by your visit."

A royal guard opened the door of the golden carriage, and the king's counselor stepped out. He had a long white beard and was dressed in royal blue. He wore gold chains about his neck and jeweled rings on his fingers. "I thank the lord of this land for his hospitality. I am the king's counselor and His Majesty has sent me on a quest to find the most valuable person in the kingdom so that he may be honored before the people as their champion."

"Oh, sir, I am most humbly honored to be chosen as the people's champion. Thank you. Oh, thank you. I do not know what to say."

While the rich man was talking, the king's advisor caught sight of the man with the wooden leg. He was some distance away carrying heavy loads of rock from one pile to another. The man's struggle in the heat, and the fact that he did not let his handicap slow him in his work, moved the counselor deeply. "Yes, yes, I am sure you would be honored if you were to be chosen," the counselor said absently. "Pray, tell me about that man over there with the wooden leg."

"Ah...oh...that is just Goodman," the rich man stammered. "He could not find work due to his handicap, and I was kind enough to hire him."

"Is that so? How did he lose his leg?"

The landowner told the counselor the story about how the man lost his leg saving the street orphan. Then he added, "I told him he was a fool."

"You thought him a fool, and yet you hired him anyway?"

"I figured if he was so stupid as to risk his life for a nothing like a homeless child, then I could make good use of his foolishness. And I was right." The rich man laughingly told the counselor how he treated Goodman.

The wise man listened intently, occasionally muttering, "Hmm," and, "I see. Please continue."

The rich man chuckled and said, "One day, I decided to test him to see just how stupid he was. I got the idea from something that happened when I was just starting out. When I was a young man, I ran into a bit of luck. I saw a wealthy old gentleman carelessly drop his moneybag in the street. I picked it up and quickly put it in my pocket. I used that money to purchase my first few acres of land, and that is how I got my start. I put a bag of gold coins where Goodman would find it. I wanted to see what he would do when he found some real money."

"What happened?"

"Goodman brought it to me and told me where he found it. I checked it to see if any of the coins were missing, but it was all there. If he had kept it and left to make a better life for himself, I would have had him arrested, but at least I would have had some respect for the man."

"Incredible," the counselor muttered.

"If you think that is incredible, you will not believe the things I hear other people say about him."

"Is that so? Please, do go on," the counselor prompted.

"Would you not rather learn more about me? After all, I am being considered to receive the king's honor, am I not?"

"Fear not, I am learning all I need to know about you," the wise man said, wearing a stilted smile.

"Very well, if you insist. The grocer told the servant who does my shopping that on one of Goodman's days off, he learned that the old woman who sells apples on a street corner was too ill to sell her goods. He immediately went to the old hag and told her to lie down on her cot and get some rest. He then proceeded to sell her apples for her. Later when it was time to close up shop, the apple woman offered to give Goodman half the money he made selling the apples for her. The fool refused, saying that she needed the money more than he did. When the old biddy started to cry and insisted that she could not accept his help without paying him something, the stupid man told her that he would only take an apple for his wages. I am told that the apple woman offers Goodman a free apple every time he comes into town now, but he refuses the gift and insists on paying."

"Absolutely incredible," the counselor mused.

"Yes it is, and there is more. I hear that on most of his days off, he takes the meager wages I pay him, and he buys fruit, bread, cheese, and candy. Then, he gets all the homeless children together, and they have a picnic. He is so beloved by the children that they follow him around while he is in town. He plays games with them, talks to them, and encourages them to help each other and take care of each other. He is some sort of hero to them. I hear that by his example, some of the merchants are beginning to help the street scum by giving them food and secondhand clothes. Some are even giving the older ones jobs. The older orphans then use their money to help the younger ones. It is insanity, I tell you. You cannot get ahead by being stupid. You have to look out for yourself, step on those who get in your way, bend the rules, and use those who are foolish enough to let themselves be used."

"You say that you allow this Goodman to eat your garbage, wear your rags, and work for half wages doing any and all jobs, without complaint, often better than your servants that you treat fairly?"

"Yes, and you know what really infuriates me?"

"I could not even begin to guess," said the counselor in a tone bordering on contempt.

"The other servants are starting to buy into his insane attitude. They seem to love and respect him more than they do me. Can you believe that? I am wealthy, powerful, and smart, but my servants defy me and give him food behind my back. They see to it that he gets better clothes and blankets when they can get away with it. Goodman is everything I hate. He is a failure, he is poor, he is stupid, and he shows weakness for the worthless. *He* is worthless! I do not want to talk about him any more. Let me take you on a tour of my land so you can get a feel for my value and worth."

"That will not be necessary. I have already made my decision. I want you and your servant to accompany me to the king's court so that I can present to him the people's champion."

"Oh, my lord, I am so honored," the rich man gushed as he kneeled before the king's man.

"Please get up. The choice is not up to me; it is the king's decision."

"I did not understand that there were any other candidates up for consideration. I assumed I was the only one."

"Please call your servant over and step into the carriage."

"Yes, of course. I will need a moment to get my personal servant and pack," the rich man said excitedly.

"That will not be necessary. I just want you and Goodman."

The rich man looked shocked. "What do you mean, Goodman?

He is filthy, he stinks, and he is in rags. I cannot have him serve as my personal servant in front of the court."

"I believe that the king would be amused by Goodman. I am afraid that if Goodman cannot come, then you cannot come either."

"I see," said the rich man. "Yes, I suppose Goodman would be an amusing character for the king to meet. He has been a mystery to me."

"Exactly so," the wise man said.

One of the guards rode on ahead to alert the king that the royal carriage was on its way back to the palace. When the coach arrived, the king was so excited that he greeted the coach personally. The first out of the coach was the wise man. "Welcome back, my valued counselor. I trust that even though your journey was a brief one that you have found the right man to serve as an inspiration and role model for the people."

"Sire, I believe I have. May I present to you, Goodman." The counselor motioned for the servant to exit the carriage. Goodman shyly stepped out and fell on his face before the king.

The king looked at the counselor with shock on his face. His mouth was agape, trying to find words to respond to what he was seeing. Flustered, the king asked, "What is the meaning of this? Is this some sort of jest?"

"No, Sire, this is no jest. May I also present to you the rich man you suggested that I seek out?" The wise man motioned for the landowner to exit the carriage.

The rich man stepped out of the coach, bowed to the king, and said, "Majesty, I am sorry for the appearance of my servant. We were bidden to come so quickly that we did not have a chance to change into something more appropriate."

"I see," said the king. "So this is the man you have chosen, and this fellow with the wooden leg is his servant."

"Well, yes and no, Majesty...I need to meet with you before anymore is said publicly."

"Very well, see to it that these two are cleaned up, fed, and rested from their journey," the king ordered his servants. "We will hold court tomorrow," declared the king and then went inside to meet with his advisor.

"Now, Counselor, explain the situation to me."

The wise man proceeded to report to the king all that had happened during his meeting with the rich man. He also told the king about the rich man's treatment of his servant. He explained to the king the man's opinions about looking out for one's self, using any means necessary to get rich, and his willingness to step on others in order to get ahead.

Then the advisor told his king what he observed of Goodman and all the stories of bravery, kindness, and selflessness that he had heard about the man. He told the king how the children loved him, and how Goodman's example caused people to show kindness and generosity to others. The counselor revealed everything to the king. Then he said, "I have brought you two very different men from which you can choose. The decision, as always, is yours."

The king nodded and dismissed the counselor. The next day at court, the king summoned the two individuals that the wise man brought to him. "My counselor has told me everything that he learned about you, rich man, and he has told me what he has learned about Goodman, your servant. Rich man, I have a royal decree to proclaim upon you. Step forward."

The rich man held his head up and walked down the long red carpet to the king's throne. He was full of pride and excitement; he was overjoyed at the thought that he was going to be recognized for his greatness. He bowed to the king and said, "I am grateful to his Majesty for this honor. I cannot begin to tell—"

"*Silence!*" the king commanded. "Sir, you are a despicable man. Your cruelty, selfishness, arrogance, and pride are quite offensive to my royal sensibilities. You, sir, offend my kingdom simply by your existence. Step aside, and be silent!"

The rich man was aghast. Confused and humiliated, he obeyed the king.

The king looked at Goodman. "Goodman, approach your king."

Goodman looked around in shock. Even though he had bathed and was dressed in nice clothes for the occasion, he did not feel worthy to approach the king. "I am just a servant, Your Majesty. I am nobody. I am not worthy to come into your presence."

"Gentle Goodman," the king spoke kindly, "would you disobey your king?" he said with a smile and a twinkle in his eye.

"Oh, oh certainly not, Majesty; please forgive me," Goodman stammered as he approached the king, bowing with each step he took.

"Calm yourself. All is well. I am going to declare you the people's champion."

"Me? Oh, but I am no champion. I am just a servant. I am no one. Surely you mean to make my master the people's champion."

The rich man could contain himself no longer. He said, "Your Majesty, you cannot be serious. This scum is not worthy—"

"*Hold your tongue, wretch, or, so help me, I will have your head removed from off your shoulders!*" The king's voice boomed out with intense rage. The rich man's face turned red with humiliation. He closed his mouth and hung his head in shame.

"Now, Goodman," the king continued. "I will not make your master the people's champion, but I will make him your servant. Furthermore, I will make you master of all he owns. Your bravery, kindness, love, positive influence on others, your humble spirit, your generosity, honesty, and positive attitude is the example that will lift up my kingdom and make it strong, healthy, and powerful. I declare that *Goodman* is the people's champion."

The people cheered. They lifted Goodman on their shoulders and carried him out into the streets, declaring to all they met that Goodman was the king's man, and that he was the people's champion. In the days that followed, Goodman's story spread throughout the kingdom, inspiring many to be better people.

It seemed to the partners that telling the story was difficult for Dark Beard. It was as if he knew each character personally, and perhaps he was an eyewitness to the events that he related. For the longest time,

Dark Beard sat quietly with a faraway look on his face. Then, quite unexpectedly, they saw tears well up in the man's eyes.

"Dark Beard, what is it? Are you all right?" Kat asked with concern.

"I am sorry. I promised myself that I would not let my emotions get the better of me when I told my story."

Carter asked, "Your story? Do you mean that you wrote the story for us?"

"No, I mean I lived it. I am the rich man from the story."

THE REST OF THE STORY

Carter, with a disbelieving look on his face, said, "You are the man who got your start by stealing a bag of gold from an old man? You are the man who tormented Goodman and held poor orphan children with absolute contempt? You are the man who was so arrogant and selfish that the king took all your holdings and gave them to Goodman?" Carter looked as if he had a nasty taste in his mouth.

Dark Beard sat looking at the table. His whole posture communicated deep feelings of shame as he nodded his head. "Yes, I was that man, but I have changed. I feel nothing but regret for the way I was. Now, I seek only to follow the example of my friend, Goodman."

Kat questioned, "Your friend?"

"Yes, my best friend. You see, Goodman wanted to give me back all my land and wealth, but the king would not allow it. He actually assigned guards to protect Goodman from me and to carry out all of Goodman's commands. One of the things the king commanded the guards to do was to make sure that Goodman did not show me any special kindness. The guards hated me so much that they did everything they could to make my life miserable. When Goodman caught them being cruel to me, he would put a stop to it. He would say, 'If I cannot show my former master kindness, at least I can forbid you from tormenting him.'

"You have no idea how much I hated Goodman," Dark Beard said with obvious pain. "I hated him when he was just a crippled servant that I kept for my amusement, but when he took all that was mine, all I had worked for all my life, I was determined to kill him the first chance I got. That is why the king sent guards to protect Goodman from me. The king sensed my rage and my desire for revenge. The more decent Goodman was to me, the more I wanted to tear him apart with my bare hands."

"But you said he was your best friend," Kat pointed out.

"Yes, I now see that he was my teacher, my hero, and my best friend. I had what you might call an epiphany." Seeing the confused looks on the children's faces, he simplified. "I guess you could say that I had a change of heart, mind, and soul. You see, the king would frequently call Goodman to court to act as one of his advisors. He also wanted to remind the people of the value of their champion. While he was away on these visits to the king, the other servants would take the opportunity to ridicule and mock me. They would say things like, 'You are not so high and mighty now, are you servant?' The head servant would give me the same type of dirty jobs that I once gave Goodman to do. Then, the servants would gather round, spit on me, and throw filth at me, all the while laughing and cursing me. They loved it when I lost my temper at them or wept in frustration."

Dark Beard smiled a crooked smile as he continued. "If I told Goodman what was going on, the servants would have murdered me; I deserved it. I was treated the same way I treated others."

Suddenly, it was as if a shadow passed over the man's face. "One day, while Goodman was away, things got so out of hand that one of the guards was taunting me with his sword. He kept saying, 'I will cut your head off, you wretch,' as he swung it in front of my face. The servants egged him on, saying, 'Do it; cut the scum's head off!

Do what the king should have done. Put us out of our misery, and cut his throat!'

"Goodman returned early that day. He saw the commotion and decided to investigate. When he got close enough to see what was happening, he shouted in horror. The guard turned his head suddenly, lost his balance, and stumbled. His sword was still pointing at my face when he fell toward me. As you can see from my scar, he almost succeeded in granting the servants their wish. Poor Goodman could hardly believe his eyes. Such cruelty was just not in his nature. Seeing his own servants acting in such a way was more than he could comprehend."

The tall man shook his head in wonder as he continued. "Goodman would come to my room while my wound was healing and visit with me. I could tell that he was a broken man. He would say to me that he felt like a failure. He said, 'The idea of me being the people's champion is laughable. If my own servants cannot show common decency to a fellow human being, then I will tell the king that he needs to find another champion.' Then he said the most peculiar thing. He told me that this was entirely his fault, and then he apologized to me. He went on to say that if he had not come into my life, none of this would have happened, and he began to weep."

"Then what happened?" Carter prompted.

"When he got control of himself, he said, 'I have had enough of this. If I cannot give you back your wealth and lands, at least I can help you get away from this constant humiliation.'

"I was overcome; I could not believe my ears. I knew that Goodman was a kind man. He used my wealth to help the community. He had a home built for the orphans in our village so that they would be cared for while they were educated and trained. I used to hold such kindness to be weakness. Yet, I see now that he was the strongest man I have ever known. He was willing to defy the king to help me escape and start my life over again. I could not let him do it. I told him that I was getting what I deserved, and that I would not let him defy the king and risk his own life for me. I told him that I was not worth it, and that I would always be grateful to him for his example to me.

"No matter whether he influenced anyone else to be a better person or not, he had reached me. That day, as I sat on the edge of my bed, I hung my head, and it was my turn to weep. For the first time in my life, I felt shame. Goodman put me to shame, and I saw myself for what I was. As I wept and begged his forgiveness, I felt all the anger, hatred, jealousy, and shame flow out of me. For the first time in my life, I felt free. Then I was aware of a hand stroking my head. When I looked up, I saw a man in a white robe. I was no longer in my room; I was here. I stood up, and the man was gone. The strange thing was that somehow I knew exactly what I had to do. I knew that I was to live in this cabin and wait for you.

"That is the first gift I was to give you—my story so that you would know it is possible for even a person like me to change. I no longer desire fortune, power, or fame. I desire to be of service to those in need. I want to help you children just as my teacher, Goodman, would help you if he were here. I know now that serving others is the source of true greatness. It took me a long time to realize it, but I finally came to see that Goodman truly was a champion and I was nothing."

Dark Beard stood, stretched, and said, "Now, how about some food. I do not know about you, but I am hungry."

The partners were a little overwhelmed by all that they had heard. Nevertheless, they nodded their agreement to some food. To their delight, it was wonderful. It was simple fare, but the bread was the best that they had ever tasted. It was still warm, and the rich butter that Dark Beard spread on the thick slices was soft and sweet. The beef stew was thick and tangy with just the right seasoning. The meat was tender, and the potatoes and carrots melted in their mouths. Dark Beard provided them with cold cups of well water that was more refreshing than any soft drink they had ever had. They ate with such zest that everyone was too busy with their meal to talk.

Finally, Carter broke the silence. "You said something about two gifts. May I ask what the second one is?"

Kat shot Carter a disapproving look to let him know that he was being rude.

"Yes, thank you for reminding me," the man said pleasantly. He reached into his pocket and brought out a large red-handled pocketknife. "I am supposed to give this to you." He handed the knife to Carter. "It has several tools that you will find useful. It has a compass in the handle, a little saw, a magnifying glass, a can opener, a little pair of scissors, a small blade, and a four-inch blade that is sharp as a razor. There are other tools—you can see for yourself what it has."

Carter was impressed with the pocketknife, and he smiled with joy as he looked it over.

"It'll be a miracle if he doesn't stab himself with it," Kat joked.

"Don't worry about me. I know how to handle stuff like this," the boy boasted.

"You mean like the way you handled the cheese grater that time you grated your knuckles so bad you could see the bone?"

"I was distracted."

"Were you distracted when you had to have ten stitches in your leg because you sliced it open with a box cutter?"

"Hmm, maybe I should have given the knife to Kat," Dark Beard said with a grin.

Carter's exasperation at being made the joke of the day came out as he said, "Come on, you guys. Give me a break, will you?"

Kat, with a self-satisfied expression, said, "Just be careful. I wouldn't want you to accidentally cut yourself and attract the witch's wolves to us."

"Come on, Hamsted; give it a rest."

The girl could tell that she was embarrassing her friend, so she let him off the hook by changing the subject. "Dark Beard, speaking of the witch, do you think she'll have her wolves nearby tomorrow when she comes for us?"

"I am sure of it. She will be using her time tonight to gather the pack. If they had been nearby today, she would have already forced you out."

"How are we going to get by her and the pack?" asked Kat with anxiety in her voice.

Dark Bead stood and said, "Stand up, and I will show you."

Carter and Kat obeyed their host and stood.

"Now grab your end of the table and help me move it off the rug." Once the rug was clear, the man pulled it back revealing a trapdoor. "There is your way out. That trapdoor opens to a tunnel that leads to a system of caverns called The Forge of Providence. Follow the tunnel straight to the cave. You will find a winding path through the caverns that leads to a dense forest. Once you are out, head north, and you will come upon a road that runs east and west."

Dark Beard laid the carpet back over the trapdoor and had the children help him move everything back into place. Resuming their seats, the man continued, saying, "Even though this will get you past the witch and her pack tomorrow, I must warn you that The Forge of Providence is a place from which few return. This system of caverns has been the testing ground of many great heroes. Stories tell that there are beings who dwell in the caverns to test those brave enough to enter The Forge. If they determine that the person being tested has some special role to play in history, they set the individual free to fulfill their destiny. It is also said that only those tested by The Forge have any chance of surviving the Valley of Shadows."

When Carter first saw the opening of the tunnel that would lead them away from the witch, he felt encouraged. Upon hearing how dangerous the caverns would be to travel, his anxiety began to grow. His fear made him feel agitated and frustrated. "That's just great! And what, may I ask, is this Valley of Shadows? Is that some other pleasant place we have to look forward to?"

Dark Beard looked at Carter with compassion in his eyes as he said, "To be honest with you, I do not know if the Valley of Shadows is a real place or just something people use to refer to difficult times. I know that you are going to face more danger ahead. And since you have made it this far in your quest, it is fitting that you travel The Forge. The responsibility has been given me to tell you that you have been and are preparing for a task that will demand every ounce of strength, courage, and determination you can muster. If you are able to exit The Forge, you will prove once again that you may be the ones who can accomplish that which few would even attempt."

"We have just come through some serious situations that almost got us killed. It sounds like you're telling us that what is waiting for us is far worse. How much more of this are we supposed to take?" Carter sounded as frustrated as he looked.

"That is up to you; it always has been your choice. You *have* come a long way, and you have succeeded where many have failed. Do you regret what you have learned, what you have accomplished?"

"No." Carter shook his head.

"Kat, you have prevailed against powerful forces. Do you feel like you have gained all that you desire from this endeavor?"

Kat sighed and shook her head too.

"If you decide to continue your quest, I must tell you that when you enter The Forge, one of three things will happen. Either you will take a wrong path and be killed, make a bad decision and be forever trapped, or you will find your way out. But, be warned, even if you do find your way out of the cave, there is a good possibility that the witch and her wolves will still track you down. I do not think that she will give up on her revenge after all the damage you have done to her. But the fact that you did not allow the wolves to get your scent from your blood will slow them down. And speaking of the blood sacrifice, there is one other good reason that you did not make the sacrifice. Those who make an offering to evil would be automatically trapped in The Forge with no chance of escape."

The man, who at one time would never have given a second thought about another's troubles, actually felt concern for the two frightened travelers. "Carter, Kat, if I could, I would come with you and risk my life to help you fulfill your destiny, but I cannot. You are on a journey that you must face alone. I am only one of those who will give limited assistance to you, and I am almost at the end of my limit. I can provide you a place to rest for a few hours. I can supply you with enough food and water to get you through the forest. I have an extra set of batteries for your flashlight so that you will be able to have light as you travel through the cave. I will stall the witch and her pack as long as I can. Nevertheless, once she burns the cabin down, she will find the tunnel and figure out where you are headed."

A look of horror came over Kat's face. She asked, "Will she follow us through the cave?"

"No, there is no chance of that. She is old, and the cave would be even less friendly to her than it will be to you. Besides, the wolves will not be able to descend the ladder."

The girl took in a deep breath and let it out slowly as she tried to calm herself. "Maybe we should start now. The sooner we get going, the farther away from her we'll be when she comes for us. If we get tired, we can rest in the cave. Besides, I doubt that I'll be able to relax much now. The sun is still up, and I'm too uptight."

"Of course, it is your decision, but I suggest that you not sleep in the cave. Once you enter, it is best that you keep moving. It would be better if you try to get some rest now while I get your supplies ready. If you do fall asleep, I will make sure you are up in plenty of time to be gone well before the witch comes for you."

"Dark Beard, what is going to happen to you? You know that the witch is going to burn the cabin down. What are you going to do? Are you just going to let yourself be burned alive? Are you going to leave through the tunnel? What?" Carter wanted to know.

The man smiled and said, "This is only the second time in my life anyone has been concerned with what happens to me, and it feels good to know that someone cares. Do not worry, my friends. No matter what happens, I am at peace. Now, I suggest that you lie down and try to get some rest."

The partners agreed, and surprisingly, they both fell asleep only a few moments after they settled onto some blankets. They were both in a deep sleep when they heard a gentle voice saying, "Carter, Kat, it is time for you to wake up. I have your supplies ready, and I have made you a little something to eat before you leave."

The children opened their eyes and saw Dark Beard standing over them. They stretched awake and sat up.

"The sun will not rise for hours, so you have plenty of time to get far away before the witch finds that you are gone. I have made you some toast with butter and honey and some warm tea to wash it down."

The children were a bit wobbly as they moved to the table. While they ate their breakfast, Dark Beard showed them a hard leather backpack full of supplies that he had prepared for them. "There are fresh batteries, dried meat, nuts, bread, and a few other items in this pack. It should get you through the forest and maybe a little beyond. I also filled your canteen with fresh water. When you are finished eating, you can be on your way. Now, do you have any questions for me?"

Carter asked, "What do you know about the adobe?"

"What adobe?"

"The adobe we're supposed to find. We were told to head east until we find an adobe."

Dark Beard shrugged and answered, "I am sorry, but I cannot help you with that. I do not know anything about it."

When the children were done eating, Kat said, "It's time we put some distance between us and the witch." She stood and said, "Thank you, Dark Beard, for all your help. And I hope that you will be safe." The girl looked at her partner and said, "You get the backpack, I'll get the canteen, and let's get this table moved before I lose my nerve."

AN OFFER YOU CAN REFUSE

The three new friends made their goodbyes, and then the partners climbed down the ladder that took them about thirty feet below ground. The manmade tunnel was very narrow; the children had to walk single file. Carter took the lead with the flashlight in hand. The walls of the tunnel were carved out of packed soil and shored up with wooden planks. The air was stale but cool, and the overall feeling was very claustrophobic.

"Normally, I would be glad to get out of this tunnel, except I'm more afraid of what awaits us when we reach the cave," Kat said in a shaky voice. "How long is this thing anyway? It seems like we have been walking for miles."

"It looks like we are at the end of the tunnel," Carter said as he came to a stop. "We've come to a dead end. There is nothing here but a wall of dirt."

"How can that be?" Kat whined. "This thing is supposed to take us into a cave, right?"

"That's what Dark Beard said," Carter responded irritably.

"What should we do? We can't go back, or the witch will get us for sure."

Carter sighed and stood staring at the wall of dirt. "Maybe this thing isn't very thick. I'll use the knife that Dark Beard gave us and try to dig through to the other side."

The boy held the flashlight in his mouth and pulled the knife out of his pocket. He looked for a tool that would be good for probing the dirt wall. Selecting a four inch pointed spike, he attacked the wall with an overhand stab. To the partner's surprise, when the spike made contact with the wall, it made a loud thud as if it was hitting a wooden door.

"That's odd," Carter said. He tapped on the wall with the spike a few more times, and unexpectedly, a door opened. The Adversary stood behind it.

Carter was so shocked that he dropped the flashlight, took a quick step back, and accidentally stepped on Kat's foot. She yelled in pain and reflexively bent forward, bumping her forehead into the back of Carter's head. Both children lost their balance and fell backward. Carter landed on Kat and knocked the wind out of her.

"Oh my, I did not mean to startle you. Are you all right?" the Adversary asked in a concerned tone that did not sound sincere.

Carter got off Kat as quickly as he could. "Kat, are you okay? Are you hurt?"

The girl was gasping for breath and unable to speak. She managed to sit up and shook her head no.

The canteen had fallen off her shoulder and was lying beside her. Carter picked it up and said, "Here, drink some of this."

Kat took a swallow, then in a weak voice said, "My foot hurts. My head hurts. And I got the wind knocked out of me, but I'll live. Just give me a minute."

"That was quite a spill you took. Are you children just naturally clumsy?" the Adversary asked snidely.

Carter's fear started to turn into anger. He stood up, turned to the Adversary, and asked, "Why are you here? Aren't you getting tired of losing to a couple of kids?"

The Adversary's tone became cold and dangerous as he responded, "You only need to lose once, and you are dead." The boy and the white haired man stared at each other with mutual dislike in their eyes. Then, surprisingly, the Adversary broke into a smile that did not reach his eyes. "Come now; I am not here to quarrel with you. I have a proposition that I believe might interest you. If your friend is recovered enough to stand, we can step into my office and make ourselves comfortable." The Adversary stepped back and motioned for the children to enter.

Carter helped Kat to her feet and then put his arm around her waist to steady her as they walked through the door. They found themselves in a large office with dark wood paneling. A large cherry wood desk and thick padded, dark leather chairs were located appropriately about the room. Strange, abstract paintings hung on the walls. The colors and images hinted of suffering and horrors that made them hard to look at.

The Adversary moved around behind the desk and sat in a luxurious chair that looked a lot like a throne. "Sit and rest awhile. You will find the chairs are very comfortable," the man said as he indicated two chairs in front of the desk.

"What is this place? I thought the tunnel emptied into a cave," Carter said as he helped Kat to her seat and then sat down to her right.

"Yes, it does. The tunnel empties into the cave right where you discovered the door to this office. This office is just a temporary construct where we can conduct our business. Once we have finished, this place will dissolve."

"I see. Then we'll be back in the cave to continue our journey," Carter speculated.

"Perhaps not; that is what I want to discuss with you. As I said, I have a proposition for you, and if you agree to it you will no longer need to continue your journey. I know that you have been through some rough experiences. You have seen people die, you have been in mortal danger yourselves, and even now, an evil woman and a vicious pack of wolves are hunting you. I can make all this go away and send you home. How does that sound?"

Carter's jaw tightened and his eyes narrowed to angry slits. "Why should we trust you? You're the cause of most of our troubles."

"Yes ... well ... maybe so, but why not give me a chance to make it up to you. Let me send you home where it is safe, and you can forget all about these past few days."

"Why?" asked Kat.

"Did the Kat get her tongue back?" The Adversary grinned as though he had just made a most clever pun. "Why what, my dear?"

"Why would you send us home? You must want something from us."

"You are a clever girl." The Adversary looked at Kat for a moment; then he turned his gaze upon Carter. "Both of you have exceeded my expectations. Nevertheless, believe me when I say that it is only a matter of time before I defeat you. Give up, and agree to forget everything that has happened from the day the storm caught you in the Dead Forest up until now. If you do, I will take you back to the day of the storm and place you outside the forest. I will make the forest disappear so that you will never find it again. Eventually, you will give up looking for it, and the terrible things you have experienced will fade from your memories. Think about it; what do you have to lose? Just a lot of terrible memories of painful experiences," the Adversary finished with a smile that attempted to reflect sincere concern, but failed.

"No, I don't think so," said Carter. "You wouldn't be offering us this deal if you weren't beginning to wonder if you really can defeat us. We have made it farther than you expected, and you are starting to have your doubts, so rather than risk defeat, you are trying to deal your way out. That's it, isn't it?"

"What difference does that make? Even if you do succeed in completing this quest, is it worth it? Has it been worth all the pain and suffering you have gone through to make it this far? Let me assure you that win or lose, there is more misery to come—a lot more. Why not end it now and go home? Do not be foolish; you are smart kids. You have nothing more to prove. Now, what do you say? Shall we put an end to all this? You will be home in time for dinner, you will sleep in your warm, comfortable beds, and none of this will ever have happened."

"I don't understand. If this isn't very important, then what's it to you? Why do you care? Carter and I know that you don't care what happens to us. So there must be some other reason you are making this offer."

The Adversary's face grew very cold and cruel. Kat and Carter knew that the Adversary's expression reflected his true feelings. "I know why he is making this offer, Kat. It's because he really doesn't care what happens to us. He knows that it's through struggle and hardship that a person grows strong. It's like that corny saying: no pain, no gain. We are growing as people and gaining strength of character and wisdom by going through these experiences. If we give up the struggle, we give up all we've gained. I'm not willing to do that. There is more to learn and more to gain. Now, if you don't mind, you are holding us up, and we want to be on our way." Carter stood to leave.

The Adversary stood and raged, "More to gain, you say? Do you suppose that I do not know what lies the Guardian has put in your heads? He has you stupid children believing that you are the youths of the prophecy, but there is no truth in it, and I will prove it by seeing to it that you fail!" With a wave of his hand, the partners found themselves sitting on the ground, in total darkness.

LIFE IS NOT A DREAM

"Turn on the flashlight; I can't see a thing," Kat demanded.

"I hate to say it, but I don't have the flashlight."

"What do you mean you don't have it? What happened to it?"

"When we stumbled outside the Adversary's office, I was so concerned about you being hurt that I forgot to look for it. With the light coming from the office, it just didn't occur to me that I had lost it. I'm sorry; it's my fault."

"Never mind that; what are we going to do without a light? We don't know how big this cave is, and without a light, we could be lost in here forever," Kat said with more than a little panic in her voice.

"Don't freak out on me. I have an idea. You still have some matches—"

"Oh yeah; those will last us a long time," Kat interrupted sarcastically.

"Just wait a minute, and let me finish what I was going to say. We lost the flashlight—"

"You lost the flashlight," Kat interrupted again.

Carter let out a patient sigh that said he was trying to hold his temper. "When I lost the flashlight we were in front of the Adversary's door. Now that it's gone, we must be near where I dropped it. If we're lucky, we should be able to find it before we run out of matches. You still have them, don't you?"

"Yes, I'll strike a match, hold it up, and you see if you can locate the flashlight. Give me a second to get them out. Are you ready?"

"Yes; go ahead."

The two were still sitting on the ground when Kat struck the match. The match flared, revealing that they were in a massive cave. Then Kat screamed and dropped the match. Dropping the match did not plunge them back into darkness. The reason for the scream and the source of the new light was standing in front of them. A man in a brown robe, with brown hair and a goatee, was holding their lit flashlight. The unexpected appearance of the man caused the partners to jump to their feet without noticing the pain from their minor injuries. The man's face looked young. It was not a kind face, but it was not cruel either.

"Who are you?" Carter demanded.

"Calm down, children," said the man. "You are in no danger from me. I simply need to explain what you are doing here and how you can get out. You and Kat sit over there on that rock."

"We will stand, thank you. And how is it that you know our names?" Kat said with her arms crossed and a look of suspicion on her face.

"Fine, have it your way. Stand, sit; it does not matter to me. Who I am and how I know your names is unimportant. What you need to do is listen to me if you want to get out of here."

Kat was starting to feel anger well up inside her. She did not know if it was anger at being in the mess she was in or anger at the attitude of the stranger, but she decided to be difficult just because she was in a mood to be difficult. "Why?"

The man looked at her and asked, "Why what?"

"Why should we listen to you? How do we know that we can trust you? How do we know you aren't here to confuse or trick us into doing the wrong thing so that we will never find our way out of here?"

"I am not here to hurt or help you. I am only here to make clear to you what you can expect. First, you will not be able to get out of here without a light. I believe this belongs to you," he said as he held the light out to Kat. But the angry girl just stood with her arms crossed. The man offered the light to Carter. "Do you want your light back?"

"I'll take it, thank you, and I will sit down." After sitting down on the rock, Carter requested, "Please tell us how to get out of here."

Before the man could say a thing, Kat turned to Carter and said, "What's the matter with you? Why are you listening to this person? Whose side are you on anyway?"

"I'm on our side, and I don't see that we have any choice here. I don't know how to get out of here, do you?" Before she could answer, Carter continued, "No. I didn't think so. Now, come over here, sit down, and let's hear what he has to say."

Kat was so annoyed that she pursed her lips, scowled at her partner, and tapped her foot defiantly. Finally, she said, "I'll listen, but I'm not going to sit."

"Fine," Carter said.

"Fine," Kat said in a nasty tone.

"That is wonderful. We are all fine now," said the man sarcastically. "This is a place of testing. You will face three challenges, and if you are successful in dealing with these challenges, you will be allowed to leave the cave. Those of us who test do not care whether you succeed or fail. We have no other interest or concern for you other than putting you to the test. Therefore, you will find us unbiased and unyielding. The letter of the law, not compassion, rules here."

"What if we're not successful?" Carter asked.

"Then we will know that you are not the youths of the prophecy, and it will matter not to the world if it never sees you again."

"What prophesy are you talking about? We do not know about any prophesy," Kat grumbled and then sat down next to her friend.

"It is not for me to explain such things to you. I am here to tell you that if you do the right thing, you will be allowed to leave The

Forge of Providence, and then you will be one-step closer to fulfill-ing your destinies."

"How will we know what the right thing is?" Kat asked in an urgent voice.

"Simple. If you do the right thing, then things will work out for you. If you do not do the right thing, then you will have to pay the price for making a bad decision."

"Is that it? Is that your big help? Make the right choice, and we'll be okay; make the wrong choice, and pay the price? We could have figured that out for ourselves," Kat growled.

"As I said, I am not here to help or hurt you. Though, come to think of it, I did find your flashlight for you," he said and then winked annoyingly. Oh, one more thing, you will want to start your journey going down the path right behind the rock on which you are sitting." Then he turned abruptly and disappeared into the dark.

Carter stood and said, "Okay, let's go."

"Go? Go where?"

"I don't know about you, but I'm going to head down the path he suggested."

"Why are you going to do that? The guy in the robe went straight ahead. How do you know he wasn't lying to us?"

"I don't know, but for now, I'm going to trust him. After all, he did return our flashlight," Carter said with a grin as he held up the light.

Kat was about to say something irritating, but stopped herself when they heard the sound of someone crying. "Do you hear that?" Carter asked as he looked around trying to decide from which direc-tion the sound was coming.

"Yes, and I think it's coming from the direction that man told us to go," Kat said as she looked behind them.

"I guess that settles it. Someone needs help, and we have to see if we can be of help. Besides, it will give us a chance to talk to someone else and see if we can get some more information about this place."

"Very well, I'll go along with that."

As the partners moved closer to the sound of weeping, they heard someone say, "I cannot reach them. Please, will someone help me get another?" Then there were more sobs and loud weeping.

"It's hard to tell where the sound is coming from. It keeps bouncing off the rocks. Should we call out and see if we can get a response?" asked Kat.

Before he could respond, Carter saw something unusual on the ground. "What's that?"

"What?"

"That blue thing with the yellow specks on it that looks like a yo-yo. I think it's some kind of mushroom."

"Yeah, I see it," Kat said. She leaned down to pick it.

"No!" Carter cautioned as he grabbed her arm. "Don't touch it; it could be poisonous."

"They are not poisonous," a weak voice said. "They are the most wonderful thing I have ever eaten. Please bring it to me," the voice said pleadingly.

"Where are you?" Carter called out.

"Pick the mushroom, and bring it to me. I am a little farther along the path. Hurry, I must have another mushroom."

Kat reached down to pick the mushroom, and again Carter stopped her. "Don't touch it. Let's wait and see what's going on before we do anything we might regret."

"But someone is in pain. Don't you think we should help?" Kat asked with concern in her voice.

"Yes, we should help, but we need to know more before we can decide what needs to be done. Come on; we're wasting time."

The friends continued toward the sound of weeping and eventually came upon a boy that was about seventeen. He looked to be in good health, but he was on his stomach lying on the ground, crying. "Thank goodness you came. Let me have the mushroom—*quick*. I need it! You did bring it, right?"

Carter stooped down next to the teenager and asked, "What's wrong with you? Why can't you get up and get the mushroom for yourself?"

"Actually, I am fine. It is just that the mushrooms paralyze me for about ten hours after I wake up. You eat them, and they are the most wonderful thing you have ever tasted. They cause you to fall asleep, and you dream the most fantastic dreams. It is as if you are really there. You dream that you can fly, that you are a superhero, or that you are rich and can do anything you want. Every dream is new and wonderful. When you wake up, all you want to do is eat another and go to sleep again. But, as I said before, you cannot move for about ten hours. You have to wait to get your strength back so you can go and get another. But since you are here, I do not have to wait. You can bring one for me and one for each of you, and we will all dream together."

Carter asked, "Where did you come from? How did you get here? Who are you?"

"I do not remember. It does not matter. All I want is for you to get me a mushroom. I need it! I am miserable until I get one."

"Why don't you gather a bunch of them so when you wake up you can just eat another?" Kat wanted to know.

"There are two reasons why that will not work. First, the mushrooms shrivel up and rot soon after they are picked. Second, when I wake, my body is paralyzed except for my mouth. I could not use my hands to put another in my mouth."

"No," said Kat.

"What do you mean?"

"She means we will not get you a mushroom."

"Why not? I am in pain. I *need* a mushroom! I will just die if I do not get one right *now*! Do you not care if I die?"

"That's not what you said before. You said that you would be paralyzed for several hours. Eventually, you will get up and get another. Can't you see that's not living? You dream about stuff that's not real. Then you lay awake for ten hours, unable to move or do anything. When you finally can do something, you just eat another and dream again," Carter said with a disapproving tone.

"You have no right to judge me. I can do whatever I want. Now give me a mushroom, or my suffering will be your fault."

"You're right," Carter nodded.

Kat looked at Carter, confused, and said, "What?"

"Good. Now get me a mushroom. I need one real bad."

"You're right. You can make your own decisions and live the way you want. You're a prisoner to your own addiction. Now, if you want us to wait with you until you can walk again, we will be glad to take you with us as we try to find a way out of here. We do want to help you. If we give you another mushroom, it will only prolong your suffering. We won't help with that."

"Please, if you are just going to leave me here, at least get me a mushroom. I just woke up, and I will have to lie here about nine more hours. Please, you have to help me go to sleep again and dream."

Kat shook her head and said, "What you need is to spend the next nine hours thinking about what you are doing to yourself. We'll go slow and leave marks on the rocks so you can catch up with us, if you decide to get out of here. We are going to leave, and we will be happy to have you join us, but we are not going to be a part of your sickness."

The boy started to cry, and then he screamed, "Get out; go away! You have no idea what you are missing. It is worth the suffering. Now get out!"

"If that's what you want," said Carter. "But remember, we're going to leave a trail for you just in case you change your mind."

NARROW IS THE WAY

As the partners started to leave, the boy began shouting insults at them, calling them evil brats, selfish, uncaring monsters.

Carter said, "Call out to us, and we'll wait while you follow our signs. My name is Carter, and my friend is Kat."

The teen cried, "I have no light; I will not be able to see the signs. There is no other choice. You have to stay with me and feed me the mushrooms. They are hard to find in the dark. Sometimes it takes me hours to find one."

Kat began to weaken and said, "I don't think I can leave him alone in the dark. He's sick. Can't we stay with him for a little while?"

"Kat, I would if I believed it would help, but you can see for yourself that he has no intention of leaving this place. He is just trying to get us to make it easier for him to feed his addiction."

Kat nodded and said, "You're right."

The teen started to beg, "Please, please do not leave me here like this. I need the mushrooms, and I need your help. I will come with you if you will just get me one more mushroom. Then I will be able to leave. Just one more, *please*."

"Carter, he has a point. He has no light. How can he follow us in the dark?"

Carter considered this and then told the teen, "If you are serious about quitting and coming with us, we'll wait with you until you're able to walk again, but we will not get you another mushroom. You have to make up your mind now; this is your only chance."

"I hate you! Go; get out of here. You are evil little children; I hate you!"

"Come on, Kat. We can't do anything for him; he's made his choice."

Kat nodded sadly and said, "I guess you're right. Do you think we can send someone back for him, someone who can help him?"

"No!" the boy shrieked. "Do not send anyone. They will take my mushrooms. They are mine, and I do not want anyone else to know they are here. Just go and leave me alone. You have done enough to upset me. Just leave me alone!"

"I'm ready to continue," Kat said sadly.

For what seemed like hours, they heard echoes of the teen crying and screaming. Eventually the sounds faded, and they found themselves standing before a large divide. From the edge, Carter pointed his light down the drop to see if he could get an estimate of how deep it was. Disturbingly, it was so deep they could not see the bottom. Luckily, enough of a ledge existed along the cliff that they were able to continue on to their left.

As they walked along the ledge, they noticed that the path grew wider and easier to travel. "Look at this," Carter said, and he knelt down and pointed the light at a footprint in the dust. "We must be going the right way. Someone else has gone this way before us."

The friends continued until they came across an unexpected sight. Two parallel ropes, one above the other, ran across the divide. They were about six feet apart, and Carter recognized what they were. "It's a two-rope bridge. I wonder where it goes."

"Who cares? You won't get me on that thing. How does it work anyway?"

"It's fun. We made one at summer camp last summer. You hold onto the top rope and stand on the bottom rope. You slide your feet in a sidestep motion to cross. It isn't easy, but it works if you're careful."

"I want to keep going along the ledge. The path is wide and level. Besides, I see more footprints up ahead."

"Hold on a minute; let's give this some thought. There wouldn't be a bridge unless it went somewhere. It's going in the direction we were headed before we got to the divide. If we cross the bridge, we can continue on in the same direction we started," Carter speculated.

"Hey, you kids. I need help," a girl's voice called from across the divide.

"Who are you? What do you want?" Kat shouted back.

"What difference does it make, *stupid*? I need help. Get over here, *now!*"

"Who do you suppose she is?" asked Kat.

"I guess she's someone who needs our help. We need to check it out."

"You check it out, Carter. You know how to cross a rope bridge. I'll wait here. When you get back, we can keep walking on the ledge."

"Okay, I'll be back as soon as I can." To the person across the divide he called, "I'm on my way; I'll be there as soon as I can cross the bridge."

The female voice called back, "It is about time. Be sure that you both come. And watch out for the rope snakes. You must cross in darkness; light makes them crazy. They are very poisonous. Now get moving!"

"What does she mean *rope snakes*? What's a rope snake? Why do we both have to go? I'm not going; I can't. I especially can't go in the dark. And there is no way I'm going if there are poisonous snakes on the ropes, and neither should you, Carter," Kat said with her voice full of fear and anger.

The female called out again, "Hurry up. I need help. Just be careful and go slowly in total darkness. The snakes should not bother you if you do not step on them or grab them."

Kat yelled back, "Why do you need *both* of us? I can't do it; I cannot cross that bridge. I hate snakes. I think you are just trying to get us killed. You are rude, nasty, and you are trying to trick us. It won't work, so just leave us alone."

"Kat, I know you're scared, but we don't really have a choice. Besides, I think this might be the right way. People don't just build bridges for nothing."

"Yes, but what about the footprints? There are several sets of footprints going the easy way. That's a clue that lots of people know the way to go. It must be the right way."

"Maybe, but it could mean that lots of people *hope* the easy path is the right way. Face it; we have to check out what's going on with that girl."

"I don't trust her. She is rude and obnoxious. Since when does someone who needs help call the people she's asking stupid? It doesn't feel right. Besides, I can't do it. I cannot go across that rope in the dark with poisonous snakes crawling all over me. Who could? It isn't right. *No!*" Kat screamed and stomped her foot.

Carter gave his friend a moment to calm herself, and then he said, "You know we have to go, don't you?"

Looking down at her feet, Kat sighed and nodded her head without looking up.

"I know it's scary. I'm scared too. Listen, I have an idea. There's enough excess rope where the ropes are tied off that I can cut a long enough piece to fit around our waists. That way if you fall, I can help you back up. How's that sound?"

Kat thought, *What if you fall and pull me off.* She decided to keep that thought to herself and just nodded her agreement.

"What is taking so long?" the female shouted. "I am caught between two huge rocks over here, and I cannot move. I need you to stop wasting time and get over here to help me. What is wrong with you people? Is it that you just do not care if someone is hurt?"

"Just ignore her, Kat," said Carter as he finished tying the rope around her waist. "Now, here's the plan: I go first; we go slowly and stop if there's a problem. We take our time and stay safe."

"What if the bridge breaks? What if a snake bites one of us? What if—"

"What if I'm the one who slips and falls?" Carter finished Kat's question.

Kat nodded shamefully. "I don't want to be a coward, but I can't help it. I'm really scared."

"I understand, but I know this is the right way to go. If we don't make it across this bridge, we're not going to make it home anyway. Come on; the more we think about it, the harder it's going to be. We need to just go for it."

The friends stepped onto the bridge. Kat's legs were shaking so bad that Carter could feel the rope vibrating. The ropes were so far apart that the partners had to reach well above their heads to grab the upper rope. "It's going to be okay, Kat; just stay close to me. I'm going to turn off the light, so don't freak out." Fortunately, the ropes were very taut, which made the bridge easier to use. Once Carter turned off the light, the darkness was total. Kat could not help letting out a little moan of fear.

"Together now; we slide our right feet and then bring our left feet to meet our right. Slide the right foot out and bring the left foot to meet the right," Carter called as the two inched their way across the bridge.

They were making good progress when suddenly, Kat's left foot slipped off the rope. Then her left hand slipped, followed by her right foot. Kat was hanging on with just her right hand. Screaming and kicking her feet, she tried desperately to get back on the footrope. Carter reached out and grabbed her around her back and under her arms. "I've got you, Kat. I won't let you fall. Reach up with your left hand, and grab hold of the rope."

"I can't! I'm going to fall! I'm going to fall!" she screamed in panic.

"No, you're not! I won't let you. Stop struggling, and do what I say. Reach up with your left hand, and grab the rope."

"Okay, I have it."

"Good. Now pull yourself up a little and get your feet back on the bottom rope. I will lift you while you pull yourself up." With Carter's help, Kat was able to get herself back on the rope bridge.

"I knew you could do it, Hamsted. Now, let's start again."

"Wait. I need a rest. I almost died! Please, Carter, let's go back."

"We can't go back now. We're probably closer to the other side than we are to the beginning. We need to keep going."

"But what about the rope snakes? How are we going to get by them?"

Carter sighed and answered, "I don't know. We'll just have to deal with it if we run into them. Now, the sooner we get going, the sooner we can get off this thing." Just as they were about to resume their trek across the bridge, they heard a hissing sound. "Kat, did you hear that?"

"Yes; it sounded like a snake hissing."

"It came from just next to my right foot," Carter reported.

"What now?" Kat asked.

"Let's just try to stay calm, wait, and see what it does. Maybe it'll go away." As the frightened children stood motionless on the rope bridge, in total darkness, hanging over a drop so deep they could not see the bottom, a deadly poisonous snake crawled slowly over Carter's feet and then over Kat's feet as it made its way along the rope.

Once the snake passed, Kat said, "I'm feeling sick. I think I'm going to throw up."

"Me too. If we were on solid ground right now, I think I would faint dead away. I'm dizzy, and this darkness isn't helping. We've got to get off this bridge."

The partners had just resumed moving across the bridge when they heard another terrifying hiss. "Stop!" Carter called to Kat. "This one is by my hand. It's touching my little finger. Kat! It's crawling down my arm. Now it's crawling across the back of my neck."

"Oh, Carter," Kat sobbed. "I knew we shouldn't have tried to cross this thing."

Carter stood gritting his teeth and trying desperately not to scream. To his horror, when the snake reached the far side of his shirt collar, it moved inside his shirt and down his back. His fear

174

was paralyzing; he could not talk, move, or think. He stood bracing himself for the burning bite that he knew would come. The snake moved to the bottom of his left shoulder blade, under his armpit, out the bottom of his sleeve, up his left arm, and surprisingly, back onto the rope. "It's back on the rope and headed for you. Don't move. It's your only chance," Carter managed to say with a trembling voice.

Kat let out a gasp that alerted Carter to the fact that the snake had made contact. "Don't move, Hamsted. Just let it go where it wants."

"It, it…knuckles…m-my knuckles," she stammered. "It's past n-now. Oh, please I hope there are no more," the girl croaked.

Carter's resolve began to weaken as he said, "I thought I was strong, but this is too much. It's all I can do to hold onto the rope. I cannot move."

Now it was Kat's turn to be strong. "No you don't. You got me out here, and you're going to get me across this crazy bridge. Do you hear me? You're not going to give up now. We've made it this far. We're going to finish it or die trying!"

"Okay, I'll be all right; let's go." Happily, they only had to take three more steps, and they were across. Once they stepped onto solid ground, they both fell down and just lay there trying to calm their rapidly beating hearts.

"So, you made it; big deal. Get off your lazy bottoms, and help me out here," the female voice said in a nasty tone.

Carter sat up, reached into his pocket, and pulled out his flashlight. When he turned it on, he saw a young woman standing a few feet away. She had long platinum blond hair, violet eyes, fair skin, and was dressed in a beige robe. She was not pretty even though she had pretty features. There was something cold and uncaring in her expression.

Kat sat up and said, "You look fine. What help do you need?"

The woman said, "I do not need any help, but you did. You needed help to get you across that bridge. This is the only way out of here. If I had not given you a good reason to cross it, you would no doubt have taken the easy path that most people take. That path along the ledge leads to a very dark place where even your flashlight would not have helped. You would have fallen off the edge of the divide that you just crossed. Everyone who takes that path ends up dead."

Kat shook her head in confusion and asked, "Why were you so rude to us? Couldn't you have just told us that the rope bridge was the only way across the divide?"

"This was your second test, and you passed it. You were willing to risk your lives to help someone who was not nice to you, and it saved your lives. If you had taken the attitude that you would only help people who are nice to you and refused to help me, you would have taken the wrong path and perished. Now you can continue on to your last test. If you pass it, you will be out of this cave."

The woman turned abruptly and started to walk away. Carter called out, "Wait! I don't understand. If that was our second test, what was our first test?"

The woman turned to Carter and said, "Your first test was handling the boy addicted to the mushrooms. You passed that test too." Before Carter could ask her another question, she disappeared into the darkness.

THE ELF AND THE GIANT

"Have you noticed that each test has gotten harder and more dangerous? I wonder what's in store for us this time," said Carter.

"What could be harder than what we just did? I mean, we almost died!"

"I might have the answer to your question, young lady," a voice from behind a rock said.

Startled, Carter pointed the flashlight in the direction of the voice, but he did not see anyone. "Who are you? Show yourself," Carter demanded.

"Certainly, I will be happy to show myself," the voice said as a man, about three and a half feet tall, stepped from around a large rock. "The next test is for you to help me get my gold back from a giant. Do you suppose that you have the courage for a challenge like that?" The little man had a long brown beard that came to a point. He wore a strange yellow hat that came to a point and leaned to the right side of his head. He had on orange overalls, no shirt, and green pointy shoes. Kat thought that he looked like a human little person trying to pass himself off as a storybook elf. Even though the little man looked a bit comical, he seemed like someone not to be trusted.

"My name is Lastooch. I am an elf, and I live in this cave. I dug a tunnel where I mine gold for a living. One day an evil giant threw me out of my mine and took it over. He has my gold, my mine, and everything I have worked for."

The whole time he talked, the little person blinked his eyes rapidly and shuffled his feet. His speech was halting as if he were trying to repeat something rehearsed.

"We're only kids. How are we supposed to force a giant to give your stuff back?" Carter asked.

"I have a plan to get my gold back, and I need your help. That is your final test. You are to assist me in recovering my gold. If you do, I am prepared to give you a bag of gold nuggets worth a considerable amount of money."

"Mr. Lastooch, do you mind if we talk this over first?" asked Kat.

"No, of course not, I expect you to talk it over. Take your time. I will just wait here."

Kat walked far enough away that Lastooch would not be able to hear them. Carter followed her and asked, "What do you think?"

"I don't know. I don't trust him," Kat said with her hands rubbing her upper arms. She added with a shiver, "It's cold in here."

"What if Lostmooch, or whatever his name is, is telling the truth? What if he really needs our help and we don't help him? We could be stuck here forever. And what do you make of his offer to give us a bag of gold?" Carter asked with a glint of greed in his eyes.

"That's part of what's bothering me. If this really is a test, why is he offering us a bribe to help him? If we help him for a reward, we'll not be demonstrating a willingness to aid someone out of kindness. And, by the way, I believe his name is pronounced Lastooch."

Carter shrugged and scowled as he started to feel a bit disappointed. "I get it. The test is to see if we will turn down the gold and help him just because he needs help, right?"

"Maybe, I'm not sure. As I said, I don't trust this guy; something about his attitude makes me suspicious."

"Yeah, he does seem a little shifty," agreed Carter. "Do you think we should tell him he doesn't have to give us anything? Maybe he knows a way out of here. We could ask him if he would show us the way out if we help him," Carter suggested.

"It wouldn't hurt to ask," agreed Kat. "Lastooch, we will help you. We don't want any reward. But if you know a way out of this cave, we would be grateful if you would show it to us when we're done."

"Absolutely; it would be my pleasure to show you the way out. That is, of course, if we are successful. Now that we have an agreement, I will explain my plan to you on the way to the giant's mine."

"Wait a second," Carter said. "You said the mine was yours."

"It is."

"But you just referred to it as the giant's mine," Carter pointed out.

"Did I? Well, I meant my mine, of course. How silly of me. He has had possession of it for so long that I guess I have begun to think of it as his. Just a simple mistake, my boy; just a simple mistake is all it was," Lastooch said with a careless shrug. "Let us be on our way, shall we?"

As the partners followed the man through the cave, he proceeded to explain that the giant would be asleep when they arrived. "I am going to sneak in while he is asleep, take the bags of gold out, and load them into a wheelbarrow that I have hidden nearby. It will take me three trips to get all the gold. If I am lucky, I will be able to get all the gold without waking him. However, if he wakes up, I will need you to create a distraction so I can escape."

"What sort of distraction will get him out of the mine?" asked Kat.

"You will hide at the top of a large pile of rocks located about fifty feet in front of the mine entrance. You will have little trouble climbing it, and you will be perfectly safe hidden among the rocks near the top. You will call out that you are hurt and need help. Since he sleeps near the entrance, he will hear you and go out to investigate. That will leave me in the clear to escape."

"Tell me something, Lastooch," Carter demanded. "If the giant is so evil, why would he leave the mine to see if we need help?"

The little man seemed to be thinking up an answer when suddenly, he tripped and fell to the ground. "Ouch! I think I sprained my ankle," he said, rubbing his left ankle. "Let me sit here a minute." After making a real show of his injury, moaning and rocking himself, he finally stood up and said, "I will be okay now; we can continue on to the mine." He walked with an exaggerated limp.

"You haven't answered Carter's question, Lastooch," Kat said, not convinced that the injury was real.

"Question? Oh, you mean, why would an evil giant care enough to come out of the mine if he believed someone was injured? Well, I assumed that was obvious. He would try to rob anyone who was injured and unable to defend himself. You need not be concerned; as I said, you will be safe upon the rocks. Now, we need to be quiet; we are almost there."

The partners noticed that the little man's limp was gone. The sprained ankle was obviously a stall while he came up with an answer. This made Carter and Kat more convinced that Lastooch was not to be trusted.

Kat whispered to Carter, "He's lying."

"I know, but what are we to do? We're almost there."

"I don't know. I don't like this. I don't like him," Kat said in a little louder voice.

"Careful; he'll hear you," Carter whispered.

"I don't care," Kat said aloud.

There was no doubt that Lastooch heard this last comment, but he ignored it. After they walked a few more feet, in silence, the man stopped. He pointed to a large pile of rocks and said, "That is the backside of the rock pile I told you about. Climb to the top, and you will see right into the mine. You will be able to see the giant sleeping. While you climb, I am going to wait by the entrance. Once you get into position, use your flashlight to signal me. I will sneak in and begin bringing the gold out. If I am in the mine and the giant wakes up, you call out for help. It is very important that you do that. If he catches me, there is no telling what he might do. Do you understand?" Lastooch waited for a response while the partners looked at each other with doubt in their eyes.

"What? What is the matter? I thought we had a deal. You are not going to go back on your word, are you? He is a giant! He stole everything I own, and I need your help! I am going to do this with or without your help," he said and stormed off.

Alone now, Kat said, "I have a bad feeling about this."

"Me too, but I don't think we have much choice. We gave our word. I say we climb the rocks and see what happens. Maybe the giant won't wake up."

Kat nodded her agreement. The two were able to climb the rock pile in about ten minutes. From the top of the pile, they had a clear view into the mine entrance. They could see a fire burning. Behind it was a giant man laying on his side. Even from this distance, they could hear loud snoring. Carter pointed his flashlight down toward the mine and waved it back and forth a couple of times to signal Lastooch. He turned it off, and they waited to see what would happen.

A moment later, they saw the little person sneak around the right side of the entrance and into the mine. They watched and wondered how long each trip would take. After about three minutes, they saw Lastooch sneaking out with several small cloth bags cradled in his arms. It took about five minutes per trip. That left just ten more minutes of torturous waiting to see if anything unfortunate happened. The partners did not want to be faced with making a decision to help Lastooch or not. They were worried that they might be helping the wrong person. After all, they only had his word, and his word did not seem very credible.

The two watched nervously as the little person finished his second trip. Everything was going smoothly—until Lastooch entered the cave on his third trip. A loud *pop* from the fire threw sparks and hot ash into the sleeping giant's face. He sat up with a yell of shock and wiped at his face with his hands. He did not seem to be seriously injured. Looking around sleepily, he rubbed the back of his neck, stretched, and then used a stick to shove some embers back into the fire. The partners continued to watch nervously as the giant man moved his blankets and bedding back away from the fire.

"He is huge," Carter whispered.

"So what should we do? Should we yell out?" Kat asked with fear in her voice.

"Let's just wait a minute. Maybe he'll go back to sleep."

To their disappointment, he stood up and yawned. Then he quickly turned his head, looked back into the tunnel, and rumbled, "Who is there?"

"Carter, we have to do something!"

"Is there someone back there?" They heard the giant call out.

"Carter!" Kat pleaded.

"Okay, together, we both yell out," Carter said and then began shouting, "Help! Help! Someone help us, please!"

Kat began calling out too, and they saw the giant turn his attention toward them. He called out, "I am coming. Hold on. I am coming." He picked up a torch, stuck it into the fire to light it, and then hurried out of the mine. "Where are you? Keep shouting so I can follow your voices."

When they saw Lastooch sneak out behind the giant, the partners stopped yelling.

"Oh no; I am too late," they heard the giant say to himself. "*Please* call out again. I am coming," he shouted. "Oh, this is terrible. I am too late. They sounded like children," he said aloud with trembling in his voice. Once again, he shouted, "Call out again, and I will come help you. *Please!*" That last please was so full of concern and passion that the children started to feel that they had done something terribly wrong.

"Oh, Carter, we have made a horrible mistake. We have to go down to him and explain what we've done."

The partners could see the giant looking about frantically as he called, "Where are you? I am coming. Please be all right. I am sorry I did not get to you in time. Forgive me. I am big and slow. Please forgive me."

Kat could not take it any longer. She called out to the distraught man, "It's all right. We're okay. We will be down in a minute. All is well."

The giant turned toward the sound of Kat's voice. He held his torch up in an attempt to see where they were. Of course, he could not see them because they were climbing down the backside of the pile.

"You are all right then? I am so relieved. I will wait here for you."

"What are we going to say?" Carter asked as they descended the rock pile.

"The truth, of course; what else can we do. We have made a real mess of things. Whatever happens, we deserve what we get."

When the two finally made it down to where the giant waited, they were amazed at how truly large he was. He had long tangled brown hair and a scruffy beard. His leather garments and bare feet made him look a bit like a caveman. However, his kind intelligent eyes made him seem very human.

"We're so sorry. I'm afraid we have made a terrible mistake," Kat said as tears welled up in her eyes.

"Now, now, little lady, it cannot be as bad as all that," the giant said in a deep booming voice. "Come, sit by my fire, and you can tell me all about it." His voice was so full of compassion and kindness that Kat could feel guilt welling up in her chest.

"We don't have time. Your gold is gone, and we need to hurry and get it back. It's our fault. We helped Lastooch steal your gold."

The giant man let out a long sigh and said, "I am afraid it is too late; he is long gone by now. Come, let us talk." He led the children into the mine.

The giant and the partners sat down around the comfortable fire. Carter spoke up, "I know that it's no excuse, but he told us that you stole the gold from him. He said that he dug this tunnel, mined the gold, and that you took it all from him. He asked us for our help to distract you if you woke up while he was recovering his gold."

"I see, and you believed him because he told you I was some sort of monster, an evil giant. Then, when you saw me, and how I look, you believed him enough to go through with it."

183

"Something like that," Carter admitted. "For what it's worth, we are very sorry, and we'll do whatever it takes to make this right."

"I am afraid that there is no way to make this right. It took me four years to mine the gold I needed to pay my way out of here, and now there is no more gold in this mine."

"I don't understand. What do you mean *pay your way out of here?*" Kat asked.

"When I found myself trapped here, I was told that if I mined twenty bags of golden nuggets, I would be set free. Today, I finished that task. After my nap, I was going to take my payment to the keeper of this place. I was so excited about getting out of here that I almost could not fall asleep. I guess I will not have any trouble sleeping now. There will not be much else to do since I am trapped here forever."

"Don't say that. We'll get your gold back. We have to. We can't just let you be trapped here forever," Kat said with desperation in her voice.

The giant put his huge hand on the girls head and patted it gently. "It is all right. I know you are sorry and you would make it right if you could. You made a mistake, and I forgive you. You need to forgive yourselves. It looks like we are *all* trapped here now. You are free to stay with me if you like. At least I will not be lonely anymore."

"I guess you're right," Carter said. "We were supposed to pass three tests in order to get out. This was our last one, and we failed it miserably. I guess that means we're stuck here too. It serves us right, but it isn't fair that you should suffer too."

"You are right about that, young man," said a familiar voice from outside the mine. The three new friends looked out and saw Lastooch approaching the entrance. "You did fail that last test miserably, and it is not fair that this kind soul should suffer on account of your mistakes. That is what happens when you do stupid things. Not only do you hurt yourself, you hurt others too."

"*You!*" Carter snarled and jumped to his feet. "It's Lastooch: the one who stole your gold."

184

"Calm yourself, Carter. Everything is going to be made right." Pointing at the giant, Lastooch said, "Taloff has passed his test. His test was to see if he could forgive someone who had done him a great wrong. Because he has forgiven you, he is free to leave this place, and so are you."

"But we failed our test; you said we failed it. Why are we being let go?" Kat asked.

"Everyone makes mistakes. You should remember, Kat, the way to handle mistakes is to feel genuine sorrow and have a willingness to make things right. You both have that attitude. *And* since Taloff has forgiven you, he has set you free along with himself. You will have plenty of time to consider what has happened here. It is time now for all of you to leave this place and fulfill your destinies." With a wave of his hand, Lastooch and the cave disappeared.

After a brief moment of disorientation, the partners realized that they were standing in a thick green forest of pine and fir trees. The sun was setting and had already dropped below the tree line. There was no sign of the cave exit, no trail, or any evidence of how the partners had arrived at their present location. They simply found themselves standing alone in the midst of huge evergreen trees.

Once they had oriented themselves to their new surroundings, Carter noticed Kat was looking around as if she were trying to locate something. "What are you looking for?"

"I was hoping that Taloff would have been allowed to join us for a while. I rather liked him. He is one of the few really kind people we have met since entering the Dead Forest."

"Yeah, you're right. I liked him too. Who knows, maybe we'll see him again." Carter looked up at the sky and said, "It's going to be dark soon. We need to get a fire started and set up camp. I don't want to scare you, but I don't want to be caught out here in these woods after dark without a fire. I'm thinking about the witch and her wolves. If they are tracking us, we do not know how close they may already be."

Catherine put the canteen down and started gathering wood. The partners worked swiftly. Before long, they had a roaring fire that chased away the dark. "Do we have enough wood to last the night," Kat asked and sat down next to Carter.

"Yes, we have some big logs that will burn all night. I'll put them on the fire before we go to sleep. Nothing will come near us as long as the fire burns bright." Carter decided not to add *unless it's rabid.* He also thought, *There's no telling, in this strange dimension, what unnatural things might be lurking in the forest that would not let a little thing like a campfire stop them.*

Kat reached over and grabbed the pack, opened it, and asked, "Are you as hungry as I am?"

Carter nodded and asked, "How long do you suppose we were in that cave?"

"I was just going to ask you the same question. We didn't sleep or eat while we were in there, but it seemed like we were in there for days." Kat bit into a piece of dried meat and said, "That tastes wonderful."

Carter chuckled at seeing his partner talking with her mouth full. That was something she never would have done at home. "I didn't realize how hungry I was, either," the boy said as he joined in the meal. "The water tastes fresh, and the meat and rolls are delicious."

The warmth of the fire and the pleasure of having their hunger satisfied with good food put the partners in better spirits. When they were finished eating, they each made a sleeping area near the fire. It was a warm night, and as they lay staring into the fire, Carter said, "Do you want to talk about what happened in the cave?"

Kat turned on her back, put her hands behind her head, and looked up at the stars. "No, not tonight, I'm tired. Let's get some sleep."

NIGHT TERROR

In his sleep, Carter thought he heard Kat scream. He sat bolt upright and looked over at her covers only to find that she was gone. Just as he was about to call out for her, he heard a desperate scream coming from the forest directly in front of him. Along with the scream, he heard growling, snarling, and yipping sounds. The terrified boy yelled, "Kat, *I'm coming!*" He looked at the fire and saw a large branch about the size of a baseball bat. Half of it was on fire and half was unburnt. He grabbed the cold end and held his torch high as he ran toward the sounds that filled the night.

He was so desperate to reach Kat that, in his haste, he fell several times over the brush and debris that covered the forest floor. He felt like he was in a hideous nightmare where, try as he could, he was unable to make progress toward his goal. Kat's screams and the sounds of what Carter knew were the witch's wolves were getting farther and farther away. Desperate, Carter yelled, "Hold on, Kat, I'm coming!" His heart pounded like a hammer in his chest as he kept trying to hurry through the thick forest only to be frustrated time and again. Kat was screaming Carter's name and pleading for help.

Then, something more terrible than the screams of terror and the vicious growls of killer wolves filled the night: silence. The boy froze. He was so intent on hearing something, anything, that he stopped breathing. He stayed focused on the forest ahead, begging in his mind for some little sound that would let him know that it was not too late to save Kat, but there was nothing. Finally, Carter breathed, and then he yelled, "Kat, can you hear me?" What he heard in response was an evil, mocking laugh that Carter knew came from the witch. The sound of that laugh and the thought of his best friend being hurt, or worse, filled the boy with rage. He gritted his teeth and yelled out, "You better not hurt her, or you'll be sorry!"

Off in the distance he could hear the witch mocking him. "I am so afraid; please, do not hurt me, little boy." More cackling laughs followed. "Do not be angry because my wolves were hungry. They could not help themselves. The girl was sweet and tender." Then, more evil laughing filled the night.

Something seemed to snap inside Carter. He reached into his pocket for his knife. He opened the largest blade and held the knife like a sword; in his other hand, he held the torch. With his jaw set in furious determination, he forged ahead. There was no fear left in him, only rage. Fire filled his eyes, and his heart slowed to a steady pounding. Carter was like a soldier who had seen his buddy killed in battle. He was so filled with hate and grief that he no longer cared if he lived or died. If his partner was dead, then nothing mattered anymore. He just wanted to do as much damage to the witch and her wolves as he could—before he fell.

The witch continued taunting and mocking Carter, and that made it easy to find his way.

Now you, the reader, may be thinking that if he had not been so angry, Carter might have realized that he was being led into a trap. Carter knew it was a trap; he just did not care.

Eventually, he came to a clearing where the body of a young girl lay, covered in blood. Carter fell to her side and gently turned her over to look into her face. It was Kat; she was not breathing. He shook her and called her name trying to revive her.

"No use; she is dead, and soon you will join her. The two of you will feed me and my precious wolves for at least a week," the witch said as she stepped out from behind a large tree. She was smiling, and her eyes glowed yellow like the eyes of her wolves. They too stepped out of the forest and surrounded the boy.

Carter felt for his knife that had fallen to the ground along with the torch. He picked up his weapons and held them out over Kat's body. "I won't let you hurt her anymore," he raged. "Stay back or I will kill you and every one of your precious wolves."

"Oh, dear me, whatever shall we do? We are hungry, and a little boy with a pocketknife will not let us eat our kill," she said mockingly. "Do you really believe you have a chance against me and a pack of wolves? Do you think we are afraid of you and your pitiful pocketknife?" the witch spat with contempt.

Carter continued pointing the torch and knife at the witch as he glanced around to see if any of the wolves were advancing on him. They were not moving, but they were crouching, ready to pounce. Their eyes were glowing, their teeth glistened, and their lips were curled back in hideous snarls. It was a terrible sight, and the boy knew that he only had seconds left to live. That realization became even clearer when he noticed that his torch was flickering out. He knew the moment the fire died that it would be over. When it finally happened, he heard the hag shout, "*Kill!*"

Carter threw himself across his friend's corpse, covered his head with his hands, squeezed his eyes shut, and braced himself for the impact of the large vicious animals pouncing on him. He dreaded the terrible pain of sharp teeth ripping and tearing at his flesh. He just hoped that it would be over quickly. However, there was nothing—no pain, no sounds, just the peaceful sound of a campfire burning. He opened his eyes, looked around, and the first thing he saw was Kat sitting up and looking at him. She was white with fear, and she was looking at her friend as if she had just seen a ghost.

Carter sat up and said, "Kat, you're okay; you're alive."

"Oh, Carter, I just had the worst dream I've ever had. I dreamt that the witch's wolves came into our camp and dragged you out into the forest and killed you. I chased after you, but I couldn't keep up. I kept falling, and when I finally found you, you were dead. You were covered in blood, and it was so real. I'm still not sure it was just a dream."

"I don't think it was. I had the same dream, but in my dream it was *you* that the wolves dragged into the forest and killed." I think it's a warning. If we're not out of this forest by the time the sun goes down tonight, the witch and her wolves will find us. We have to break camp now and get moving." Carter looked up at the sky and observed, "The sky is already starting to lighten. It will be light enough for us to travel by the time we pack up and put the fire out."

The children worked quickly—they were eager to be on their way. Carter checked the compass in the knife handle and then pointed north. "If we head north, we'll come to the road heading east. I hope we're out of the forest by the time we reach the road."

"Why don't we head northeast and come out farther up the road?" Kat suggested.

Carter scratched his head and said, "I considered that, but if the forest ends before we hit the road, then heading straight north will get us out of here faster. I'll feel better once we're back on the road. Out here, I feel lost and spooked. I don't like thinking about what might be hiding behind the trees and bushes."

"Good point. Let's get out of the forest as fast as we can," said Kat as she shouldered the canteen. The partners said little as they struggled through the dense forest. The going was slow and exhausting, but the children were determined to reach the road before nightfall.

BATTLE AT
IRON WOODS

The partners struggled on, taking few rest stops because they knew the witch and her wolves were determined to make them their dinner. They figured that if they made it out of the forest before dark, they might find help. There were only two hours of daylight left when Kat asked, "Carter, what if we don't find shelter or help? And even if we do, what is to keep the wolves from coming after us again?" Kat sounded breathless as she struggled next to her partner.

"We can't worry about that now; we have to keep going. One thing is for sure: we don't have any chance at all if they catch us in the forest."

"Couldn't we climb a tree? Wolves can't climb trees, can they?"

"No, they can't, but you're forgetting the witch. She could set the tree on fire, and then what would we do? No, our only chance is to get to open ground and hope we find shelter or someone to help us."

"Oh, I hate playing the victim. I don't like feeling helpless and at the mercy of that old hag and her pets!" Kat snarled.

"Hold on a minute," Carter said thoughtfully, and stopped. "You're right, Kat. We are running and panicked about the witch, her pack, and whatever else might be stalking us in these woods. And what have we done to prepare for a possible attack? In our dream warning, or whatever it was, we were helpless because we didn't have any weapons."

Kat shrugged and said, "Yeah, so where are we going to get weapons?"

Carter brightened up and said, "We have a forest full of resources. Where do primitive cultures get weapons to survive against wild animals and to hunt for food?"

Understanding began to dawn on Kat's face. "We can make spears, staffs, maybe even bow and arrows."

"Now you're talking, Cookie," Carter said jokingly. "Since we're in a hurry, I suggest we each find a staff and I'll carve the ends into points. That way we can hit and poke."

Within thirty minutes, the partners had two sturdy staff about six feet long with sharp points carved at each end.

Kat felt the heft of her staff, swung it around to get a feel for its balance, and declared, "I feel safer already. Just having something in my hands that I can swing makes me feel like I am ready for anything."

"Maybe we'll get a chance to practice some moves later," Carter said as he tested his staff. "Anyway, I still think our best bet is to get out of the forest as soon as we can."

Just as the partners started north again, they heard loud booming footsteps and the sounds of breaking branches. Turning toward the disturbance, they saw part of the forest on their southwest side shaking and tree tops waving violently. Instinctively the children held their staffs ready to repel whatever came through the wood at them. With a cry of relief and joy, they greeted the humble giant, Taloff, as he came into view.

"I am glad that I found you," Taloff rumbled. "I have much to tell."

"We were wondering if we would ever see you again," Kat beamed. "Where have you been, and why were you looking for us?"

"I am here to help you. When we left The Forge, I found myself in this forest. You were nowhere to be seen. I called out for you, hoping you were close enough that we could meet up again, but someone else answered my call. A man in white who calls himself the Guardian was camping nearby. He invited me to join him and he was kind enough to feed me and give me drink. We talked about you, and he told me that you were on a quest that could bring radical change to all the people. Then he told me that you were in grave danger and in need of a champion to help you. Then he asked me if I was that champion. I told him that I did not know if I was a champion, but that I would do whatever I could to aid you."

"What did he say," Kat asked.

Taloff smiled and said, "He said, 'Spoken like a true champion.' Then he told me about the witch and her wolves tracking you. He said that they would catch up with you sometime tomorrow morning."

"Does that mean that even if we travel all night that we will still not be clear of the forest?" Carter asked apprehensively.

Taloff sighed and said, "It means that they will catch up with you whether or not you clear the forest, but do not despair. I know about this witch and her monsters. Before I was trapped in The Forge, I wandered this land for many years."

"What land is this, Taloff? "Does this existence have a name?" asked Kat.

"This world is called Dearth."

"That sounds like where we came from. We came from Earth. And this place is called Dearth—how funny."

Taloff smiled a sad smile at Kat and said, "I see that you do not understand. The name of my world is a very sad one. Dearth means deficiency, want, or lack. Perhaps you have noticed that there is a shortage of kindness and compassion in my world, but that is not all. The very fabric of existence here lacks stability. Things change, disappear, and move around mysteriously. Some say that this lack of stability is a reflection of the weakness in the character of its people."

Before the children could respond, Taloff continued, "Every place in Dearth has a name. I am only familiar with the names of the places I have traveled and a few I have heard others mention. This forest is called Iron Woods because there is something in the soil here that makes the trees strong like iron. The staffs you have made for yourselves are impressive. How is it that you were able to sharpen the ends? The wood is so strong that no ordinary knife would have been able to shape those points."

Carter explained that he used the knife Dark Beard gave him. "I had no trouble at all carving the points. In fact, it was so easy that I was worried that the wood may have been too soft to be used as a weapon."

Taloff laughed at this and asked, "Have you tried breaking the staff over your knee? If you have not then I suggest you not bother; you will only injure yourself. Once we get a fire started, I will show you how to temper the points and make them even harder. Few things are as strong as an iron wood point tempered by fire."

It was decided that the trio would make camp where they were, and that they would make their stand against the witch there too. The area was relatively clear of plants and debris. With a bit of tidying up, they had a clearing large enough for a fight.

Once they were set up for the night, Taloff surprised the children with a pack of food sent by the Guardian. They had dried meat and fruit along with fresh, cold water.

Once they had eaten their fill, Taloff showed the partners how to fire harden their staff tips.

"Taloff," Carter asked, "can you give us some pointers on how to use these staffs?"

"The staff is my weapon of choice. I will be glad to teach you some basics. First, you have to know your enemy. Fighting animals is different from fighting men. There is a different strategy and a different psychology. You will not be fighting ordinary timber wolves either. The witch controls a pack of six dire wolves."

"Dire wolves?" Carter choked. "But I learned in my science class that dire wolves went extinct thousands of years ago."

Taloff raised his eyebrows and said, "Perhaps where you come from they are no more, but here there are still a few running around. They are larger than average wolves, and their teeth are larger. They are not as intelligent as timber wolves, but what they lack in cunning, they make up for in ferocity."

"When they come for you, ignore the witch. Her power is in the animals she controls. The Guardian told me that you already took care of her crows."

The partners smiled uncomfortably. "That was an accident," Kat said. "We did not mean that to happen."

"Accident or not, you seriously weakened her powers. I hear that the former Valley of the Gods is beginning to bloom and blossom with natural beauty now that the scarecrows and crows are cleared away. If we can destroy her pack, she will be done for. She will hurt no one ever again."

"Taloff, did Guard say anything about Dark Beard? Did he make it out of the cabin alive?"

"Is that the man who gave you the knife?"

"Yes," Kat said hopefully and sat up straighter.

"No, I am sorry, little one. His name never came up. I only remember Carter referring to him as the man who gave you that magnificent pocketknife. Now, I think it is time we started our fighting lessons."

Late into the night, Taloff worked with the partners teaching them basic staff fighting moves. The giant was impressed at how fast they learned. Both children were well coordinated, quick, and surprisingly strong for their ages.

When he felt that they had learned enough of the basics, he instructed the partners on strategy. "We will stay here by the fire and make our stand. We want the fire burning brightly—the higher the better. This will make the pack nervous and keep them from sneaking up behind you. When the witch shows up, she will have the leader at her side. I want you both to stand with the fire to your backs, and confront them.

"Remember what I taught you about how to use your staffs. Remember your war cries and make them fierce! Show no fear. You are mighty warriors who have exited The Forge of Providence! You are ready to take on anything. Now get some sleep. I will watch over you and keep the fire burning bright."

The partners found it impossible to sleep knowing what they were to face. Every night sound from the forest made them jump. It was the longest night of their lives. The waiting was unbearable. They wanted the sun to rise so that they could face their enemy. The night wore on, and as the dawn drew close, the partners were finally able to catch a little sleep.

Once the sun was up so were the partners. They turned to Taloff and he put his finger to his lips to warn them to silence. He stood, nodded to them, and then he hid himself in the forest. The partners felt their stomachs flutter as if a hundred butterflies were fighting to escape them. It was time that they take their places. Taloff told them that when they saw him move into the forest to hide, that it would be the sign that the witch and the wolves were near.

They quickly wadded up their sleeping gear and tossed it out of the way. They picked up their staffs and stood listening to see if they could catch where the witch would emerge.

"I see you were expecting us. So kind of you to have breakfast ready," The witch cackled as she stepped out of the forest shadows across from the partners. Standing next to her, on her right, was a large brutish animal. Its eyes were flashing yellow. Its mouth was open to reveal large sharp teeth. It emitted a low rumbling growl. "I see you have some sticks for my pets to play with. Were you hoping to play fetch with them?" she taunted, and suddenly, five more dire wolves appeared out of the shadows. They stood near the witch facing the children with piercing yellow eyes.

"Actually, we were hoping to play stick the pig with them," Carter said without humor. The partners were standing like soldiers at attention with their staffs set vertically at their sides. In spite of their anxiety over what was to come, they had hard-determined looks on their faces.

The witch's confidence seemed to falter slightly. "It would have been much easier if you had just made sacrifice to the gods."

"Enough talk, hag. We tire of you and your stupid games," Carter said viciously.

"I see that you have gained courage by surviving The Forge, but still, you are no match for my pack. And just so there will be no myths about how you fought courageously against my pack, I will let my champion kill you first," she said to the boy. "And then I will let the rest of the pack play tug-of-war with the girl. The wolf with the largest chunk of her, wins. The hag looked down at the monster that came almost to her hips. The wolf, with large strands of drool falling from its massive mouth, looked into the face of his mistress. The witch commanded, "Kill the boy!"

Quick as a flash, the beast turned toward Carter, took two running steps, and sprang for his throat. Carter was ready for the attack. He stooped down on one knee, with one end of the staff anchored in the ground; he angled the other pointed end at the giant wolf. The beast let out a single surprised scream of pain as it impaled itself on the staff. Carter let the momentum carry it over his head, and it landed in the raging fire.

Carter pulled the staff free of the carcass and turned back to meet another attack. The witch screamed with shock and rage. "First the gods and the protectors and now you have taken my most precious companion!" With eyes wild with fury, the hag screamed at the pack, "Kill them! Kill them both!"

However, the pack seemed a bit cowed. They were looking at each other and at the witch. They wanted orders from their leader but he was gone. The witch controlled the leader of the pack, and the leader of the pack controlled the five females that were left.

Adding to the creatures' confusion, the partners began spinning their staffs hand over hand. The sticks were distracting them and making them more skittish.

The hag was beside herself with rage and grief. She shrieked, "What are you waiting for? Kill them. They killed your leader!"

Hesitantly, and with far less confidence, the pack began to look for a way past the spinning staffs. Crouching low to the ground, one bold wolf moved close to Kat on her left side while the others spread out making false charges at the partners. They were careful to keep out of the reach of the spinning staffs. On one of these charges, the bold wolf got careless and when it was within reach of Kats staff, she let the momentum of the spinning stick catch the animal a solid blow on top of its head, taking out an eye. The beast rolled back howling in pain. Another wolf on her right saw its chance to breach the girl's defenses. Taking stock of her small victory, Kat took her eyes off the other wolves and was slow to start her staff moving again. Her right side was open. Luckily, Carter, who stood on her right side, saw the animal leap with its jaws wide open and determined to sink its teeth into some part of the girl. Quick as a flash, Carter brought his staff down as hard as he could on the back of the animal's neck. The loud crack that followed was not from a breaking staff. The dead wolf's momentum carried it into Kat's right side, knocking her down and out.

Carter moved in front of Kat and crouched into a defensive stance with his staff held across the front of him. He was facing three wolves now, alone. The witch feeling confident that the battle was over, moved closer to the remainder of her pack as they stood facing the boy. "You children put up a brave fight, but you really had no chance. Because you have fought well, and because I feel my revenge is about to be satisfied, I am feeling a tinge merciful. Put down your staff, boy, and I will see to it that your deaths are quick."

Unexpectedly, Carter stood erect, held up his staff, and let out with an impressive war cry that shocked the pack and the witch. As he shouted, he raised and lowered his staff. All eyes were on him, so they did not see the giant step quietly out of the woods behind them. When Carter saw Taloff draw closer, he intensified his distraction. He started twirling his staff again as he shouted at the witch, "It is not your revenge that is about to be satisfied, it is justice that will be satisfied for all those you have tormented and killed!"

The witch's rage filled her again, and she screamed, "Kill them now!" Before the wolves could make a move, two huge hands reached down from behind them, grabbed two of the remaining three wolves by the scruff of the neck and lifted them high in the air. Taloff cracked their heads together and tossed their limp carcasses into the fire. Upon seeing the giant, the witch screamed, clutched her chest, and ran for her life.

The remaining wolf had enough sense to save itself and ran in the opposite direction from the witch.

Carter stooped to check Kat. She was already starting to come round. As Carter checked her for wounds, the girl asked groggily, "Is it over? Did we win?"

Carter smiled at her and said, "Yes, it's over, and we won. It didn't even take that long."

Taloff laughed and asked, "Are you disappointed that the battle did not last longer? The way stories are told and retold, eventually, this battle will have lasted long into the night. The witch's six wolves will be sixty, and you will have killed them all without my help."

Carter smiled and then said to Kat, "Looks like you are going to be sore for a few days. Nothing is broken and your wounds are superficial."

"What happened to the witch? Did we kill all her wolves?" Kat wanted to know as she sat up and looked around.

"Taloff was right," Carter said. "As soon as she saw him, she ran off." The giant man had explained to the partners, as they were devising their strategy, that if the witch knew he was with them, she would wait until they separated to attack. If she thought she only had two scared kids to deal with, she would be over confident. Taloff was their secret weapon. The signal for him to strike was when Carter raised his war cry and distracted the pack.

"What happened to the wolf I hit? Did I kill it?" Kat asked as she looked over her shoulder. The wolf was gone; it had crawled off into the forest.

"There is no need to worry about the witch anymore. Her power is broken. She will not last long without her creatures to care for her. That is the good news," Taloff said with a smile. "Now I have some bad news; it is time for me to leave you."

The children looked disappointed. Kat said, "Can't you stay with us for a little longer? Why do you have to leave so soon?"

"I too wish I could spend more time with you, but I have done what I was chosen to do, and now it is very important that you continue your quest. The Guardian said something to me that did not make a lot of sense, but it struck me as important. I cannot tell you his exact words, but it was something about an important person or persons that Dearth needed. He said he hoped the partners would be able to save them. I wish I could be more help, but I am afraid that I do not really understand why you are even here, unless..."

"Unless what?" Carter asked.

"I almost forgot the prophecy," Taloff said with a thoughtful smile.

Kat wrinkled her brow and said, "This isn't the first time we've heard a prophecy mentioned. What is it?"

"It's nothing really, and yet... There is an old prophesy that has been around for so long that most people do not even talk of it anymore. It goes something like this: Dearth will want no more when the wooden limb lifts up the kingdom, and two youths of alien realm, sow seeds of life in the taken. Maybe the prophecy has something to do with you. You said that you come from a place called Earth, so you come from an alien realm. I do not know, but maybe you are the ones who will make Dearth just a name and not the definition of this world."

Carter had a troubled look on his face as he stared down at the ground thoughtfully. "I wonder what it all means. What does it mean for us, if anything," he mused.

Taloff shrugged and said, "I am sorry I cannot be of more help. I have never given it any thought. As I said before, no one even talks about it much anymore."

"What about you, Taloff, what will you do? Where will you go?" Kat asked with a touch of sadness in her voice.

"I think I will travel to the southern kingdoms. I hear that there is a great champion there called Goodman who has brought many wonderful things to life in that part of Dearth. I wish to see this for myself."

When the partners heard the name Goodman, they gave each other a knowing look. "We know of Goodman," Kat said excitedly.

"The man, Dark Beard, who gave us the knife, is a friend and student of Goodman's. The story of Goodman and Dark Beard is an exciting one. Let us tell you about it before you leave."

The partners spent a pleasant hour telling Taloff the story of Goodman over breakfast. When Kat was feeling well enough to travel, they made their goodbyes, and then went their separate ways.

THE BELOVED LOST

The partners traveled the rest of the day through the thickest part of the forest. They were both eager to discuss the prophecy that Taloff recited to them. However, the forest was so thick that Kat needed help due to her injuries. The partners had to concentrate on what they were doing. As the sun began to set, the forest began to thin. Carter checked his compass and said, "We're still heading north. We might see the eastern path sometime tomorrow. If you are feeling up to it, I would like to keep traveling until it gets dark. Then we can use the light of the flashlight to set up camp."

"That's okay with me. Walking is helping me keep from getting stiff from the bruises and sprains I got when the wolf clobbered me."

Just as Carter was about to call a halt for the night, he stopped and said, "Hey, look there off to the right. I see a light."

"Yeah, I see it too. It looks like a light from a window. Maybe it's a house where we can stay the night."

"It does look like a house," Carter agreed. "Of course, there's no telling who or what might be in there. Let's go peek in the window."

It was dark enough now that Carter had to use the flashlight to see their way to the house. "When we get close, be quiet."

"*You* be quiet too; you're the clumsy one."

Carter turned to his friend and said, "Shush."

As the partners approached the house, they could see that it was a small, one-room cabin made of unfinished wood. It was the same size as the cabins in the Dead Forest. The children crouched down below a window that was located a few inches to the left of the front door. As they kneeled in the dirt, they heard a woman crying. "Let me peek in first. You stay down," Carter ordered in a soft whisper. Slowly, he rose up, took a brief look, and ducked back down.

"What did you see?"

"I saw a woman crying."

"What else did you see?"

"Well, that's about it. She's sitting on a bed, crying."

"You're some detective, Carter. You stay down, and let me take a look."

Kat took a few seconds longer than Carter did to scan the room. When she ducked back down she said, "I don't see anything too unusual about the place. There's a wood burning stove at the back of the house and some shelves of dry goods to the left of the stove. There is a chest at the foot of the bed. The room looks warm and clean, but there is something rather strange. The woman is about my mom's age, but she is crying, rocking back and forth, and hugging about a dozen rag dolls of different sizes. Her lips are moving; she's saying something as she's crying."

"Okay, Nancy Drew, what's she saying?"

"I think she's saying, 'My baby, my baby,' over and over again."

"What do you make of that?" Carter asked.

"I don't think there's anything dangerous in there. Maybe we can help her; she seems very upset. Let's talk to her."

"Okay, but first we need to hide the staffs. I'll put them around the side of the cabin," Carter said. Once he had taken care of their weapons, he knocked on the door.

The door opened just a crack, and the woman peered out with red, swollen eyes. In a shaky voice filled with grief, she asked, "Yes? What do you want?"

Carter cleared his throat and said, "My friend and I were camping in the forest a few miles back. We thought we heard wolves and got scared. We left the forest, and we were hoping to find shelter until morning. We hate to bother you, but my friend is really scared."

The woman opened the door a little wider to get a better look at her visitors. "Why, you are just children. You should not be out at night in these wilds." She sniffed, wiped at her eyes with the back of her hand, and opened the door the rest of the way. The woman appeared to be in her mid thirties. She had short dirty-blond hair and brown eyes. She was slightly overweight and had a pleasant oval face. She was wearing a simple white cotton dress with a yellow apron.

"Come in; you cannot stay out in the dark all night. My name is Agaphy. I am sorry that I do not have beds for you; the stone floor is cold but clean. You can spread your bedding out near the stove and make yourselves comfortable. Are you hungry? I have some soup leftover from dinner. It will just go bad if someone does not eat it."

The partners felt warm and safe with the sad woman. It touched their hearts to see her trying so hard to make her guests feel welcome in spite of her sorrow. "We really appreciate this," Kat said as she spread out her blanket. "We hate to be a bother, especially when you are feeling sad."

"Oh dear, does it show? I am sorry, but I am beside myself with grief. One of my babies has run off, and I do not know where he is."

"Babies? You have children?" asked Kat.

"Oh, forgive me. Where are my manners? Let me introduce you to my babies. I did not get your names."

"I'm Kat, and this is Carter."

"Are you brother and sister?"

"No, we are just good friends. We have lived next to each other most of our lives."

"I see. Well, Kat, Carter, these are my babies," the woman said with pride in her voice. She reached over and scooped up the little rag dolls and cradled them lovingly in her arms. "This is Kat, and her friend, Carter. They are going to spend the night with us. Say hi to them, and tell them that you are glad they are here." Agaphy paused as if she was actually expecting the dolls to obey. After a moment of silence, she said, "You will have to forgive them. They are always shy around strangers. After they get to know you a little better, they will be all over you."

A sad look came over the woman's face. She sat on the bed and looked as if a profound sorrow weighed her down. She buried her face in the bundle of rag dolls and began to weep. "I am sorry, but I cannot help myself. Please forgive me. It is just that the loss of my little one is more than I can bear."

This display of emotion—over a missing rag doll—confused Carter. It appeared to him that this woman really believed that she had lost a real human child.

Kat sat down on the bed, put her arm around the woman, and said, "Please don't cry. Tell us what happened; maybe we can help."

Through sobs and gasping sounds, she said, "I have looked everywhere. I tore my house apart. I had just finished putting everything back when you knocked. He is just gone. I do not know what to do, and the others do not know where he is either."

"When was the last time you saw your baby?" Kat asked.

The woman calmed a bit as she tried to compose herself enough to answer the girl's question. "Today, at lunchtime, we went out under the big tree in front of our home to have a picnic. We had such fun; the children laughed and played all afternoon. When it was time for a nap, we came back into the house, got on the bed, and went fast to sleep. When we woke, we all gathered around the table for a late afternoon snack. It was then that I noticed one of my babies was missing. I just figured that he got up during naptime and was playing a hiding game. But when I could not find him, I knew it was serious. I tore the house apart looking for him, but I did not find him. He has just vanished! I believe my heart will break, and I will die," the woman said as she started to cry again.

Carter did not know what to make of the woman and her obses-
sion with the rag dolls, but he had an idea. "If you ladies will excuse
me for a few minutes, I'm going out for some fresh air."

The woman ignored the boy, but Carter saw his friend give him
a dirty look that said *Boys have no feelings.* When Carter stepped out
into the night, he pulled out his flashlight and headed for the large
tree where the woman had picnicked. He looked around the tree,
and then he heard a rustling sound coming from a bush nearby. He
went to investigate and found what looked like a tangle of old dirty
yarn. Upon a closer look, he could tell that it was one of Agaphy's
rag dolls. He picked it up and discovered that it was the smallest,
dirtiest, and most ragged of the dolls he had seen. He shrugged
and took it back to the house. When he reached the front door, he
knocked lightly and opened it. The woman and girl were still sitting
on the bed talking quietly.

"I found something outside by the tree. Is this what you've been
looking for?" Cater asked as he held out the handful of tangled yarn.

The woman looked to see what Carter had in his hand. She
gasped, put her hand over her open mouth, and sprang off the bed.
She grabbed the doll away from the boy and held it to her heart.
"You have found him! You have found him! Oh, my precious, precious baby—mother is so sorry. I looked and looked for you, but this
young man found you," she said and began to cry again. This time
she was crying tears of joy. "We must celebrate; we must have a party.
That which was lost has been found! My life has been made full
again, and I have emerged from the Valley of Shadows.

"You," Agaphy said as she turned abruptly toward Carter. "You
are the hero of the day, and we will never forget you. You are part
of our family now, and you will always be welcome here." Then the
woman squeezed the doll to her cheek and said, "Mommy loves you
so much, you precious, precious thing.

"Come now; we must prepare for the party. Kat and Carter, you
do not have to do a thing. We will take care of everything, so sit
right there while we prepare refreshments. Later, we will sing songs
and play games. Oh, this is wonderful!"

"If you don't mind," Carter said, "I'd like to take Kat outside and show her where I found your 'baby.'"

"Whatever you wish, dear; you can do anything you want. I owe you my life."

Carter headed for the door. Kat got up to follow. Once they were outside and a little removed from the house, Carter asked, "What do you make of that? Is she insane? She actually believes that those dolls are alive and are her children. I have never seen anything like it before."

"Oh really, and where have you been the past few days while I have been here in loony tune land?" Kat asked with her arms crossed. She was rubbing warmth into them as she talked.

"Well, you got me there. But seriously, do you feel it's safe to stay the night here?"

"I don't know why not. She considers you her hero. Why would she want to hurt us? No, she's just lonely. Living out here in the wilderness without any human contact has caused her to create her own little fantasy family to keep her company. Let's go inside, have a little play party, get some sleep, and then we can be on our way tomorrow."

Carter nodded, and then said, "Did you hear what she said about emerging from the Valley of Shadows? It must be just a saying people use here for feeling sad or depressed."

Kat shrugged and answered, "Maybe, let's ask her."

When the friends got back in the cabin, they found the small, wooden table covered with a clean, red cloth. There were cups of milk and white, square cloths placed around the table. Each cloth had a piece of nut bread on it. The dolls were placed around the edge of the table, and the woman was seated at the head. "Come and have some cake. My little ones could not wait; they ate theirs already. I hope you do not mind. Children are so impatient, you know."

The partners found the nut bread to be sweet and tasty. The milk was cold from being outside. Everything was good, except for the feeling that the dolls were watching them. It was the strangest feeling; it felt like real people were staring at them.

When they finished their refreshments, they sang songs that the woman taught them. She explained that these were some of her children's favorites, but she apologized that they would not sing in front of strangers.

At one point during the party, Kat did ask Agaphy about the Valley of Shadows. The woman confirmed Carter's suspicions that it was just a saying.

Finally, after the party died down, it was time for bed. The partners were more than ready. They were exhausted; unfortunately, they would be unable to sleep in the house.

After their hostess blew the candles out, and the room was plunged into darkness, the partners could hear soft shuffling sounds and little clicking noises coming from all around them. It sounded like dozens of mice were moving about the room. Kat exclaimed, "There are mice in here. I felt one touch me on the cheek!"

Carter sat up, reached for his flashlight, turned it on, and pointed it around the room. Yet, there was no sign of any mice.

"It is okay, you two." Agaphy chuckled. "There are no mice in my house; my children are playing in the dark. Just ignore them, and they will go to sleep."

"Look, Kat," Carter said as he pointed the light at different locations around the room. "The dolls are scattered around. They were on the bed before the lights went out. Do you suppose she threw them around the room in the dark?"

"Hey, Carter, I heard that. I would never throw my precious children. What kind of a mother do you think I am? You do not have to worry. They will get tired in a few minutes and go to sleep."

As soon as Carter turned off the light, the noises started again. This time they could hear what sounded like tiny voices laughing. "Carter," Kat whispered, "this is creeping me out. I don't think I can take any more of this house."

"Wait a second, Kat. I'm going to turn the light on and see if I can catch them doing something." Just then, there was a loud click followed by the sounds of little voices laughing. Carter pointed the flashlight in the direction of the sounds and turned on the light. Even though he did not see anything move, he could tell that the dolls had shifted locations in the dark. They were not where they were the first time he turned on the light. "That does it. I'm sorry, Agaphy. We had fun, and I'm glad we were able to help find your 'baby,' but it's time for us to leave," he said as began packing his gear.

"Me too, Agaphy," Kat said as she joined her partner in packing.

"I know that children can be such a nuisance sometimes. I quite understand. There is a small tool shed just a few feet beyond that big tree out front. You can lock yourselves in there, and you will be safe until morning. I do hope you will come back and have breakfast before you leave. I appreciate all you have done for me."

"We'll see, Agaphy. We need to be on our way early, so maybe we'll see you, but don't plan on us. It has been … interesting," Carter said as he opened the door and stepped out into the night, with Kat following close behind.

Carter and Kat woke just as the sun cleared the horizon. They had gone to sleep in the tool shed near the house, but now that they were awake, they saw no evidence that the shed or house ever existed. "I don't get it," Kat said. "I was tired, but I remember setting out my blanket in a shed."

"We did. We're in the same place we were last night. There's the big tree near where I found the doll. Why is there no sign of the buildings? The ground isn't even disturbed," Carter observed as he reached around with his right arm to scratch his back. "Well, so much for having breakfast with them before we head out," he said with a touch of sarcasm. "I'll get our staffs."

"Good thing you thought of that, I would have forgotten them," said Kat.

"Oh no, they're gone too," Carter said with disappointment in his voice.

Kat shrugged and said, "Maybe we don't need them anymore. Hey, look at this," she called. Carter turned back to where his partner was standing and saw that she was holding a crude wooden plate with nut bread and two cups of cold milk. "I found these on that big rock next to where we were sleeping. It's the same cake Agaphy served us at the party last night."

"What?" Carter walked over to check out the items. "It just gets curiouser and curiouser."

"Where did you get that one?" Kat asked with a frown.

"It was in a book I read. Let's pack up and then eat our cake on the move." Carter suggested.

When they finished breaking camp, Carter looked back at where the house used to be, held out his cup of milk, and said, "Thank you, Agaphy, for the breakfast, and I hope you and your children will be happy—wherever you are." He drank the cup dry, and the two continued on their trek.

THE LAMB

About half an hour into their morning hike, Carter said, "Do you think that prophecy Taloff mentioned could really be about us?"

"Hold up a second," Kat called. The two stopped and as she tied up a loose shoelace she said, "Several little bits and pieces I have heard are making me question what it is we're really doing here. Dark Beard said that we were preparing for a task that will demand every ounce of our strength and courage. Then Guard told Taloff that we were on a quest that could bring radical change to the people. Obviously, our quest isn't just about us gaining maturity and wisdom like I was beginning to think."

The two started fighting their way through thick dead brush again, heading north. "Right," Carter agreed. "And I got the feeling from Dark Beard that us going through The Forge wasn't just a way to evade the witch. It sounded to me like we were supposed to prepare for the Valley of Shadows by traveling the cave. Yet, Agaphy said that the Valley of Shadows is just a saying to describe feeling really bad."

"Even the first tester we met in The Forge said something about us proving we were the youths in the prophecy."

"Actually, I believe he said that if we failed, it would prove that we are not the youths. The fact that we made it does not necessarily mean that we are the ones," Carter said with a grunt as he pushed a large clump of dry brush out of his way.

"I don't know, Carter. This whole thing seems to be getting bigger, more confusing, and more dangerous all the time."

"But it seems to be getting more important all the time too. How did that prophecy go? Do you remember?"

"I think it was something like, two youths will plant some seeds in something stolen or taken."

Carter shook his head and said, "What about the wooden limb lifting up the kingdom?"

After a moment of contemplation, Kat said, "Goodman has a wooden limb."

"Yeah, you're right! I was thinking a wooden tree limb, but it could mean a prosthetic limb. Goodman became the people's champion because the king of the realm wanted someone who was an inspiration. He wanted someone who would provide something the people needed that would lift up the kingdom."

"I think you're right, but what does it mean?"

"Wait a minute. Didn't the Adversary say something to us about Guard wanting us to think we were the two youths?"

Kat nodded and said, "That's true, I remember now. I didn't understand what he meant. I just thought he was talking about us being young and stupid or something like that."

"If we are the two youths mentioned in the prophecy, then why didn't Guard tell us? Don't you think that he would mention something that important?"

Kat sneezed when a cloud of dust and pollen floated up to her face as she stepped on a clump of dead wildflowers. She sniffed and responded with, "Maybe Guard had his reasons for not telling us. Maybe he didn't think we were ready to hear everything all at once.

This is starting to feel pretty overwhelming, but not as much, now, as it would have been if we heard about it the first night we met him."

"Maybe," Carter said as he slapped at a large fly that bit the back of his neck. Then he said, as if thinking aloud, "What is supposed to be taken or stolen? And who took it? Are we supposed to find it?"

"Maybe it's in that Valley of Shadows place?" Kat offered.

The partners went on discussing and speculating about the possible meaning of the prophecy until the heat of the day and the density of dry brush made it too exhausting to converse. At times, the brush was so thick that they had to spend long minutes finding ways around the more dense patches. The going was so difficult that it did not allow for small talk. Finally, toward the early afternoon, the way thinned out enough for them to quicken their pace.

When they started getting hungry, talk turned to food. "I don't know about you, but I'm hungry enough to eat a lizard," Carter opened the topic.

"Well, if you want a lizard, there are plenty of them running around here. I would much rather have a hotdog covered with mustard, mayo, and chili," Kat said with a dreamy smile on her face.

Just then, Carter's stomach let out with a loud growl of agreement. "You're killing me, Hamsted. You know that's my favorite food—next to pizza. What do you suppose our chances are of getting chili dogs out here?"

"Based on what we've had to eat since we've been on this adventure, I'd say slim to none. Think about it; we've had green veggie pudding, stew, dried meat, nut bread cake, wild berries, and, oh yes, we had junk food from the gas station where we met Mr. Stewborn."

"Don't forget the cookies we had at the inn and the roasted birds and waffles we got from Guard," Carter added.

"I have to admit that the most normal food we've had on this trip has come from Guard. Oh, wow! It must be my imagination, but I smell hotdogs."

Carter sniffed the air and smiled. "I smell them too. Where's that coming from?" Carter stood upon a large rock, shielded his eyes from the sun, and scanned the horizon. Pointing directly north, he almost shouted, "There, I see the eastern road, and there's something shiny along side of it. It looks like a hotdog stand. It has to be Guard. Come on; let's hurry."

When the two eager children reached the hotdog stand, they were out of breath and dripping with sweat. In spite of their fatigue, they wore big smiles, and they greeted the Guardian enthusiastically. Guard was dressed in a white apron and a paper hat. He had a long fork in his hand, which he used to serve up hotdogs. "You two look hot, thirsty, and hungry. Sit over there at the table with the sun umbrella, and I will serve you all the cola and hotdogs you can eat."

The partners were glad to have a chance to sit in the shade, and the anticipation of the promised lunch had their mouths watering. "You do not have to talk just now. Go ahead and eat, drink, and relax. You have had an exhausting day, and the day is not over yet."

The Guardian placed two hotdogs, fixed just the way they liked them, in front of each child. Then he put large bottles of ice-cold cola next to their paper plates. Finally, he put a large bag of potato chips in the middle of the table. Sitting down with them, he smiled as he watched the partners eagerly devour their lunch.

"While you enjoy your food, I want to tell you that the most important thing for you to do is stay on the eastern road until you reach the adobe."

Carter took a long drink of cola, and then he said, "Now that we don't have the witch to worry about, that should be a cinch. Sounds a lot easier than the other things we've been through."

"I am glad you feel confident. Anyone want another hotdog?" Guard asked as he got up and went back the stand.

"I'll have another if you don't mind. How about you, Kat?"

Kat shook her head and said, "No, thank you; two has always been my limit no matter how hungry I feel. But I would like a couple to take for later, if possible."

"I already wrapped several for you to take, and I have a couple extra bottles of cola for you as well. Take what is left of the potato chips, and you are set for the rest of the day."

"This is great; it's like a little bit of home," Kat said as she packed the food.

"Yes," Carter added. "Thank you. It's just what we needed."

"You are very welcome; you have earned it. I must say, you are both quite extraordinary. Solving the People Rule Inn riddle, exiting The Forge, and destroying the witch are all quite impressive feats. Yes indeed, you two are quite extraordinary." The Guardian wore a look of satisfaction and confidence on his face as he spoke.

Carter was about to ask Guard about the prophecy, but Guard forestalled him by lifting his hand and saying, "I know that you both have many questions. Once you reach the adobe, much will become clear to you. I must warn you that the Adversary will come at you with increased determination to lead you astray, to quit your quest, and see you fail. He has much to lose if you succeed."

Suddenly, there was a terrific disturbance east of them on the road. The children turned toward the disturbance and saw a sea of white moving toward them. The partners stood and stepped upon a mound, which was next to their table, to get a better look. "It looks like a herd of sheep," Carter said.

"It may be sheep, but it isn't a herd of sheep. It's a flock of sheep," Kat corrected.

"Whatever," Carter said, annoyed at being corrected. He turned back to the Guardian to ask him about the sheep, but Guard, the hotdog stand, table, and umbrella were gone. "I have to stop turning my back on that guy," Carter mumbled to himself.

"We might as well make ourselves comfortable. It's going to take a while for that flock to pass," said Kat.

"It's obvious that we can't go around it; it's huge. Maybe we can walk through it. No, they're too close together. We need to just sit tight until they pass."

Kat responded with, "Hmm, I think that's what I just said."

It took a good hour and a half for the flock to pass. And even though the partners enjoyed watching the sheep and the sheep dogs work the flock, they were relieved to be out of the noise, dust, and smell. "It's about time…Let's get going; we're wasting daylight," Carter urged.

Fully rested, they made good time on the hard-packed dirt road.

"Carter."

"What?"

"I get the feeling someone is following us."

"No, it's just your imagination. After having the witch following us for so long, you still feel like we're being followed," Carter explained.

"I see; so you're saying that there isn't a sheep following us?"

"What?" Carter exclaimed as he turned to look behind him. "What the…How long has it been following us?"

"I guess ever since the flock passed and we started traveling again. But I didn't notice it until just now."

"Shoo. Shoo. Go back to your family," Carter said as he motioned with his hands at the sheep.

The sheep just walked calmly up to the children and stood looking at them.

"He's just a little guy; he isn't fully grown. Carter, we have to take it back to the flock."

"You've got to be kidding. Do you know how much time we'll lose if we go all the way back? Besides that, the flock is still moving. We'll have to go all the way back, catch up with the flock, and then travel all the way here again. It'll take the rest of the day."

"I know, but Carter, it's the right thing to do."

"This is great! This is a real nice situation. Okay, I give up. Let's take the baby back to its mama," Carter said sarcastically.

"It's okay little fellow; we'll take you home," Kat said lovingly as she patted the sheep on the head.

The partners started back up the road, heading west. When they looked back to check on the sheep, they saw that it hadn't moved. "Come on; let's go home to your mama," Kat encouraged as she slapped her leg as if she was calling a dog.

"What's wrong with it?" Carter spat. "Is it deaf?"

"I don't know. Maybe we'll have to use a rope and lead him back."

Suddenly, as though the lamb understood what the two were planning, it ran up the road.

"Now what's it doing?" Carter growled.

"I don't know, but it's like he understood what we wanted to do, and he ran away so we couldn't catch him."

"Look, this is taking way too much time. I say we keep heading east, and if the sheep is supposed to follow us, it will."

"Okay, but let's keep an eye out for him. He's so young, and I don't want him to get hurt."

"Within reason, I'll go along with that, but I don't want to be a babysitter to a sheep," Carter grumbled.

With that settled, the partners continued journeying east. The sheep fell in behind them and stuck close to its new "flock."

Later that night, when they made camp, the children enjoyed the hotdogs Guard had prepared for them. Even though the cola was warm, they drank it gratefully. Their new companion enjoyed the clumps of green grass scattered around the campsite. When everyone was finished eating, the little sheep settled in between the children like a family pet. Even Carter was beginning to like their new companion. The partners sat looking at the fire and ran their fingers through the thick wool.

"What should we call him?" Kat asked.

"You think we should name it?"

"It's better than calling him the sheep. Let's call him Jessie."

"Why Jessie?" Carter asked.

"Because he looks like a Jessie."

Carter thought about it a minute, and then said, "I don't know what a Jessie looks like, but I guess it's as good a name as any. All right then, Jessie it is."

The next day's travel was rougher than the partners had expected. The eastern road narrowed to nothing more that a rugged trail. The trail, though straight, was bordered by steep, rocky cliffs. Sharp rocks protruded up from the floor of the path; deep holes and cracks pocked its surface.

"This path is almost impossible to walk. If it wasn't for Jessie letting us steady ourselves by holding onto his wool, we would be in real danger of twisting an ankle or breaking a leg."

"That's true. You are a very good sheep, Jessie," Kat purred as she patted the sheep's head.

"Even with Jessie's help, this path is really tough," Carter complained. "Hey, look up ahead. I think I see a side road."

The three travelers made their way to a break in the large rock walls. Off to the left ran a wide paved road with a sign that read "Adobe Road."

"This is wonderful. We've finally made it to the adobe. This road will take us right to it," Carter said excitedly.

"I don't know, Carter. It looks great, but Guard said to stay on the eastern path until we come to the adobe."

"We did. This is just the road that leads up to it. I'm sure of it; it makes perfect sense."

"Does it make sense because the road looks easier to travel or because you're sure it's the right way to go?"

"Both. Now let's get moving," Carter said curtly.

Unsure, but in no mood to argue, Kat followed her partner. Jessie walked along side of her.

"What a relief; this is much easier than that horrible trail. Look at all the room we have; it's so wide and smooth."

Kat had to admit that the new road was much more pleasant to travel, but she could not help feeling that something was not right about their decision to take the side road.

The same type of high rocky formations that bordered the eastern trail bordered the new path. As the three travelers continued down the side road, it started to narrow, and the quality of the road began to deteriorate rapidly. Suddenly, a terrifying sound filled the air. It was the roar of a mountain lion.

"Where did that come from?" Kat demanded as she grabbed onto Carter's arm.

"Look! On that rock," said Carter, pointing. "Look at the size of that thing; it's huge. It's looking right at us! Don't move. Don't run or he will chase us down and kill us for sure."

"Carter, it's moving toward us! *What should we do?*" Kat shrieked.

Just then, the huge lion jumped off its rock and charged straight for the children. At the same instant, Jessie ran past the partners directly at the lion. The sheep distracted the predator, and it grabbed Jessie by the back of the neck, turned, and ran with the little sheep hanging limply from its slobbering mouth.

Kat screamed, "Jessie, *no!*"

"Come on, Hamsted, we've got to get out of here *now!*"

"What about Jessie?"

"We can't save him; he sacrificed himself for us. We've got to get out of here!"

Kat did not want to leave Jessie to the mountain lion, but she knew that Carter was right. They could do nothing for the lamb. The partners ran as fast as they could back to the eastern path. Once there, they sat on a rock and tried to calm themselves.

"It's my fault," Carter said, angry with himself. "I had to insist that we take an easier path. It just seemed so right at the time."

"No, Carter, it wasn't just your fault. I went along, even though I felt it was a mistake. I could have refused to go. I'm just as much to blame as you; we both did the wrong thing for our own reasons, and it got Jessie killed," Kat said with tears welling up in her eyes.

"Do you think, somehow, Jessie knew we were going to be in danger, and that's why he came along with us? It's almost as if he was here to save us from ourselves."

Kat wiped her eyes with the palms of her hands and sniffed. "I don't know, but I do know that if we hadn't made a bad choice, he wouldn't have died. Let's get out of here," Kat said bitterly as she stood.

The two traveled in silence, lost in their thoughts and private feelings of guilt and grief. Later that day, the partners heard voices coming from up the road.

CULT OF THE DETOUR

"Carter, there are people up ahead."

"Yes, but what kind of people? Let's move closer. I want to get an idea of who they are. There's too much dead brush in the way to get a clear view of them."

Moving closer, they found that the group was made up of average looking people of all ages. They looked tired but seemed to be in good spirits. "Good thing they stopped for a rest, or we might not have caught up to them," Carter said.

"Well, what have we here?" a deep male voice boomed from behind the partners.

The two turned quickly to see a nice looking man in his thirties standing with his hands on his hips and a bit of a smile on his face. He had a thick head of blond hair and an angular, clean-shaven face. He had sun-tanned skin, and he wore dark sunglasses. He was dressed in camouflage-green pants and shirt and wore black combat boots. He was tall and muscular.

"Who are you?" Carter demanded.

"I am Jud Rack. And you are?"

220

"I'm Carter, and this is Kat. Who are all those people, and where are they going?"

"We are travelers just like you, and we are headed the same way you are. Would you care to join us? It makes traveling on this path a lot easier when you are not alone."

"I don't know. What do you think, Kat?"

"Maybe for a little way, and we can see how it goes. We can always separate if we don't fit in with the group." Kat looked to Rack for confirmation that they could leave whenever they wanted.

"Of course you can. Travel with us for a while, and see how you like us. Come. I want you to meet someone who will make you feel very welcome."

As the new acquaintances made their way to the group, Rack waved and called out, "Hey, everyone, I have found some new travelers who will be joining us."

Upon hearing this news, everyone stood up smiling and waving, and some even applauded. Many shouted things like, "Welcome," "Good to have you," and, "Make yourselves at home."

As they approached the group, made up of about seventy people, Rack said, "They are just children; we do not want to overwhelm them. You will all get a chance to meet them. This good looking young man is Carter, and this cutie is Kat."

Blushing, Kat noticed that all the adult women were smiling at her as if they were wishing she were their daughter. The men smiled and nodded politely.

"Ms. Jez, will you make our new friends feel welcome and help them get to know everyone?"

A portly, round woman in her forties stepped forward. She had a round face and black hair streaked with gray. Her brown eyes were wide with joy, and her large, red lips were open in a broad smile. She was wearing a brightly colored sack dress with a floral design. Her arms were open wide as if she wanted to gather the two children to her large bosom and smother them with love.

At the sight of Ms. Jez rushing toward them, the partners took a quick step back. "Now, Ms. Jez, I know you are a loving person, and you would like nothing better than to adopt these adorable children, but they are a little scared. I have a feeling that they may have been through some traumatic experiences that have made them cautious around strangers. Go slow, and let them get to know us."

Ms. Jez put her hands to her plump cheeks, and said in a rather high-pitched voice, "Of course, I am sorry. It is just that you are so precious, and I just want to scoop you up, squeeze you, and take care of you."

"We appreciate your warm welcome, and we're glad for the company, but we're not sure we'll be staying with your group for long. As for taking care of us, Kat and I have been taking care of each other for quite some time now. We'll be fine."

Kat quickly added, "We're grateful for your concern, and we are looking forward to getting to know all of you."

"Okay, everyone, it is time for us to head out," Rack said in an authoritative tone.

"Come, children," said Ms. Jez. "Walk with me, and we will talk."

The going was even slower now that the partners were traveling with the Rack group. Ms. Jez required lots of assistance, and it quickly became clear that one of the reasons Rack put the partners with the large woman was to assist her over the rough path. Though the partners were a bit frustrated at being manipulated into helping the woman, they did appreciate the information they were getting from her; she talked nonstop.

"Rack is the most wonderful leader; he is so good to us. Everyone we meet along the path is welcome to join us. He is patient, wise, and he really knows his way around here. He even knows a shortcut. Everyone is excited because he said we will arrive at the shortcut before nightfall."

"Shortcut?" said Carter. "What shortcut?"

"Oh, it is so exciting. Rack told us about a shortcut that will take us around the worst part of the eastern path. He said it is a solidly packed dirt road with a minimum of dust and no obstacles. It goes southeast then northeast, and ultimately, it will bring us back to the eastern path. I think that is wonderful. We will be able to travel much faster and avoid the terrible hardships of this miserable path."

"Tell me, Ms. Jez, can we trust this Rack fellow? I mean, we had a bad experience earlier today taking another path. We were almost killed by a huge mountain lion," Carter confided.

"Did you take the Adobe Road path?"

"Yes."

"We would have taken that path too if not for Rack. He always tells us not to be deceived. He said there are many dangers in wandering off the eastern path. He told us about the mountain lion on that road, and now you are here to confirm that he was right. You must tell your story tonight when we break for camp."

Later that night, they made camp at the beginning of the short-cut. While everyone sat around a campfire eating and talking, Ms. Jez spoke up and said, "Our new friends have something to share with us. While we were traveling together today, they told me how they took the side road marked by the Adobe Road sign." The partners did not get to tell what happened to them with the mountain lion because Ms. Jez proceeded to tell the whole story as the children had related it to her.

When she finished telling their story, one man from the group stood up and said, "That is why we are fortunate to have Rack with us. He warned us about that side road and kept us from danger. Now there can be no doubt in anyone's mind that we are doing the right thing by taking the shortcut tomorrow."

With that said, something odd happened. Everyone turned and looked at a young man who was around twenty years old. He had shoulder-length, black hair and wore a thin mustache. He had bushy eyebrows and kind eyes. He had brown skin and wore jeans and a dirty, yellow shirt. He had a look of concern on his face, and he shook his head doubtfully. After seeing his reaction, some snorted with contempt, and others sighed in exasperation.

Before Carter could ask Ms. Jez who the man was, Rack stood up, and said, "As I have said before, I have led many people on this shortcut. In fact, most people travel this easier way rather than struggle with this difficult and painful section of the eastern path. Why should we struggle when we can simply go another way that is quicker and easier? Only the simpleminded, the mentally disturbed, or those who are confused would continue down such a difficult, unyielding road." After a dramatic pause, Rack finished up with, "It is time for us to get some sleep; we are all exhausted from our travels. Tomorrow promises to be much more pleasant."

Everyone was quick to obey their leader and settled down to sleep. The camp fell silent, and Carter whispered to Kat, "What do you think about the shortcut?"

Just as she was about to answer, everyone in the camp said, "*Be quiet!*" at exactly the same time.

The next morning everyone was up by sunrise. While the partners packed their gear, Carter asked Kat again, "What do you think about the shortcut idea? Should we go with them or keep on the path?"

"I've been thinking about that most of the night. I didn't sleep very well. It seems to me that if everyone else is going on the shortcut, it must be the right thing to do. It sounds like a lot of others have gone that way, and I don't see any evidence that there has been much foot traffic on the eastern path beyond where we stopped yesterday."

"I agree. If this takes us to our destination faster, then I want to do it. I want to get to the adobe as soon as possible, and it seems like it's taking forever to get there."

"So, children, are you going to join us on the shortcut?" Ms. Jez asked as she walked up to the partners.

"We're in a hurry to get where we're going, so I guess we are," said Carter.

"Wonderful. I am so happy to hear that. And since I will not need your help traveling on this easier path, you can meet some of the other children while we travel."

Carter and Kat had noticed a few children traveling with the group. Most of them seemed either too young or too old to want to have much to do with the newcomers. During the early part of the day's journey, none of the children seemed interested in meeting the partners. Carter and Kat decided to hang back and walk by themselves. Then, about three hours into the day's trek, a group of four children, made up of two boys and two girls ranging in ages from ten to fourteen, approached the partners and started walking behind them.

Kat looked back and said, "Hello. Why don't you come up here and walk with us?"

The children just laughed and continued following the partners. After a few minutes of this strange behavior, Carter stopped, turned around, extended his hand, and said, "Hi, my name is Carter, and this is Kat; we would like to be friends."

The children stood with their hands at their sides and stared at them. Carter put his hand down, and said, "Why are you treating us this way? Have we done something to make you not like us?"

The oldest, a tall lanky girl with freckles, long orange braids, wearing a sack dress with a pastel design, said, "You have not done anything to make us dislike you; we just do not like you. Nobody here likes you, not even the adults."

As they stood looking at each other, an adult from the group yelled back, "Hey, you kids keep moving."

Carter and Kat turned around and started walking again. The other children continued walking behind the partners. Kat asked, "Why don't you like us?"

"Because you are different. We know that you are not from this place, and we do not understand why you are here."

Before the partners could respond, they heard one of the younger children say, "But, Sessy, what about Raymud? He likes the strangers."

"Shut your mouth, Kessen!" said Sessy in a very angry voice.

Carter was getting angry, and he got the urge to stir things up a bit. He stopped, turned, and said to Sessy, "So, you're not only rude and a bully, but you're a liar as well; is that it, Sessy? Not everyone hates us like you said. What kind of stupid little games are you playing?"

Carter crossed his arms and stared the older girl directly in the eye. All the children were looking at Sessy with their mouths wide open and with a bit if fear in their faces. By the look of rage on the older girl's red face, and the reaction of the other children, Carter figured that Sessy was not used to being spoken to in such a manner. Finally, without a word, the infuriated girl stomped off in a rage. The other children followed after her, except for Kessen. When the others were out of earshot, Kessen said, "Things are not going to be good after that. I am afraid you are in trouble."

"We've been in trouble before. Tell me, Kessen, who is Raymud?"

"He is the other person nobody likes. He is the brown skinned man with the mustache," answered Kessen.

"Why doesn't anyone like him?" Kat asked.

"Because he is different too, and he never agrees with Rack. Rack acts as if he likes him, but he hates him, and all the people know it. I got to go. I am probably going to be in trouble for talking to you," she said as she ran on ahead.

"I'm getting the impression that nobody in this group is who they seem to be. Maybe this Raymud is an exception. I think we have been making things too easy for these people. What do you say, instead of walking in the rear where we can't hear what they're saying, we walk in the middle of things and see what happens?"

"Carter, don't we have enough troubles without you making things worse?"

"Didn't I see a little grin of satisfaction on your face when I put that bully, Sessy, in her place?"

Kat gave a half smile and said, "Yes, but this is walking into the hornet's nest, and you will take a stick and whack it until we get stung to death."

"No, no stick. I'm going in armed only with attitude and a sharp tongue. Now let's go."

"Here we go again," Kat said with a sigh.

As the partners approached the group, they noticed that Sessy was talking to several adults and pointing at Carter.

"Hello, everyone; isn't it a beautiful day?" Carter beamed with self-satisfaction.

The adults, who just a few seconds ago were talking and laughing, were quiet now. They smiled coldly at Carter and nodded.

Carter looked around, saw Raymud walking off to the side by himself, and shouted, "Raymud, how's it going?"

Raymud looked at the boy and smiled. "It is going quite well, my friend. How are things with you?" he called back.

"Things were going well until I was told by one of these fine, friendly people that nobody here likes us except you."

All of a sudden, the people stopped walking. Their cold smiles changed to looks of warning. It was clear that Carter had landed a solid blow to the hornet's nest.

Raymud gave the boy a look of admiration, and said, "It is true that I like you and Kat. That is why I am going to tell you a secret, even though it may get me killed."

Immediately Rack appeared out of the crowd and said, "Here now, why has everyone stopped? We have a long way to go, and we need to make the most of our daylight."

Raymud stepped closer to Rack and asked, "Why is that, Rack? Where are you leading these people? You and I both know you are a liar. You do not intend to lead anyone to their intended final destination. I know this path, and I know where it goes. It is a huge circle that will take days to walk and even longer for anyone to notice that it goes nowhere." Raymud addressed the people as he continued, "This man cannot be trusted. If you continue to follow him, you will never find what you are looking for."

Rack's face contorted into a look of rage. He screamed as he pointed his finger at Raymud, "*You are the liar!* You would deceive these fine people and have them destroy themselves struggling on that impossible eastern path. It is *you* that cannot be trusted."

"Why? Is it because my skin is darker than yours? Or is it because I have a different opinion than the mighty Rack?"

One of the people shouted, "You are not of us. You would destroy us on the eastern path, but it is you that should die!" The people shouted their agreement and picked up rocks. However, before anyone threw a stone, the group looked to Rack for approval. No one would dare act without the leader's go-ahead.

Rack stood looking at Raymud with intense hatred. Finally, the leader said, "Put the rocks down. It will do no good. I know who you are now, Guardian. Take your two brats and go. These are my people; they will do as I say. You have no influence here."

"Guard, is it really you?" Kat asked with surprise.

Raymud turned to the partners and said, "Did you enjoy the hot-dogs I fixed for you the other day?"

"It is him; it's Guard!"

"That's enough! You three get out of here. These people want to travel east, and you are wasting our time."

Guard looked around at the people and said, "If anyone wants to turn back, you are welcome to come with us."

Ms. Jez stepped out of the crowd and said, "What? You want us to go back to that horrible eastern path? I almost died trying to travel on that. No, I need an easier way to go."

Then the woman turned to the partners and said, "You are *bad* children. I knew there was a reason why I did not like you. I am glad to know who you really are. Go away from us! You are not of us," she said contemptuously, and then she spat on the ground in front of them.

"Come along, my faithful followers. It is time we continue our journey," Rack called out. It was as if they were in some sort of trance; the group turned in one smooth motion and continued up the dirt road.

The three that stayed behind watched the group until they were out of sight. When the children turned to Guard, he was no longer in the persona of Raymud. He had returned to the form that was familiar to the partners.

"Guard, you look so sad," Kat observed.

"Yes, it makes me sad to see how people are so easily led astray. Those people will never find what they are looking for now, and that is sad."

"But what about us, Guard?" Kat asked. "We were tricked into taking the shortcut too."

"I must say, I am a little surprised that after your incident with the mountain lion, you were so easily taken in again. Nevertheless, the important thing is that you have decided to turn around and get back onto the right path. Every person makes mistakes. Not every person seeks to correct his mistakes. Those who have decided to continue in their error will be disappointed in the end."

"Guard?"

"Yes, Carter?"

"Can't you make people go the right way and do the right thing? They may resent you, at first, but ultimately they will be glad when they arrive at the right place."

"No one can force a person to go the right way or do the right thing and then expect that they will end up in the right place. A person has to decide for himself or herself to do the right thing and go the right way in order to come to a good end."

It was Kat's turn to ask Guard a question. "But, Guard, why were they so angry when we decided to go a different way than they chose?"

"People do not like to feel that they might be making a mistake in their choices. It threatens their sense of security when others disagree with them. It makes them afraid and uncomfortable, and that makes them angry. The way to help people change is the way Goodman does it. He never tells people what they have to do. He lives his life demonstrating the power of love. When people experience the exceedingly superior value of the people rule being applied to them, it can touch the deep empty places in their hearts. I know that all this is not clear to you now, but by the end of your adventures, perhaps you will understand."

The partners did not notice when the Guardian left them. When they arrived back at the difficult eastern path, they realized that he was gone. "Did you see when Guard left us?" asked Carter.

"No. I didn't even notice he was gone until you asked me just now."

THE NEEDLE'S EYE

Even though Carter and Kat were not anxious to start struggling on the eastern path again, they felt strangely relieved. Their relief came from knowing that no matter how hard the path was to travel, they knew they were back where they belonged.

The path became even more difficult, the farther they traveled. This was because the five hundred feet high sheer mountainous cliffs that ran along both sides of the path were coming closer together. The cliffs consisted of shiny, red brick colored rock. The surface of the cliffs was so hard and smooth that no plant could take root. The cliff walls allowed no breeze to find its way into the deep ravine. The heat was stifling, though the shaded areas did provide a bit of relief. A feeling of claustrophobia set in as the passage began to twist and turn around sharp cornered edges and narrowed to a mere three feet.

Up ahead, the partners heard a man yelling in rage. "It sounds like somebody is having a bad hair day," Carter quipped as he wiped sweat off his brow with the back of his hand.

"Carter, be serious. This doesn't sound good."

"You're right. Maybe someone needs help. Come on; we have to deal with it. We can't go back."

Kat sighed and joined her friend. By the time they reached the source of the commotion, the path was only two feet wide at its widest. Some places, where the rock stuck out, were less than a foot and a half apart. It was clear that an average adult man would have trouble getting through.

It was at one of these incredibly narrow places that the partners saw the angry, frustrated man. His puffy, purple face was dripping with sweat. He was wearing a thick coat that extended out from his body several inches, and on his back he carried a large backpack. It was obvious that he was upset because he could not fit through the narrow space with the load he was carrying.

The young travelers watched as the enraged man struggled and strained to squeeze through the impossibly narrow passage. So intense was his effort that he did not notice the children.

"Excuse me, sir," Kat called out. The man did not respond. He just continued struggling. "*Sir!*" Kat shouted.

This got the man's attention. He stopped and turned toward the partners. He looked to be in his sixties. He had gray hair with a bald spot on the back of his head. He had sad eyes, and his face was full of worry and fear. When he first turned to the partners, he looked as if he was coming out of a dream. He rubbed his eyes and said, "You stay away. You cannot have my money. I worked hard all my life for it, and nobody is going to take it from me."

Carter responded, "Mister, we're not interested in your money. In fact, we didn't even know you had any money until you told us. We wanted to know if maybe you needed some help."

"Hah. You just want to trick me into giving you some of my money. You will offer to help carry some of it for a small fee. Then, when you get through the Needle's Eye, you will run away with it, knowing that I will not be able to catch you. I am not stupid. I know about people like you. I have worked with people like you all of my life."

Kat spoke up, "Sir, we weren't going to charge you for our help. As my friend said, we don't want your money. We just want to know if we can do anything to help you through ... What did you call it?"

"Don't play innocent with me; you know that this is called the Needle's Eye. I figured there would be people like you hanging around here looking for a way to take my money. Now, go away! I have to get through this pass."

"Mister, if you don't want our help, fine. But I have to tell you, you are not going to make it through that pass with what you're carrying. You will have to leave some or all of it behind if you want to move on past this place. That's just a simple fact," Carter said respectfully.

"Carter." Kat nudged the boy. "Look up there." Kat pointed to a large, flat rock formation directly above the struggling man. "There is a message carved into the rock."

"I see it. It says, 'Attention: No wealth needed beyond this point.'"

"You are lying! You want to trick me into leaving my money behind so you can have it. It is not going to work," the man raged, and then he made another desperate effort to squeeze through the narrow passage.

Carter answered, "We aren't trying to trick you. You can see for yourself; the sign is easy to read. I'm surprised that you missed it."

The man screamed, "*Go away!* I have to get through, and I am not leaving my money, so quit trying to trick me."

"If you don't want our help, will you at least let us pass? We need to get through as well," Carter tried to talk over the man's screams of rage and frustration.

"*Go away!*"

"How are we going to get past this guy? I don't think he's going to listen to reason," said Carter.

"I don't know. He does seem to be out of touch with reality, and he might even be dangerous." After a moment of consideration, Kat continued, "Here's an idea. He believes we're trying to trick him, and we aren't. Maybe we should try to trick him, and he won't think that we are." A crafty gleam twinkled in her eye.

"Hey, Hamsted," Carter said with pride, "now you're starting to think like me."

"This is no time for insults. We have a real problem on our hands that calls for some clever thinking for a change," Kat said with an annoying smirk.

"Okay, genius, what's the plan?"

"Well, it seems like the one thing this guy loves is money."

"Duh, you think?" Carter taunted.

"Yes, I do," said Kat, unruffled. "We can go to that wide space back a way that is still close enough for him to see. We need to trick him into believing that we found some of his money on the ground. If he buys it, he should come running over to claim his beloved property. When he gets close enough to push us aside to get at it, we quickly run past him to the passage. He will be so focused on what he thinks is on the ground that we'll be in the passage before he realizes there's nothing there."

"That might work. I know exactly what to do. Follow my lead. Stay here, and wait for my signal." Carter casually walked back to the wide area. Even though it was only about four feet wide, it was enough space for the partners to accomplish their ruse. When the boy reached the spot, he checked to see if the man was paying any attention to what he was doing. Luckily, it looked like he was exhausted from his struggles and was taking a rest. While he rested, he occasionally glanced back to see what the children were up to.

"Kat!" Carter called just loud enough for the man to think that he was not supposed to hear, and that got his full attention.

Carter glanced at the man, and the man looked away. When he motioned Kat over, Carter saw that the man glanced out of the corner of his eye and saw the gesture. Kat proceeded to play her part and casually made her way to her partner. Once there, the two stood close together and looked down at the ground. "Do we have his attention?" Kat asked.

"Give me a second, and I'll tell you." Carter stretched his arms up, turned his head from side to side as if he were working stiffness out of his neck. Actually, he was getting a glance at their target, who was not only looking at them, but had actually moved out of the narrow passage to get a better look. Carter said, "Yes, he's very interested in what we're doing." Then he said, "Point down at the ground." When Kat pointed, Carter grabbed her wrist, as he had planned to do, and then he glanced at the man as though he was checking to see if they had been caught. "He's watching; that should get a reaction from him."

Carter was right. As soon as he saw Carter grab his partners hand as if he was trying to stop her from giving something away, the man yelled out, "Hey, you kids, what are you doing there?"

Carter turned and said, "Nothing. There isn't any mon ... I mean, there isn't anything on the ground."

"Yes there is; there is money over there. I accidentally dropped some, and it is *mine*! Keep your greedy hands off it!" the man said as he charged straight at the partners. As he forced himself between the children, they were already moving past the angry man. They were at the passage by the time he realized there was nothing on the ground but rock and debris. When he realized that he had been tricked, he turned and ran as fast as he could after the children. "*Stop*, you little thieves. You picked up my money. You tricked me into thinking that there was still more on the ground so you could get away with what you found. I want it back!"

The partners were far enough into the Needle's Eye that they were out of the man's reach. Try as he could, he was not able to get at them. "When I get through this pass, I will hunt you down and take what is mine," the man said through tears of rage.

"Sir, we're sorry we had to trick you. We didn't find any of your money. It was all an act to get you away from the passage. We needed to get by you," Kat said with kindness that the man did not deserve.

"I do not believe you. I am going to count my money. If any of it is missing, I will track you down."

"Mister, with all due respect, because you are unwilling to leave that wealth behind, your journey ends here," Carter said with the wisdom of a sage.

Those words hit the man with such force that all the fight, rage, and desperation seemed to leave him at once. He nodded at the two, stepped out of the passage, sat on a rock, and hugged his pack. A blank look came into his eyes.

In their haste to get by the rich man, the partners had forgotten to pick up their pack and canteen. The children had set their burdens down during their conversation with the agitated man. They did not notice their oversight until after they were through the narrow passage. "That's just great," Carter growled. "We left the rest of our water, flashlight, and most everything Dark Beard gave us back there. Well, it's probably a good thing we forgot it. It would have been difficult trying to get through the Needle's Eye carrying that stuff."

"Didn't you have the knife in your pocket?" Kat asked.

"Yes. I still have the pocketknife; do you still have some matches?"

"I have a few."

"It wouldn't be a good idea to go back; let's keep heading east. Who knows? Maybe we'll run into Guard again, and this time he'll have pizza for us," Carter said with a half smile.

"Right and he'll have ice cream for dessert," Kat played along.

The two had decided that further discussion about the prophecy and their possible role in it was futile without more information. They had discussed it from every angle they could think up and finally decided that they would wait until they reached the adobe to find the answers that the Guardian had promised.

After about a mile beyond the Needle's Eye, the path became wider and less cluttered with dried brush, rocks, and chuckholes. Even though it was still a dirt road and closed in by large, towering rock cliffs, it seemed less claustrophobic.

"This sure is an improvement over what we've been dealing with the last couple of days. I'm glad I don't have to carry that heavy pack anymore either. This is like the first day we left the Dead Forest and headed down the road. It was easy walking, and we didn't have anything to carry. We did just fine," Carter said optimistically.

"I have to admit, I do feel kind of free, but I'm a little worried too. We don't have any water or food, and I don't think we'll find any wild berries like we did on the first day. On the other hand, Guard always comes through for us. And then there's that sign back there that said we do not need any wealth beyond the pass. What else could that mean other than our needs will be met?" said Kat.

Carter shrugged and said, "We'll see."

When the partners finally decided to stop for the night, they settled into a hollow place in the side of the north rock wall. It was warm from the stored heat of the day. They needed that because even though they had matches, they had nothing to make a fire with.

"I'm so thirsty," Kat complained.

"Me too, and I sure would like a piece of that pizza right now," Carter said. Then he looked up as if listening to see if there would be a response to his request. After a moment, he continued, "I guess there's not going to be any pizza tonight."

"I just realized something. That sign back at the Needle's Eye could have meant no wealth was needed here because there is nothing here to spend it on," Kat said cynically.

Carter frowned and said, "I've been thinking about that rich man back there."

Kat moved from a sitting position and lay down with her head propped on her hand as she rested on her elbow. "What about him?"

"What's going to happen to him? I mean, he can't move on until he gives up his wealth, and he obviously values it more than moving on to his final destination."

"Why is that do you think?" Kat asked.

"It's what he worked for all of his life. He put his time, energy, and life into it. To leave it behind would be to admit that he wasted his life, and his life had no value or meaning."

"Carter, how do you come up with this stuff? Sometimes you are a real pain in the neck. Then other times you seem wise like someone much older."

"I saw it in his eyes, Kat. When he was sitting on that rock hugging his pack, he had realized that he spent his life working for something he couldn't take with him. He knew at the end that he had wasted his life."

"I know you're right," said Kat with sadness in her voice. She turned over and said, "I'm going to sleep now. It's the only way I will be able to forget how hungry I am."

Carter stood up and headed out toward the road. "I'm going out to look at the stars. I'm not going to be able to sleep just yet."

Kat was almost asleep when she heard her partner call to her, "Kat, come here!"

"No, I've seen stars before," she groaned sleepily.

"Come on, Kat; you've got to see this."

"Oh, this better be good."

PARADISE CITY

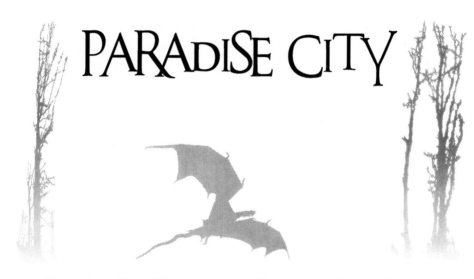

"Look there, Kat, off in the distance," Carter pointed down the road. "What do you see?"

"I can't see anything." Kat yawned. "My eyes are blurry; I was almost asleep."

"Just take a minute and focus. It's way off in the distance, and it's very faint."

Kat rubbed her eyes, yawned again, and tried to focus as best she could. "I see city lights!"

That's right. It looks like we don't have to worry about starving to death. If we leave at sunup, we should be there by late afternoon."

Carter's prediction was right. The partners were heartened by the thought that when they reached town, they would find help. They traveled fast on the good road and arrived at the city limits an hour before sunset.

"Look at that sign, Carter."

Carter read aloud, "Welcome to Paradise City, Congratulations on Reaching Your Final Destination."

"I don't understand. I thought our final destination was an adobe building," Kat said with a confused look.

"Maybe the adobe is here in Paradise. If this is our final destination, it must be here."

"That makes sense. Maybe we're almost finished with our journey, and we can go home."

"Maybe," Carter said doubtfully.

"You don't think so? Or, you hope it isn't?"

Carter shrugged and said, "I don't know; maybe both. It really doesn't matter what I think. If we're close to the adobe, then maybe we're near the end of our journey. And yet…"

"What?"

"Well, for a long time I assumed that finding the adobe would be the end of our journey. But now with all this prophecy stuff, it could be that finding the adobe may be just the start of the most important part of our quest. I have the feeling that everything we've been through up until now has been preparing us for something big. Think about it. How is just our reaching the adobe going to impact Dearth? There has to be more to it."

Kat, annoyed, said, "You'd like that, wouldn't you? You'd be happy to just keep on traveling from one adventure to another."

"You have to admit that this has been exciting. Up until now, all of our adventures around where we live have just been pretend. But this, this is the real thing. We're living a storybook fantasy adventure. What's back there at home for us? Do you remember the day we left? You couldn't wait to get away from your house. You were waiting on the porch for me, and you were annoyed that I hadn't gotten there sooner."

"I miss my mom, Carter. Don't you miss your parents, even a little?"

"Yes, of course I miss them, but we're going to see them again. Right now, we need to focus. We are about to enter a new situation, and we have to be on our toes."

"Go figure, even in 'paradise' we have to be on our toes," Kat remarked sarcastically.

"Just because it's called paradise doesn't mean that it is. And just because it says that it's the final destination doesn't make it so," Carter pointed out.

"Whether it's paradise or not, I bet they have food and drink."

"Agreed; let's head in and see if we can get some help." They only had to walk a few more feet through a clump of trees before they saw the entrance to the city. "Look at that. It looks like a huge theme park," Carter said excitedly.

"You're right. Even the entrance looks like a gated ticket booth. Do you think we have to pay to get in the place?"

"Nope, remember that sign at the Needle's Eye? It said we don't need wealth here. Let's get moving; I've got to see this place." Excited, Carter ran to the gate.

Kat ran after her partner, but for some reason she did not share her friend's enthusiasm.

"Welcome to Paradise City. We are glad that you have made it to the final destination," a beautiful young woman greeted them. She was dressed in a white robe that was so bright it almost hurt their eyes to look at. The woman had long golden hair, pale blue eyes, and milky white skin. Her face was so beautiful that the partners wondered if perhaps they were looking at an angel.

"I know that you have many questions. Since you have an eternity to find out all you want to know, I am just going to tell you a few basic things to get you started. My name is Petrah, and you will see many messengers that look like me around Paradise. They will assist you with all your needs."

Petrah reached below her counter and pulled out two booklets. "Here is a map for each of you. You will find every pleasurable and exciting experience ever conceived of for man's amusement here in Paradise. There is no need for money; everything is provided as a reward for making it to the final destination.

"Since you both look hungry, thirsty, and in need of cleaning up, let me point you to the first building on the right there on Gold Street. That is a luxury hotel, complete with a restaurant, room service, laundry service, and an information center," the messenger finished with a beautiful smile.

"That's a good idea," Kat agreed. "I don't know what I want to do first: sleep, eat, or bathe."

"I know what I am going to do. I'm going to get a large glass of ice water."

"Now that *is* a good idea."

"I can help you with that too. Over on the left, just beyond the city gate, there are several water fountains with cold, pure water."

The two thirsty children ran to find the fountains. They quickly located a row of white stone blocks. Each block had water shooting up about three inches at its top. They drank for a long time, stopping occasionally to breathe.

Finally, Carter said, "This is the best water I've ever tasted."

Kat stopped and added, "I think I could stand here forever and just drink water."

"Yeah, that's strange, isn't it? I'm sure we have had enough to drink, but I still feel like I could drink more."

"I'm for getting something to eat. I'm hungrier now than I am thirsty," Kat declared.

Carter took one more long drink, wiped his mouth, and said, "I'm ready; let's check into the hotel."

When the travelers turned their attention to Gold Street, they stopped and stared in wonder. "Look at that, Kat. I've never seen anything like it before. The buildings are strange and beautiful."

Kat nodded and added, "The buildings are all different sizes and shapes, and the colors are so brilliant they shimmer. I bet they actually glow at night."

"A person could spend a lifetime exploring this place. I just know that every one of those beautiful buildings holds wonderful delights to experience," Carter said in a dreamy, faraway voice.

Even though Kat was amazed and excited about their new surroundings, she was not sure that things were what they appeared to be. Kat was also starting to get a little concerned about Carter's attitude. He did not seem to be as focused on their goal of finding the adobe as he was before. It appeared as if he had other things on his mind.

Though she was concerned, Kat decided now was not the time to be negative. She figured that after they were cleaned up, rested, and fed that there would be plenty of time to discuss their situation. "Come on," she said. "Maybe we can explore later."

The hotel was as magnificent as they expected it would be. The lobby had a very high ceiling with enormous crystal chandeliers hanging in various places. There were beautiful golden pillars placed throughout the lobby, and the walls had intricate colorful designs painted on them, which were a delight to the eye.

The service personnel were all messengers like Petrah. They looked so much alike that it was impossible to tell them apart. The partners ended up treating them as if they were all the same person.

The other patrons or residents of Paradise were all different ages and races, as you would expect. Everyone seemed happy and friendly. They also appeared cleaner than the partners, which made Kat uncomfortable. She was glad when she finally got to her room so she could take a bath.

The partners' rooms were next to each other on the sixteenth floor. The rooms were identical. Each had a large living room complete with arcade games, widescreen video systems, computer, and a sound system that filled the room with any type of music desired. There were luxurious couches, chairs, and tables placed around the room as well. Both rooms had refreshment bars fully stocked with all types of sweets, desserts, and beverages.

The bedrooms were equally luxurious. The king-sized beds (dwarfed by the massive rooms) were so comfortable that once you laid down on them it was almost impossible to make yourself get up.

The bathrooms were a wonder to behold. The bathtub was so large that you could almost swim in it. It was fully equipped with Jacuzzi and stocked with an assortment of soaps, bubble bath products, lotions, shampoos, and perfumed oils. Everything imaginable for grooming was available.

One of the most exciting things about the accommodations was the monstrous sliding glass window in each living room. The partners had magnificent views of the colorful city. From the six-teenth floor they could see a far distance, and every bit of it was breathtaking.

Outside the windows there were massive balconies furnished with appropriate chairs and table. The partners could sit, relax, and enjoy the unbelievable views while consuming rich, decadent refreshments. Both partners had a similar thought that they could be happy for the rest of their lives just sitting out on the balcony and looking at the beauty of Paradise.

When they were finished bathing, their clothes were already back from the laundry, repaired and cleaner than new. Carter was ready long before Kat to go down to dinner. Kat made him wait out in the hall where he sat on a luxury settee. When she was finally ready, they hurried down to the dining room.

Dinner was splendid. The dining room was equipped with round tables covered with bright, white tablecloths. The utensils were pure silver, their goblets were crystal, and the plates were gold. The clean, white marble floors literally gleamed. There was no menu because, as the messenger who waited on them explained, they could have *anything* they wanted.

Kat ordered bacon, sausage, scrambled eggs, toast, and hash-brown potatoes covered in ketchup. Carter ordered the same thing. "I know it's dinner time, but I've been wanting a breakfast so bad that I just couldn't help myself," Kat explained.

The food was brought to their table almost immediately. "You don't have to explain it to me, Kat. I agree. This really looks good."

The friends were so hungry and delighted with the delicious food that neither of them spoke until they had scraped their plates clean.

"That was scrumptious, and I don't even feel full. I could stay right here forever and just eat," Carter declared.

Suddenly, Kat had a strange feeling in the pit of her stomach. It must have shown on her face because Carter asked, "Kat, are you all right? You look like someone just walked over your grave."

"That's the fourth time you or I have said that."

"Said what?"

"When we were drinking the water earlier, I said that I could stand here and just drink forever. You said when we first looked down Gold Street that a person could spend the rest of his life exploring this place. On our way down to dinner, talking about the beautiful view of Paradise all lit up at night, we agreed that we could spend the rest of our lives just looking out the window."

Carter, annoyed, grumbled, "Okay, I get it. And I just said that I could spend the rest of my life just sitting here and eating. What's your point?"

"Don't you catch a theme here? We cannot spend the rest of our lives in this place. What about the prophecy, the adobe, and Guard? What about going home eventually? It's like you don't care anymore about what we're supposed to do."

Carter shrugged and said, coldly "We don't even know that the prophecy has anything to do with us or if it's even real. If it's so important and if it has anything to do with us, why doesn't Guard just tell us? And so what if we don't find the adobe or never go home again? Would that be so terrible? I mean, look around you, Kat. This is paradise; enjoy it. I am. I'm going to order that pizza we were talking about earlier, and I bet it will be the greatest pizza I ever tasted."

"You aren't serious, are you?" Kat asked, concern filling her voice.

"About ordering the pizza? You bet I am. In fact, I'm going to order two extra large meat pizzas, and I bet I will be able to eat both of them and still not feel full."

Kat was discouraged by her partner's response, and she did not know whether she should stay with Carter and try to get through to him, or if she should just go to her room and cry. She decided to stay. She could not believe that Carter, who could be so wise at times, was actually this far gone already. Kat had to believe that he would come to his senses. She sat and watched while he ate his pizzas. Then she watched while he ordered three hot fudge sundaes and ate every bit.

"Come on, Kat; aren't you going to have something? It's really good."

"No, thank you. I'm not hungry anymore."

"That's odd; you haven't eaten nearly as much as I have, and I feel hungrier now than when we sat down."

"Well, I'm glad you find something about this place to be odd," Kat said, annoyed.

"Don't be that way; have some fun and enjoy. It's on me." Carter laughed, and then corrected, "Actually, I guess it's on the house." Then he laughed even louder.

Kat stood up, barely able to contain her anger, and said, "I'm going to bed." Then she stormed off to her room.

After that, Carter felt a little down. It always disturbed him to see Kat hurt or upset. He felt such a brotherly affection and protectiveness toward his best friend that if anyone hurt her, Carter always came to rescue her. Now, it seemed he was the one responsible for hurting her. It was like having a cold bucket of water thrown into his face, waking him from a dream. He did not feel hungry anymore.

Without warning, he saw out the corner of his eye what looked like a walking skeleton headed toward his table. He jumped and turned toward the figure. He saw a messenger bringing another pizza. "I am sorry, did I startle you? I just thought you might like another pizza," she said, smiling warmly.

Carter's heart was pounding; he was visibly shaken. "Oh dear, I see that I really did startle you." The messenger seemed more suspicious now than concerned, and that made Carter even more uneasy.

The boy quickly got back on his game and said, "Oh…no…I was daydreaming and wishing you would bring me another pizza, and there you were, bringing me one. It just surprised me, that's all." Carter smiled.

"I see," said the messenger, but she did not seem convinced. "We aim to please. Enjoy your pizza." Her tone was cold.

What's going on here? Carter wondered. He decided to eat the pizza, even though he did not want it. He wanted to talk to his partner, but he thought it would look suspicious if he just left the food untouched. He decided that since he was going to be in the dining room for a while anyway, that he would try to catch a messenger out of the corner of his eye and see if the image of a skeleton would reappear. He whispered to himself, "Okay, Carter old boy, keep it cool. If you see something scary, don't let on that you did." He continued eating while he experimented by looking at the servers out of the corner of his eyes. However, the servers always appeared normal regardless of how he looked at them.

Maybe it was just my imagination, he thought. He stopped trying to see a skeleton image and focused on finishing his pizza. He wanted to go up to Kat's room and apologize. Then, it happened again. When he was not trying, a messenger, waiting on a table nearby, came into his peripheral vision. He saw the shape of a fleshless, white skeleton. He did not move his eyes, but when he tried to concentrate and get a better idea of what he was seeing, the vision cranged back to the image of Petrah.

It could be my imagination, but this sort of thing has never happened to me before. I have to finish this food and talk to Kat, he told himself. When he was through eating, he went to his partner's room. He knocked, but there was no answer. He knocked again, louder. "Hamsted, I know you aren't asleep, and I really need to talk to you."

"Go away. I am too asleep," she said in a husky voice.

Carter felt bad because he knew that she had been crying. Still, he could not help smiling at her comment that she was asleep when obviously, she was not. "Come on, Kat. It's me, Carter. I'm back, and I need to talk to you; it's important."

At first, there was no response, and then the door slowly opened. Carter could see, from Kat's red eyes and nose, that she had really been crying hard and long. "Boy, Hamsted, we're supposed to be in paradise, and you're bawling your eyes out," he said, smiling at her. "That should be all the proof we need that we aren't in paradise."

Kat opened the door a little wider and asked, "Do you mean it?"

"Yes, you're right. There's something wrong about this place."

"There is?" Kat sniffed.

After he finished telling her what happened in the dining room, after she left, she said, "That's scary, Carter. If you're right, and it isn't just your imagination, there is a real serious implication here."

"What's that?"

"I'm surprised at you, Toby," Kat jibed her partner. "You're usually the one who sees what's going on before I do. Think about it. If the messengers aren't what they appear to be..."

"Then nothing here is what it appears to be," Carter finished. "Oh, this is not good; this is really bad. If this whole place is an illusion, then we still haven't had anything to eat or drink," Carter said with increasing anxiety.

Kat nodded and said, "That's why no matter how much we eat, we don't feel satisfied. We weren't really eating anything."

"More important, we haven't really had anything to drink. That means we haven't had any water for two days now, and we were on short rations as it was. Kat, we have to get out of this place immediately. If we wait much longer, we'll not have the strength to travel, and we'll die here." Then Carter added thoughtfully, "That's the purpose of this place. It's an illusion put here to distract us until we die and never make it to the adobe. Let's go. We have to head east down Gold Street until we come to whatever it is this place is trying to keep us from reaching."

As the partners exited the hotel, a messenger approached them. "Good evening, you two. It is a beautiful night for a walk. Where are you going?"

"We're going to take a stroll down Gold Street. It's so beautiful we just have to see as much of it as we can," said Carter in his friendliest manner.

"That is a wonderful idea, but let me caution you. Since this is the final destination, there is nothing beyond Gold Street—nothing at all."

"What do you mean there's nothing?" Kat asked. "There has to be something beyond the street: desert, dirt, jungle, swamp, something."

"Actually, there is only nothingness. Since there is nothing beyond paradise, anyone who wanders into the nothingness becomes nothing too," the beautiful creature warned.

The messenger no longer had the bright, friendly look that the partners were used to seeing; she became stern and cold. Then suddenly, Kat gasped. "Something wrong, my dear?" the messenger asked with a nasty looking smile that changed her whole face. The messenger knew that Kat had caught a glimpse of what she really was.

Carter looked at his partner and said, "You saw it, didn't you?"

"What are you really?" Kat asked.

"I am a messenger, and I am telling you, do not venture beyond Gold Street, or you will be sorry."

"I don't believe you," Carter said boldly. "You are a lie. You pretend to be beautiful and pure, but underneath you're...What are you, death? Whatever you are, you're a lie and a liar. This whole place is a lie." Carter called out to the people walking by them, "If you stay here you will all die. It's an illusion to keep you from your true final destination!" The people just waved and smiled. Some laughed as if it was supposed to be a silly joke. "It's true I tell you. This place is not the final destination. You need to head east, now!"

Kat touched Carter's shoulder and said, "Carter, they aren't real either. They're just part of the scenery."

"Yes, you're right, Kat. I understand it now. This whole place was created just for us." To the messenger he said, "Nothing is real except for you. And I don't care what you are because we're leaving right now." Carter turned and headed east down the street.

"You are wrong!" the messenger called after them. "You are both wrong, and when you step into the nothingness, you will know it. It will be just a brief moment, but you will know just the same. When that happens, I will hear your scrams of despair, and I will weep for you."

Carter looked back over his shoulder and snarled, "Weep for yourself, liar!"

After what seemed like a couple miles, they came to the end of Gold Street. They knew it was the end because there was nothing else except a wall of total darkness. "This looks like nothingness to me, Carter."

Carter nodded. "I'll say. I don't see anything at all. I don't even see stars. It looks like the ground just stops, and then there is nothing. What do you think?"

"I guess it's a matter of faith. Either we believe that the Guardian has told us the truth, and we keep going east until we find the adobe, or we believe the messenger. I, for one, believe Guard. But seeing this really makes it hard."

"Do you remember when the Guardian touched you that day he showed us Stewborn's ashes in the burned out house?"

Kat nodded. "Thank you, Carter. Yes, I do trust him, and I believe we should step into the darkness. It doesn't mean I'm not afraid, but I believe it's the right thing to do." Kat took her partner's hand, and together they stepped into the darkness.

THE WAREHOUSE

The act of stepping into the darkness was terrifying simply because the partner's did not know what to expect. They braced themselves for something traumatic. Maybe they would fall forever or drift endlessly in empty space, or maybe they would blink out of existence. Yet, all that happened was that they found themselves back on the eastern road. The road stretched on behind them and before them. Huge rock formations still ran along both sides of the path. The partners would not be able to veer off the road even if they wanted to.

"I must say, that was anticlimactic," Kat broke the tension.

Carter snorted and said, "Yeah, I expected more than this."

"Are you disappointed?"

"Actually, I'm thirsty and hungry. While we were in that illusion of paradise, I didn't feel it as much. Now that we're no longer under the influence of the illusion, I can feel the full weight of my need. How about you?"

"Yes, I'm really feeling it. I also feel dirty again. You're a sight, Carter, and I'm sure I look like a mess too. Even the bath and our clothes being laundered was a lie."

"I'm tired," said Carter. "But since we're dehydrated and weak from lack of food, I think we should travel now and try to find water. When the sun comes up, it's going to get hot. We will need to take shelter and rest."

"I know you're right, but I'm so tired and weak that if we don't find food and water soon, I'm not even going to be able to travel at night."

"I understand. There's enough moonlight we can see the road. This section is in good shape; we should be able to travel safely. I just wish I hadn't left the flashlight in the pack." Carter hesitated and then asked Kat, "Do you need to rest before we head out?"

"Yes, but let's go anyway. If I sit down now, I don't think I'll be able to get up again."

"I hear that," Carter agreed.

The partners traveled only a quarter of a mile when, on the right side of the road, they saw a lit sign above a doorway carved into the side of a large mountain of rock. The sign read "Free Supplies and Equipment for Eastern Path Travelers: Sponsored by the Guardian Group."

"Kat, look at that! I knew Guard would come through for us."

"You did, did you?" said Kat with a snort.

"Okay, so maybe I had some doubts. I suppose you knew something like this would be waiting here for us," Carter said skeptically.

"Of course I did."

"Whatever you say, Hamsted. Let's go in and see what they've got."

Even though the store was carved into a mountain of rock, they had to go through double doors made of dark tinted glass, to enter. Once inside, they saw a warehouse filled with racks of every type of equipment and supplies a person would need to survive in the wild. Looking down the center isle, the place was so large the partners could not see an end to it.

"Carter, do you see that sign?"

"How could I miss it? It's the first thing you see when you enter; it's huge." Hanging from the sealing, ten feet from the ground and directly in front of anyone who entered, was a large sign lettered in bright red print. It read "Caution: The rock that surrounds this warehouse contains a rare type of radiation that only affects living flesh. You are safe from damage if exposure is under twenty-four hours. Gather what you need quickly, and leave this facility within a twenty-three hour period."

"That should give us plenty of time to get what we need. Hey, there's a sign that says, 'Shower and Laundry Facilities.' We can get cleaned up for real after we get something to eat. And look," Kat said sounding energized. "There's a rack of bottled water up ahead on the right, and next to that there's some pouches of food. Let's start there. I'm so thirsty I can hardly swallow, and I'm so hungry I could eat a bug."

"A big bug," Carter agreed.

The numerous food products available on the racks included dried meat and fruit, crackers, cereal bars, dehydrated eggs, milk, and much more. The product labels contained no other information other than listing the contents.

Sitting on the rock floor, picnic style, Carter said, "Now that was good. I haven't felt this full since we ate hotdogs with Guard."

Kat responded with, "Yes, this food is pretty good, but it isn't as delicious as the food we had in Paradise City. Still, it's a lot more filling," she said with a sly smile.

"Now that I'm full, I'm feeling sleepy." Carter yawned.

"Me too, but I want to get a shower and wash my clothes before I try out one of those sleeping bags over there."

Carter yawned again and said, "Sounds good, but I don't want to sleep too long. I want to have enough time to search this place and make sure we don't miss anything we might need."

The warehouse was fully equipped with male and female facilities. It took the partners around an hour and a half to clean up and do their laundry. Now that they were full, clean, and groomed, they felt invigorated.

"Carter, I'm not sleepy now; how about you?"

"I could do a little shopping. I suggest that we start by checking out those backpacks over there, and then we can focus on filling them with what we need. We'll probably carry mostly food and water."

While the partners collected their supplies, Kat commented, "Do you think very many people use this place? I mean it's spotless and fully stocked. Usually when people are around, things get a bit messy. When we ate, we left empty food packets and plastic bottles on the floor. The food shelves we went through are no longer neat."

"Yes, I guess we should straighten up before we leave," Carter agreed.

"I think so too, but that isn't my point. Where's the evidence that anyone has been here besides us? Do you think there is a janitorial service or something?"

"I don't know, Kat. What difference does it make?"

"Just curious I guess."

Carter laughed. "The fact that this place is here at all is a curiosity. But leave it to you to ponder the deep mystery of who cleans the place."

"That's not what I meant, Carter. Just never mind; let's get our sleeping arrangements worked out," she grumbled.

They did not know how long they had been asleep when a loud crash woke them with a start. "What was *that?*" Kat gasped.

"I don't know," Carter whispered. The partners sat in their sleeping bags, tensely waiting for what might follow. "Did you notice where it came from?"

Kat shook her head. After a few moments of silence, they heard banging that sounded like metal hitting against metal, followed by what sounded like a cross between a moan and a growl. "It's coming from somewhere way in the back. What do you think it is, Carter?"

"Well, I don't think it's the janitor."

"Carter!" Kat sounded frightened.

"Maybe it's a traveler like us who came in while we were asleep. Or, maybe someone was already here before us, and they were asleep until now."

The next thing the children heard was the sound of shuffling footsteps accompanied by a strange metallic tap. "Carter, what if it finds us! Should we hide?"

Carter stood up and called out, "Hello. Is anyone there?" He got an immediate response to his question. A loud snarling growl of rage met the partner's ears. The shuffle tap, shuffle tap quickened.

"That was a smart move, Carter. Whatever that is, it's headed right for us, and it doesn't sound happy that we're here." Kat stood up and looked ready to run.

"Just wait. We didn't do anything wrong, and we have as much right to be here as anyone else." Her friend sounded more angry than scared.

"I know that, and you know that, but does *he* know that?" Kat asked as she pointed at a shadowy figure. The partners could see someone or something down the main isle headed toward them. It was still not close enough for them to make out whether it was human or animal. The sounds it was making did not sound human, but as it drew nearer, it looked like it was a seriously deformed man walking with the aid of a walking stick.

"It's just an old man," said Carter with some relief in his voice.

"Carter, there's something seriously wrong here." Kat was right. The man was covered with huge blisters, and his skin was peeling. He had no hair and he was wearing no clothes. The creature was so gruesome that the girl buried her face in Carter's shoulder to block out the sight of him.

As the creature came closer, it made hideous noises from what must have been a throat as diseased as its skin. The whites of the eyes were solid fiery red. The open mouth was toothless and drooling. The walking stick turned out to be an oversized machete.

The creature stopped about twenty feet away from the children. "What are you?" Carter asked with terror in his voice.

With a voice that was so rough and watery that it was difficult to understand, it said, "I traveler. You eat my food, drank water. You steal my things."

"We're travelers too. The sign outside said that the supplies are free and sponsored by the Guardian Group. This is for all travelers," Carter reasoned.

"*No!*" The man shouted and began to move closer to the children. "I here first. It free; I claim all. It belong me. You steal it. I kill you!" The man lifted the machete to strike the children down, but when he lifted up the huge knife, he lost his balance and fell to the floor. When he did not move, Carter quickly reached down and grabbed the machete that had slipped out of the man's hand.

Kat looked down at the pathetic, broken man lying in a heap and asked, "Is he dead?"

Before Carter could answer, the body began to shrivel up and slowly turn to dust. Then the dust dissolved so that there was no evidence that the man had ever been there.

"What's going on here?" Carter wondered aloud.

"He was a traveler," said a familiar voice from behind the children.

"Guard!" the partners said simultaneously. "What happened to him? Why was he so ... ?"

"So sick?" Guard suggested. "He lost sight of the journey and his final destination. His desire for the things put here to assist travelers blinded him. He came to value owning the tools, the food, and the equipment more than using them to gain that, which is far more valuable. His desire for the *things* kept him here. Eventually, the radiation from the rock surrounding this building destroyed him."

"But, Guard, why didn't you warn him? Why didn't you make him leave before he got sick?" Kat asked accusingly.

"He *was* warned. You saw the warning sign when you entered the warehouse. Everyone sees it, and there are warning sighs posted all around the place as constant reminders. I am sure you saw them."

"Yes, I saw them, but I still don't understand why you do not make people do the right thing," Kat persisted.

"Life is about making choices. I cannot force anyone to do anything against his or her will. I have not forced you in your decisions; you have always been free to choose what to do. Sometimes you have chosen wrong, and sometimes you have chosen right. Much of what happens to you in life is determined by the choices you make."

"Guardian, is the adobe our final destination?" Kat asked with a bit of pleading in her voice.

"I don't know. As I said, it is your choice. For that poor fellow, who just died here, this was his final destination. It was not the destination intended for him, but it was, by his choice, his final destination."

"Well, is the adobe our intended final destination?" Kat asked a bit annoyed.

"No. Once you reach the adobe, you will have to make a very hard choice. The choice is so difficult that if I had confronted you with it when we first met, you would not have been able or willing to attempt it. And now, you have struggled, fought, contended with difficult and evil circumstances, and emerged victorious. You have proven that if anyone can succeed in fulfilling the prophecy, it is you two."

Carter jumped in with, "So it's true then. We are the two youths in the prophecy."

"I believe you are, but prophecies are funny things. You never really know who they relate to or what they mean until they are fulfilled."

"Can you at least tell us what equipment we will need for the next leg of our journey?"

"All I can tell you is travel light, and take whatever you need to be prepared for anything."

"That's no help at all," Kat grumbled.

"What's that I smell?" Carter asked. "It smells like maple syrup."

"Yes, and hot chocolate." Kat smiled in spite of herself.

"You will find sausage, bacon, eggs, and waffles prepared just the way you like them. I thought you would like a good breakfast before you headed out today. I have everything ready for you in the eating utensil section."

The partners looked over at the area Guard mentioned. "Thank you, Guard. Will you join us for break—" Carter did not finish his question because when he looked back to address the Guardian, he was already gone. "I keep forgetting not to turn my back on that guy. He does that every time," Carter grumbled.

Kat shrugged and said, "Let's eat. I'm hungry." After she took her first bite of the delicious food, she said, "I don't know if it's because I'm so hungry or if the food is just exceptionally good, but this tastes as good as our fake breakfast we had for dinner in Paradise City."

"I'll say," Carter agreed as he stuffed half a waffle, dripping with butter and syrup, into his mouth.

"Carter." Kat chuckled. "You're dripping stuff all down your chin; be careful. We cleaned up just last night. I don't want to wait while you wash up again. I want to get out of this place as soon as possible."

"Don't worry about me. You should see yourself. You have sausage grease all over your mouth. And I have to say, Hamsted, it looks pretty disgusting." Then Carter pointed his finger down his throat and made gagging noises.

The girl wiped her mouth with a napkin, put it down, and stared down at her plate.

"What's wrong? I was just kidding you because you were getting on me when you were messy too."

"It's not that. I was just thinking about that man who died. Here we are eating and having a bit of fun when just a few minutes ago someone was suffering and dying right in front of us."

"Yeah, I guess so. It doesn't seem right that we should just act as if it never happened. But he did bring it on himself, and he tried to hurt us. Still, we all make mistakes, and he certainly suffered for his. I feel bad for him too."

"I still think about Mr. Stewborn sometimes," Kat said as she looked up at her partner.

"So do I, but I guess it's important that we learn from their mistakes as well as our own. I'm beginning to understand Guard when he says we are responsible for a lot of what happens to us in our lives. Nobody forced Stewborn into that stone house, and nobody forced that traveler to stay here until he grew sick and died."

"I know, but it's still hard to see people suffer, no matter the cause."

Carter sat up straight, brightened, and said in an encouraging tone, "Kat, we have been through a lot. We've seen and experienced some intense and frightening things, and it looks like we are in for some more. So, we should have some fun while we can. That's why Guard made us this breakfast. He did it so we could relax and enjoy ourselves for a time, and that's what I'm going to do. I'm going to enjoy this great food, and then I'm going to go on a shopping spree. I'm going to shop till I drop, or at least until I can't carry anymore."

Kat smiled and said, "I guess you're right. We don't know what's coming next, and it feels good to just take a moment and enjoy something simple like breakfast."

It was late morning when the partners left the warehouse. Their backpacks were crammed full of stuff they were convinced they would need. Not surprisingly, after walking a few miles with the heavy packs, they decided to go through their stuff and eliminate things that they agreed were not essential. They repeated this process two more times. By the end of the day, they felt that they had finally trimmed their supplies to the real necessities: food, half the number of water bottles they had started with, rope, matches, two sleeping bags, plastic tarps, hats to keep the sun off their sunburned heads, sunglasses, two flashlights with extra batteries, and warm jackets. Carter still had the knife that Dark Beard had given him.

That night when they made camp, they ate well around a warm fire and slept soundly in their new sleeping bags. When the sun came up the next day, they were rested and in good spirits.

Around noon, the rock formations and piles of boulders lining either side of the path finally opened up, and the travelers found themselves in a valley.

"Kat, do you know what kind of ground this is? It's adobe."

"Is that an adobe building up ahead?" Kat pointed off to the right.

"All I see is a clump of trees. No, wait...I see it now. I'm not sure; it's so far away. But it has that look to it—kind of like an old mission. Let's check it out."

THE ADOBE

"Yes," Carter said excitedly as they drew closer. "That is an adobe. It looks like pictures of the Alamo I've seen in school. There's a painted sign over the front door that reads 'Adobe Orphanage.'"

"It's awfully quiet for an orphanage. Where are all the kids? Do you suppose it's abandoned?"

"There's only one way to find out. Let's go in and take a look around," Carter said eagerly.

The partners stepped onto the wooden porch and knocked on the door. When there was no answer, Carter gently pushed the door open and called out, "Hello! Is anyone home?" When there was no response, he pushed the door the rest of the way open and stepped over the threshold.

Kat followed, and they found themselves in a vestibule. There were small benches along the walls to the left and right and another door straight ahead. Kat stepped forward and opened the second door. Inside was a small lecture hall. There were about twenty wooden chairs set up in rows facing a wooden lectern. The girl called out, "Hello, is anyone here?" This time they heard someone moaning behind a closed door located behind and to the right of the lectern. "It sounds like someone's hurt." Kat moved toward the sound.

Carter, close behind her, cautioned, "Be careful."

Kat slowly pushed the door open and found a man dressed in black laying face down on the floor. He was in a small office furnished with a wooden desk and chair. Books lined the walls. Upon hearing the door open, the man turned over with a great effort and several loud moans.

He had a kind face, a receding hairline, and black hair graying at the temples. His eyes were small, and his nose was large. He had a bloody gash on the left side of his forehead and a bloody lip. "The children have been taken! Please help me to my chair; I am too weak to stand without help," he said in a feeble voice.

With great effort, the partners were able to help the man get to his chair behind the desk. "Thank you. My name is Harfet. I would like to know your names."

"I'm Kat, and this is my partner, Carter."

Harfet's eyes widened. "Did you say *your partner*?"

Kat smiled and answered, "That's right. Carter and I are partners; at least that's how we define our relationship. Why do you ask?"

"Because, the Adversary said he was taking the children to the Valley of Shadows, and if I ever wanted to see them again, I would send the partners to him. Was he referring to you?"

Carter and Kat shared a look, and then Carter said, "Yes, the Adversary has been trying to destroy us for several days now. I assume he has taken your orphans hostage because he knows we will come after them."

"No, more likely he hopes you will not go after them. The Valley of Shadows is a terrible place filled with things you cannot imagine. He would want you to be haunted by guilt and shame for saving yourselves. I am sure that is his plan. Even if you attempt to rescue them, you will soon turn back and give up your mission because of the horrors you will encounter. He is counting on your fear and doubt to defeat you."

"The Valley of Shadows, you say?" Carter shared a look with Kat. "We thought that was a saying people used to describe their sorrow."

"Yes, for a long time people have used that saying to describe their deepest darkest feelings of sorrow and desperation. Not everyone knows that the saying is also the name of the most cursed, cruel, evil place in all of Dearth. And if you have traveled much in Dearth, you know that is saying something truly incredible. Most of Dearth is lacking in love and compassion."

Kat asked in a soft voice, "Will you tell us about the children?"

"The children are all from one family. Their parents died of an illness within a day of each other. I found the children a little over a month ago, living alone. The oldest, Marista, who is ten, was taking care of her little brother, Shawnter, who is five, and her sisters, Rebee, who is seven, and Leana, who is eight. They were hungry, dirty, and frightened. They lived up in the rocks in a cave about five miles from here. I knew the family and visited them regularly. It was on one of my visits that I found the children living alone.

"The orphanage has not had any children in it for several months, so I visit the people who live in the surrounding area to see if I can do anything to assist them. Sometimes they need a little first aid; sometimes they need some food that grows in my garden. Sometimes they just need to see a familiar face to let them know that they are not alone." Harfet paused, sighed, and continued, "And sometimes, they need someone to take their children when they can no longer care for them."

Harfet focused on the partners and said, "But this is not your concern; this is my responsibility. I am the children's guardian, and I must try to rescue them." Attempting to stand, Harfet swooned and fell back into his chair. He tried again to stand, but this time he fell back, unconscious.

Kat shrieked, "Oh no! He's dead!"

Carter felt for a pulse in the man's neck. "He's not dead; he fainted." Carter shook the man and said, "Sir—Mr. Harfet—wake up!"

Eventually, the man opened his eyes, and in a weak voice he said, "It looks like the Adversary made sure that I would not be able to go after the children myself. I have a couple of broken ribs and a few bruised organs."

The broken man looked at the partners with worry and said, "How can I ask you to risk your lives? You are just children yourselves. No, I will not allow it. There must be another way."

Kat asked, "Is there another way?"

He looked down and shook his head.

"That settles it then. The only chance those children have is if we go," Carter said.

"You do not understand. The Valley of Shadows is a place where few, if any, return. The children are lost to me. And you should not fall into the trap of feeling guilty because there is nothing you can do for them. No one would expect you to risk yourselves on an impossible task."

Kat pointed out, "You are willing to risk yourself on an impossible task. If you were able, would you go?"

Harfet nodded and said with determination, "Yes, I would. And when I am able, if the children have not returned, I will go."

Carter asked, "Sir, what do you know of the prophecy?"

"Prophecy?" Harfet looked at the boy with an expression that was both quizzical and thoughtful. "Are you referring to the prophecy of when Dearth will want no more? Have you two survived The Forge of Providence?" Harfet looked hopeful.

Carter nodded and said, "Yes." And before the man could ask, Carter said, "We are from alien realm too—a place called Earth."

In Harfet's growing excitement, he forgot his injuries and stood. He groaned and fell back into his chair panting in pain. Then he smiled and asked, "Are you the two youths from the prophecy?"

"Some think that we might be. Who can know for sure until the prophecy is fulfilled?" Carter said with a sly look.

"But what about the first part of the prophecy that talks of the kingdom being lifted by wooden limb?" The man's eyes shifted to the side as if he were trying to figure something out.

"Have you heard of Goodman?" asked Kat.

"I know the story of Goodman. Is he real? Did it really happen?"

Kat smiled and said, "Yes, it really happened. We met the rich man who was Goodman's former master."

Harfet almost forgot his condition again as he leaned forward, his eyes wide with wonder at all the exciting things he was hearing. "But I understood that his former master was an evil, selfish man—a true child of Dearth. I also heard that he ran off and no one has seen him since."

Kat told Harfet what really happened to the man they knew as Dark Beard. When he heard of the great conversion of Dark Beard he declared, "It must be true then. The prophecy is being fulfilled in my time. And if you are the two youths, then my little orphans must be the taken."

"Tell us, Mr. Harfet, where is this Valley of Shadows?" Carter asked.

"If you continue east through this valley, which is known as Dearth Valley, it is the next valley over."

Kat took a deep breath and said, "That settles it. We're going to go rescue the children. We've been set on an eastern path ever since we began this journey. It looks like we're still supposed to journey east. Mr. Harfet, is there anything you can tell us that will help us?"

Harfet said, "There is a wise man who knows more about the Valley of Shadows than anyone else around here. Go to him and learn what you can before you enter the valley. You will find him living near the entrance of the cursed place. Travel east until you come to a natural tunnel in the rock mountain. That is the entrance to the Valley of Shadows. But before you enter the tunnel, travel north until you see an ancient oak tree that has a tree house built in its branches. The wise man lives there. If you call up to him using his name, he will know that I have sent you, and he will allow you to enter his home. His name is Losmoon.

"That, my brave friends, is all I have to offer in the way of assistance. I would plead with you not to go, but it is clear that you are determined to do this thing. It would be a lie to say that I am not glad of it. I pray that your journey will be short and successful."

"How about you?" Carter asked. "Will you be all right?"

"It will be several days before I am able to do much more than feed myself. As I said before, when I am able to travel, if there has been no word of the children, I too will go after them.

"You are welcome to eat and rest here before you continue. There is food in the dining hall. If you will assist me, we will enjoy a bit of refreshment together."

As the partners shared a bowl of rabbit stew with Harfet, he explained that the journey to the tunnel that leads to the Valley of Shadows was a day's walk. He also informed them that the wise man's tree house would be another two-hour walk. It was midafternoon when the young travelers left the adobe. They walked four hours before they made camp under a large tree. Neither of the partners recognized the type of the tree. Under its branches was a ground-hugging plant that looked a lot like seaweed. It was thick, soft, and made a nice cushion on which to sleep.

The children were exhausted and agreed to bed down and wait until morning to eat. The night was warm, they did not need to build a fire, and they slept on top of their sleeping bags. In a matter of minutes they fell into a deep sleep.

As they slept, an unexpected thing happened. Very slowly, the seaweed like vines began to move over the bodies of the sleeping partners. Some of the vines wrapped around their wrists and arms. Some wrapped around their ankles and legs. Even more frightening, some wrapped around their throats.

A Seaweed Tree

The next morning, Carter was the first to wake. "Kat," he called gently. He did not want to startle her more than she was going to be once she discovered their situation.

"Oh, do we have to get up already? Can't we sleep in today?" Kat said groggily. She did not open her eyes. "I'm so exhausted; I can't even move my body."

"Kat, I don't want to alarm you, but it isn't because you're exhausted that you can't move your body."

"Hmm? What do you mean?" Kat asked as she opened her eyes. "What? Carter! What's happening?" The frightened girl was wide awake now and struggling to free herself from the vines that had her tightly bound to the ground.

"Hamsted!" Carter yelled at her. "Stop struggling. The more you struggle, the tighter the vines get. Just relax, and they will hold you firmly, but they won't strangle you."

Kat got the message and stopped immediately. Panic was already threatening to overwhelm her. It took all her self-control just to make herself keep still. "Carter, I can't move."

"Just try to stay calm. I think these vines are part of this tree. It's some sort of Venus flytrap tree."

"You mean … this tree is going to *eat* us?"

"It already is eating us. The nodules along the vines behind each leaf are bladders filled with digestive juice. The juice slowly seeps through the vines and digests whatever it has caught. Then, as the victim dissolves, it seeps into the ground and feeds the roots of the tree."

"Carter, how can you possibly know all that?"

"My skin is starting to burn where the vines are touching me. At first, it just felt itchy, but now it is starting to burn. What's odd is that I can hear the tree talking to me in my mind. It told me what it's doing, and it even apologized for it."

"Okay, that makes me feel much better," she said sarcastically. "Carter, I'm starting to feel my skin burn too. Please, you must have an idea of what we can do."

"Kat, you have to calm yourself. I do have an idea. I don't know if it'll work, but it's our only chance. I have been working my hand into the pocket where I keep the knife. I have it in my hand, and I'm trying to open the blade. It isn't easy opening a pocketknife with only one hand, but I believe I can do it."

"Yes, Carter, you must do it. Please hurry!"

"Once I get the knife open and out of my pocket, I have to be careful not to pierce the bladders. The digestive juice is an acid that will burn whatever it touches. If I can get between the bladders and just cut the vines, I may be able to free my hand enough to cut my way out of this. What I don't know is how the tree will react to having its vines cut. If we're lucky, it doesn't feel pain. There, I got the knife open. I'm going to cut through my pocket. I cannot see what I'm cutting because I can't lift my head. Can you see my right pocket?"

"The vines are holding my head, and I can't see it."

"You can turn your head toward me by applying gentle pressure. Too much will cause the vines to tighten. You have to turn very gently—and I mean very gently—then they will move and adjust slowly. It may take fifteen minutes to turn your head all the way toward me. I hate to say it, but this is going to take a while. The problem is that the longer it takes the more damage the digesting vines will do. It's going to get worse before it gets better."

It took more than twenty minutes for Kat to turn her head toward Carter. By the time she was facing the right way, she was in so much pain from the vines digesting her skin that she could not help crying. The tears were blurring her eyes, and she choked out, "Carter, I can't see to help you. I cannot stop the tears; they are blurring my vision."

"It's okay, Kat. I'm having the same problem. I'm going to do the best I can by feel." Carter used the time it took Kat to turn her head, to position the blade in his right hand so it slid under the vines that were wrapped around his wrist. He had the blade pointing up his arm with the sharp side out. "I'm going to start sawing by moving my wrist back and forth. Hopefully I won't be cutting into any bladders."

"Be careful, Carter."

"Here goes nothing," the boy said as he made his first attempt to cut the ties that had him bound. Surprisingly, the vines were easy to cut. Thankfully, there was no reaction from the tree or its vines. Encouraged by the positive results, Carter became a bit careless as he continued. Eventually, he did nick one of the bladders. At first, the boy did not even notice what he had done. However, when his upper leg started to feel cold, and then began to feel warm, he realized what he had done. "I cut one of the bladders, but it doesn't hurt. It just feels warm. I need to hurry and get free so I can wash it off with some water. Now it's starting to burn."

Carter kept cutting as he gave a report of what he was feeling from the digestive juice that was eating into his upper thigh. "Now it's really burning." Suddenly, Carter screamed out, "It feels like a red hot iron! My leg! My leg! It burns!"

"Carter!" Kat called out in helpless despair.

Without thinking, he reached out with his free hand and wiped at the juice, but as soon as he did it, he realized he had made another mistake. "Great, now my hand is starting to burn," he said through gritted teeth.

"Thank goodness I am not too late," the children heard an out-of-breath voice say. "You poor boy, try to stay calm. I know you are in terrible pain, but everything will be all right," said a very old man with deep wrinkles around his eyes. He had white hair and a white beard. He wore a wide-brimmed hat and a blue jumpsuit. He used a gnarled walking stick, and he had a cloth bag slung over his left shoulder.

The man kneeled down beside Carter and put his hand on the boy's forehead. Carter felt comforted, and he calmed down enough to stop struggling. "Now, I need to treat the burns on your leg and hand right away, or they will continue to get worse," he said as he reached into his bag. He took out a dark blue bottle and a clean, white cloth. He poured some liquid from the bottle onto the cloth and began to clean the serious wounds.

"I will need to treat both of you once I have cut you free. Everywhere the vines have touched your skin must be cleaned and neutralized, or you will suffer much damage and become sick from the seaweed tree's digestive juices."

The old man used Carter's knife to free the children and then proceeded to treat their wounds. When he was finished he said, "I suggest that we move to a nice safe shade tree located around that mound of dirt up ahead."

After they settled around the shade tree, Carter announced, "The pain is gone. Thank you for your help; we would have died if you had not come along when you did. My name is Carter, and this is my friend, Kat. I would like to know your name, sir."

"My name is Losmoon, and I did not just happen by. I had a dream two nights ago that two very special children would visit me on a matter of great importance. In my dream, I saw you camp under the seaweed tree and become trapped. As soon as I woke, I gathered what was needed and came as quickly as possible. I travel slowly, as you can imagine. I am sorry that I did not arrive sooner, but let me assure you that this treatment will heal the wounds from the seaweed tree and will leave no scars."

"Mr. Losmoon, you must be very tired and hungry," Kat said. "We're grateful to you for your help. Will you share some of our food?"

"Thank you for your kind offer, Kat. I will share a meal with you, but I insist on eating my own food. You will need all you have for your journey."

"Do you know about our journey?" Carter asked.

"I saw in my dream that you come from alien realm. You intend to journey into the Valley of Shadows to rescue children who have been *taken* by the Adversary. I sense you have journeyed The Forge of Providence, and I sense a power in you that I have not witnessed before in any other. You were seeking me out because you wish to learn what you can about the valley and receive any aid that I might be able to give you."

"You've given us pretty good aid already," Kat said.

"I'll say," Carter agreed.

"You are welcome."

The partners got comfortable and started eating. The wise man said, "I am going to build a fire and make us some tea. It is delicious, and it will make you feel stronger for your day's travels."

"Will you be coming with us as far as the tunnel?" asked Kat.

"You were right when you said I must be tired. I will spend the rest of the day and most of the night right here under this tree, resting. It is a bit of a journey back to my tree house."

"Of course, I'm sorry. I wasn't thinking," said Kat, a little surprised at herself.

"It is all right, my dear. It is the effects of the seaweed tree. The vines give off chemicals that disorient as well as digest. By the end of breakfast, you will be back to your old self."

"Why is it called a seaweed tree?" Carter asked with a mouth full of dried apples. Kat shot him a nasty look and said, "Don't talk with your mouth full, Mister Manners."

Carter swallowed and smiled sheepishly. "Sorry, I'm hungry; we didn't eat last night."

"No need to apologize," said Losmoon. "The tree gets its name from the digestive vines that had you bound. You may have noticed that they look a lot like seaweed. The tree gets most of its food from animals that eat the tree's sweet fruit that falls to the ground. The fruit contains a chemical that induces a deep sleep. When the animals eat the fruit, they fall asleep, and then the vines wrap them as they did you. The tree has no fruit now because it is out of season. It is rare that people are caught in its trap. Oh, there is the occasional intoxicated person who falls asleep under the tree and an occasional young child who wanders away and gets lost, but that does not happen very often."

"And then there is the unwitting stranger who has never seen a seaweed tree and makes camp under it," Kat added.

"True, but I must tell you that seaweed trees do have value. The fruit is so effective at inducing sleep that people sundry it—use it for curing insomnia and pain relief. It also keeps the vermin population down. Most of the animals that the tree traps are the small ones that carry diseases.

"But that is not the information you are looking for is it? It is time we talked of the Valley of Shadows." Losmoon paused for a moment and then continued. "It is a place of darkness. Thick, low-hanging fog covers the sky. The ground is black dust in places, black rock in others. Black water flows in rivers into black bogs filled with many dangers. The air is thick and heavy, making it hard to breathe. You will feel an oppressive weight of sorrow and despair fall on your hearts at times. You must be strong and trust each other, help each other, and never forget the deep friendship that binds you."

"Will there be other people there besides the children?" asked Kat.

"Yes, there are individuals who dwell in the valley, but most who dwell there are not to be trusted. The darkness has entered their being. They eat the things of the valley and drink its dark water. They are a part of the valley."

"What sorts of creatures will we run into?" asked Carter.

"There are things far worse than the seaweed tree in that dark place. Evil beings that thrive on fear, hate, anger, greed, and selfishness will seek to destroy you. These beings are powerful. However, the fact that you are entering the valley to rescue innocent children will work to your advantage. Use your courage, selfless motives, and loving concern as your shield. These things will keep you strong and hinder the valley's influence over you. Do not be deceived or side-tracked. Do not lose sight of your mission to save the children."

"Mr. Losmoon," Kat asked, "how will we find the children?"

"The children are imprisoned at the eastern end of the valley. Your journey will ever take you east."

"Is there anything else you can tell us?" Carter asked.

"Do not eat or drink anything from the valley. Be careful whom you trust. Remember all that you have learned during your travels." After a brief pause, he continued. "Traveling the Valley of Shadows is a frightening prospect; you will be facing and contending with great evil. Of course, you do not have to do this; it is your choice whether or not you continue the journey. But know this. I believe you can succeed. I believe you can survive the valley and rescue the children."

"Why?" Kat asked.

"Why do I believe it?"

"Yes. Why do you believe we can succeed in this?"

"Because, as difficult as this all seems, anyone could be successful if only they had courage, faith, love, compassion, and were determined to succeed."

"Then why don't you go?" asked Kat.

"Because this is *your* quest. We all have a part to play. Mine is to provide you the assistance I am providing. Yours is to go and find the children. The Adversary would not release the children if I went. He wants you, and you have to decide if you will go. I know that you must be special because you have made it this far. You obviously have wisdom, determination, courage, and all the things I mentioned that would give you success. You must employ all those qualities to succeed in the valley. And if it is not already clear to you, it is not only the orphans that need you, all of Dearth needs you."

The three sat quietly as the children pondered what the wise man had shared with them. After a time, Kat broke the silence. "This tea is delicious, and I do feel better." She sipped at her tea again.

Carter finished his tea and began organizing his pack. He asked, "How long will it take us to walk through the valley?"

"If you could walk straight through the Valley of Shadows to the end, it would take you a day and a half if you averaged ten hours a day travel. The truth is, you will have much to contend with, and that will delay your journey."

Carter stood up and waited for Kat to pack. "We thank you for all your help," he said.

"I wish you success, and I want to send you off with one final word. The Valley of Shadows is a very difficult place. The moment you emerge from the tunnel and enter it, your first impulse will be to give up due to the overwhelming oppression you will feel. I implore you to remember the children. They are in the worst part of the valley, and you *are* their only hope."

"Don't worry, sir. We'll get to the children," Carter said. "If you're ready, Kat; we need to be on our way." The new acquaintances parted company, and the partners resumed their travels.

Carter and Kat had little trouble finding the entrance to the tunnel. With the help of their flashlights, they made their way through the mountain. The children were encouraged with how smoothly their journey seemed to be going. That sense of encouragement was short-lived. The moment they stepped out of the tunnel, it felt like they had just stepped into Death's living room. Deep feelings of sadness fell so heavy upon them that they knew they would never be happy again. Powerful fingers of fear reached into their innards with such intensity that they wanted more than anything to turn and run back the way they had come.

THE VALLEY OF SHADOWS

"Carter, this place is worse than I imagined. I can hardly breathe. I want to leave!"

Carter wanted desperately to grab his friend's hand and flee, but he struggled with all his might to stand his ground. The boy reached over, took Kat's hand, and squeezed it tight. Then he said, as much to himself as to her, "Feelings cannot kill. Think, Kat, why are we here? We are here to rescue the little children. We need to let that purpose fill us and overpower the feelings of dread and fear. Try to picture them in their desperation. We are their only hope."

As they stood, hand in hand, struggling against forces threatening to overpower them and turn them from their purpose, they began to feel a glimmer of hope and courage take root.

After a time, Kat let go of Carter's hand. She looked at him with dread in her face.

"I know," Carter said sympathetically. "This is far worse than anything I had imagined too. Even now, it's all I can do to keep from running as far from here as I can."

Not surprisingly, Kat turned quickly away from Carter and threw-up. Seconds later, Carter did the same.

Emptying their stomachs actually made them feel better both physically and emotionally. The feeling of relief made it possible for them to take in their surroundings. It was a dark place and not just because the sky was covered with dense clouds. It was dark because something was missing. In fact, many things were missing. There was no sound. There was no wind, no buzzing of insects, or bird song. It was like wearing headphones with no music playing.

Love and compassion were obviously in short supply because that is what caused the intense feelings of fear and sadness.

"Carter, I think I see shadows moving in the distance." The fear in the girl's voice was palpable.

"I'm scared too. I mean, I'm really scared," Carter said with uncharacteristic candor.

"Are you?"

Carter nodded as he gave a weak smile. "Yes."

"I feel such sadness, and my heart feels heavy. I don't think I can do this anymore." Kat sounded ashamed.

"I know you can, Hamsted, and this is how we are going to do it. It's a day and a half walk straight east. We are going to put one foot in front of the other, and before you know it, we'll be at the end of our journey. I know we can do this. Are you ready?"

Kat heaved a deep trembling sigh and nodded. With that, the two were off. They took five steps on the hard black ground, and then they saw Guard standing in front of them.

The children were so relieved to see the Guardian; they shouted with joy and ran to meet him. "Boy are we glad to see you," said Kat with such relief in her voice that it made Carter chuckle.

"And as always, I am glad to see you as well. I am especially glad to see you because I have some very good news. You have successfully completed your quest; you are finished, and it is time for you to return home. You made it to the adobe, and you were willing to go beyond what I asked you to do by going after the orphans. You have demonstrated your courage, your selfless attitudes, and your wisdom. There is nothing more for you to prove."

With a confused look on her face, Kat asked, "What about the children being held by the Adversary?"

Guard smiled warmly at her and said, "You do not have to worry about the children. I will take care of them. They are no longer your concern. Now, let us get you back home. You must be anxious to see your parents."

Carter turned a questioning look toward Kat. She returned the boy's look with a little shrug. Carter said to Guard, "That's great, but we're going to miss those delicious pancakes you made us back at the warehouse. I was hoping to taste those pancakes and strawberries one more time. Tell me, Guard, were those buttermilk pancakes?"

"Yes, I always use buttermilk in my pancakes. I am glad you enjoyed them."

Carter pursed his lips and shook his head. With a sigh of exasperation he said, "Let's get going, Kat; we have some children to rescue."

When the two started walking east again, Guard asked, "What are you doing? You are through; it is time for you to go home."

The children stopped, turned to Guard, and Carter said, "Nice try, Adversary. Guard didn't make pancakes for us at the warehouse. He's never made us pancakes and strawberries. He made us waffles with maple syrup."

The Adversary immediately changed to his familiar appearance. He had an ugly look of contempt on his face as he said, "You think that you are very clever. I was just trying to spare you the terrible experience of passing through the Valley of Shadows."

"No you weren't," Carter flung back. "You were trying to keep us from sowing seeds of life in the taken."

The Adversary looked like he had just been punched in the nose. "So you think you have figured out the prophecy, do you? Do you even know how to plant seeds of life in the taken?"

"All we know for sure is that we must rescue the orphans or die trying," Carter said in a firm voice.

"Very well then, you will surly die long before you even find them."

Carter turned to his friend and said, "We're wasting time, Kat; let's get moving."

The partners did not look back. They just focused on traveling east. It did not take long before the travelers had to slow their steps. They came upon ground covered with two inches of black dust. The dust was so fine that their quick pace was stirring it up and causing a dark dust cloud to surround them. Their eyes began to itch, and they struggled with fits of coughing.

"This is unbearable; I can't breathe," Kat croaked.

"We have to slow down," Carter said between bouts of coughing. "Tear off part of the bottom of your shirt and make a filter mask to cover your nose and mouth. We need to pick up our feet and place them down flat. Try not to raise any more dust."

After they both took a swallow of water and covered their faces with cloth, they started out again. "At this rate it will take us forever to get across this valley," Kat observed.

"What choice do we have? This air is thick and hard to breathe as it is, and now we have to contend with this black dust. I actually think it could coat our lungs and suffocate us if we're not careful." Carter sounded worried.

After about a half-hour of struggling to make their way across the dust covered ground, Kat said, "Carter, what are we going to do when we need to take a rest? Better yet, how are we going to sleep?"

"I don't know. I've been trying to figure that out myself. If we don't find a clear spot that's not covered with dust, we will have to keep going. There's no way we will be able sit or lay on this stuff; it's too dangerous."

"I hate to say it, but if we turn back now, we can get out of this. We don't know how far it goes, and we're not making very good progress. At this rate it could take us a couple of days before we find a clearing where we can rest."

Carter stopped and asked his partner, "Are you saying you're ready to give up?"

"Well, what good is it going to do if we die out here? We won't be able to save the children if we're dead from breathing this dust. You know as well as I do that if we get too tired to go on, we'll fall down and end up getting a lung full of this stuff."

Carter looked down at the ground as he pondered the situation. After a moment, he said, "Let's see if we can shove enough dust to one side with our feet to clear an area where we can sit down. If we can, we'll be able to get some rest."

It was no use. Each time they shoved the dust aside (in an attempt to expose the solid ground underneath) it flowed back into place. Trying to displace the dust was stirring it up again and causing the children to cough.

"This is hopeless," Kat said. "Do you have any other bright ideas?"

Carter nodded as he coughed up dust. Once the dust settled, he said, "Actually, I do have a bright idea."

"I can't wait to hear this one."

"I think we should run."

"This place must be getting to you; you're losing your mind. If we run, we'll stir up more dust than ever," Kat said with a raised voice.

"You're right. We'll stir up more dust than ever, but we'll be out in front of it. As the dust rises with each step, we'll already be past it. As long as we keep running, we'll be able to breath without choking on it."

"I have to admit, that does make sense. But do you believe we can run with our backpacks in this heavy atmosphere?"

"We can jog and see how fast we can go. Hopefully, we'll be able to go fast enough to keep in front of the dust. I figure we'll cover more ground, and if we're lucky, we'll be out of this stuff before we run out of steam. Or, we might find a clear space or a large rock on top of the dust where we can get some rest."

"I don't know, Carter. This might go on for miles. We could end up so exhausted from running that we collapse, and if we collapse, out of breath, gasping for air in a cloud of this dust, we'll choke to death. The same thing would happen if we were to stumble."

"I know it's dangerous, but everything we've done so far has been dangerous. We're at the end of our quest; we can't give up now."

"But, Carter, this is the worst. Death and madness fill this place. I can feel it trying to overwhelm me with fear and doubt. I don't think I can do it," Catherine said with tears welling up in her eyes.

With pain in his heart for his friend, Carter watched as a single tear ran down the girl's cheek and fell to the ground. Then, something odd happened. A fizzing sound came from their feet where the tear landed. Looking down, they saw the dust compact into a round disk about six inches in diameter.

Kneeling, Carter touched the disk and found that it was like a crust. It was brittle and easily broken, but it did not create a dust cloud when it was disturbed. Carter reached into his backpack and pulled out a bottle of water. He opened it, sprinkled a few drops around, and watched as the dust compacted into the same crust.

"Look at this, Kat. We can walk on the crust that's created by moisture. We need to put some thick, damp cloths around our shoes. As long as the cloth stays moist, we should be able to walk on this dust without much trouble. This is how we will cross the plane. We can tear off the flaps that wrap around and cover our sleeping bags when they're rolled up and tie them around our shoes."

Kat wiped her eyes and gave a weak smile. "It might work. I wish there was something that would work to make my dark feelings go away," she said as she joined Carter in preparing the foot coverings.

"Do you remember how it felt when we thought Guard was here to help us? Up until the time I realized it wasn't Guard, I felt good. I felt lighter, safer."

Kat smiled a genuine smile as she remembered how she felt when she thought Guard had come to them. "It was the same for me. It was the best I've felt since I've been in this awful place."

"That's your answer. We need to generate positive feelings by creating our own little environment of joy and confidence."

Kat, sounding encouraged, asked, "How do we do that?"

"Let's start by lightening up. As we travel through this miserable dust plane, we'll tell funny stories and be silly. You start and tell me something that will make me laugh. I know. Tell me your most humiliating experience."

The partners found that their wet shoe idea worked perfectly. As they walked, a constant fizzing sound came from their feet as the dust compacted into the brittle crust. They did not have to use much water; even a very small amount was enough to cause the dust to turn into the crust.

They were able to make good time and left a conspicuous trail that resembled a road. They walked for approximately three hours, stopping only to remoisten their shoe coverings every half-hour.

Carter's idea of telling funny stories and being silly to lift their spirits seemed to be working too. Kat insisted that Carter tell something on himself first. After a little coaxing, he finally agreed. "That week, last year, when you were home sick with the measles, I had to give an oral report in health class, and I had to give it right after lunch. That day at lunch, they had my favorite—cooked spinach. I ate my spinach, and everyone at my table gave me theirs to eat. I cannot believe that I am the only one who likes that stuff.

"I was running late because I wanted to finish the last of my spinach. I put my tray away and ran to class. I sat down just as the bell rang. Mrs. Hanley called on me right off, but I didn't care. I had my report done, and I was excited about it. I knew I had it aced, so I got up all full of confidence and swagger. I began to speak authoritatively on the subject of dental hygiene. As I talked, the kids started laughing at me. I was standing in front of Mrs. Hanley's desk, facing away from her toward the class. She kept telling the class to settle down, but no matter what she did, the kids were getting worse. They were laughing so hard that they couldn't stop. I turned around to look at Mrs. Hanley for support, but as soon as I faced her, she began to laugh too. I was so frustrated that I started to get angry. Finally, the teacher held up a small mirror she kept in her desk, and I could see that I had big chunks of spinach caught in my teeth. I looked like I had about three teeth missing, and it was nasty looking. Then, to make matters worse, Tom McCoy yelled out, 'Hey look! Carter has tarter!' Kids were laughing so hard they were falling out of their seats. I was so embarrassed that I hid out in the boy's bathroom, between classes, the rest of the week."

The thought of Carter getting up in front of his class all puffed up and full of himself, and then having his teeth look disgusting without his knowing it, was too much for Kat. She laughed so hard that she forgot all about where she was. It was so fun to see her laughing again that Carter could not help laughing along with her. It was not that the story was all that funny; it was more that the contrast between the silly situation of the story and the serious situation they were in exaggerated the humor and met their need for an emotional release.

The effect of the children laughing and feeling positive had an amazing effect on their environment. The atmosphere surrounding them lightened to the point that it was easier for them to breathe. The oppressive feelings of dread and sorrow lifted, and they felt like their old selves again.

"Come on, Kat; it's your turn now. I want to hear something really embarrassing that happened to you."

Kat sighed and said, "I was never going to tell you this story." With a shrug she began, "Last summer vacation when I spent a month at my Cousin Amber's house, we went to a party thrown by a friend of hers. The friend was a boy named Patrick that she liked and wanted to impress. She wanted to tell Patrick that I was a singer and that I was going to try out for a TV commercial in New York. I didn't want to lie to him, but she insisted that she would tell him the truth after I went back home. She said it would be like a joke just between us, so I said I would play along. I didn't know that Amber had already told him the lie over the phone when he invited her to the party.

"The night of the party, Patrick announced to everyone that he was going to have a celebrity sing for them. It never occurred to me that he was referring to me. After we had been there for about an hour, he called for everyone's attention and said that it was time for the entertainment.

"He called Amber up front and told her to introduce her famous cousin, Catherine. He had a piano, and his mother who played, all ready to go. There were at least thirty kids there, and they were all looking at me. I was petrified. You know I can't sing a tune no matter how simple the song is. I cannot even sing 'Mary had a Little Lamb.' I didn't know what to do.

"Then, Amber calls me up in front of everyone. I was in a daze. She announces that for my first song, I would be singing 'The Jokes on Me,' and everybody started to laugh. I was in a panic, and all I could think to say was, 'I don't know that song.' Everybody laughed even harder. Then I realized that the joke *was* on me. Patrick and Amber had cooked the whole thing up to pull a punk on me at the party. Everyone there was in on it but me.

"At first I was furious at Amber and a little hurt, but everybody was impressed with how I handled myself and told me what a good sport I was. I had a great time after that. Now that I can look back at it, I laugh about it. It was pretty funny."

Carter had a good chuckle over it too, and he had to admit that he would like to have been in on that one. "Why wouldn't you tell me that story? That was funny, and you came out of it looking pretty good."

Kat shrugged and said, "I don't know; I guess I just don't like looking foolish. Why didn't you tell me about your oral-hygiene-report fiasco?"

Carter smirked. "You got me there. I don't like looking foolish either." Then he added, "Especially to you."

That last statement made Kat feel good, though she did not know why.

"Carter, what's that over there?" Kat pointed to a large, black shape that rose about two feet above the surface of the dust. It was about eight feet long and six feet wide. "It looks like a flat rock."

Carter nodded and said, "That's what it is. This is great; we can make camp on it and get some sleep."

The partners were glad to have a place to sit and lay down for the night. As they settled in for the night, they ate by the light of one of their flashlights. The dark valley grew much darker as night fell. With the coming of night and feeling the weight of their fatigue, the oppressive sense of fear and sadness threatened to return. As soon as they finished their modest meal, the partners slipped into their sleeping bags and pulled them over their heads, just as little children pull their blankets over their heads when they are afraid of the dark.

"Carter," Kat said in a small, scared voice. "I'm afraid to go to sleep."

"Me too."

"Can we turn on a flashlight?"

"I have a better idea. I have a box of candles that I picked up at the warehouse." Carter got up, fished around in his backpack, and then brought out a plain, black box that contained five white candles. They were four inches long and about the diameter of a nickel. He lit a match and warmed the bottom of a candle until it was soft. Then he pressed it firmly down on the rock surface between them. He lit the wick and announced triumphantly, "There; a mini campfire. That should burn for at least three hours. It's so dark here that the flame seems brighter than normal."

Kat smiled at the flame and said sleepily, "Thank you, Carter; it's perfect."

The moment they closed their eyes, they fell fast asleep. They woke at the same time. The candle had burned out, and they were bathed in darkness.

"Kat, are you awake?" Carter whispered.

"Yes, and I feel like we're being watched."

"I feel it too," Carter confirmed, and then they both sat up.

As soon as they moved, they heard the sound of thousands of voices all around them whispering, "Murderers!" over and over again.

The partners jumped to their feet and looked into the darkness. At first, what their eyes saw confused their brains. After a moment of concentration, they began to see thousands of dark figures, in human form, come into focus.

A MATTER OF LIQUIDATION

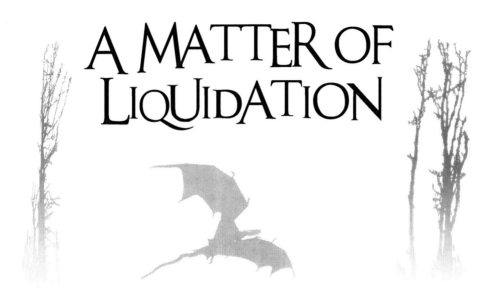

In the deep darkness that surrounded the partners, they could see even darker human shapes. It was possible to see facial features and other details because they were darker and denser than the darkness of the night. It was like looking at a strange three-dimensional painting created by darker paint on a black background.

Once the children's eyes adjusted to the scene, they noticed a strange shifting on the faces. The facial features constantly changed from one set of features to another. The changing was not synchronized, so the individual faces changed at different rates.

"Carter, look. Their faces are mimicking our features and changing back and forth from your face to mine!"

"You're right," the boy said as he instinctively reached slowly down into his backpack.

Kat called out, "Who are you? What are you? What do you want?"

In response to her questions, the whispering stopped. The faces continued to morph between Carter's and Kat's facial features, but one face froze into Kat's face. It stepped forward and said, in the same whispering voice, "We are the People of the Dark Earth. The black dust covering this plane gives us physical form. We need it in order to survive. During the day, we exist as disembodied spirits in a sleep state. When night comes, we awaken and merge with the dark earth of this plane to take the form you see us in now. We need every particle of the black earth. Those unable to take form, perish. Thousands of my people are no more because of you. The moisture you poured out on the ground has destroyed large portions of the precious black earth. For this, you will die a lingering death."

Upon hearing the results of their actions, Kat felt overwhelmed with guilt and grief. "We didn't know. We had no way of knowing what would happen if we used water to travel over the dust," Kat said with deep remorse in her voice. "We don't belong here, Carter. We've made a mess of things and hurt innocent people."

"Hamsted, get a hold of yourself," Carter said firmly. Then to the spokesperson, Carter said, "Before you kill us, tell me something. What would you have done to us if you found us here, and we had not destroyed any of the dark earth?"

The face of the spokesperson morphed and took on Carter's features, and then he said, "We kill all who we find in our plane."

"I see, so you have killed many of our kind."

"Yes."

"Interesting," Carter mused. "We, in ignorance and completely without intention of harming anyone, do something that leads to the death of some of your people. You, on the other hand, intentionally kill our people just because you happen to find them here. And you call us murderers."

"Yes. You are not of us. You are not our people; you are nothing. Killing your kind is nothing more than ridding ourselves of a nuisance. But killing you after what you have done will be a most gratifying experience."

"You hear that, Kat? These are the beings you are mourning." Carter slipped a bottle of water into Kat's hand behind her back. While the creature had been talking, Carter was removing bottled waters from his backpack and loosening the lids. Now that each of the partners had one, Carter said, "I have a proposition. I propose that you step aside, let us leave, and we promise never to return. But if you insist on killing us, I must warn you that my friend and I have open bottles in our hands with enough water to destroy three times as much of your precious dust as we did yesterday." Carter held up his bottle and said, "Kat, let them see what's in your hand. Be careful; just a few drops slopped over the top will do considerable damage to some of these fine individuals."

Upon seeing the bottles, a unified gasp of fear came from the dark beings as they quickly moved back away from the partners. "Ah, that's better," said Carter smugly. "I see that the ground is clear of dust since you have taken it up to assume your forms. That will make it much easier for us to travel. We should be out of your plane in no time."

Kat handed Carter her bottle to hold while she rolled up the sleeping bags and packed their stuff. Carter stood with open bottles in each hand grinning confidently at the creatures in front of him. The creatures' facial features continued to shift as they kept a close watch on the partners.

"Kat, when you're done packing, hand me a flashlight." Once the two were loaded and ready to move out, Carter turned on the light, and the dark forms shrieked and moved even farther away. The light apparently was painful to the People of the Dark Earth. "This is going to be easier than I imagined," Carter said with a sneer as the children moved off the rock.

They had not gotten far when they heard the dark figures call out, "*Stop!*"

The partners turned around to see the spokesperson approach. "Put out the light. I have something to say."

"Now, you *stop!*" Carter said as he raised his bottle of water. "I will only lower the light a bit. Say what you have to say, and be quick about it."

The spokesperson still held Carter's features on his face. He stopped and said in a loud whispery voice, "You may escape our wrath, but I promise you that you will not get far once you reach the Doom Marsh. Moon hound trackers will hunt you down. The trackers are exceedingly cruel. They are completely blind, but they can hear a heartbeat several feet away. They can track anything with the help of their moon hounds. The hounds have no ears, but their eyesight in near total darkness is as clear as a hawk in bright sunlight. They sense fear; some say they can smell it. Lest you assume I am telling you this to warn you, let me assure you that I tell you this so that your fear may begin to grow with each step you take toward the marsh. You will have no chance against the trackers and their hounds. Once they find you, they will turn you over to their taskmasters, who will make you slaves and force you to work in their gold mines. No one lasts a year in the mines. You will wish that you had let us kill you. Your death at our hands would have been lingering, but it would be over in a few hours. Now you will suffer and die over a matter of months. It is not too late for you to surrender yourselves to us."

Carter wore that annoying look that made Kat furious when he used it on her. It was a look that communicated, *I know something you don't. I have a trick or two up my sleeve.* This time the look did not annoy Kat; it made her proud that she had a friend who was not easily intimidated.

Carter responded with, "You may be right. These trackers may catch us, and we might find ourselves wishing that we had surrendered to your tender mercies. Still, I think we'll take our chances."

As soon as they turned to head east, the People of the Dark Earth were gone. Carter knew that they were in their human forms somewhere because the ground was still clear of the dust.

"Where do you suppose they went?" Kat asked with a shiver.

"I don't know, but I don't think we need to worry about them anymore."

"What if they decide to try something before we leave the plane? They may decide to sacrifice a bit more dust and choke us," Kat said as she glanced around nervously.

"Think about it. If they do something to us, and we fall with these open bottles, the water will destroy a lot more dust than we did yesterday. Do you remember what happened when we tried to move the dust aside to make a clear area?"

"Yes, it wouldn't stay; it all flowed evenly back over the ground."

"That's right, so when those beings return to their spirit forms and leave the dust, it will flow evenly back over the ground. That means that it will flow over any water we leave on the ground. Two bottles of water would make a good-sized puddle. There would be lots more dust destroyed if it was to flow over that much water. Do you remember what just one drop did? No. They won't chance doing anything to us that would cause us to drop these bottles."

"That makes sense, but what do you think about those trackers and their hounds?"

Carter shrugged and answered, "So far, every problem we've encountered has had a solution. I believe that if we put our heads together, we'll come up with something. If we can't, maybe something will present itself in the nick of time. And don't forget Guard. He has been helpful in supplying what we need when we need it."

Kat nodded and said, "That's true. You know, I actually feel more confident about our chances. I don't know if it will last, but I don't feel quite as afraid at the moment."

"That's a good thing because, apparently, the moon hounds can smell fear. I have to admit that I feel pretty good myself."

Carter reached into his pocket and pulled out Dark Beard's knife to check the compass. Since the partners entered the Valley of Shadows, they had no road to follow, and they could not see the sun. Carter had to depend on the compass to keep them headed east.

After a couple hours of travel, Kat observed, "It must be almost morning. It seems to be getting a bit lighter. I can see the outline of trees on the horizon. At least, I think they're trees."

By this time, the plane had given way to a more hilly landscape. Strange monolithic rock formations were scattered about, and there was still no vegetation.

"Look, Carter. There's a path up ahead."

The boy took out the pocketknife and checked the compass again. "Good. It heads straight east. Let's take a break. We should make good time now that we have a clear path to travel."

It was light enough that they no longer needed a flashlight. Low dense clouds still covered the sky. Patches of moving fog, which came up from the ground, glided about like ghosts.

The partners climbed up onto a rock formation, which was flat on top, and settled in for a rest and a bite of food. When they finished eating, they were about to continue on their way when they saw something or someone approaching from the direction they had just traveled. It was too far away to tell what or who it was.

Kat, straining to see, said, "I think it's a person, a small person. It looks like a child."

As the individual drew closer, Carter said, "It's small, but I don't think it's a child. Whatever it is, its eyes are glowing yellow."

THE LITTLE BULLY

Carter was right. The thing that approached was no child. It was a little over four feet tall with a round head on top of a thin body. It looked a bit like a child's stick figure drawing. Instead of clothes, dark gray strips of cloth wrapped it like a mummy. It had straight, black hair that reached its shoulders. The face, hands, and feet were the only parts of the body that were not covered. The skin was ghostly white. The eyes were larger than normal. The eyelids were black, and there were dark circles under the eyes. The nose was almost nonexistent with nostrils visible at the end of a slight bump. The lips, though clearly formed, had no color. The darkness of the valley kept these details hidden from the partners until the strange-looking individual came closer.

"Hello there," Carter called out.

"I need to speak with you," it said in a voice that was much deeper than expected.

"We were just about to resume our journey," Carter said a bit nervously. "But I suppose we can spare a moment." The partners climbed down, and once they reached ground level, Carter introduced himself and Kat. "What shall we call you?"

"I will not tell you my name. You may call me anything you like."

"That's a strange response," said Kat. "Why won't you tell us your name?"

"You would like that; you would like to have power over me. Well, I am no fool. I tell my name to no one I do not trust. As I said, you may call me whatever you like."

The children shared confused looks. Carter asked, "What do you want with us?"

"You are going to help me with a problem that I have, and I am going to help you with a problem that you have."

"Oh?" Carter said skeptically with a raised eyebrow. "What makes you think we need your help?"

"I know that you plan to cross the marsh. Without my help, you will never evade the trackers. If you do not help me, I will turn you over to the trackers and collect the bounty they offer for strangers like you."

"I know what we can call you," Carter growled. "We'll call you Stinky. Because you really are a little stinker, aren't you?"

"It matters not to me; call me whatever you like. Know this, you will help me, and since the task that needs doing is on the other side of the marsh, I am forced to help you as well."

Kat asked, "What do you need us to do?"

"I am not going to tell you that either."

"I don't understand. Why won't you tell us what you want us to do?" Carter asked, his anger beginning to bubble to the surface. "I don't like this. I don't like any of this."

"I do not care. I do not have to tell you anything. I am not going to tell you anything I do not want to tell. You will help me because you have no choice. You need my help, and if you do not do what I want, I will set the trackers on you. Further discussion is a waste of time. My need of you is urgent; now get moving."

Carter was so angry that he almost did not care about the consequences of letting loose with a display of rage that would have been disastrous to their mission. He took a step toward Stinky with his hands clinched into fists. Luckily, Kat was more in control of her emotions. She put her hand on the furious boy's shoulder to stop him. "I know how you feel, Carter, but we really don't have a choice here. We need help getting through the marsh. This may be the answer to our problem; let's not mess it up."

Carter stood clinching and unclenching his fists and breathing hard as he tried to get control of himself. Finally, he calmed a bit and said, "You win, Stinky. But I warn you, if you want us to do something that is cruel, hurtful, or immoral, we won't do it."

Kat agreed with Carter and added, "If you want us for something that goes against what we believe is right, you're wasting your time. It would be to your advantage to tell us, now, what you need us for so that you'll know if we will do it or not."

"No," said Stinky. "Follow me. We are going to a tunnel that will take us through the most dangerous part of the marsh." Stinky turned and headed southeast without even looking to see if the partners were following.

The partners walked a few feet behind their guide so they could talk without being overheard. "I don't like this," Carter growled. "We're not traveling the road, and we're letting this 'person' manipulate us."

"I know, but what else can we do? At least we're going to get safe passage through the marsh. She needs us for something on the other side, so we can trust her that far. Don't you think?"

"I don't think we can trust that person at all. She, if she is a she, is up to something. She's too secretive. Why won't she tell us what she wants us for?"

"Obviously she doesn't trust us. This is a very dangerous place, and I'm sure it's a survival thing for her."

Carter harrumphed.

They only traveled about a quarter-mile when Stinky stopped, turned to the partners, and said, "From this point on, you will have to be blindfolded."

"Blindfolded!" Carter exclaimed. "What are you up to, Stinky? Why do we have to be blindfolded?"

"Only my people are allowed to know where the secret tunnels are located. If word got out to the trackers where they are, my kind would be at great risk. Inside every entrance to the tunnels there is a guard that will kill anyone, not of our race, who enters."

Kat beat Carter to the punch, asking, "What's to keep the guard from killing us?"

"That is why you need to be blindfolded. I will tell the guard that I have urgent need of you, and I blindfolded you so that you cannot reveal the tunnel's location."

"Will that be enough? Will the guard let us live and let us pass?" Kat asked with growing doubt in her voice.

"You do not need to be concerned. You will survive, though I cannot guarantee that the guard will."

Now it was time for Carter to jump in and say, "Hold on there. Are you telling us that if the guard will not let us pass that you are going to kill him?"

"What do you care? He is not one of your people. I will do what needs to be done."

"*No!* That's not acceptable. You can turn us into the trackers if you want, but we will not be a part of murder," Carter said firmly. Kat nodded her agreement, fervently.

"I don't understand what difference it makes to you. You killed hundreds, maybe thousands, of the dust people. What is one marsh dweller to you?"

"We didn't know that our actions would harm anyone. What we did was unintentional. What you're asking us to do is be part of cold-blooded murder," Carter tried to explain.

"I am not asking you to participate. I told you I would take care of it. All you have to do is stay out of my way and let me do what needs to be done."

Kat said, "That's what we cannot do. We cannot stand by and let you kill someone when we know that's your intention."

For the first time since they met Stinky, the creature seemed to show some emotion. Even her voice reflected the exasperation she was feeling when she said, "I do not understand you. I will only take lethal action if the guard is not reasonable. If he insists on killing you, are you saying that you will not let me defend you?"

"No," Kat answered in a patient voice. "We're saying that we will not go with you if there is a chance that someone will be killed because of us."

The emotion in Stinky's voice intensified as she said, "I will turn you into the trackers; make no mistake about that."

"Do what you need to do. We have survived plenty of tough situations during our journey. We'll take our chances," Carter said defiantly. "Now, Kat, let me see; that eastern path we saw earlier should be that way." Carter pointed back the way they had come. "If we head straight north, we should pick it up again."

Stinky quickly warned them, "That path is heavily patrolled. The moment you reach it, you will be captured."

"Then you better hurry on ahead and alert them that we're coming," Carter mocked. "Come on, Kat; we've wasted enough time today." The two turned and started to walk away.

Stinky appeared to be a bit shaken. Thus far, she had been in charge of the situation. Now she was about to lose her help. "*Wait,*" she called out. "There is no need for you to sacrifice yourselves. I can get you through the tunnel without hurting anyone. It will be more difficult and costly, but it can be done."

The partners stopped, turned to face Stinky, and Carter spoke. "If you are lying to us, we will have no more to do with you no matter what you do or threaten to do. Is that understood?"

Anger and frustration crossed Stinky's face as she said, dangerously, "Yes, I understand."

The children could tell that they had broken part of the hold that Stinky had over them and that she was not happy about it.

Besides her anger, something in her eyes made the partners feel uncomfortable.

Carter, feeling empowered by the turn things had taken, decided to push the limit. "We might come with you, blindfolded, if you tell us what it is you want us to do when we get past the marsh."

The strange little person stood staring at Carter with intense yellow eyes. Slowly, the eyes began to glow and grew brighter until they actually caused dark shadows to form on the creatures face. It was such an eerie, frightening sight that it made Carter feel like stepping back. Deciding that showing fear would cause them to lose the advantage they had won, he stood firm.

Carter sensed his friend's fear growing, and he reached over and put his hand on her shoulder to reassure her. That was all she needed to let her know that the plan was to stand firm and see who blinked first. She took a deep breath, set her jaw, and let a determined look fill her eyes.

After a very tense moment, the glow in Stinky's eyes began to fade. "My sister fell into a tar pit on the far side of the marsh. I am not strong enough to pull her out. She will die if I cannot get help to free her," she said with warning in her voice.

Kat put her hands on her hips and said, "That's it? That's the big secret you wouldn't tell us? If you had told us that you needed help to save your sister's life, we would have gone with you gladly."

"Yes," Carter agreed. "We will be glad to help you, but I don't understand why you don't get your own people to assist you. Surly you must have friends and family who are able to go with you to save your sister. Why did you come all the way on the other side of the marsh to seek out strangers to bully and threaten into helping you? That doesn't make sense; you're not telling us everything."

"Carter's right," Kat said suspiciously. "What are you really up to?"

"I have told you the truth. I have no family other than my sister. Among my people, there is no such thing as friendship. There is only power and greed. If you have enough wealth to pay people off or enough power to force them, you can get what you want from others. I am not wealthy, and I am not powerful by myself. With my sister by my side, we are more powerful than most of our people."

"I get it." Kat smiled knowingly. "You and your sister have made enemies, and they probably prefer that you be separated. So, of course, they wouldn't help you."

"I think you're right, Kat. I wouldn't be surprised if her own people put her sister in the tar pit for revenge or punishment for crimes they may have committed."

"If that's true, I'm not sure we should be helping her. We may be going against their laws," Kat observed.

"No! That is not what happened. My sister fell into the pit by accident. It is as I have said. No one will help us because nobody among my people cares about anyone but themselves and their immediate family."

"If what you say about your people is true, and if your sister is anything like you, it doesn't sound like she is even worth saving," Carter jibed.

Suddenly, the small creature's eyes started to glow brilliant yellow. She opened her mouth, and a high-pitched noise came out. It grew in volume, intensity, and pitch. At first, the sound just hurt their ears, and the partners clapped their hands over them, trying desperately to block out the noise. As the pitch continued to rise, they were no longer able to hear the sound, but the pain in their heads became unbearable. They fell to their knees and eventually dropped over, unmoving.

THE TUNNEL

Carter opened his eyes, but saw nothing. He could not move his hands. "Carter, are you awake?" Kat asked in a shaky voice.

"Yes. What's happening?"

"I will tell you what is happening," Stinky growled. "I am through trying to do this the easy way. There will be no further discussion. I blindfolded you and tied your hands. I have ropes tied around your necks like leashes. I will lead you like animals. You will come with me, or I will leave you tied up here while I go and get the trackers to take you into custody. Now, get to your feet and start moving." Carter felt a vicious tug on the rope around his neck. At the same time, he heard Kat grunt in pain.

"Okay, you win," snarled Carter. "You don't have to torture us; we will come with you willingly."

"It does not matter to me how you come. You will come with me, and I will treat you any way I wish. This would have been much easier if you had been reasonable. Now the time for reason is over. Keep silent, and get moving."

Walking blindfolded over unfamiliar territory without the use of your hands, while being viciously pulled with a rope tied around your neck, is a very difficult way to travel. At first, it was obvious that Stinky was taking her frustration out on the partners; she did not attempt to lead them around obstacles or holes in the ground. The children fell several times, and their travel began to slow due to minor injuries they were receiving because of the rough treatment. The more the partners slowed the more vicious and cruel their leader became in the way she pulled and tugged at the ropes. The little creature was surprisingly strong. Finally, it seemed their captor had decided that she had punished her captives enough. "We are going to rest for a while and eat. When we begin traveling again, I think things will go a little easier for you."

Carter had plenty of bitter comments he wanted to shout at Stinky, but he bit his tongue. The memory of the painful piercing sound she made to render them unconscious was something he did not want to experience again. He had no doubt that their captor could kill them with her sonic voice weapon.

After they settled in and got comfortable, Stinky gave them some food from their packs. "Make no mistake," she said, almost as though she could read their minds. "I can kill you with the sound of my voice. I also have other quicker, painless ways to kill. However, I do not want to kill you; I need you. I give you my word that if you agree to help me get my sister back, I will not harm you further. The rest of our journey is rough, and I need you rested and cooperative to make good time. Time is of the essence, as you can imagine. I need to get my sister out of the tar pit soon, or she will die."

Carter was so angry at how Stinky was treating them that it was all he could do to hold his tongue. He was afraid to open his mouth because of what he would say. Kat knew her partner well, and she knew he was struggling with his rage. She, on the other hand, was in control of herself, so she said what Carter could not. "We give you our word that we will do what we can to help you rescue your sister. We also promise not to purposely hinder or slow the journey, but we want one promise from you."

Stinky stiffened and asked curtly, "What?"

"Promise us that you will not kill the guard or anyone else because of us—unless there is no other choice."

Stinky grunted her agreement and then turned to Carter. "The girl has given me your promise, but I have had no indication from you that you will honor what she has said. Will you honor this agreement?"

All Carter could bring himself to do was nod his head to indicate that he would.

"Very well then, I am satisfied. As a show of good faith on my part, I will move the rope leashes from your necks to your waists."

"Thank you," Kat said weakly.

Once they were on their way again, the children could tell that the terrain had changed. They had to deal with vegetation now. The vegetation grew thicker as they moved closer to the tunnel. Stinky had to use more verbal warnings and directions as she guided her captors around and through bushes, trees, and tall grass.

They had traveled for several hours without rest when their guide finally said, "We have arrived. I will remove your blindfolds." To Kat she said, "I need you to help me open the entrance, so I will free her hands."

"What?" Carter sneered. "You don't trust me?"

Stinky ignored Carter and she untied Kat. When she was finished freeing her, Stinky showed her where, in the tall, thick grass, to reach down and find a hole big enough to stick her hands. "Feel how the hole moves forward? Stick your fingers under, and when I say lift, we will lift the trap door." The small person moved to the right of Kat about three feet, reached down into the thick grass, and then said, "Lift." Together they lifted the heavy, grass-covered trapdoor.

It looked to Carter like a three-foot square piece of the ground tilted forward. He thought to himself, *I never would have known that there was a trapdoor under that thick vegetation if I hadn't seen it.*

"Hurry, this is the entrance. We need to close it as soon as we can before someone sees us." There were stairs leading down into the dark. Once the trap door was shut, Stinky said to Kat, "I have to tie your hands again. The guard must think that you are my property if we are to have any chance of getting by him without violence. He is at the bottom of these steps."

"I can't see anything," Kat said. "It's so dark."

"Do not concern yourself with that. I can see in the dark," Stinky said as her eyes began to glow. The yellow glowing eyes were creepy the first time the partners saw them, but here in the total darkness they caused chills to run down their spines. The two glowing orbs and the shadows they created on the nasty little person's face were beyond sinister looking. "We have to go down several steps, so watch yourselves."

After descending several dozen steps, they found themselves standing on what felt like a cobblestone floor. The air was stale and humid. Carter reached out to touch one of the walls and found them to be made of the same cobblestone surface as the floor. Off in the distance the children could see a flickering light. "That light is where the guard station is located," their captor explained. "The guard knows that we are here, and even now he is ready to confront us. I will call the password so he will know that it is one of his people who has entered." Stinky opened her mouth and called a series of high-pitched sounds down the tunnel. After a moment, she said, "That is strange. He is supposed to respond. We must tread carefully; there may be danger up ahead."

When the three travelers reached the source of the light, they discovered that it was a torch hanging on the wall across from a room. The room was carved into the side of the tunnel, and it appeared to be a small office. The furnishings included a wooden desk and stool, a cot with a blanket and pillow. A candle in a holder sat on the left side of the desk, and a wooden box sat on the right side of the desk. A metal cup, a plate with a bit of meat on it, and a half loaf of dark bread sat in the center of the desk.

"I do not like the look of this," Stinky muttered. "You two stay here. I am going to check up ahead. Do not try anything. I can track you down better than a moon hound," she said, and then she was gone.

Carter looked around and said, "Do you notice anything strange about this place?"

"I don't know what you mean. It's all strange to me," Kat grumbled.

"This is supposed to be a guard post. Wouldn't you think there would be weapons in the corner or on a rack hanging on the walls?"

Kat shrugged and said, "I don't know. Stinky doesn't have any weapons that I can see, but she is lethal without them."

"Good point. But, still..."

The partners heard a whisper come from the hall, "Hey, you in the room, be quiet."

Kat looked at Carter and mouthed, "Is that Stinky?"

Carter shook his head, put his index finger to his lips, and turned toward the door. Unexpectedly, a little person (that looked a bit like Stinky) peeked into the room and then stepped into the doorway. He had short, black hair, and he was wrapped in the same mummy fashion as their captor. He was a few inches taller, a few pounds heavier, and had a more masculine look than Stinky. To Carter's surprise, the little guard looked terrified.

"Are you the guard of the tunnel?" Kat asked.

"Quietly, quietly, whisper your softest voice; she must not hear us. There are no guards here. This is a toll tunnel; anyone who pays the toll is free to travel here."

Kat looked confused and said, "We were told that this was a safe passage through the moon hound tracker's territory and that it was a secret known only to your people."

"Is that what the evil one told you? The trackers know about these tunnels, but we are safe in here. The trackers are afraid of confined spaces. The tunnel entrances and exits all begin and end beyond their territory. They never leave the marsh for any reason. It is a sacred place to them, and they believe that if they leave it, they will become sick and die. So you see, these tunnels are quite safe from the trackers; there is no reason to keep them secret."

"Then why—" Kat started.

"Quiet!" the toll taker interrupted. He leaned his head back out into the corridor and looked both ways. Satisfied they were still alone, he said, "You cannot trust her or her sister; they are evil outcasts. You should get as far away from that one as you can. Let me cut your ropes." The toll taker reached into his pocket and pulled out a knife. He stepped forward, but before he could cut Carter's bindings, something odd happened. The man froze. Carter looked into his yellow eyes; they glowed for a moment, and then they faded and went dark. He dropped to the floor in a heap, revealing Stinky standing behind him.

"Are you all right?" Stinky asked with phony concern. "It is a good thing I got back in time. He would have cut you up real bad if I had not been here."

"What did you do? Did you kill him?" Carter knew that he had just watched the life go out of a person's eyes, and it upset him deeply. "You did, didn't you? You killed him."

Kat stooped down to see if there was anything she could do to help the toll taker, but it was too late. She stood, looked at the murderer, and said, "You aren't just a stinker; you're evil."

The little person stiffened and asked, "How did you discover my name? Did the guard tell you?"

Just then, something occurred to Kat. "Evil is your name. And no, the one you murdered didn't tell us. I knew what it was because evil is as evil does. What you have done since we met you has revealed your true name and nature—Evil."

"I prefer to be called Ev."

"Your preferences are of no concern to us, Evil," Carter spat.

"Why did you kill him?" Kat asked with sadness in her voice.

"He was going to harm you; he had a knife and was headed right for you. I told you that we might have trouble with him. As I said, this tunnel system is a closely guarded secret, and I had no choice. Why, did he say anything before I got here?"

It appeared that Evil had not heard any of the conversation between the toll taker and the partners. Or, was it that she *had* overheard and was testing them to see if they would be truthful about what he told them. Carter decided to play dumb, and before his partner could say anything to the contrary, he said, "He walked in and wanted to know what we were doing in his office. He already had the knife in his hand, but we didn't realize that he was going to kill us. I guess we owe you an apology."

Kat turned to Carter and saw him wink at her. She nodded and said, "Yes, I'm sorry too. It all happened so fast I didn't realize that we were in danger."

"I need you, and I cannot afford to lose you. It is time we get moving. Travel goes quickly and easily through the tunnels. We will be moving through total darkness, so it is best I keep you bound so I can lead you. You would be lost without me," Ev said in a tone of warning. "The tunnels branch in many directions. Even if you could see in the passages, you would not know which way to go. You could exit in several dangerous areas. So you see, you need me as much as I need you."

As they traveled the tunnels, there were a few zigzags, but as far as the partners could tell, they were generally headed in one direction. "Ev, I was wondering," Kat inquired. "Won't there be a guard posted where we exit? I mean, aren't the exits also entrances that require guarding? Will that be a problem for us?"

"You do not need to concern yourself with that. I know a secret exit where there is no guard."

"We have been walking in darkness for hours. Can we take a rest?" Carter asked.

"No."

"Oh, that's right. I forgot. Time is of the essence," Carter said snidely.

"Yes."

The children could not communicate with each other without Ev hearing, so they traveled in silence, thinking of their options. Since their captor was not one to share information and since the information she had given them appeared to be lies, it seemed that their only option was to wait and see what came next. Carter, in spite of himself, could not help but admire the cleverness of the little creature in the way she did not give out any more information than was needed. The fact that Carter could not even speculate about what he might do to free himself and Kat, from their circumstance, had him feeling totally trapped. Ev was in complete control of the situation. The boy had to admit that they were in a tough spot, and unless something happened that gave him an advantage, they were in serious peril.

Carter let out a sigh as he decided that he had to be ready for the unexpected. Thinking of the unexpected, he suddenly realized that Ev probably did not know about the flashlight in his pocket. He remembered how the People of the Dark Earth backed away from the light and wondered if all the creatures born in this dark valley might be sensitive to bright light. It would make sense if they were. *That must be why Ev's people have eyes that glow*, Carter speculated. *The faint light from their eyes illuminates their surroundings so they can see. A person with eyes sensitive enough to see by such faint light would most likely be blinded if a flashlight were shined directly into their eyes. Yes*, Carter concluded, *I need to be ready when an opportunity presents itself.*

"We have arrived," said Ev, breaking into Carter's thoughts. "There is a secret door hidden in the wall here that leads into a cave where it will still be dark. It is only a few hundred feet more to the cave exit."

The children heard a click and a scraping noise as Ev opened the secret door. She pulled on the ropes and said, "Come." They had not traveled more than a few steps into the cave when Ev announced, "It is night now. We will eat and rest in here until morning. There will be no fire. That way you will not be as tempted to try anything foolish. I can still see you even if my eyes are darkened." To demonstrate, their captor let her glowing eyes fade so that to the partners there was total darkness. They could not see where they were, and they could not see their captor. They had no choice but to stay put until morning.

After a fitful night of restless sleep, Kat heard Ev say, "It is morning; time to wake. We will eat and then get under way again. Your hands will remain bound, and you will stay on the leashes until we arrive at the tar pit."

This last announcement disappointed Carter. He would need his hands free to use his flashlight. *But what will I do if the light does blind? All I can do is hope that the right circumstance presents itself and that I will know what to do. I must be careful not to waste what may be our best chance by acting hastily. On the other hand, if I second-guess myself too much, I may miss my best opportunity by hesitating.* Carter grimaced as he thought, *There I go over thinking everything again; all I can do is my best.*

Ev was right about it being daytime. The children could see again even though everything was still darker than the darkest storm-covered sky they had ever seen. It was so dark that it was difficult to tell colors. The area outside the cave was thick with leafy plants and trees, but the green leaves looked almost black. Strange sounds from animals and creatures never seen by the two adventurers before filled the thick air. "What are those sounds coming from?" Kat ventured a question.

"Most of the high-pitched noises are coming from different plants around here. A few of the more desperate cries come from creatures dying as plants devour them."

Kat shuddered and said, "Where we come from, it is the animals that eat the plants."

Ev looked a bit surprised. "Do the plants cry out when they are eaten?"

"I have never heard a plant make sounds before. What about these plants near us? Are they dangerous?"

"Everything in this valley can be dangerous if you do not know what you are doing. That is why you were foolish to come here. You are lost to all you have known. Now come, and do not touch anything. We will be heading into the marsh, and the deeper we travel into the marsh, the more danger we risk."

"Did you say you're taking us into the marsh? I thought the whole idea of traveling the tunnels was to avoid the marsh and the moon hound trackers?" Carter protested.

"That is true. Using the tunnels has reduced our risk of running into them. Unfortunately, my sister is trapped just inside the eastern edge of the marsh. We have to risk it. We have to save her; she is all I have. Now, I have said too much. Keep silent, touch nothing, and do not try my patience," she snarled and gave a vicious tug on the leashes.

The brush, shrubs, and trees all looked vastly different from anything the partners had ever seen before. The place was so alien that it could have been on another planet. There were plants with flowers as large as the tires on a midsized car. They grew on top of sturdy stems with large leaves that twisted around into spirals.

There were shrubs growing in shallow watery areas with leaves that grew out from unseen centers, and the plants were in the shape of a perfect sphere the size of a small house. Each leaf was shaped like a dagger blade with a needle-sharp point. The points secreted clear, white liquid that dripped continuously into the water. At one point, Kat saw a large insect, about the size of a humming bird, fly within a few inches of one of the dagger shaped leaves. The leaf shot forward and skewered the unfortunate creature. The insect made a chirp of pain and then quickly dissolved into a gooey liquid that ran down the leaf and disappeared into the heart of the plant.

One of the most disturbing things they saw in the marsh, was a large rodent, about the size of a house cat, lassoed by a vine covered with razor-sharp thorns. The vine came up out of the wet ground, wrapped itself around the creature, and pulled it under, leaving only a red splash of blood behind.

"This is a horrible place," said Kat with a hint of panic in her voice.

Ev snorted with contempt. "This is the nice part of the marsh. If you had tried to travel through the heart of the marsh and a tracker did not capture you, you would not have lasted more than a few minutes. Of course, you would be better off dying at the mercy of the marsh than being captured by the trackers. Speaking of trackers, there is one now."

BETRAYED

"I was beginning to wonder if you were going to come back," said an unnaturally harsh voice. "I see you come bearing gifts. It is a good thing too; your sister isn't doing well."

"Hey, what's going on here?" Carter demanded.

Quick as a flash, a huge canine head, bearing inch-long razor sharp teeth, moved within two inches of Carter's face. The filthy animal was emitting a low, rumbling growl that said very clearly that it would like nothing better than to rip out the boy's throat. The stench of the beast's breath was enough to make Carter gag. The animal had large, glowing, yellow eyes, a long snout, and an elongated head with no ears. It had no fur, just a dark gray hide.

Carter froze, and after a tense moment, a harsh, gravelly chuckle came from the tracker. The tracker was standing beside the moon hound holding onto a harness similar to what a guide dog for the blind might wear, but it was not made of stiff leather. It was looser and longer, like reigns used to steer a horse-driven wagon.

The tracker was husky and muscular. He stood a little over five feet tall. He had a large, bald head. Coarse, black hair covered his face and body except for where his eyes should have been. In place of eyes, he had two round bald patches. The ears were shaped similar to human ears, but they were larger and sat a bit higher on the head. He wore strange, dark green, scaly leather pants and vest.

"I would not raise my voice if I were you, slave," the tracker rumbled. "Even though he has no ears, he and I have a psychic link. He knows what I think, and I know what he thinks. Right now, he knows that you do not understand your situation. He is trying, in his gentle way, to communicate to you that you belong to us and that you better not try anything stupid." The hound turned his head toward his master and then backed off the boy.

"If my sister dies because—"

Before Ev could finish, the tracker broke in with, "I have nothing to do with your sister's situation, and you know it. You were the one who pushed her into that tar pit, so save your threats for someone who fears your measly powers. I suggest that if you want her back that you use my new slaves to retrieve her before she dies. And be quick about it. I want to get this new property back to the mines."

"Very well," Ev spat. She gave a sharp tug on the rope leashes and said, "It is time that you two repay your debt to me for getting you safely through the marsh."

"Are you serious?" Kat barked. "This is your idea of getting us safely through the marsh?"

"You are wasting your breath on her, Kat," Carter said with cold contempt. "You said it yourself, evil is as evil does. What else can you expect from evil except lies and betrayal? It sounds like she even betrayed her own sister. I'm sure her sister didn't agree to being pushed into a tar pit."

"That is enough; shut your mouths. We are at the rescue site. My sister is over there." Ev pointed to her right.

The partners turned to see a shiny black tar pit about the size of a football field. The bank was about three feet above the tar. Approximately fifteen feet from the bank stood a small person that looked a lot like Ev. She was stuck in the tar up to her thighs. Her shoulders were slumped, and her head was turned to one side, resting on her left shoulder. She looked weak, tired, and ready to give up and lay down in the tar.

"Sister," Ev shouted. "Sister, are you all right? I have brought your ransom. We will get you out of there and go home."

Ev's sister slowly raised her head. She looked as if she were in a trance and having a hard time focusing. "Sister, it is me, Ev!"

"Ev?" the pathetic creature moaned weakly.

"Yes, look at me! Look at me!"

Eventually, the trapped sister was able to focus and look around at her surroundings. "Ev?" she said again as her eyes lit on Ev's face. "You came back. I did not think you were coming back. It has been so long, and I am so tired. But you came back for me."

"Yes, I came back, and I need you to focus. We are going to throw you a rope. I want you to put it around you, and we will pull you out. Do you understand?"

"You pushed me into the pit. I did not think you would come back," the sister said with a sad look on her face. "There are things that live in the tar—awful things!" she said with growing anger and clarity.

"Yes, that is good sister; you get angry. It will give you strength." Ev turned to the partners and began untying their ropes. "We will need every inch of rope. I will tie the leashes to the rope that I used to bind your hands. I will make a loop and throw it to her. Once she has it around her, the three of us will pull her out. Do not try anything foolish. Even if you were to escape us, you would not last five minutes in the marsh. Do you understand?"

The partners nodded while they rubbed circulation back into their wrists.

"Sister, I am going to throw you the rope. Put the loop around you and up under your arms," Evil said as she threw it within reach of her sister.

"At night they come to the surface. I had to beat them off for hours at a time. I have been bitten and stung. I am dying because of you!"

"No, sister, you are not going to die. Put the rope around you, and we will pull you out. I will treat your wounds. Now hurry. We can talk more about what really happened later."

"Yes, we will talk," said Ev's sister as she put the rope around herself. "Pull me out! I have business with you, Evil," she snarled.

While they worked, the tracker and his hound stood on the bank. The hound watched everything that happened with great interest. Carter assumed that if there was a psychic link between the animal and tracker, that the tracker might be able to get a picture of what was going on through his hound's eyes.

Even though Ev's sister was small, it was difficult for the three of them to extract her from the tar pit. It had a firm hold on her. Once the sister was out, Carter and Kat could see that her legs and thighs were swollen. She must have been in a lot of pain, but her anger seemed to overshadow her pain and fatigue.

"Give me one of your water bottles and one of the cloths I used as a blindfold," Ev demanded of Kat. The girl obediently fished around in her backpack, came up with the items, and handed them over. Ev proceeded to clean her sister's lower body, revealing nasty open wounds. "You can take your new property now and leave us. I no longer have need of them," Ev called over her shoulder to the tracker.

A nasty *growl* erupted from the moon hound. Ev jumped to her feet and turned on the tracker. "Well? You heard me. Take the brats and go. I have fulfilled my end of the bargain. We are through with you," Ev snapped.

"I know you believe that you are very clever, but I am more clever than you," boasted the tracker. "I know why you pushed your sister into the pit. When you sensed my presence, you came up with a plan. You decided to push your sister into the pit knowing that neither you nor I would be able to rescue her. That left me with a choice. Either I chose to take you as a slave, or I let you go get two others to take your place. That way, if I agreed to let you go and get two others to help you rescue your sister, I would end up with two slaves instead of just one, and you would be free to go. That was a clever plan. My plan was to let you think that I had accepted the risk of losing my only piece of property in the hope of getting two slaves. I decided to take a chance that if you did return with two slaves, I would take them, and after you rescued your sister, I would take her and you as well. It paid off, and now I have four slaves. It was hard trusting you to live up to your end of the bargain. After all, anyone who did what you did to your own sister could just as easily take the opportunity to escape and not return. Tell me, why did you come back?"

"I'll tell you why she came back," Ev's sister snarled. "She came back because she needs me. My sister does everything with herself in mind; she cares for no one but herself. She only risked coming back for me because she has made so many enemies that, without me, she would not live very long. Alone, she is powerful, but she is not powerful enough to escape the wrath of our people. Together, we are almost invincible." To Ev she said, "Here is a big surprise for you sister: I am through with you."

"Where you are going you do not have to worry about your relationship. All four of you may as well get used to the idea that your lives, as you know them, are over. Finish treating your sister. It is time we traveled," the tracker commanded.

Ev knelt back down and started working on her sister's wounds again. Carter could see the anger and contempt in the eyes of Ev's sister as she watched Ev work on her.

Maybe this is the time to act, he thought. *If I shine the flashlight directly into the hound's eyes, it might stun the beast. But what about the tracker, he can't see light. If we're lucky and the light stuns the hound, the tracker, who shares a link with the animal, might be stunned too. Then what? Do we just make a run for it? That won't work. The moment I remove the light, they will be on us in a flash. No, if this is going to work, we need the sisters' help. Since they are captives too, it shouldn't be a problem. But what if they have their own plan? After all, they do seem to have abilities that can disable and even kill. Why is the tracker not more concerned about what the sisters might do?* Luck seemed to be on Carter's side as his question was about to be answered.

Ev said, "If you were not immune to my powers, tracker, you would be dead already."

"Yes, it is a pity that you cannot sing me to sleep with your lovely voice or kill me with your touch of death," the tracker said smugly. "Your sister seems to be ready to travel. Tie her hands, and then do the same to the brats. I am eager to get back to the mines. My masters will want to reward me for my skillful capture of four slaves in a single hunt."

From the time of the rescue up to this point, everyone was lined up along the bank overlooking the tar pit. The tracker and the hound were on Carter's left. Kat was on the boy's right and slightly in front of his right arm, so the hound would not be able to see Carter reach into his pocket. The sisters were two feet to the partner's right and behind them sitting on the ground. The hound had a straight line of sight to the sisters and, fortunately, it was focused intently on what they were doing.

As Ev began to tie her sister's hands, Carter slowly reached into his pocket and grasped the flashlight. His heart was pounding so hard that he was sure the tracker would hear it, and his fear was so intense that he was sure the hound would smell it. He was right; the hound turned and looked straight at Carter. In that same instant, the boy pulled the already lit flashlight out of his pocket and pointed it directly into the hound's eyes.

SAVED BY THE LIGHT

His hand was shaking so badly that he had to use both hands to steady the light. What happened was better than Carter had expected. The hound and tracker froze as stiff as statues; the light paralyzed them. It was as if their whole system had been short-circuited. Since Kat did not know what Carter had planned, his action took her by surprise. "Carter! How did you know the light would do that to them?"

Something else happened when Carter brought out the light. The sisters let out with loud gasps. "I never suspected that you had such a weapon at your disposal," said Ev. Carter thought he heard a touch of respect in her voice. "If I had known, I would have taken it from you when I rendered you unconscious."

"Kat, please hold the light, and be careful not to let it slip from the hound's eyes." Kat took the light from her partner, and the boy turned to face the sisters. He was surprised to see that they were turned away from the light and their hands were covering their eyes. "Interesting, very interesting," Carter mused. "Your eyes are so sensitive that you cannot even look at the reflected light. This is a very helpful bit of information."

"Quick; you must push the hound into the tar pit," Ev's sister said. "If you do, the tracker will go in with it. They will be stunned for about five minutes after the light is off. When they come around, they will send out a mental call to nearby trackers. The rescue will take a couple of hours. Trackers are not very smart. We can escape now. I will lead you out of here and take you anywhere you wish to go."

"What about your sister?" Carter asked.

"Tie her up and leave her here for the trackers; she can spend the rest of her miserable life as a slave in the mines."

"Sister! You do not mean that," Ev pleaded.

"Carter, you can't do that," Kat said.

Carter looked at his partner and asked, "How are you doing with that light?"

"I'm doing all right. There must be a better way of dealing with Ev than leaving her to these beasts."

Carter asked Ev's sister, "What's your name?"

"My name is Shadow. I have been the shadow of Evil all my life. It is time for me to follow my own path and forsake hers. From this day forth, I shall be known as—"

Before her sister finished, Ev exclaimed, "*No!* Sister, do not declare it. I implore you!"

"Seeker, I shall be known as Seeker. I will seek that which gives me peace." Then Seeker said to her sister, "I have never been at peace being a part of your hateful and cruel ways. Pushing me into that tar pit was the final betrayal. I am through with you, Evil, now and forever."

Kat looked back over her shoulder and said, "Seeker, I don't think that leaving Ev here for the trackers will give you peace. I find that doing what is right and lawful brings peace more than taking revenge. Is there someone in authority among your people who will take Ev into custody and see to it that justice is done?"

The sisters still had their eyes covered and their heads turned away from the light. Carter could see that Ev was feeling trapped, and he feared that she was getting ready to act. "Ev, I wouldn't try anything If I were you. We have another light, and I am not afraid to use it. If you force me to, I *will* tie you up and leave you here."

Quick as a flash, Seeker's hand shot out and touched Ev's throat. Ev slumped over her sisters legs. "She will be unconscious for three or four minutes. Please turn off the light, and I will gag her and tie her hands while you two push the hound into the pit. It really is safe to turn off the light."

Kat said, "Carter, it's up to you."

"Go ahead and turn it off, but be ready to turn it back on—quick."

Kat took a couple of steps back from the hound's head, and then she switched the light off. Just as seeker had predicted, the tracker and his hound remained frozen.

"Like I said, you have about five minutes before they start to come around. I suggest that you get them into the pit, now."

It was a good thing that the hound and tracker were standing only a foot from the ledge. "Let's make a run at the side of the hound and use our shoulders like a football blocker. Kat, if you and I hit the hound at the same time, we should be able to knock it into the pit. But be careful that the momentum doesn't carry you in with it." Carter stood about twenty feet back and said, "Let's try from here. I'll hit it near the rump; you hit it at the front shoulders. I'm going to count to three, and on three, we charge at it. Are you ready?"

"As ready as I'll ever be," the girl said and took her stance, ready to charge.

"Here we go then: One—two—three!" The partners ran and hit the hound a solid blow. Surprisingly, it was easier than they had expected to topple the beast. Both of the children fell on the ground and slid forward with half their bodies ending up over the edge of the bank. Carter had the hardest time keeping from sliding all the way down into the tar. With a bit of help from Kat, the two made it back on their feet.

"You were right about the tracker," Carter said to Seeker as he looked over into the pit. "The tracker must have a tight grip on that harness because the hound pulled him in as it fell."

314

"Ev is secure," Seeker announced as she stood up. "Oh," she groaned and swooned. She touched her forehead and said, "I am afraid that I am not very strong yet. Just let me stand here a moment until my head clears."

Carter hastened to Seeker's side and asked, "Are you going to be all right? Here, lean on me." Just then, Ev opened her eyes. "Kat, Ev is regaining consciousness. Will you take the rope and lead her while I help Seeker?"

Seeker smiled at Carter and said, "Thank you. Let me put my arm around your waist, and we can get out of here."

"Come on, Ev," Kat ordered. She gave a tug on the rope; the other end was tied around Ev's hands. "Get to your feet if you don't want to be left behind for the trackers."

Since Seeker tied Ev's hands in front of her, she was able to get to her feet without help. The little creature was so furious at being gagged and tied that her eyes glowed bright yellow. The hate that came from the evil creature was frightening in its intensity. Reluctantly, she cooperated rather than be left to the cruelty of the trackers.

The going was slower leaving the marsh than it was entering it. Seeker needed frequent rest stops. Once they were far enough from the marsh that they were no longer in danger of being captured by the trackers, Seeker said, "I am sorry, but I must stop and rest for the night. I need food and sleep. I will be better tomorrow."

"That's good because I'm exhausted," said Kat. "Let's make camp here. The ground is dry, and there are lots of little trees scattered around. I have never seen miniature trees like these before."

"Yes, it is safe here. The trees are called moss trees because, as you can see, the tiny leaves make the tree look like it has moss instead of leaves growing out of it. That one over there," Seeker pointed to a moss tree that was nearly seven feet high, "is tall enough for us to sleep under. We can tie Ev to it, and we will be able to get some rest."

After securing their prisoner to the tree, it was agreed that it would be safer and more comfortable for the valley dwellers if they did not have a campfire. Carter did light one of his candles so that the partners would be able to see.

After everyone was settled in for the night, Carter handed out food from his backpack. "What about Ev?" the boy asked. "Is it safe to remove the gag so she can eat?"

"I do not understand why you care. She was going to give you to the trackers, and knowing my sister, I am sure that she was not gentle with you."

"That's true. Your sister's name fits her." Kat proceeded to tell Seeker about their experiences with Evil.

"After all that—the betrayal, the lies, the abuse—you still care enough about her welfare that you would not leave her for the trackers? You still care if she is hungry?"

"That's the point, isn't it? She is cruel, selfish, and hateful. We are not like her. I got the impression that you do not want to be like her either. If we treat her as she treated us, we would be no better than she is. Seeker, you said that you were no longer going to be your sister's shadow. You said that you were going to seek that which will give you peace. If you are going to be true to that commitment, then you must treat others the way you wish to be treated, not the way they treat you."

At first, Seeker did not respond. She looked as though she was trying to grasp the concept. After a moment of contemplation, she said, "Carter, take off the gag; she can feed herself. I will move next to her, and if she tries anything, I will not hesitate to end her life." To Ev, Seeker said coldly, "Do you understand me?" Ev gave a curt nod. "Go ahead, Carter."

Ev ate and drank in silence. When she was finished, the gag was replaced.

"Seeker," Carter said, "we still haven't decided what to do with your sister. Do you have an idea that you haven't shared with us?"

"Yes, I have an idea. Perhaps I will tell you about it tomorrow. Right now, I need to rest. I am tired to the point of passing out."

"Me too," Kat said with a yawn. "Are you sure Ev cannot escape?"

"She is quite secure. Now, I really must sleep," Seeker said, her eyes already closed.

"Carter, do you think one of us should keep watch? Carter? Carter?" Kat got no response because her friend was already asleep. "I guess if everybody is comfortable enough with the situation to be asleep already, I guess it's okay for me to go to ..." Kat mumbled as she drifted off to a deep sleep.

When the partners awoke the next morning, they were dismayed to find that both Ev and her sister were gone.

Carter went directly to the rope used to secure Ev; it was lying on the ground by the tree trunk. "It's been untied, but I can't tell if Ev got it lose somehow or if Seeker untied her. It's even possible that someone else came into camp and untied Ev and took them both. I slept really hard and didn't hear a thing."

"Same here. It doesn't look like they took any of our stuff."

"You're right; it's all here, even the flashlights."

"Should we go after them?" asked Kat.

Carter shook his head. "No, our priority is the orphans. We don't know where the sisters went, nor do we know the circumstances of their leaving. Seeker may have gone willingly; she might have been the one who set Ev free. We'll probably never know what happened. Let's have something to eat, pack up, and head for that road that goes east. If things go smoothly, we might be able to reach the orphans by tonight."

Kat snorted. "Things go smoothly here? I doubt that very seriously."

Things did go smoothly for the partners for most of the morning. They found the road they were looking for in just a little under half an hour. Then they walked the road without incident until they came to a large city. When they arrived at the city gate, their troubles started up again.

GATEKEEPER'S TOLL

An enormous rock wall surrounded the city. The road the partners were traveling led right to the city gate. The gate was open, and human guards were stationed on either side. The children were allowed to pass unharassed. Inside the gate, to their right, was a sturdy table. Sitting behind the table was a large muscular man with pale white skin, a shaved head, and intense, brown eyes. He had a high forehead with bushy, black eyebrows. His teeth were yellow, and two were missing. A deep scar ran from under his left eye to the corner of his thin mouth. He wore studded leather armor. A broadsword and a large knife hung from his belt.

When he saw the partners, he broke into a broad smile that made them feel very uncomfortable. "Welcome to our humble city. I am the gatekeeper in charge of gate security. What business do two outlander human children have here in Omagora?"

Carter cleared his dry throat and said, "Actually, sir, we are just passing through."

"Just passing through ... Just passing through," he said thoughtfully. "I must inform you that if you are not here on business, and you are not here to visit someone you know, we have a law that says everyone who is just passing through must pay a toll. Your toll will be one hundred gold pieces—each."

Carter's mouth dropped open in shock. He stammered, "W-we don't have two hundred gold pieces. We don't even have one gold piece. There must be some other way we can get permission to pass through your city. We are on an important mission to rescue some orphan children being held by the Adversary."

"I see," the gatekeeper mused. "I tell you what I will do. I will let you," he pointed at Carter, "pass through the city, and I will take the girl as your toll."

"*What?*" Carter blurted out. "You can't be serious."

"I am very serious, and I am doing this for your benefit. You see, I am going to present the girl as a servant to the king's family. She will be well taken care of and have a very useful life. Otherwise, street gangs will take her captive and kill you. This way she will be safe, and so will you. Since you have nothing of value now, you will be ignored by those who would kill you for the girl." The gatekeeper's caring look almost seemed genuine.

A look of stark terror came over Kat's face as she said, "Excuse me, sir, I appreciate your kind offer, but we must stay together. If there is no other way for us to pass through your city, then we'll have to go around it."

"Yes," Carter agreed. "We will just have to go around the city. Can you tell us which way is the shortest way around?"

"Nonsense," the gatekeeper responded. "There is no way you will survive on the outskirts of the city. Besides, once you passed through the gate, you were already subject to the toll. Even if you are foolish enough to go around the city, or if you just go back the way you came, you still have to pay the toll. Since the only thing of value you have is the girl, you are required to surrender her. I am sorry, but that is the law."

"Carter," Kat pleaded. "Please don't leave me here!"

Carter looked over his shoulder out the gate as if he were thinking about making a run for it.

"I would not recommend that you try to escape. The guards will have a crossbow bolt in your back before you get ten feet down the road. They will chase down the girl, and she will still be the king's property. Now, the only reasonable thing for you to do is to pass through the city; your toll is paid," the gatekeeper said in a very business-like tone.

Kat looked like a deer caught in headlights. Carter felt helpless and at a loss for a solution to their problem. Then, he got an idea. "Did you say that if we each had one hundred gold pieces that our toll would be paid?"

"Yes, that is the toll price."

"Kat, check your backpack and I'll check mine. Maybe we do have the gold after all. Remember the money we found in our pockets when we needed food?"

"Yes," Kat said with a hopeful look. She put her pack down and searched through it. "I don't have any gold, do you?" the girl asked her friend with such desperate pleading that it almost made Carter choke up. He shook his head sadly.

"I don't understand why Guard isn't helping us. This can't be happening," Carter said to no one in particular.

"You can take the girl's bag. Everything she needs will be provided for her."

The gatekeeper motioned to a guard holding a crossbow. "Secure the girl."

The guard responded quickly and moved toward the children. He took Kat by her arm and pulled her toward a cage located across from the gatekeeper's table on the other side of the gate. The cage was made of wooden poles about two inches in diameter. Rawhide straps held the poles together. Kat went without a struggle; she seemed resigned to her fate.

Her partner stood by helplessly and watched them cage his best friend like an animal. Strong emotions of anger, hatred, fear, frustration, sorrow, loss, and guilt filled the boy.

"You are free to go now," the gatekeeper said coldly to the distraught boy.

"Would it be all right if I said goodbye to her?" Carter asked in a weak, pathetic voice of defeat.

"Very well, but be quick about it. I do not want you hanging around the gate. Do I make myself clear?"

Carter understood exactly what he meant. He did not want Carter standing around looking for an opportunity to free Kat. The boy picked up their packs and walked over to the cage. It was obvious that the gatekeeper and guards were not concerned about the children trying anything. They did not even watch them as they talked. Kat stood dejected, behind the bars looking at her friend. He said to her in a low voice, "I'm going to get you out of this, Hamsted. I promise you, if it is the last thing I ever do, I will get you out of this." Kat looked at her friend and smiled weakly. "Hamsted, I mean it! Don't give me that look."

"Carter, you must rescue the children. I have served my purpose. I am the toll paid so that you can go on and do what we came here to do. You cannot let this stop you. That's what the Adversary wants; he wants us to give up. That's something you cannot do. Besides, it looks like I get the better end of this deal. I'm going to live in a palace, while you have to face the Adversary alone."

"But, Kat—"

"No, partner, this is the way it's supposed to be. Now go. I don't want you to see me cry."

Carter checked and was relieved to find that the guards were not watching them. The boy positioned himself and the packs he carried so that he could reach into his pocket without being seen. "I am going to give you Dark Beard's knife; put it in your pocket," he whispered.

"No, Carter, you might need it. You have a job to do, and you need all that we have to help you succeed."

"Kat, I need *you*. I need you to help me succeed. Now take the knife, and put it in your pocket," Carter insisted. "If you get a chance to escape, disguise yourself as best you can. Use one of those blankets to cover yourself and walk like an old woman. Don't talk to anyone. I will get a room at the first inn I find down this street. I will wait until noon tomorrow. If you do not show up, I'll try to rescue the orphans by myself. If I succeed, I'll come back for you."

Kat said, "Goodbye, Carter. If you ever make it back home, tell my mother that I love her and that I'm sorry."

"You're scaring me, Hamsted. Don't think like that. You have to be determined to do whatever you can to escape. If I can figure out a way, I'll rescue you. In the meantime, if you find a way out, take it."

"Time is up," the gatekeeper announced. "Move along boy, and do not let me catch you hanging around here, or I will have you arrested for breach of contract. Your contract with me is that you are passing through. That is what you will do. Now get moving."

"Carter!" Kat pleaded as she grasped the boy's hands before he could let go of the bars. There was such desperation and fear in her eyes that it almost drove Carter to do something foolish. He suddenly had the urge to run at the gatekeeper's table and strangle him. Seeing the rage in Carter's eyes, Kat said, "No, Carter, you have to stay free; it's the orphan's only chance—it's my only chance."

Carter took a deep breath and was able to retain control. Then he said, "I know you're right, but you have to do all you can to escape. Promise me that you won't give up."

"I said leave! I have been more that generous letting you have private time alone. Now, be on your way." The gatekeeper was leaning forward to communicate that the next thing he would do would be to get up and forcibly remove Carter.

"Yes, I will try to escape. If I do, I will look for you at the closest inn down this street. Now go before you get arrested too."

Carter stood for a moment longer looking into his best friend's eyes. Then he turned his head and shot an unfriendly look at the gatekeeper. Turning back to Kat, he said, "I'm sorry this is happening to you." Then, he let go of the bars, and headed up the street with his head hung low. He looked and felt like the weight of the world rested on his back. He walked slowly as tears of frustration and guilt ran down his cheeks.

ROOM AT THE INN

There were no sidewalks. Everyone traveled by foot on the filthy, litter-strewn street. The citizens were mostly, if not all, human. It was not always easy to tell because the people wore drab earth-tone blankets. Some wore them like a cape and hood that hid their gender as well as their species. On the other hand, all those who wore them like a poncho and those who used them like a toga appeared to be human.

The faces Carter could see looked pale and sickly. No one smiled and everyone—men, women, and even the few children—he saw were walking, standing, or sitting alone. He did not see any groups or couples anywhere.

The buildings that lined the street were crude structures. Some were made of stone, some of wood, and some were nothing more than roughhewn tables set under roofs made of wooden planks, covered with straw and held up by poles. There were no signs on any of the buildings. Structures that were closed-in had large open doors that allowed passersby to peek in and see the goods offered for sale.

Carter walked about two blocks beyond the city gate, and he did not see anything that even remotely resembled an inn. He decided to ask directions from an old man sitting on a wooden stool along the side of the street. He was staring at the ground. "Excuse me, sir, can you tell me if there is an inn nearby?"

The man did not look up; he just stuck out his hand as if he were begging for a handout.

"I'm sorry, but I don't have any money."

The man looked up at the boy and said, "I need something to eat to give me strength."

"Oh, I have some food I can give you." Carter reached into his backpack and pulled out his last bag of dried fruit. The bag was a third full of apricots. He had planned to eat them for his lunch, but after what had happened to Kat, he had no appetite. The boy handed the bag to the old man, who quickly consumed its contents. When he was finished, he threw the bag down and resumed staring at the ground.

Carter waited for a moment and then cleared his throat in an attempt to let the man know that he was waiting for his information. The man did not move. "Sir, would you please tell me where I can get a room for the night?"

"Go away, and leave me alone."

After what had happened to him at the gate and now suffering this rude treatment, Carter wanted to take all his frustrations out on the old man. He felt like blasting him verbally with several choice words and phrases he had heard his dad use when he got mad at his computer. Nevertheless, the boy decided it would not be the right way to handle the situation. Instead, he said, with as much sincerity as he could muster, "I hope you have a good day, sir, and I'm sorry if I disturbed you."

The man looked up at Carter with confusion on his face; he nodded and looked back down at the ground. Carter wondered if perhaps the man was suffering from some malady that caused him to be confused or unaware of what was really going on around him. He was glad that he did not add to the man's suffering.

Carter decided to try his luck with one of the shopkeepers. Two doors past the old man there was a building that looked to be made of adobe. Taking this as a good sign, Carter entered and found that it was a garment store. There was only one table in the shop displaying about a dozen of the drab colored blankets used by the citizens to cover their bodies. In the back of the store, a middle-aged woman sat on a chair. She had long, black hair streaked with gray and a large nose. She had a broad smile that revealed several missing teeth. The look in her eyes did not match the warmth that her smile attempted to project. "Welcome to my shop, stranger. Your garments are unlike any I have ever seen before." She stood, saying, "Let me help you pick out something that will allow you fit in better."

Standing just inside the door, he told the woman, "I'm sorry, but I don't have any money. I was just hoping that you would tell me if there is an inn nearby where I can get a room."

The shopkeeper's smile vanished, her eyes went cold, and her hands balled into fists. "What kind of game are you playing at, little boy? You come in here acting as if you want to buy something, and then you say you are looking for an inn, but you cannot buy anything because you have no money. How are you going to stay at an inn if you have no money? Why are you here? I want you out of my store right now! Do not come back; you will not like what happens if you do."

Carter turned and exited the shop as quickly as he could. Once he was out on the street again, he stood and wondered, *What is the problem with these people? Are they all insane?* Then he remembered where he was, and he mumbled, "Oh, that's right, I'm in the Valley of Shadows." Across the street, he saw a boy who looked to be about his own age. He was sitting on the ground whittling on a piece of wood. Carter wondered if he might do better asking a kid for help. Figuring that he did not have anything to lose, he started across the street. As Carter approached, the boy dropped the piece of wood, jumped to his feet, and pointed his knife at Carter. "What do you want? Stay away from me, or I will cut you. I will cut you!"

Carter stopped dead in his tracks and put his hands up with his palms forward. "Hold on there. I just wanted to ask you a question. Please put the knife down."

"You would like that. I put the knife down, and then I would be at your mercy. I am not stupid, and if you do not back off right now, I will cut you!"

"Okay, okay, I'm leaving," said Carter. He walked backwards, keeping his eyes on the kid. Once he was back on the other side of the street, the kid stooped down, picked up his wood, and started whittling again.

I guess I'll just have to look around until I find a place to stay, he thought. *I don't dare ask anyone else.* Luckily, Carter found a place three more blocks up the street. It was the largest building he had seen since he arrived in Omagora, and there was a smell of cooked food coming from inside. Entering the front door, he found himself in a small dining hall. There were four men, each sitting alone, eating. The only furniture in the place were eight tables with a single chair at each one. There was a thin, grizzled man standing beside a door in the back of the hall. He looked at Carter and asked, in a nasty harsh tone, "What do you want?"

"I would like to talk to someone about getting a room for the night. You do have rooms for rent, don't you?"

"Do not get smart with me boy. Everyone knows that this is the only inn in the area. A room and a meal are five coppers."

"I believe that I might have something that is worth more than five coppers for trade."

"I doubt that, but I am in a good mood today. I will look at what you have to offer. Bring it here."

If he is in a good mood, Carter thought, *I sure wouldn't like to see him in a bad one.* The boy reached into his pocket as he moved toward the innkeeper and pulled out a full box of matches. He figured that since everything he had seen in the city was rather primitive, that it was a good bet that these people did not have easy access to anything as sophisticated as matches. "In this box I have thirty matches," he said as he slid the box open.

The innkeeper looked into the box, saw the wooden matches, and said, "What is this? Is this some kind of stupid joke? You expect to get a room and a meal for little wooden sticks?" the old man roared, blowing his bad breath in Carter's face.

Quickly, Carter pulled out a match and struck it on the side of the box. It immediately blossomed into a bright yellow flame. It startled the man, and he gasped. Then he broke into a greedy grin. "My boy, I had no idea that these little pieces of wood were magic."

"No, not magic. They're just matches, and each one will only flame once."

The old man asked, "Will the maychees flame without the box?"

Luckily, the matches were the strike-anywhere kind. "Yes, they only need a rough surface. I will let you try one, and they're called matches, not maychees," Carter corrected. "Here is a *match*," he emphasized the word as he handed him one. "Be careful and do not press too hard when you strike it."

The old man's eyes were wide with wonder as he took the match. Looking at it as if it was some powerful device, he asked, "Can I release the flame by rubbing the tip on this wall?"

"Yes. Just do what you saw me do on the side of the box."

The man's hand was actually trembling as he struck the match on the wooden wall. When it ignited, the innkeeper let out with a squeal of excitement. "I must have some of these maychees."

Seeing the man's reaction, Carter realized he had a valuable treasure. Originally, he intended to give the innkeeper the whole box for a room, but now he figured he could get more for them. "I tell you what. I will give five matches instead of five coppers for the room."

"Done," the old man said. "But would you not like to stay more than one night, my young friend?"

"I might want to stay another night, but I'm not sure my business will keep me here that long. I tell you what. I'll sell you as many matches as I have here for one copper each."

It looked as if the man was about to agree to the price, when suddenly, it occurred to him that he was about to make a purchase without trying to get a better price. He immediately took on an attitude of feigned indifference. Carter had been to a few swap meets and flea markets with his dad, and he recognized the look. He and the old man were going to haggle over the price of the matches.

"I do not know. The maychees only work once, and a copper is too high a price to pay for something that will only work once. Tell me, how many maychees are in the box?"

"This was a full box, and as I said, there are thirty in a box. There are twenty-eight left," Carter explained.

"I will pay one copper for three maychees. Since you had thirty to start, I will give you the room for five, as I agreed, and eight coppers for the rest. That way, you are actually getting the room for the equivalent of two coppers, and I end up paying for the sample maychees you used to demonstrate."

Carter was too tired to check the man's math, and since he had originally planned to offer him the whole box for a room, it was a good deal. He realized that he could easily talk the innkeeper into paying a copper for each match because he knew that he wanted the matches really bad. The boy figured that the man was probably planning to sell them for double or triple the price he would spend for them.

"I tell you what. I'm tired, and I really don't feel like a long, drawn out haggling session. I'll give you the box of matches for the room and fifteen coppers. That is my only and final offer. Take it, or I will just take the room for the five as we agreed."

"Well, I am being cheated, and there is no denying that, but as I said before, I am in a good mood, so I will give you the room and fourteen coppers."

"Done," Carter said, and held out his hand for his money.

"First the box, and then I'll give you the money."

"No, I want my coppers, and then I'll give you the box when you take me to my room."

The innkeeper smiled at Carter and nodded. He reached into a leather pouch that hung from a belt wrapped around his dirty, white, toga-like garment. He brought out a handful of coins, counted out thirteen copper coins (about half the size of a penny) and put them into the boy's hand.

"The agreed upon price for the matches was fourteen coppers and a room," Carter growled.

The innkeeper had already put the extra coins back in the pouch. "Yes, well, let me tell you what I am going to do for you. I am going to have a hot meal prepared for you with food that comes from outside the valley. You do come from outside the valley, is that not true?"

"Yes, but—"

"I wager that you have not had a decent, hot meal since you have been here, have you?"

"No, but—"

"Well, food from outside the valley is very expensive and costs an extra copper."

"Very well; take me to my room, and I'll be down in an hour to eat."

The old man smiled triumphantly and said, "A wise choice. Follow me, and I will take you to your room, and I can get my maychees."

"They're called ... Oh never mind."

The innkeeper led Carter through the back door that went into the kitchen. They passed through to the outside. Behind the main building there were seven wooden cabins lined up in a row. They looked like the ones the partners found in the Dead Forest. The innkeeper took Carter to the end cabin located at the far right. It was empty; it had no furniture. Carter glanced around and asked, "What's this? Are you kidding me? Where's the bed? Where's the washroom?"

"You wanted a room; here it is. You have your own bedroll, and the washroom is inside the main building on your left across from the kitchen. Now, give me my maychees."

"Fine," Carter grumbled. "Here are your maychees," he said mockingly. "Does the door even have a lock on it?"

"Just close the door, and you will see that there is a strong piece of wood that will slide into a slot in the frame. Now, I am off to see to your meal." He left cradling his box of matches as if it held precious gems."

Alone now, Carter felt guilty that he had a safe place to spend the night and was about to have a meal prepared with food that came from outside the valley. He thought about Kat at the mercy of the gatekeeper and his guards. He wanted desperately to go back and protect her, but he knew that would accomplish nothing. The gatekeeper would arrest him and lock him up with Kat. Carter had to stay free if there was going to be any chance of rescuing the orphans. It was just that he was struggling with that old guilt about leaving Kat in the Wilson barn with a broken leg. *Can I leave her again if she doesn't escape,* he wondered. *Even though I would be doing it for the orphans, I don't think I can just leave her here. Yet, what else can I do?*

Finally, in frustration, he said aloud, "Guard, where are you when I really need you?" He listened, but there was no response.

With a sigh, the boy turned to his thoughts again. *I guess it's a good thing that I have a meal waiting for me. This way I can save the food I have left, and I will be able to give Kat an extra portion. I'm sure she won't eat the valley food, so she will be hungry when she gets here. If she gets here,* he corrected himself. *What if she doesn't escape? I guess I'll have to deal with that situation when the time comes for me to decide to leave, or give Kat more time to escape.*

When it was time for Carter to have his dinner, he went into the dining hall and found a table in a back corner. He moved the chair so that he sat with his back to the wall. There were four other men and two women, each dining alone at the single tables. It was quiet because no one talked; each person focused on his or her own table. Carter found that if one of the patrons caught him looking in his or her direction, they would shoot him a dangerous look.

They were all eating some sort of stew, black bread, and water. When the innkeeper brought Carter his dinner, it looked the same as everyone else's. "Is this the food that comes from outside the valley?"

"Yes, of course. That is what you paid for, is it not?"

"But it looks like the same thing everyone else is eating."

"It is the same thing; everyone wanted something different, so they all ordered the imported plate. It happens sometimes," the old man said with a shrug.

Carter was suspicious and was not sure if he should eat the food.

While he was trying to decide, he heard a disturbance come from a table in front and to his left. He looked up and saw one of the customers, a man, holding his throat and choking.

THE STORY OF OMAGORA

The other customers passively watched the man as he struggled. Carter had learned the Heimlich maneuver in his health class a couple of weeks before he had given his disastrous report on dental hygiene. The pale man's face was beginning to turn blue. He stood up and looked at the door as if he were about to run.

Carter got out of his chair and approached the man before he could bolt, and said, "I know how to help you."

The struggling man turned on the boy, holding a knife that he picked up off his table. Even though his eyes were bulging, his face was blue, and his tongue was hanging out, he slashed the knife back and forth in an attempt to keep the boy away from him.

"Please, sir, I can save you! I just need to get behind you. I know what to do," Carter pleaded.

"Forget it, boy," Carter heard the innkeeper's gruff voice. "He is a goner. I have seen it before. The food is stuck too deep; he will be dead in a few moments. Let him die in peace."

When the choking man was near unconsciousness, he dropped the knife. He held his throat with both his hands, and his eyes began to roll up into his head. Quickly, Carter got behind the man. Luckily, the people from this town were thin, and the boy's arms reached around the man. He locked his hands together into a tight ball and squeezed. Nothing happened, and everyone in the room was waiting to see what the "crazy" boy was doing. Again, Carter squeezed, pulling as hard as he could with his balled fists up into the man's abdomen. This time, he heard a loud choking cough as a large piece of vegetable flew out of the man's mouth. Carter let him go, and the man coughed and gasped for air. The man's color returned to normal, and he sat back in his seat, trembling. When he was able to speak, he made an announcement to those present in the hall. "The boy and I have business to discuss." To Carter, he said, still as though he was making an announcement to the group, "I will move my table beside yours so that we can discuss our business in private."

As Carter's new contact moved his table and chair next to his, the man said, "I am grateful for your service to me, but I did not ask for it. I will not give you more than two gold pieces."

"I do not want money for saving your life. I did it because I knew how and you needed help; that's all."

The man looked confused and asked, "Is this a new approach to doing business?"

"No. It's just that I want something other than money. I want information. Why are the people so rude, and why is it that nobody seems to care about anything? Has it always been like this? By the way, my name is Carter. What's yours?"

The man sitting next to Carter looked to be around forty years old. It was hard to tell for sure because everyone looked unhealthy and used up. He had dirty, shoulder-length, brown hair, intense eyes, and a large mouth. He had a clever look about him that made the boy think the man he saved was someone who knew his way around.

"My name is Houtdec, and no, things were not always like this. This was once a great and prosperous city.

Carter was surprised at this revelation and asked, "What happened? This is the worst city I've ever seen. It's filthy, crude, and everyone stays to himself. Why is that? Why are there no couples walking the streets, and where are the families? Why doesn't the king do something about it?"

"Since you will not take money as a reward for saving me, I will pay part of my debt by telling you the story of Omagora.

"Twenty years ago, Omagora was a beautiful thriving city ruled by a kindhearted king and his beautiful wife. The king's love for the people and his wisdom was a rich and rare thing in Dearth. At the peak of his rule, the city teamed with commerce, the streets were filled with happy people, and families flourished. The city was the exception in Dearth. While people struggled and scraped by everywhere else, we had a leader whose dearest desire was the welfare of his people.

"In his wisdom, the king declared that all people regardless of their age, gender, beliefs, or species were born equal in value. He made a decree that he would not tolerate any sort of favoritism. Thus, everyone had equal opportunity to seek happiness and follow his or her dreams in an atmosphere of fairness.

"As in any free society, there were those who prospered far beyond others. The majority of the people made comfortable livings and raised happy families. Even those who labored and served in menial jobs had enough to live modestly, and they took pride in their work. Those who were unable to work for a living due to age or circumstance were taken care of by family or the kindness of others.

"I was a sandal maker, and my business was successful and gratifying. It supported me, my wife, my son, and eight other families in my employ. We loved and respected each other; we were one big family.

"Little did we know that this would all change. One sad day, a man with white hair, dressed in a white robe appeared and declared that he was a holy man come to aid the city in finding even greater prosperity and happiness for all. Something about the man caused people to take him at his word. The people cheered him, ushered him to the palace, and begged the king to give him an audience. The king was always open to his people and open to making things better for them, so he gladly received the man in the white robe.

"The man flattered the king with words of praise and encouragement. He told the king that in all his travels he had never seen a wiser king or a more satisfied people. He said that Omagora was a wonderful city. He convinced the king that it would only take a few simple changes to make it perfect. The king invited the man to stay in the palace and serve as his advisor. The man in white agreed.

"At first, Vardrayes (as he called himself) made little, harmless suggestions, such as, a day of celebration to show gratitude to all who labored doing jobs that were menial and low paying. He told the king that those who labor with little hope of bettering themselves needed to be encouraged so that they would know how much people appreciated their service.

"The king loved the idea and left the details to Vardrayes. It turned out to be a great success, and it seemed to encourage an even closer bond between our citizens. The king was so pleased with his new advisor's work that he let him have a free hand to do whatever he thought would make the city perfect. Many of his actions and activities involved charitable events and new policies that, on the surface, seemed to enhance the lives of the poor and take care of the helpless. These actions were well received and made us love the king even more, and Vardrayes was as beloved and respected as the king.

"One day, Vardrayes went to the king and told him that the harmony and joy of Omagora was in danger of being destroyed. This greatly disturbed the king. His advisor explained that there were those outside the city who envied and resented Omagora's prosperity. He convinced the king that the city needed a great wall built around it, and that the king needed an army to protect the people against those who were plotting to destroy them. The king trusted Vardrayes and authorized the project to secure the city.

"In order to finance the project, taxes were raised and men recruited to build the wall and staff the army. We trusted our leaders, and even though the heavy taxation and drain on our labor force was a burden, the majority of the people were supportive. Within seven years, the wall was completed and the army was well trained. Everyone was relieved to have the security project in place. We felt safe and looked forward to some well-needed tax relief. However, the tax relief did not come. The army had to be maintained; the wall needed guards. Yet, that was not the worst of it. Vardrayes convinced the king that the only way to have a truly perfect city was for the people to own everything equally. He told the king that taking all the wealth of the city and redistributing it equally to everyone was the only way to make Omagora a paradise on earth. 'Think about it,' he would say. 'Everyone is of equal value as you yourself have said. The people love each other, and they will come to see that since they are all equal that they should share equally in the prosperity of the city. What could be more logical?'

"The king was getting on in years, and his mind was no longer sharp. This, along with his trust in Vardrayes, led him to agree to the plan. He did not realize that it would destroy his city. The soldiers' duties changed from protecting the people to enforcing the counselor's new plan. They walked the city dressed in black-studded leather armor and flowing, black capes. They wrapped their heads with black leather straps and wore hoods, allowing only their eyes and mouths to be seen. They carried long, black staffs in which they were well trained. Hundreds of them went out into the city to enforce the collection and redistribution of the wealth. The poor were delighted, but the business community and the wealthy were devastated. Employees quit by the thousands, destroying essential businesses. There was no longer a reason to work since everyone got the same amount of wealth. There was no reason to have a business or have a farm or work at a job if no matter how hard you worked, you would receive the same rewards as those who did nothing.

"The city descended into chaos as food ran out and goods became scarce. Some of us tried to keep our businesses going on our own, but without warning, the enforcers would drop into the businesses and take most of the money, leaving only a small amount that they said was the legal amount allowed for citizens to have.

"It became clear to everyone that the enforcers were keeping large sums of money for themselves while they punished any resistance. They were skilled at breaking bones, and sometimes skulls, with their staffs. People were terrified of the enforcers, but eventually their anger and hatred at what had happened to their lives grew to outweigh their fear. Even the poor, who had more money than they had ever imagined, saw the evil of what had happened to the fabric of society. Money, if there is nothing to buy, is worthless. The poor realized that they had been cheated along with everyone else.

"There were riots in the streets. The mobs were able to kill some of the enforcers, but the well-trained, heavily armed enforcers crippled and killed hundreds of our people. They took great delight in their work as they brutalized women and children. Unrest and rebellion went on for several years.

"In an effort to quell the rioting, a new law made it illegal for two or more people to be together in public. The only way people could come together was if they were doing business. If the enforcers caught a group of people together, they would demand proof that they were doing business and not conspiring to cause trouble. If they failed, they were beaten mercilessly. It got so bad, people would attack anyone who came within a few feet of them, for fear that an enforcer would accuse them of conspiracy. Even families would spread out and walk on opposite sides of the street from each other in order to avoid even the appearance that they were together.

"The king died of a broken heart as he saw his beautiful city ruined by disease and starvation. Slowly, it deteriorated to what it is today. His evil work done, Vardrayes took his army of enforcers, moved to the far eastern end of the valley, and built a dark stronghold on an island in the middle of a black lake.

"I, like many others, am alone now. My wife and son are dead, and the few friends I had that are still alive, are friends no more. Now that the enforcers are gone, and the money distribution program is gone, we have nothing left. Somehow, the precious metals we used for currency have disappeared. There is little doubt that the king's advisor and his army took it with them when they abandoned the city. Now, we just live on the scraps of our past. We just get by the best that we can—alone and hopeless."

Houtdec's story fascinated Carter. When the man finished his tale, the boy asked, "Why, if Vardrayes and the enforcers are gone, are things still so bad? Why don't you and the citizens come together and rebuild your society?"

"The people are defeated. Their spirits are broken, and their bodies are weak and sickly. They live in fear that Vardrayes and his enforcers will return. Since it was during times of prosperity that he came, the people continue to live as they did when he went away. They resist change and any efforts to better their lives because of the fear that if things were to get better, he would return."

As their talk continued, several of the patrons in the dining area began to shoot looks at them. The innkeeper, who kept a close watch on everything that went on in his establishment, approached the pair and said, for all to hear, "I hope there is business taking place here. If not, you will find yourselves bloodied and thrown out." In response to this, there was a murmur of agreement and nodding of heads from those seated around them.

"The boy is being stubborn," said Houtdec with convincing annoyance. "I offer him two gold, and he says now that he will take five. At least that is down from the ten he wanted at first. It is a good thing too, because I do not have ten gold. Who has that much nowadays?" he asked and looked around at the others in the dining hall. Some nodded, and all went back to their dining.

"He is right, boy," the innkeeper said to Carter. "I doubt he even has five gold. That is a tidy sum. You best find a reasonable compromise and finish your business," he said and then walked away.

"The people will enforce the laws; if they get the idea that we are not doing business, they will come together and beat us. The people are especially mistrusting of strangers like you. We all know that you are from outside the Valley of Shadows because of your sun-touched skin. Since the evil times of the king's advisor, the people look upon all strangers with suspicion. For that reason, you must be especially careful."

Without warning, Houtdec slammed his hand on his table and shouted, "Be reasonable, boy. I do not have all night to haggle with you!"

The outburst startled Carter, but he understood the game they were playing. He played along by raising his voice as he responded, "I don't have all night either, and I will not settle for less than four gold."

Lowering his voice so that only Carter could hear him, the man asked, "What else would you have from me? I would gladly give you gold or anything that I have. I will ever be in your debt."

"I still don't understand. Why doesn't the king exert his leadership and rebuild?"

"As I said before, the king died of a broken heart."

"I remember you saying that, but I mean the present king. The one who took over after the old king died."

Houtdec looked a bit confused by the question and answered, "There is no king now. The king had no heir, and there was no effort to crown a king because Vardrayes had complete control long before the king died."

This bit of information deeply upset Carter.

Houtdec could see that his savior was shaken. He asked, "Why does this news trouble you so?"

"When I arrived at the city gate, I was not alone. I had a friend with me; her name is Kat. The gatekeeper insisted on keeping her as toll for my being able to pass through the city. He said that Kat would be presented to the king, live in the palace, and serve the royal family."

The man sighed heavily and shook his head sadly. "I fear that your friend is lost to you. The gatekeeper is an eccentric fellow who is capable of anything."

"Please, you have to help me free her. She is my best friend, and I need her to help me rescue the orphans," Carter pleaded desperately.

"Orphans? The city is full of orphans. What do you mean that you need to rescue them?"

Carter explained to Houtdec about the Adobe Orphanage and a bit about their troubles with the Adversary. He told him about their mission to rescue the four children.

"This Adversary you speak of sounds like Vardrayes," said Houtdec.

"Yes, I am sure that they are one and the same. Wait a minute. I just realized that 'Vardrayes' is 'Adversary' with the letters changed around."

"If that is true then it means you are headed for the stronghold of Vardrayes. That is impossible; you will never make it. First, you will not be able to leave the city through the eastern gate without a pass from the gatekeeper. No one can leave the city without the gatekeeper's permission. Second, even if you were able to find a way out of the city, there is no way to cross the lake to the island where the stronghold is located. And freeing your friend is simply not possible."

"Houtdec, you seem like a man who knows his way around. You have survived your family, many of your friends, and you ran a successful business. I find it hard to believe that a man like you has no connections, no ambitions other than surviving, and no resources at your disposal. You must be able to help. If not you, then who can I turn to?"

"Look, Carter, I owe you, but I have little that I can give or do. For the very reasons you listed, I have given up. Grief, anger, and hatred fill my life. I am no better than any other citizen of Omagora. I must admit, though, seeing your passion for your friend and your determination to save the orphans has stirred up old feelings in me that were dead. It is as if when you saved my life, I was reborn. I want to help you. I want to help anyone I can. I remember now how my life was never as full and satisfying as when I created something useful for others. True, they were just sandals, but they were of good quality, and they were useful to my fellow citizens.

"Now we are getting somewhere," Houtdec said aloud, smiling. "You drive a hard bargain, boy, but I respect that. I could use your skills to assist me with some other business dealings I have."

Playing along, Carter said aloud, "Perhaps. Tell me what you have in mind, and if it pays well enough, we might make some sort of arrangement."

"That should buy us another twenty minutes," the man said with lowered voice. "I tell you what I can do. I can go to the gate and see if your friend is still there. If she is not, I can bribe one of the guards to tell me where she is. Would that be helpful?"

Carter nodded and then asked, "Would you go tonight, and if she is still there, watch her? If you see them move her, you could follow them and then report back to me."

Houtdec nodded and answered, "Yes. It will be my pleasure."

"Thank you, sir," Carter said, with tears of gratitude welling up in his eyes. "I told Kat that if she did not find a way to escape and find me here at the inn by noon tomorrow that I would try to rescue the orphans alone and then come back for her. But if there is no way to leave the city without permission then I feel justified in focusing my efforts on getting her back. I was not going to leave without her anyway."

"Very well, I will leave now. If she is still at the gate, I will watch her. If I see them move her, I will follow her. If she is not at the gate, I will find out what they did with her. You must stay here, and wait for me no matter how long it takes. I swear to you that I will return with news.

"Do not eat any of the food the innkeeper tries to feed you. He will tell you that his food is from outside the valley. He is a crook and a liar. If you brought any food or water from outside the valley, eat that.

"One more thing, never call me sir. The person who saved my life has a right to call me by my name no matter how old he is."

"Tell me, Houtdec, what would happen if I ate food or drank water from the valley?"

"Because you are from outside the valley and were not born here, you would get so sick that you could die and be glad if you did. If you survive it, then you would be able to eat it without getting sick. Even so, it still tastes foul no matter how much you season it. I hope your friend has not consumed any of the valley's food or drink."

Before Carter said another word, Houtdec stood up and said in a loud jovial voice, "Done and done gladly. I will be in touch with you when I have business that requires your assistance. I wish you a goodnight." Then he left the dining hall and disappeared into the night.

Carter got up from his table, went to his room, and ate some of his food. He spent a very lonely, sleepless night as he thought about Kat and imagined all sorts of horrors she might be suffering.

SWEET REVENGE

Sitting in the back of her cage, Kat tried to think of ways she might escape. She tried to remember movies where she had seen prisoners escape. Most of those involved tunneling or overpowering guards. Her cell was a six-foot cube in full view of her captors. Even with Dark Beard's knife, it was unlikely that she would be able to free herself from her prison. She thought, *A chance might present itself during transfer from here to the palace. I will just have to wait and see if an opportunity presents itself.*

With the subject of escape decided, she turned her thoughts to food and drink. Because Losmoon had warned the partners not to eat or drink anything that came from the valley, she and Carter had been careful to consume only what they brought with them. Unfortunately, the gatekeeper refused to let her keep her pack. She wondered what would happen if she ended up with no other choice but to eat what came from the valley. Remembering all that she had seen and experienced since being in the Valley of Shadows, the thought of eating food or drinking water that came from this horrible place made her stomach turn. She decided that she would have to be starving before she ate valley food.

It was exactly two hours after the gatekeeper locked Kat in the cell that he paid her a visit. He stood in front of her cell wearing a rather nasty grin as he asked, "Are you comfortable?"

The girl was in no mood for games; she just glared at the man and refused to answer.

"I have some information that may cheer you up. I am going to set you free."

This statement caught Kat by surprise. "Are you serious?"

"I am being perfectly serious. What do you say to that?"

"What about living in the palace, serving the king, and all that stuff you said?"

"Oh that. Well there is no king, and the palace was torn down years ago."

"So why did you tell us all those lies and lock me up if you were just planning to let me go?"

The gatekeeper put on a mischievous smirk and asked, "Have you noticed how many people have entered the city since you have been here?"

"I haven't seen anyone enter."

"And you probably will not see anyone for weeks or even months come to the gate again. I get bored, so when someone does come along, I like to have a little fun," he said with a chuckle.

What she just heard made Kat so angry that she wanted to tell this despicable man exactly what she thought of him. She wanted to hurt him the only way available to her. Before she opened her mouth, she saw something that caused her to change her course of action. She saw a look of satisfaction on the man's face. She realized that he was hoping that she would lose it; he wanted to see her pain. This was his payoff. Everything that he did was to cause her to do what she was about to do. *I will not give him the satisfaction*, she thought.

Kat smiled brightly and said, "I see; it was all a big joke. You sure had me going there," she said with a little chuckle. "That was a good one. It reminds me of another joke that was played on me by my cousin—"

"I am not interested in your story," the gatekeeper cut Kat off gruffly. A look of disappointment replaced his smugness. Kat was sure that the disappointment cut deep, especially if he had to wait months at a time for a victim to wander into his little net. She also knew that he would try to make her pay for robbing him of his payoff.

"One of my men overheard your plan to escape and meet your friend at the inn by noon tomorrow. I know that if you do not show up by noon, he will continue without you. By midnight, he will be well out of the city, and then I will release you. You will be stranded here with no way to care for yourself," he snarled, and then waited to see if he had put a scare into the girl.

Kat decided that the time to play along had come. If she did not at least look upset by this last piece of news, there was no telling what the bully would do in an effort to inflict pain on her. "I see," Kat said sadly, hung her head in a posture of brokenness, and began to weep softly.

"Your sniveling will not move me." The old smugness was back in the bully's voice, and it was all Kat could do to keep from laughing. She felt safe now because she knew her partner. She thought about the night when she broke her leg on a ghost hunt with Carter, and he ran off in fear believing that a ghost was chasing him. When he found out that he had left his friend back at the barn alone in the dark with a broken leg, he suffered painful guilt feelings for a long time. The girl knew that the guilt of that night would not allow him to leave her again. *Carter will wait for me*, she said to herself, *regardless of our agreement. When I show up at the inn, we will continue on to the Adversary's stronghold.*

Kat decided it would be wise to put on a good show for the gatekeeper. She did not want him to think that she was not suffering enough. He might decide to keep her for a few more days and try to find ways to punish her for robbing him of his fun. Catherine Hamsted always wondered if she could act. Now was as good a time as any to find out if she could be convincing.

"Please, you must think of the orphans. We are on our way to—"

"Yes, I know; you told me that already. You are passing through to rescue some orphans. I care not about such things. Your friend will move on, try to rescue the brats, and he will fail. You, on the other hand, will live. You will live in this miserable stinking town with the thought that you lost your friend and failed to accomplish what you came here to do. Every day you spend here will be an evil reminder of what you have lost. When you finally give up and surrender to despair, you will become just another miserable dweller of Omagora," he sneered.

Throughout the rest of the day, he glanced over at Kat. He had such a look of satisfaction when he saw the "pain" he was causing that it was as if it was feeding a hunger, and he was savoring every delicious moment of the girl's "suffering."

Kat was hugging her knees to her chin and rocking herself back and forth. She made little mewling noises. While she was putting on her act for the gatekeeper, she was thinking, *I should get an academy award for this performance; he's totally buying it.*

Then it occurred to her that if one of his men overheard the conversation between her and Carter, why did the gatekeeper not take the knife away from her? Either he forgot about it, or his spy did not hear everything that they said to each other. Carter did whisper when he slipped her the knife. It was a good thing that the gatekeeper did not take the knife because, even though she no longer needed it to help her escape, they still might find it useful before their adventure ended.

The time passed slowly as the girl sat in her cage. She had plenty of time to think back over all the things they had been through since entering the Dead Forest. *How many days have we been on this adventure*, she wondered. She shrugged and decided that it really did not matter. What did matter was how many more days would it take to finish it. She was tired of being frightened, but she had to admit that she would do it all over again. She agreed with Carter that what was happening to them was incredible. What they were learning and experiencing would change them forever. She smiled to herself as she thought, *Life at home, if we ever make it back, will be different*

346

because we will be different. We will be stronger, wiser, and have greater understanding. Yes, we have found treasures in this wretched dimension. Treasures that will serve us well the rest of our lives.

"I dare say you have learned much, my little Kat, and there is much more to learn," said the Guardian.

Kat lifted her head and turned to see Guard sitting next to her. "Guard!" she squealed.

"Shush. Only you can see me. Put your head down again so they can't see you talking to me."

"What do you want?" the gatekeeper growled, thinking that Kat was calling out to him.

"Won't you please let me out sooner?" she whined to the gatekeeper.

"I may keep you longer, but I will not let you out sooner," he said with an evil grin.

Kat put her head back on her knees as though she was going to cry again.

"Not bad, not bad at all. You are quick. You covered your slip and used it to make him think that you were pleading with him to end your suffering. He will feed on that tidbit for a while."

Kat smiled and said, "It seems such a long time since I've seen you. I suppose you know that Carter and I have been separated."

"You do not need to worry about that. You and Carter will be back together soon. Even now, he is sending a man named Houtdec to watch over you. When the gatekeeper sets you free, Houtdec will contact you and take you to Carter. I am telling you this so that when he presents himself to you, you will know that it is safe to go with him.

"Now, as I said before, there is still much for you to learn. I have come to teach you a lesson on revenge."

"But I don't plan to take revenge on anyone. Do you think that I mean to take revenge on the gatekeeper?"

"No. I know that you do not want to take revenge on anyone. Nevertheless, I want to encourage you to do just that. I want you to take revenge on the gatekeeper."

"Oh, I get it; you're the Adversary posing as Guard again. You didn't fool us the last time, and you aren't going to fool me this time. Just go away!" Kat said with anger and disappointment in her voice.

"I will not go away because I am the Guardian," he said as he put his hand on the girl's shoulder. Kat immediately felt the same loving peace and strength that she felt the first time he touched her, and she knew without a doubt that this was the Guardian.

"Guard, I'm sorry that I doubted you. Explain what it is that you want me to do."

"That is better. Let us commence with our lesson on revenge. Think for a moment. What could you do to the gatekeeper that would make him feel ashamed of himself for what he has put you through?"

"I don't know that there is anything I or anyone could do that would make him feel ashamed for what he has done to me. If I had the power or ability to hurt him physically or could enlist someone to hurt him physically, he might regret that he picked on me. But I don't think that would make him feel bad about what he has done. He would most likely get angry and seek to do me real harm. He has all the power and resources. I have nothing."

"I would not say that you have nothing; you still have Dark Beard's knife."

"Yes, but you don't expect me to use the knife on him, do you?"

"I think that the knife is the most effective means available to you."

"I'm not going to stab the gatekeeper!"

"I am glad to hear that because stabbing him will not make him feel ashamed of what he did to you."

"I'm confused. You said that I should use the knife on him. If you didn't mean stabbing him, did you mean I should just cut him?"

"I do not want you to hurt him, physically. I want you to do something that will cause him the pain of regret and shame. That kind of pain can change a person for the good. Hurting a person to make you feel good does not make things better; it makes things worse."

"How can I do that?" Kat asked, confused. She got no response. "Guard, how can I use the knife to make him feel regret for what he has done to me?" When there was still no answer, Kat turned her head to look at Guard. He was gone.

Cat sighed and said to herself, "I guess that means I'm supposed to figure it out for myself."

"You are right, Kat," said Guard. The girl could not see the Guardian, but she could hear his voice in her mind. "I will give you a hint; remember Beth."

At the mention of that name, a flood of memories came over her. She had not thought about Beth in a long time. Her experience with Beth taught Kat a hard lesson, and it was bittersweet remembering how she had learned it.

Beth had attended the same school as Kat for only four months. Her family moved a lot, and she started at the school in the middle of the term. Beth and Kat were both in the fourth grade. Kat had three girlfriends that she had gone to school with ever since the first grade. From the first day Beth started at the school, the four friends decided to have some fun at the new girl's expense. They talked about her plain clothes and laughed about how she wore the same outfit to school every day. It was obvious to the four friends that Beth was from a family so poor that they could not afford to buy her enough clothes to wear something different each day. What did escape them was that her one outfit was always clean and neatly laundered.

Kat still felt shame and guilt as she remembered that after seeing Beth wear the same clothes to school for over a week, she stopped Beth in the hall, between classes, and in front of all the children she said, "Beth, you look so nice today. Is that a new outfit?" All the children laughed, and Beth turned scarlet with embarrassment.

After that incident, most of the children in the school giggled when Beth walked by them. Kids would point at her and say things that she could not hear, but she could hear the laughs that followed the comments. Beth stayed to herself, ate alone, and sat alone during recess.

One day when Kat was having an exceedingly rough time at home with her mother, she ran out of the house, yelling, "I've got to go to school, Mom, or I'll be late." She was in such a hurry to escape the contentious situation that she skipped her breakfast and forgot her bag lunch. This happened during the winter when several of the children were home from school sick with colds and flu. Two of Kat's girlfriends were twins, and they were both home with the flu. The one friend that was at school that day laughed at Kat when she heard the story of how she forgot her lunch.

Kat asked her, "Do you have an extra cookie or something I could have? I'm starving."

Her friend just shook her head and said with a sanctimonious air, "No. Being hungry is good for you. It will teach you to make sure that you have all your things before you leave the house. Besides, I'm hungry too. I need all my food to get me through the rest of the day."

"I can't believe you're treating me this way. If you had forgotten your lunch, I would share with you," said Kat with disappointment in her voice.

"But *I* didn't forget my lunch," her friend said with a superior attitude.

"Fine! Thanks for nothing," Kat snarled. She got up from the table, stormed out into the empty hallway, and sat on the floor, resting her back against the wall. After a few moments of brooding, she heard the cafeteria door open. She looked up expecting to see her friend coming out with a change of heart and an offer to share her lunch, but instead she saw Beth.

Beth sat on the floor on the opposite side of the hall facing Kat. Kat snorted with contempt and looked down. Her legs were stuck straight out, and her hands were folded in her lap.

After a few moments of silence, Beth asked, "Would you like to share some of my lunch?"

Kat looked up at the girl and asked, "What? Are you serious?"

"I overheard what you said about missing breakfast and forgetting your lunch. I have half a sandwich and an apple you can have."

Beth was so sweet and sincere in her offer to share her lunch that Kat felt something in her chest grow heavy and her throat tighten. "Why?" Kat managed to croak out.

"Well, I ate half my sandwich and my cookies. I'm full. I know how it feels to be hungry, and I just thought that you would like a little something to get you through—"

"No, I don't mean that," said Kat. Tears were starting to pool in her eyes. "Why are you being kind to me? I have been rude and mean to you since you've been here."

"If I had been mean back to you, would it have made you like me and change the way you were treating me?"

Kat shook her head slowly. "No, it would have made me want to hurt you even more. I think that if you had been mean to me, it would have allowed me to feel okay with treating you poorly."

"I wouldn't feel good about myself if I hurt you, and you certainly wouldn't feel better about me. I would lose two times over. On the other hand, being kind to people makes me feel good. Perhaps if I'm kind to you, then you might forgive me for what I did to make you and your friends hate me. Whatever it was, I'm sorry. Will you forgive me?"

For the longest time, Kat just sat and stared at Beth. When she finally spoke, she said, "I will not forgive you."

Beth dropped her head and said in a sad voice, "Oh, I see."

"I will not forgive you because you have done nothing that needs forgiving. It should be me asking you for forgiveness. I always thought of myself as a good person, but the way my friends and I have treated you shows that I am not the person I thought I was." Kat began to feel hot tears of shame roll down her cheeks. "You did nothing to deserve what we did to you."

At this point, Beth got up, sat down beside Kat, and put her arm around her shoulders as she wept. Beth stroked Kat's hair and said gently, "It's okay; don't cry. You are a good person, Kat, or you wouldn't be so upset over this."

"I'm truly sorry, Beth. Can you ever forgive me?"

"On one condition, that you eat the sandwich and apple," Beth said with a warm smile.

Even though Beth was only at the school for another six weeks, after they became friends, Kat spent more time with her during those weeks than she did with her old friends. Kat's old friends could not understand why, all of a sudden, Kat seemed to prefer

Beth's company to theirs. They felt that Kat had betrayed them. She tried to explain to them that Beth was actually a very nice person. She wanted them to get to know her and let her become part of their group. They would not even consider it, and soon after, Kat became the target of their ridicule as well. The two new friends just shrugged it off, and since nothing the three old friends did to provoke Kat and Beth worked, they finally gave up trying.

Things were never the same between Kat and her three girl friends; even after Beth moved away, the girls considered Kat a traitor. Kat's friendship with Carter made the loss of her girlfriends seem less painful. She spent more time with him, and he was glad of it because he never really approved of those three.

Kat's mind raced as she thought, *I understand now. That's what Guard wants me to do with the knife. I'm supposed to give it to the gatekeeper as a gift. It may not do any good, but it will sure confuse him. This is going to be exciting. Maybe I should give it to him now. No, if I do that, he will think that I am trying to bribe him to set me free. I'll wait until he opens the cage and sends me on my way. Before I walk away, I'll give him the gift.*

But what if we need it to help us rescue the orphans? I guess if we still needed it then Guard would not have led me to give it to the gatekeeper. Maybe the primary purpose of the knife is to be a gift for the gatekeeper. Come to think of it, the knife was a gift given to us by a man who was at one time very bad. And the kindness of another changed him. It is fitting that another man in need of some kindness should have it.

PIERCING THE HEART

The time finally came for Kat's release. It was midnight, the next day, when the gatekeeper swaggered up to the cell door. "Your friend is long gone by now. It is time for you to start your new life as a permanent resident of Omagora," he said as he unlocked the cell.

Kat stood up, dusted herself off, and walked out. "I have something I would like to give you before I go."

The gatekeeper furrowed his brow and said, "What do you mean?"

Kat reached into her pocket, pulled out Dark Beard's knife, and handed it to the man. "It's a special knife that has some useful tools. That is a compass," Kat pointed out. "It is a navigation tool; it always points north. There are different sized blades, scissors, a saw blade, file, a blade sharpener, and other things you might be able to use," she said with a warm smile.

"Why are you giving this to me? This is very valuable. If I had known that you had it, I would have taken it from you. I suspect you know that. I do not understand what you are doing."

"I know that your job is long and boring. I thought that you could use this to help pass the time. Maybe you could carve wood, use it to make repairs, do leather work. I'm sure that you can find a use for it."

"I believe you are serious. You are giving this to me because you actually care. I have never met anyone like you. I have had people curse me, spit on me, and threaten me. I usually have a good laugh and then let my men beat them before I let them go. But you, what am I to do with you? This is unexpected and uncomfortable. No one has ever made me feel uncomfortable or sorry for hurting them before."

"You don't have to do anything with me. I will just go and try to make the best of things. I do hope you like the gift. It made me feel good to give it to someone who can make good use of it. Do you like it?" asked Kat expectantly.

The gatekeeper nodded and said with some emotion, "Yes, yes I like it very much. The knife is a marvelous tool that would be worth a fortune in this town. Tell me your name."

"My name is Catherine Hamsted, but everyone calls me Kat. What's yours?"

"I am called Casbar. Kat, since you have shown me a kindness, I am going to do something for you. The truth is that your friend is still in town. If he has gone to the eastern gate, he will not be able to leave without a pass issued by me. Come," Casbar commanded as he moved toward his table, took a piece of paper, and wrote something on it. "This is a pass giving you and your friend permission to be together, travel together, and exit at the eastern gate. I hope that you do not have too much trouble finding your friend," he said and handed the pass to the girl.

"Thank you for this," said Kat.

"I am not sure that I am doing you any favors. If the Adversary that you mentioned is who I think he is, then you have little hope of rescuing anyone from him. I suspect this Adversary is someone we call Vardrayes. He is an evil being who destroyed Omagora some years ago. Then he built a stronghold on an island in the middle of the black lake east of the city. There is no way to get to the island."

"There must be a way," said Kat.

"I have heard rumors that the remains of a stone bridge lay just beneath the surface of the water. Of course, no one would cross the ruins, even if they did exist, because of the danger. They would be unstable, full of gaps that would require some swimming. When you consider that the creatures living in the black lake are monstrous, it would be suicidal to try crossing it."

For the first time since Kat had met the gatekeeper, he smiled a genuine warm smile at her. "I do hope that you and your friend will be okay. Is there anything else I can do for you before you leave?" asked Casbar.

The girl nodded and said, "I have a favor to ask."

"Ask it."

"Please be kind to people who come through your gate. I think you will find it much more gratifying."

"I will think about it."

Kat turned to leave, and then she hesitated.

"What is it that you wish to say to me, child?"

Kat looked into the gatekeeper's eyes and said what Beth had said to her. "I know that there is kindness in your heart, or you would not have felt uncomfortable or sorry for hurting me."

"Perhaps, I will have much time to think about it, and you. Now go and find your friend, and if you are successful in rescuing the orphans, come back and tell me of your adventure."

"Whether we succeed or not," said Kat, "it is unlikely that we will pass this way again. But I will never forget you. I will always think of you smiling at me after we became friends. You have a very nice smile when you are kind. It is a powerful thing when you help people. It allows you to win their gratitude, and that feels a lot better than incurring their wrath and hatred. I challenge you to give it a try and see if it is not so."

The gatekeeper listened to Kat's words thoughtfully, and when she finished talking, she turned and walked away. He watched her disappear down the street and then, smiling, he looked at his new knife.

Torchlight lit the dark streets. Passing the entrance to an alley, she heard a man call to her, "Kat, I have a message from Carter."

The girl stopped and turned to see who had addressed her, but all she could see were dark shadows. There were no other people around her, and she said, "I can't see you, Mr. Houtdec. Where are you?"

"Never mind that now. Turn around, lean against the wall, and pretend you are pausing to rest. It is important that we not be seen together. Carter will explain later. By the way, how did you know my name?"

"That's not important; please, I need to see Carter."

"Very well, I am going to step out of the alley. You wait until I get several feet ahead of you, and then follow me, but try not to look like you are following. When you see me go into the inn, find a place outside, and wait. I will send Carter out to you. Do you understand?"

"Yes."

There were only a few people out and about at the time Kat and Houtdec walked down the dimly lit street. When Houtdec reached the inn, he disappeared into the main entrance. Kat sat down on a wooden bench next to the door. After a few minutes, Carter came out of the inn carrying their backpacks. Kat jumped up, but before she could say a word, Carter held up his hand and shushed her. "Please have a seat, young miss," he said in a louder than normal voice and motioned with his hand toward the bench. Assuming that the reason for Carter's peculiar behavior would soon be revealed, she obeyed. Carter sat down next to her and said in a lowered voice, "Don't say anything yet. I need you to play along."

Not long after he sat down, the vigilant innkeeper peeked out of the door to see what was happening. This caused Carter to go into his "doing business" act. "Miss, might I interest you in this fine pack? You look like someone who could use a pack to carry her things."

Kat was a little befuddled by Carter's behavior, but she played along as best as she could. "I don't know. I suppose I could use a pack. How much do you want for it?"

Before Carter could answer, Houtdec approached the innkeeper at the door and said, "Do you mind? My new apprentice is trying to do some business. If you expect us to be able to afford your high-priced rooms, you do not want to scare away our customers." The old man cleared his throat indignantly and disappeared back into the dining hall. Houtdec nodded to Carter and followed the innkeeper back inside.

The partners were alone now. "Kat, I'm so glad to see you. How did you escape?"

"I didn't escape; the gatekeeper just let me go. It's a bit of a story, but if you don't mind, I haven't had anything to eat for two days now. I'm very hungry and thirsty."

"I'm sorry," said Carter. He handed Kat her pack. "I was so glad to see you that I forgot that you would be starving."

While Kat ate a couple protein bars and drank a full bottle of water, Carter reported, "I have some bad news. We cannot get out of this city without a pass from our old friend the gatekeeper. I haven't been able to figure out what to do about getting past the guard at the eastern gate."

While Kat ate hungrily, she pulled out their pass and handed it to Carter.

"What's this?"

"Read it," she said with her mouth full.

"This is a pass from the gatekeeper. It says we can meet together, travel together, and exit the eastern gate. How did you get this?"

"I had a little help from Guard and Beth."

"Beth? Beth who?"

"Never mind that now. I'll tell you about it later. Right now, I want to get out of this city."

"I agree with that, but first, I need to talk to Houtdec and tell him goodbye."

"Who is he anyway?"

Now it was Carter's turn to tell Kat, "Never mind that now. I will tell you about him later." Carter stuck his head into the inn and called, "Houtdec, I need a bit of help here if you don't mind."

As the man headed outside, he said to the patrons in the dining hall, "New apprentice. He needs a bit more training before he can do business without me holding his hand." A few chuckles and some knowing nods from the patrons let Houtdec know that he was safe to meet with the partners.

"Kat," Carter said. "This is my friend, Houtdec. Houtdec, this is my partner, Kat." The two greeted each other, shaking hands.

"I'm grateful for your help," Carter continued. "But it's time for us to be on our way. Kat was able, somehow, to get a pass from the gatekeeper, so we can travel together and leave the city."

"Yes, I saw that. I would never have thought to give the old boy a gift. It was obviously the right move. I do not think that the gatekeeper has ever shown a kindness to anyone before," he said to Kat. Turning to Carter, Houtdec said, "Remember, even if you leave the city, you still need to find a way across the lake to get to the island stronghold."

"The gatekeeper told me something that, if it's true, might give us a way across," Kat announced.

"That must have been some gift you gave him," Houtdec said, scratching his head. "Anyway, if you two do not mind, I would like to escort you to the eastern gate. Even though there are not many people on the streets at night, the ones that are can be trouble."

Carter beamed as he said, "We would like that. Any help we can get is most welcome. But do you think it will be safe for all of us to travel together?"

"No. I will follow you in the shadows. If you run into trouble, I will create a diversion so you can run on ahead. If I do not get a chance to talk to you again before you leave the city, I want to thank you for not only saving my life, but also for giving me back my life. I am even thinking that I might pay the gatekeeper a visit and see if the two of us could work together to turn things around for our people." Houtdec shrugged and said, "Stranger things have happened."

"Why wouldn't it be safe for us to travel together?" asked Kat. "I always thought that there was safety in numbers."

"Not in this town," Carter said. "In this town there is only safety in singles. I'll explain that to you later, also. It looks like we both have a lot to tell when we get out of here. Are you finished eating?"

"Yes, but, is there a little girl's room around here I could use? It has been awhile..."

"I'll take her back to the facilities, Carter. You wait here. Kat, whatever I say as we walk through the dining hall, just play along."

When the three friends were ready to travel, Houtdec gave the partners a torch to light their way. Carter was relieved that he did not have to use a flashlight. No doubt, technology that advanced in this primitive environment would raise too much attention. As planned, the partners headed up the main street with Houtdec following, unseen.

The farther they moved away from the inn, the more quiet and scary things became. While the torchlight made the path easy to see, the shadows between the buildings and behind objects were harder to penetrate. When they started hearing shuffling, bumping, and scratching noises coming from both sides of the street, Kat clutched Carter's arm tightly with both of her hands. "Kat," Carter said softly, "you're cutting off my circulation."

"Sorry," she apologized and let go of his arm. They stopped for a moment, and Carter rubbed his arm while Kat watched. When they were ready to move again, they saw a man blocking their way.

DEATH AT THE EASTERN GATE

"What are you kids doing together out here at night?" asked a tall thin man in an accusing tone. He was standing about thirty feet in front of them, and it looked like he was holding two squirming creatures, one in each hand. The darkness and the distance made it hard to make out details.

Carter was about to mention their pass when the man lifted his hands and pointed the animals' heads at the partners as if he were aiming weapons. The creatures had glowing yellow eyes similar to Evil and Seeker. It looked to Carter like the creatures were some sort of snakes with legs. They had pointed snouts, and as soon as the man held them out, the creatures opened their mouths and made hideous high-pitched squeals. At the same time, blue-white sparks gapped between the upper and lower front teeth, making loud snapping sounds. It looked and sounded exactly like the arcing spark that a stun device would make.

"How do you like my pets? When I let them go, they will chase you down, sink their teeth into you, and kill you with their lightning. It is only fitting that you should die—being together as you are. I am sure that you are up to no good. When you are dead, I will strip you of your valuables and clothes. I will sell your things for a tidy sum; that will be my reward for executing two troublemakers. I suggest that you do not run. It will make things easier for me and for you; it will be over quickly."

As the man stooped down to release the electric creatures, Carter yelled out, "Wait a minute. We have a pass from the gate-keeper allowing us to travel together and leave the city."

This caused the man to hesitate, chuckle, and then say, "That pass is worth more than the total of your possessions." With a smile of self-satisfaction, he said aloud to himself, "This is a good night's work. Yes indeed, a very good night's work."

The time it took for the thief to make his last gloating comments gave Carter enough time to reach into his pocket for his flashlight. He figured that if the light worked to stun the moon hound that it might stun these yellow-eyed creatures as well. However, he did not have a chance to try it. Just then, Houtdec came running out of the shadows and slammed, full force, into the man's back, knocking him to the ground. The man fell on top of the lightning creatures. Though the man's weight crushed the creatures to death, before they died, they used their last "spark" of life to sink their teeth into him and kill him. It was not, as he had promised, a quick, easy death. The man screamed and shook violently for what seemed an eternity before he fell silent.

Long before his screams died out, the three friends had moved on quickly to avoid being caught up in any trouble that the death scene might attract. When they were far enough away, Houtdec explained, "Anyone within earshot of that fellow's screams will hide in fear for some time. You are safe to travel now; we are not far from the Deserted Land. That is a large area between the eastern gate and the populated area of the city. People call it the Deserted Land because nothing will grow on it, and anyone who tries to live on it, or who stays on it for even a few days, ends up getting sick and dying. It is safe to travel through, but I would not recommend spending even one night on it."

Their new friend put his hand on Carter's shoulder, squeezed it affectionately, and said, "This is where I leave you. I wish you good luck in your efforts to rescue the orphans."

"Thank you, Houtdec, for saving our lives back there. I guess that makes us even," Carter said as he reached out to shake the man's hand.

Houtdec took the boy's hand and held it firmly as he looked him in the eyes. "Even...no...what you have given me is far more precious than saving my life. You helped me find myself again. For that, I will forever be in your debt."

He let go of Carter's hand, and turning to Kat, he said, "I am in your debt as well, young lady. Watching you, I learned a valuable lesson about the power of generosity, forgiveness, and kindness. For the first time in many years, I am looking forward to tomorrow. You two have given me weapons I can use to fight the dark brokenness of my people. I want to do for them what you have done for me. I am not sure yet how to apply them, but I am eager to try."

"We wish you well in your efforts to save your people," Kat said.

"I will never forget you, and I thank you for all your help," Carter added.

When the partners found themselves alone again, Carter asked, "What did you give the gatekeeper? You didn't have anything except the... Oh, don't tell me. It was Dark Beard's knife, wasn't it?"

Kat smiled, shrugged, and said, "Like you said, it was the only thing I had. Guard came to me and suggested I give it to the gatekeeper. I figured that perhaps it was the main purpose of the knife. It paid off; we got a pass and information on how we might cross the lake to the island."

Carter nodded and said, "Yeah, I guess you're right. We got what we needed from it, and since Guard suggested you give it to him, that means we probably don't need it anymore. But it sure was an awesome knife."

As the two continued toward the eastern gate, they filled each other in on what had happened to them during their separation. Talking and catching up made the time pass quickly, and before they knew it, they found themselves standing before huge wooden doors. To the right of the gate, there was a wooden guard shack.

"Should we knock and wake the guard or wait until morning?" Kat whispered.

"Let's wait until morning. I think it is safer to spend the night here rather than trying to find a place to camp out there." Carter nodded toward the gate.

The partners laid out their bedrolls across the road from the guard shack. Carter lit a candle and put it between them as he did their first night in the Valley of Shadows. They slept well, as it was very quiet. There were no insects or other wildlife this close to the Deserted Land.

When the children woke, they agreed that it felt like it was rather late in the day. "Why didn't the guard wake us? Would he still be asleep?" Kat wondered aloud.

"I guess so," said Carter. "It looks like we might have to wake him after all. How about we have a bite to eat, pack our stuff, and see if he comes out on his own."

Kat agreed with the plan, and it only took them about twenty minutes to eat and pack. When the guard still had not shown himself, Carter called out, "Hello in there. We have a pass to leave the city, and we need someone to open the gate." When there was no response, Carter knocked on the door. Again, there was no response. "I'm going to open the door and enter. Is that all right?" Carter called through the door, but there was still no response.

Kat stood behind Carter as he opened the door.

Inside the cabin, they saw a wood burning stove and a cot with someone under a dark green blanket. The partners stepped into the plain wooden shack, and Carter said, "Excuse us, we are sorry to wake you, but we have a pass to leave the city." When there was still no response, Carter stepped up to the cot and put out his hand to shake the person awake. When he touched the blanket, a skeleton hand slipped out and fell to the floor. Startled, Carter jumped back. Kat let out with a small scream and then put her hand over her mouth. Carter screwed up his nerve and pulled the blanket all the way back revealing the skeletal remains of the gate guard.

"What do you think happened to him?" asked Kat.

"Look around. Do you see any evidence of food or supplies here? I suspect that this guy died from neglect and has been dead for at least a couple of years. He took his post here, and then he was forgotten. No one came to supply him, check on him, or relieve him. Nobody in Omagora takes responsibility for anything. I'm sure everybody assumes that somebody else is taking care of things, and as a result, nobody is taking care of things. This poor guy stuck by his post waiting for relief that never came, and he just sickened and died. At least that's the way it looks to me."

"That makes sense. So, how are going to get out of here? Do you think we can open the gate? And if we do open the gate, is there a way to secure it again so that something or someone dangerous doesn't enter the city? I would feel awful if we were responsible for letting something or someone in that ended up causing the city more problems than it already has," Kat said.

"I don't know. The only way we would be able to keep the gate closed is if we climb over the wall. Let's leave this poor guy to his rest and see if we can find a way out of here." Carter led the way out of the shack and gently, almost reverently, closed the door. Turning to Kat, he said, "We still have the rope. If we can climb to the top of the wall and then tie the rope off, we can let ourselves down on the other side. Then, we could throw the rope up and over so it hangs down on the inside."

"That sounds like a good plan, but how are we going to climb the wall? The wall is smooth, and the gate doesn't appear to have any hand holds."

Carter scratched his head thoughtfully as he pondered the situation. "Hmm, I guess we either try to open the gate and just leave it open, or we use the wood from the shack to make a ladder. I noticed that the floor is made of wood, so if we just use the floorboards, the shack will still protect the remains of the guard. The problem is that we don't have any tools. We need something to pry up the floor, and then we can use the rope to lash the rungs to the ladder."

Searching the area for something that might help them with their project was discouraging. "There just isn't anything out here. There're no trees or dead branches to use to make poles. Even the rocks are too little to use as a hammer to break up the lumber." Carter looked at Kat, and he could tell that she knew what he was thinking.

"We really could have used Dark Beard's knife right about now," Kat said with a touch of guilt.

Carter tried to make her feel better by saying, "No, don't say that. You got the pass with it."

"Come on, Carter. We didn't need the pass. There is no one to stop us from leaving the city. There never was. And now we can't even cut the rope to make the ladder."

"Wrong. We will use a candle to burn the rope instead of cut it."

"What about the floorboards? How are we going to pry them up? How are we going to cut them to size even if we do pry them up?" Kat asked with some emotion.

"Those are good questions. Let me think about it for a bit. Carter folded his hands in front of his face and then moved them to the back of his head. Resting his head in his hands, he looked up at the sky as if he was seeking solutions to their problems in the ever-present dark clouds of the Valley of Shadows. After a moment, he said, "There's a wood burning stove in the shack. There might be a metal poker or something that was used to shove the coals around." Carter went back inside to have a look. Lying on the floor behind the stove, he found an iron rod. "Ah-ha, now we're getting some-where," he said triumphantly as he brandished the rod. "We can use this like a crowbar and pry up the floorboards."

"That was pretty good thinking—for a boy," Kat was feeling encouraged by the find and could not help teasing her friend. It had been so long since they just kidded around with each other that it felt good to have a little moment of normalcy back in their relationship. "Now, I have an idea I want to check out," she said as she approached the cot and knelt down.

"What are you doing, you crazy female?" Carter asked half joking, half concerned.

The blanket that covered the remains of the gate guard went all the way to the floor. Kat lifted the blanket, looked under the cot, and said, "I was thinking that guards are armed, so maybe he has a sword or knife under his bed. It's too dark. I can't see anything. Will you hand me a flashlight, please?"

Carter fished his flashlight out of his pocket and handed it down to the girl.

"Nothing but dust," she reported. "How about under his pillow?" she asked as she stood up. The children ended up searching the entire cot and the surrounding area until they finally discovered what they were looking for. Under the thin mattress, they found a two-edged short sword. One edge was serrated, and both edges were very sharp.

"We can cut rope, chop and saw wood with this thing," Carter said with glee. Then he added, "Not bad thinking for a girl."

"Nope, not bad at all," she agreed.

All of a sudden, Carter and Kat found themselves standing on the other side of the locked eastern gate. Their supplies and equipment, still packed up, were lying on the ground next to them.

VERY TEMPTING

"Amazing!" the Adversary exclaimed. He was standing on the path blocking the partner's way. "I must say that I am impressed. I never thought you would make it as far as Omagora let alone make it successfully through the city, and yet, here you are. I could see that you were going to spend the whole day working on a ladder of some sort to scale the wall, so I decided to help you speed things up and just bring you over. It would have been such a waste of energy. If you think that something as simple as this gate could keep me out, then you really are naïve."

"We don't need nor want your help," Carter snarled. "Let us pass!"

"Not so fast. Do not be so eager to die," the Adversary said in a less-than-friendly tone. "I want you to know just what you are risking if you make the wrong decision and what you have to gain if you make the right one. I suspect that the Guardian may have tempted you into taking this journey by suggesting that you might find treasure. Behold," he said with a wave of his hand. Instantly, a monstrous pile of shiny gold coins, that reached as high as the city wall, appeared next to the Adversary.

The partners' mouths dropped open in awe at the sight. There was more wealth piled in front of them than any two families would ever be able to spend in several lifetimes. The children walked over to the edge of the pile, grabbed handfuls of gold, and let the shiny yellow metal slip through their fingers. Feelings of sheer greed filled them, and it was exhilarating.

"It is yours," the Adversary said. "There is more wealth there than you will ever need to fulfill every dream you have for yourselves and for your families. With this treasure, you can do anything, buy anything, or help anyone you want. With it comes power, security, excitement, and adventure."

"But we can't carry all this gold. Even if we could, how would we explain it? Nobody is going to let a couple of kids keep this. People will take it, steal it, and others will make sure that we won't be able to do what we want with it," Carter said, struggling with his desire.

"Not a problem, my boy, not a problem. I will transfer all this gold to the Dead Forest. Since you two are the only ones who can find it, see it, and enter it, the gold will be safe. You are the only ones who will have access to it."

"All this, mine," Carter whispered to himself.

Kat heard Carter's statement, and she noticed that he said *mine* not *ours*. "Wait a minute, Carter; something's not right here."

"I can do anything I want with this gold—*anything!*" Carter said as though no one else existed.

"Tobias Carter!" Kat shouted. "What has come over you? This is not right, and you know it." Kat picked up a single gold coin and looked closely at it. "Where did this gold come from?" she demanded from the Adversary, but before he could answer, she continued. "This gold belongs to Omagora, doesn't it?"

"What difference does it make? It is yours if you want it. Just say the word, and I will move the gold to the Dead Forest and return you to your homes right now."

Carter shook his head as if he were coming out of a trance and then looked closely at one of the gold coins. "These coins have a king's likeness on one side, and on the other they are engraved: Omagora. This is the missing wealth of Omagora that you and your enforcers stole."

The Adversary shrugged and said, "So what if it is. It is mine now, and I will give it to whomever I wish. Like I said, if you want it, I will give it to you and return you to your homes. On the other hand, if you insist on trying to rescue the orphans, let me assure you, rescue is quite impossible. You will die long before you reach them. Why throw your lives away when I am offering you the wealth of a kingdom and a wonderful life? Anyone would be thrilled to accept such an offer. Most people would be screaming and crying with joy to have so much. What is wrong with you that you cannot see that this is the only reasonable thing to do?"

"Screaming and crying," Carter said as if he were trying to recall something. "I remember, before we ever entered this valley, we came across a man who was screaming and crying. Do you remember, Kat? It was on the eastern path, and he was screaming and crying because he could not take his wealth with him through a narrow passage. Rather than leave the wealth behind so that he could continue his journey, he stayed with it and missed his intended final destination."

"I remember," said Kat. "And if we let this wealth keep us from our intended final destination, we will be as devastated and miserable as he was."

The Adversary was beginning to lose his composure. He said, "You do not know what devastation and misery awaits you if you do not start being reasonable. This insane single-mindedness of yours is simply not normal; it is suicidal."

"Let me explain it to you," said Carter. "First, the gold is stolen, and we do not take what does not belong to us. Second, we are committed to seeing our responsibilities through to the end. Third, if there really were no chance that we could succeed, you would not be trying so hard to buy us off. Fourth, you are wasting our time, and we want to be on our way, so if you will excuse us ..."

The Adversary regained his composure and said, "Since you seem determined to commit suicide, I have decided that I would like to give you a fighting chance. I will answer, truthfully, one question you ask of me. You can ask something that might make it easier for you to locate the children, set the children free, or maybe you might want to ask how to get to the island. All I want in return is that you give me one of your flashlights."

"No, Carter, don't fall for it; it's a trick."

"I'm sure it's a trick, but it may be worth it. If we ask the right question, we might be able to get a key piece of information that will make this rescue possible. We have got to be careful and think about what we want to ask."

"We only have two flashlights, what if we get separated? They not only help us find our way around, they're also weapons," Kat pointed out.

"That's true, but what good does it do us to find our way around if we don't know where to look? I say we give him a flashlight and then ask him where in the stronghold he is holding the children. We will stay together and just use one flashlight."

Kat turned her head so the Adversary could not read her lips and whispered to her partner, "Since he didn't ask for the batteries, let's remove them from the flashlight we give him—it'll be useless."

Carter smiled and whispered, "Good thinking." The boy reached into the backpack, took the batteries out of a flashlight, and then handed it over to the Adversary. "You got yourself a deal; here's a flashlight."

The Adversary took the flashlight from the boy and said, "You really are a couple of foolish children."

Taken aback, Carter asked, "What do you mean?"

The Adversary laughed and said, "What do I mean? Not a very good question to ask, but since I promised you an honest answer, here it is. You are foolish because you just wasted your question and lost a flashlight." He crushed the flashlight in his hand and let the pieces drop to the ground. "You are foolish because you do not see that if you are so easily outsmarted, that there is no way you will prevail against the powers that reside in the fortress, let alone cross the dark waters which are filled with their own horrors."

"I'm so stupid! I can't believe I fell for that," Carter moaned.

"It's okay, Carter; he tricked you. Let's get out of here before we do something else stupid. No offense," she added.

"No, you're right, Kat. I was stupid and overconfident. Let's get out of here."

The partners walked away from the Adversary and headed for the lake. The Adversary called after them, "What is wrong with you? No matter how I try to save your lives, you stubbornly insist on death. You do not have a chance. This is my final offer. It is not too late; you can be home in a snap of my fingers and possess the wealth of a kingdom. Do not throw your lives away!"

It took the partners a good portion of their day to struggle over and around black obsidian rock formations that erupted from the ground. Some were sharp like knives while others were odd shaped lumps covered with sharp points and edges. It was unavoidable to pass through the obsidian garden without suffering torn clothes and cut skin. By the time the partners reached the lake, they looked quite ragged and bloodied. Luckily, their wounds were not serious. As miserable as they felt, when they reached the lake they forgot all about their wounds. The sight of the strange body of water was quite unsettling. It was as black as tar and as still and smooth as glass.

"I've never seen a body of water like this before. There is not a single ripple on the surface," Carter observed. The boy looked up at the sky and said, "Let's make camp, and tomorrow we'll try to figure out how to cross over to the island."

"I hope we'll be able to see the island in the morning. All I see now is black water."

The next morning, the children woke early. They ate and broke camp. "That's the last of our food. We still have one bottle of water left. I hope we will be able to locate and rescue the orphans before our strength gives out," said Kat.

Carter stepped a few feet toward the lake. He stood on his tiptoes, and even though there was no sun in the sky, he shielded his eyes with his right hand as he took in their surroundings. The place was desolate. There were no plants, no sounds of wildlife, and nothing to see but black sand and black water.

Kat, looking out over the lake, said, "I think I can see the island. It's hard to make out because the island is black like the water. It's sort of like a black shadow on the water's surface. Do you see it?"

Carter moved beside his friend and said, "Yes, I think that's it. It looks like there's a large building in the middle of it. Do you see that? It's not quite as dark as the island."

"I think so. How far away do you think the island is?"

"I'm guessing it's about a mile off shore, but it could be much farther. Depending on how large it is, it could be several miles away," Carter said with a shrug.

"How are we going to get there? I don't see any evidence of a rock bridge, and there is nothing around here we can use to build a raft."

"We can start by walking along the shore, and maybe we'll see some evidence of the bridge. If the rocks are black, like everything else around here, we will have to look very carefully to see them below the surface of the water."

"Let's use the flashlight. Maybe the light will penetrate the water enough for us to see the remains of the bridge."

"Okay, we'll try that. A good place to start would be straight ahead in the direction of this path." Carter walked to the water's edge and shined their remaining light into the water. "The water is clear as glass. The dark sand and sky makes the water look black. I don't see anything nearby. I'll wade out a little and see if I spot something."

"Be careful, Carter. I don't like the looks of this lake. It gives me the creeps."

Carter took off his shoes and socks, rolled up his pant legs, laid the pack down, and said jovially, "Everything in this valley gives me the creeps." Then in a more serious tone, he added, "But I have to admit, this lake is super creepy. Well, here goes nothing," he said, stepping into the water. "That's odd. I thought the water would be cold, but it's body temperature." He walked out about fifteen feet and the water was just above his ankles.

"There aren't any rocks here. Maybe farther out when it gets deeper I'll see the remains of the bridge." Carter waded out another thirty feet. Yet, no matter how far he walked, the lake remained the same depth. When the boy reached fifty feet out, he called to Kat, "I don't know how far we'll have to go before it gets deeper, but it's possible that the water is the same depth all they way across. I'm coming back to get you; let's see if we can just walk to the island."

"No, you stay there," Kat called back to Carter. "I'll come out to meet you." She took off her shoes, socks, and rolled up her pant legs. "I'm going to consolidate our supplies into one backpack." She put her and Carter's footwear in the pack and then hoisted it in place. She waded out to her partner and handed him the backpack. Then together they continued toward the island.

After walking another hundred feet or so, Kat said, "I have a funny feeling about this. Nothing about this lake is anything like I was told. There doesn't seem to be a need for a bridge, and it doesn't look like it's filled with monsters. Maybe we're the only living things in the lake. Is it possible that a lake this large is only one foot deep at its deepest point?"

"I don't see why not, and if it is this shallow all the way across, any monsters lurking under the surface can't be very large. Of course, when it comes to monsters, they really don't have to be big to be deadly."

"That's a cheery thought," Kat said with a shudder.

"Well, here's another cheery thought: the water's getting deeper. At first, it was just above my ankles, and now it's halfway to my knees. Granted, that isn't much considering how far we've come. All the same, if it continues at this rate to get deeper, we may be in trouble before we get to the island. That's not to mention that the cuts and scrapes we got yesterday, in the obsidian garden, are seeping blood into the water. If there is anything in this water to fear, I think it will have no trouble finding us."

By the time the children had traveled another quarter-mile, the water line was at Carter's knees. It was hard to walk in the deeper water, and the children's legs were getting tired. The water was shallow enough that they could sit down and their heads would still be above water. However, their gear would get wet.

"Let's rest our legs," Carter said looking around cautiously. "I don't want to stay in one place too long though. I have a funny feeling something is about to happen."

Kat nodded and said, "Yeah—I think you may be right—I feel it too."

Rested, the two continued. By this time, they were able to make out some details of the stronghold. It was large and ominous. It had several watchtowers and a high wall surrounded the entire compound.

When the partners came within one-third mile of the island, the water level had risen to their waists. Suddenly, Kat yelped and blurted out, "Something brushed against my leg!"

"Are you sure?"

"It did it again! There's something in the water!"

Carter was a couple of steps ahead of Kat. He reached back and said, "Take my hand, and we will make a run for the island."

Taking her partner's hand, she yelled, "Run? Are you kidding?"

"We'll do the best we can; run!"

Since the water was waist deep, they were not able to move much faster than before. What did happen because of their "rush" to the island was that they stepped off an underwater drop-off. As a result, they found themselves paddling desperately to keep their heads above water. Their forward momentum, along with their paddling motions, carried them away from the shallow water.

"Carter! I only know how to dogpaddle," Kat cried out in terror.

Carter was struggling to keep from being pulled under by the backpack, and trying desperately to hold onto their flashlight. "I'm coming, Kat!" he called. Carter decided to lose the backpack. He stuck the flashlight in his pocket, wiggled out of the pack, and let it sink. After freeing himself, he tried to locate his partner. To his horror, Kat was nowhere to be seen.

MONSTER IN THE DEEP

Carter whipped his head around in every direction trying to get a fix on his friend. He shouted hysterically, "Kat! Kat! Where are you?" Realizing she was under water, he pulled the flashlight out of his pocket (Thankfully, the light was waterproof.) and went below the surface to look for her.

It did not take long to locate Kat, but what Carter saw terrified him far more than what he expected to see. He expected to see Kat struggling to reach the surface. Yet, what he did see was his friend struggling to free herself from the long tongue of a monstrous fish-like creature. What he saw was so horrible that he thought he was having a nightmare. But it was no dream. The fish was real, and it had a massive mouth, rows of sharp teeth, and huge, bulbous eyes on either side of its head. Its body was massive and was so long that Carter could not see the end of it. Anywhere you might expect to see a fin, there was a large, webbed hand at the end of what looked like stubby, thick arms.

Carter realized that Kat was screaming as she struggled because there was a long stream of bubbles rushing out of her open mouth.

Her eyes were wide with terror. Soon she would inhale a lung of water, stop struggling, and the creature would have its meal.

Even though the boy knew that the situation was hopeless, he swam to his friend's rescue. As predicted, Kat became motionless; the creature drew her into its mouth and then turned its attention on the two-legged creature with a glowing eye, Carter. Tobias was so distraught at seeing his best friend eaten by the monster that he no longer cared what happened to him. All he wanted to do was try to hurt the thing that took Kat from him.

He swam straight for one of the creature's huge eyes, intending to smash it with the flashlight. Unfortunately, before he got more than a few feet from his target, the thing's tongue whipped out and wrapped itself around Carter. Quick as a flash, it drew him into its mouth and swallowed him whole. The thought that went through the boy's mind as he was drawn past rows of sharp teeth was, *I hope my mom doesn't miss me too much.*

Carter held his breath as long as he could while he was forced deep into the creature's digestive system. He knew that he would have to breathe soon, and then he would drown like his friend. At this point, he really did not care. He figured that drowning would be quicker and less painful than being slowly digested. When he finally reached his limit, and was no longer able to hold his breath, he exhaled. At that very moment, he fell into a chamber or cavity of some sort that was about the size of Stewborn's car. It was full of air and had about six inches of water on a slippery rubbery surface. The stench was overwhelming, and when the boy took a deep breath, he gagged almost to the point of vomiting. The smell of digesting creatures that littered the "floor" of the chamber was similar to the smell of four-day-old rotting meat that had been sitting in the hot sun.

It did not take Carter long to realize that Kat was only a few feet beyond him. He rushed to her body and turned her over so her face was out of the watery muck. He grabbed her by the shoulders, pulled her to a sitting position, and began shaking her violently. When the girl remained unresponsive, Carter reached around and began to beat on her back, and then he shook her again. When he screamed into her face, "Kat! Wake up." She opened her eyes, opened her mouth, and vomited a stomach full of water right in Carter's face. Then she began to cough and choke violently, expelling more water.

The combination of being vomited on, along with the ghastly stench of the creature's insides, caused Carter to empty his stomach too.

To make things worse, while the children were trying to get control of their nausea, the monster began to swim. Since its swimming motions required it to move its entire body from side to side and up and down, the children, along with other half-dead creatures, were tossed around uncontrollably. There was nothing to hold onto, and the motions were so violent that they slammed the children into the chamber walls and into each other.

Carter held onto the flashlight as long as he could, but eventually he lost his grip on it. After what seemed like an eternity, the monster stopped. The chamber was dark now because the flashlight was lost and covered with semi-liquid digested matter. Carter crawled around on his knees, running his hands through the muck hoping to catch a glimpse of the light. As he searched, he realized that he did not hear his friend. "Kat, are you okay; where are you?"

When there was no response, Carter quickened his search for the light as he continued to call out to his friend. Finally, he found it, but something was wrong. Up to now, the light was very bright; now it was dim. It was much too dim to be a weapon against creatures sensitive to bright light, yet it was bright enough for Carter to make out his surroundings. He tried shaking it and gave it a whack, and that caused the light to go out. He shook it again, and even though it came back on, the light was still dim and had a tendency to flicker. He stopped playing with it for fear that it might stop working altogether.

He focused on finding Kat and found her at the farthest end of the chamber. She was unconscious again. Her breathing was very shallow, and Carter feared that she would not be able to survive another beating like the one they just took. He did not know what to do. There was no way out of the stomach of a monster, and there was no way to keep a monster from moving whenever it wanted. *Is this it*, he wondered. *Is this the end?*

"Carter?" Kat said weakly. "I'm sorry."

Carter looked down at his best friend and said gently, "Sorry for what, Hamsted?"

"I'm sorry I gave Dark Beard's knife away. If we still had it, maybe we could cut our way out of here or something. But now, I guess we're at our final destination."

"You did the right thing, Kat. You used the knife wisely while I threw away one of our flashlights. Even if we did have the knife, it wouldn't do us any good in here."

"We could have at least given it a stomach ache," Kat said weakly and closed her eyes. "I'm so tired."

"Kat," Carter said firmly. "I don't want you to give up. I need you. I can't rescue the orphans alone."

"Haven't you heard, Carter? We aren't going to rescue the orphans. A lake monster has eaten us. Have you ever heard of any-one who survived being eaten before?"

"Actually, I have."

This caused Kat to open her eyes again. "You really have heard a true story about someone who survived being eaten?"

"I'm a little fuzzy on the details, but I seem to remember hear-ing something about a guy on a boat who went overboard during a storm. Maybe it was a whale watching cruse or something because he got swallowed by a whale and three days later he was found alive on a beach."

Kat smiled feebly and said, "Carter, I can't make it three days. I'm not sure I can make it another three hours."

"Sure you can, Hamsted. You are as tough as any guy I have ever known; you can do it. Maybe this thing is asleep and it'll be still for a while. Try to get some rest, and I'll go to work finding a way out of here. Everything's going to be okay; I promise."

Kat said softly, "Sure it will, Carter." She closed her eyes and fell asleep.

"You sleep, my friend," Carter whispered. He knew there was no possible way out of their situation. He decided to use what was left of the dying flashlight to watch over Kat as she slept. Sitting beside her, knowing that she might never wake again, knowing, too, that he was living his last moments, he took her hand in his and wished he had done it before she fell asleep.

As Carter sat in the slimy muck and breathed the putrid stench-filled air, he thought he heard the rushing of water coming toward him from the direction of the mouth. Turning his head quickly toward the sound, he saw a wall of water rushing at him and Kat. He had no time to respond. The water picked up the partners and carried them down the length of the long, rubbery, slimy tube of the monster's insides. After what seemed like a wild water ride at some perverse theme park, the children were emptied out of the wet darkness onto the floor of a large indoor docking area.

They were no longer in the monster, and they were no longer in water. They were on a stone floor that was two feet above the water level. To their left was a large stone wall lined with burning torches. Straight ahead, about twenty feet away, was a set of stairs leading to an upper level. Behind them and to their right was the black water of the lake. Carter correctly assumed that an opening along the cliffs of the island gave access to the docking area.

Carter quickly located his partner, who was laying face down on the stone floor some fifteen feet beyond him. He gently rolled her over and checked her breathing. To his relief she was still alive. He gently rubbed her forehead and smoothed back her hair, and eventually she opened her eyes and asked, "Did you find us a way out, Carter?"

"No, but we're out of the monster. We're inside an underground docking area. I suppose it's an entrance to the Adversary's fortress."

"Indeed it is, Carter," said a familiar voice.

PREPARING FOR BATTLE

Seeing the broad grin and look of relief on the boy's face, the Guardian said, "I'm glad to see you as well." His eyes shifted to the girl. "It looks like our poor Kat has been injured from all her adventuring."

"Can you help her?" Carter pleaded. "I'm afraid she is badly hurt, and she took in quite a bit of the lake water when we were swallowed by the monster."

The Guardian knelt down next to the girl. He put his hand on her forehead and said, "I am proud of you, my brave girl." Looking back at Carter, he said, "I am proud of you both. You have come so far. No matter what you encounter, you persevere. That is a rare thing in two so young."

The Guardian turned to Kat, with his left hand on her forehead and his right hand on her shoulder, and closed his eyes. After a moment, Carter heard Kat take in a deep breath, and then she smiled. Guard let go of her and asked, "Feeling better?"

Kat sat up and answered, "I feel much better, thank you. My mom would say you should bottle that, and you would make a fortune."

Guard smiled and said, "Seeing you feel better is all the reward I need. Speaking of feeling better, I have brought you a little surprise.

Look there." Guard pointed to a large raft supporting a lunch counter. The raft was tied to the mooring posts of the dock, which, until now, had been empty. Menus, stools, and a variety of glass-covered shelves displayed pies, cakes, doughnuts, pastries, and much more. "Come and order anything you want. Since you are on the last leg of your adventure, you will need all your strength and wits about you."

The Guardian stepped up onto the raft and took his place behind the counter. The partners did not notice when the old man's white robe changed to a short-order cook's white uniform, apron, and hat, but by now the children were used to strange happenings when Guard was around.

The children stood looking eagerly at the welcome sight. It is true that they wanted to jump aboard and enjoy the meal that they knew would be delicious, but they hesitated. Kat spoke up and said, "Guard, we're filthy. We stink of rotting fish and vomit. Surprisingly, I'm hungry, but I don't think I can eat unless we can clean up."

"Oh, is that all? For the sake of time, let me help you with that." Guard snapped his fingers, and the children, as well as their clothes, were as clean and in the same condition as the day they entered the Dead Forest. Even their shoes and socks, that were lost when Carter cast off the pack, were back on their feet. As a bonus, all their cuts, scratches, and bruises were healed as well.

"You can either look at the menu for suggestions, or you can just tell me what you feel like eating. I know you are hungry for some good food after living off skimpy survival supplies."

"Wow!" Carter beamed as he took his place at the counter. "I never thought being clean and wearing clean clothes could feel so good. This is the best I've felt since I entered this valley."

"I agree," said Kat, joining her partner. "I'll go first because I'm hungrier than Carter. I want a cheeseburger with mustard, ketchup, and mushrooms. I'll have fries and a double chocolate, chocolate malt," Kat ordered. As soon as her napkin was unfolded and placed in her lap, Guard had her food set in front of her. When she saw her order already prepared and ready to eat, she joked, "I'll have to recommend this place to my friends. The service is fast and friendly, and the food looks great."

Carter was so relieved to have his friend back to her old self—after thinking she was going to die—that he couldn't help but wear a big grin on his face. "Let me try one of those fries," he said as he helped himself to Kat's food. Instead of taking just one, he took several and smeared them in the ketchup that she had squeezed on the side of her plate.

"Hey, watch it, Toby. Order your own food, and keep your hands off mine," Kat said with mock anger.

"Okay, let me see. I think I'll have … doughnuts! That's what I want: maple bars, cinnamon buns, and lots of different kinds of doughnuts."

"Good idea, Carter. I want some of those too when I'm finished with my burger."

Guard said, "You can have anything you want to eat, although you do need to be at your best for what lies ahead."

Carter thought about it for a moment, and then he said, "Maybe I should start with a bowl of chili covered with cheddar cheese. I want crackers and a big, cold glass of milk."

Guard smiled approvingly as he served the boy.

Carter said, "I can't believe that after being as sick and nauseated as I was a few moments ago, that I can even look at food. But I'm hungry enough to lick the bowl clean." After serving the children, the Guardian joined them as he ate a turkey and Swiss cheese on white bread.

As one might expect, the partners overdid it a bit. When they were finished stuffing themselves, they leaned back from the counter and rubbed their full bellies. "That was the best chili I've ever eaten, and the doughnuts were as fresh as if they had just been made. I don't think I've ever eaten that much food at one time," said Carter.

Kat had not eaten as much as her partner, but she was feeling the pressure too. "I couldn't eat another bite if you paid me," she moaned.

"Usually I do not encourage such excess," Guard said as he stood looking at the children from across the counter. "However, this will be your last meal before you return home."

"Are we really that close to finishing our adventure?" Kat asked with a bit of excitement in her voice.

"Why don't you tell them the truth, Guardian?" Carter and Kat heard the Adversary's voice directly behind them. Startled, they jumped off their seats and turned to face him. It was the first time that they had seen the Guardian and the Adversary in the same place at the same time, and it was rather exciting to see these two confront each other.

"I was wondering if you would pay us a visit while we picnicked on your dock," said Guard. "Would you like to join us for a bite to eat?"

The Adversary snorted contemptuously and said, "You are avoiding my challenge, Guardian, and I understand why. You do not want to admit your true purpose in egging on these two brave children."

"Then please enlighten them," the Guardian invited.

"You pretend to care about these innocents, and you act like you want to help them. Yet, what you really desire is for them to continue to struggle desperately against forces they have no chance of defeating. You relentlessly encourage them on toward certain defeat and death, all for your own amusement."

The Adversary looked at Carter and continued. "If this Guardian really cared for you, he would help you find your way home where you are safe and loved. I can do that for you. Just say the word, and I will have you back home in the blink of an eye. On the other hand, if you continue to follow this deceiver, who calls himself 'the Guardian,' you will encounter still more horrors that will ultimately end in your deaths, or worse."

After a dramatic pause, he looked at the Guardian and sneered. "How ironic that he who calls himself the Guardian has been suspiciously absent during every crisis you have encountered. Only after you have narrowly escaped with your lives does he show up. Where has he lived up to his name? How has he been your guardian? You are intelligent children. I cannot understand why you put your trust in someone whose only contribution to your situation has been to feed you your favorite foods, pat you on your heads, and send you on your way again to encounter still more hardship and suffering."

Carter hated to admit it, but the Adversary's points made a kind of sense; there was logic to his words. Nevertheless, the boy knew deep down in his heart that the Guardian really cared about him and Kat. The Adversary was the true deceiver.

"What do you think, Carter, Kat?" Guard asked. "He makes sense, does he not?"

"Yes, he makes sense," Carter agreed.

"Carter?" Kat seemed confused. "What are you saying?"

"The Adversary is making sense."

The Adversary smiled triumphantly as he responded. "Finally, you have seen reason. I knew you were an intelligent boy."

Carter addressed the Adversary, "Your words have truth in them, but what you're saying is not correct. The Guardian points us to the right path. He provides what we need to continue our journey. He watches over us to give us the support we need to stay on the right path, and he helps us make sense out of what we learn." Carter looked at Guard and saw him smiling with pride at the boy's wisdom.

"As for your phony concern," Kat added, "we know that you would not be so eager to have us quit our journey if we had no chance of success. It becomes more obvious all the time that you are worried that we will succeed. And speaking of being in crisis situations, you created and/or used many, if not all of them, to hurt us or lead us down the wrong path. How is that supposed to be helpful and caring?"

The Adversary knew that he had failed once again to deceive the children into abandoning their mission. He decided to drop the pretense as he said sarcastically, "That was just my gentle way of trying to convince you that you would be safer and happier if you turned back and went home. I thought that you would especially like my little surprise entrance to the fortress. There is nothing like being eaten by a monster to bring one face-to-face with his, or her, mortality. I knew you would eventually find a way to the island, so I just made it a bit more interesting for you. I see that I have failed to help you see reason. The one thing you do not seem to understand yet, is that I cannot and will not allow you to succeed. There is too much at stake! Therefore, I will leave you with these final thoughts: I welcome you as my guests. I am not a gracious host, and it will be my pleasure to heap as much misery as I can upon you as you journey through my fortress. No matter what you think about your chances of success, I promise you that you and the orphans will never see your homes again." With that said, the Adversary disappeared.

The partners turned to face the Guardian, and as they sat back down, Kat asked, "Is it true that we will fail to rescue the orphans and that we will never see our homes again?"

"What do you think?"

"Well, he keeps making threats against us, and yet, here we are. We're still making progress."

"Yes indeed; you are still making progress. What the Adversary is communicating is what he hopes will be, not necessarily what will be. The truth of the matter is that it is up to you. If you make good decisions, based on love and doing what is right, you will succeed. Even if you fail in the eyes of others, you still succeed."

"But what if we make the wrong decision?" asked Carter.

"Then make it right if you can, and if you cannot, then make the next decision the right one. Learn from your mistakes and from your successes. Let what you have learned be your guide, and follow the people rule.

"I am going to ask you a question, but before you answer I want you to think back and remember all you have learned from your travels and from the examples set for you by brave companions you have met along the way. What is the ultimate application of the people rule?"

The partners looked down into their laps as they thought back over their adventures. It was not hard to come up with the answer. When they looked up at the Guardian, he could see on their faces that they had the correct answer.

"Dark Beard showed us," Carter said.

"Jessie showed us too," added Kat.

Carter said it, "To give your life for another."

"Yes, Harfet was willing to sacrifice himself for the orphans."

"Houtdec and Taloff risked their lives for us too," Carter added.

The Guardian smiled and nodded. "It is the ultimate act of love.

It is so powerful that it can plant seeds of life in the heart of the one who experiences that love shown to him or her."

After a time of contemplating the implications of what had just been discussed, the Guardian said, "I found your flashlight. It needed a little repair and some new batteries, so I fixed it up for you. It should be good for several hours." Guard handed it to Carter.

"This is a safe area. Stay here until you feel ready to brave the fortress. Just remember, the longer you wait, the longer the orphans will suffer in their captivity."

"Then we must hurry," said Kat as she stood.

"Only if you are sure that you are ready. You need to take care of yourselves, first, so that you will be at your best to help others," the Guardian exhorted.

"I'm ready, Carter, what about you?"

The boy stood up and said, "Now is as good a time as any to brave the unknown."

The partners turned and stepped onto the dock. This time the two expected that when they turned back to look at Guard that he would be gone, and they were right. There was no sign of the raft or Guard.

"I have one more thing to say to you before I leave." The Guardian startled the children; they turned back to the docking area. Guard was back in his white robe.

"The orphans are scattered throughout the fortress. Your mission is to find them, bring them back together, and rescue them. If you succeed, I will meet you in the Dead Forest. Now, go with my blessing." The Guardian put a hand on each of the partner's heads, smiled encouragingly, and then vanished.

A FINE KETTLE OF FISH

The partners stood alone on the dock bathed in torch light. Carter said, "Well, Kat, we're about to begin a new adventure. I feel a little like I did on the day we left the Dead Forest, except now we have knowledge and experience that we didn't have before. Not only that, but we know exactly what our mission is."

"Are we just going to talk about it, or are we going to do it? Why are you stalling?" Kat asked caustically.

"Is something wrong? Why are you talking to me like that?"

Kat sighed and said, "I'm sorry, Carter. I think it's just fear and fatigue talking. We have been through a lot already, and we're about to step in it again. I just want to get on with it."

"You got it; let's just get on with it." The boy headed for the steps that took them to a heavy wooden door. It opened easily for its size, and they found themselves looking out over a large courtyard. What they saw in the courtyard was both terrifying and impressive. As far as their eyes could see, there were row upon row of soldiers standing at attention, holding thick, powerful staffs at their sides. They were dressed in black-studded leather armor. They wore black, flowing capes. Black leather straps covered their faces, and hoods covered their heads. "They are the Adversary's enforcers," Carter whispered to Kat. "There are thousands of them, but something's wrong. They're facing our direction, but I don't think they've taken notice of us. They're so still."

"Carter, I don't think they're breathing; maybe they're just statues."

"You stay here; I'll take a closer look." Carter took out his flashlight and carefully approached the nearest soldier. When he was standing directly in front of the man, Carter turned on the light and pointed it in the man's face. To the boy's surprise, the enforcer opened his eyes and shifted them straight at him. Carter took a step back.

In a weak, raspy voice, the enforcer said, "Keep the light on me. It will give me enough energy to speak to you."

Carter swallowed noisily and asked with a shaky voice, "Are you unable to move?"

"When Vardrayes no longer had need of us, he put us in a state of suspended animation. We are mentally aware. We feel things physically, and we can hear each other's thoughts. The physical and emotional pain of this living hell is slowly driving us mad."

Kat joined her partner and said, "I don't understand why this is happening to you. We thought that you were the enforcers who served Vardrayes. We heard that you were loyal to him and aided him in the destruction of Omagora."

"It is because we were his enforcers that we suffer this horror now. We should have known that if he would betray the king and the people of Omagora that he would not hesitate to betray us. We were fools, blinded by our own greed and lust for power. He used us to destroy our homeland and then take all the wealth of the city (which he promised would be ours), and then he imprisoned us here with nothing but our guilt and shame as our reward—for eternity. Now go, and warn whoever will listen: do not trust Vardrayes. Turn off the light. It burns me. I cannot bear the light any longer!" the enforcer screamed.

Carter quickly turned off the light, and immediately the soldier closed his eyes. "Oh, Carter," Kat pleaded. "Isn't there anything we can do for them? They must be in such agony."

Carter shook his head sadly and said, "I don't think there is anything we can do. It's their final destination. Come on; let's check out that large building over there to the left. I see a door."

The partners walked up to the door of a large stone building. The entire fortress was made of stone. They heard children's voices inside. It sounded like a party, and at the same time, it sounded like a riot.

Carter knocked on the door. When there was no answer, he tried the handle. It opened to a large hall filled with children of all ages. Colorful balloons, streamers, and a large banner that read "Welcome Partners" decorated the place.

"There are our guests of honor," said a clown as he made his way through the children to greet the partners. The children fell silent and watched to see what would become of the newcomers.

"Welcome! Come in and join the fun." The clown grabbed the partners by the front of their shirts and pulled them into the room. The door slammed shut behind them.

The clown was wearing a puffy, white costume covered with large, colorful polka dots. He wore a whiteface and had a bald head except for a five-inch long spike of red hair sticking straight up out of the middle of his head. He had a large, red-painted mouth and a red ball nose. Everything about the clown looked like a fun-loving birthday party clown—except for the eyes. The eyes peeked out from under a heavy brow, painted black. They were cruel, piercing eyes filled with murder. When the clown released Carter and Kat, the partners turned and tried to escape, but the door was locked.

"You do not want to leave so soon. We are having fun. Right, children?"

The children looked frightened as some nodded and others said, "Yes," timidly.

The clown raised his voice and used a threatening tone as he repeated, "I said, we are having fun, is that not right, children?"

This time the children yelled a forced, "Yes."

Turning back to the partners, the clown said, "You are just in time to participate in our dunking game." He smiled, grabbed his nose, and squeezed it twice. It made an annoying honking noise. He laughed hideously, and then he grabbed Carter's and Kat's hands with a vice grip and dragged them to the back of the room.

The partners found themselves standing in front of a carnival-dunking tank. It was the kind where a person sits on a plank above a glass tank of water. When a second person hits a small target on the side of the tank with a ball, it causes the plank to collapse and dunk the person sitting on it into the water below. Usually, the individual sitting above the water taunts the person who is throwing the ball. They might say things like, "You can't hit the broadside of a barn," or, "You throw like an old lady." When the annoying person is dunked, it causes lots of laughter.

"This is my favorite game, and the kids love it too. Right, kids?"

Again, the children, except for the partners, forced a weak, "Yes."

It was clear to Carter and Kat that the children were terrified, and when they got a good look at the dunking tank, the reason for their fear became obvious.

"What are those things swimming around in the tank?" asked Carter. "You can't be serious about dunking a kid in with those things."

"Well, I thought they would add a bit of color—if you know what I mean—and so far I have been right. Every time someone gets dunked, the water turns red." The evil clown honked his red nose twice and laughed his hideous laugh. "Besides, it makes it so much more exciting for everyone when there is a little danger to the game. I put over a hundred flesh-eating sharpies in the tank. I think they are rather beautiful."

"They're ugly! They have no color. They have big eyes and big mouths full of sharp teeth. They are hideous, and so are you!" Kat snarled.

"Maybe you will feel differently, Kat, when you see them in action. Let us get on with the game. But first, I will repeat the rules for our guests of honor. I pick a person to sit in the dunking machine, and then I call on a volunteer to throw. The thrower gets three tries.

If the thrower fails to dunk the person, then the thrower takes the person's place in the tank. If the thrower hits the target, causing a successful dunk, the thrower is then exempt from any further play. So, dunk and you will not be dunked; fail to dunk and you may find yourself being lunch for the sharpies. Are we all clear on the rules of the game?" Before anyone could answer the clown said, "Good." Then he honked his nose twice and laughed.

"Alrighty then—enough talk—let us have some fun. The next person to sit in the tank is … Marista. Where are you, child? Come and sit on the plank." The children backed away from a girl with long, black hair and wearing a simple, white blanket similar to the type of dress found in Omagora. She stood alone now, with her hands over her face, crying and saying, "I do not want to play. I do not want to be eaten."

"Carter," Kat whispered, "that's one of the orphans—the ten-year-old."

"We need a volunteer to be the thrower," the evil clown called out excitedly.

"Me," Carter volunteered and raised his hand. "I want to be the thrower."

"Now that is what I like to see: eager cooperation. Carter, my boy, it is good to see you jump right into the game. I just know that you will do your best." To Marista, he said, "Come along now, girl. Do not make me come and drag you to the booth."

"Carter, what are you doing? If you knock her in the tank, she will die, and if you don't, you will be the next one to sit the plank!"

"Trust me," he said. Carter walked over to Marista, put his arm around her shoulders, gently guided her to the tank, and whispered in her ear, "Don't worry. I am here to rescue you and your sisters and brother. I promise that I will not dunk you."

The girl lowered her hands enough to look at Carter. The boy smiled at her, and she smiled back behind her hands where the clown could not see. When they arrived at the tank, Carter helped the frightened girl onto the plank.

BEYOND THE DEAD FOREST

"Way to go," the clown said as he slapped Carter on the shoulder. "I like your initiative. Everyone, I want you all to pay attention to this boy. He is smart, and I know that he will not disappoint us. You should all follow his example. Here you go," he said and handed Carter three baseballs. "Stand behind the red line and hit the target dead center." The clown stepped back, smiling and dry washing his hands as he said, "This is going to be great! Make sure you all stand where you can get a good view."

Kat was standing a little behind her partner to his left. She whispered to him, "I sure hope you know what you are doing."

Carter wound up and threw as hard as he could, missing the target by three feet over the top. Marista had her eyes closed and gasped when she heard the ball wiz by. She swallowed hard and put her hands over her face.

"Take your time, boy. You have two throws left. You got the power; now you just need to zero in on that target," the clown coached.

Again, Carter made a big show of winding up, and then he pitched the ball as hard as before, only this time the ball was three feet under the target.

"Careful now, boy; you only have one throw left. All you have to do is throw the ball between your last two throws. Come on now, you can do it. I would hate to see you up in the tank."

This time Carter looked at the clown and then at the ball in his hand. "Enough of this pretending," he said and tossed the ball up and over the tank. An unbelieving gasp came from the children. They had never seen anyone deliberately miss and willingly face the danger of the tank before.

"Ah shucks; I missed. I better take my place in the tank." Carter walked up to the dunking machine and assisted Marista down. When her feet were firmly back on the floor, she hugged Carter around the neck and said, as she cried, "Thank you, thank you. You saved my life. I do not understand why you did that, but thank you."

"I do not understand it either," the clown said angrily. "For your foolishness you will take the girl's place, and I am going to pick the thrower this time. The thrower will be Catherine Hamsted."

Carter protested, "I thought the thrower had to volunteer."

"Funny, but I could have sworn that I heard Kat volunteer," the clown said. Then he turned his evil eyes on Kat; his expression communicated, *You had better accept, or else*... "You did volunteer, did you not, Kat?"

"No," she said defiantly. She could hear Carter heave a sigh of relief as he settled himself on the dunking plank. She could also see that the clown was about to make her sorry for her defiance; however, before he could respond, she added, "But I was going to volunteer."

The clown laughed a hideous laugh and said, "I like you partners. It is going to be sad to see one of you die."

From the dunking tank, Carter called out, "What are you doing, Hamsted? You have to dunk me now, or you will be up here with someone throwing who will be trying to dunk you. You can't take any chances; you have to dunk me!"

Carter looked down to see if there was a way he could throw himself into the tank and sacrifice himself if he had to. But part of the mechanism included a trapdoor located under the plank that would open only when the ball hit the target. His next idea was to egg her on and make her mad enough that she would want to dunk him.

Kat received her three balls and took her place behind the red line.

Carter yelled, "Come on, Hamsted! You throw like a girl. You couldn't hit the broad side of a barn."

Kat smiled and said, "Hey, Toby, at least I can throw as well as you. Watch this." She threw the ball high over the dunking machine. "That looks about as good as the on-purpose misses you threw."

"Come on, Kat. Please don't do this. You have got to hit the target, and you will be out of the game and free to rescue the rest of the orphans."

Kat ignored her partner as she readied her second ball and said to the children standing around, "I am going to show you how to win this game." Again, she threw the ball way over the top of the tank. She took her third and last ball and said, "If we all agree to miss for each other, then we all win. The game is over, and no one will die in the tank." She wound up for her last throw and shouted, "If we miss, we win!" Then she threw her last ball over the tank.

Then, something wonderful happened, and all the children began to applaud, laugh, and even started to chant, "If we miss, we win. If we miss, we win."

As Carter climbed out of the tank, he could hear the clown shouting, "Wait a minute. Everybody quiet down. There is no rule that says you can win by everyone missing on purpose."

Carter walked up to the clown, and everyone quieted to see what the boy would say. "You're wrong. You failed to mention one very important rule: the people rule."

Suddenly, the clown's evil eyes flashed an angry yellow. "Do not mention that rule here!"

"Why not? Is it because you are afraid to let these others hear about it?"

The clown did not answer. Instead, he waved his hand across his face, as if he were erasing a blackboard, and everyone in the great hall vanished except for the clown, the partners, and Marista. "Very good...I must say that is very, very good. You have won this round, and for your prize, I will take you to one of the other orphans. I would like to see your people rule help you with that one," the clown said with a sneer. He lifted his right hand high in the air and then slowly lowered it. As it came down, so did the light, until there was nothing but darkness.

MIRROR ON THE WALL

The darkness lasted only a moment, and then they found themselves in a large children's bedroom. The room was filthy, full of cobwebs and dust. It had no doors or windows. A double-flame, gaslight chandelier hung in the middle of the ceiling, providing dim light.

Disturbing paintings of children at play covered the walls. One of the paintings depicted four children swimming in a pond. The youngest appeared to be drowning while the other three stood by pointing and laughing at the dying child. In another, three children were in a bedroom. One little boy was in bed, sick. The other two children were jumping up and down on the bed causing the sick boy much distress. In yet another, a girl was sitting under a tree pulling the wings off butterflies and making a little pile of wings in front of her. These three "works of art" are the only ones that will be described to the reader. The other more gruesome and troubling renderings will not be discussed.

The bedroom contained a large bed that consisted only of a frame and mattress. Next to the bed was a night table. Last, and most significant, a large full-length mirror hung on the wall across from the foot of the bed.

Looking around, Kat said, "Why have you brought us to this awful room? I thought you were taking us to one of the other orphans."

"And so I have. I have brought you to Leana. She is here."

The partners and Marista glanced around the room and under the bed. "She's not here," Kat insisted.

The clown laughed hideously and said, "You are looking in the wrong places. Look in the mirror."

The mirror reflected the room, the three children, and the clown. Carter said, "I see only our reflections."

Addressing the mirror, the clown said, "Leana, show yourself. I have brought your sister and some friends to visit you."

To the children's surprise, they saw a frightened little girl crawl out from under the bed. She favored Marista except she had short brown hair and sad eyes. She was dressed in a filthy, light blue robe, had dirt smudges on her face, and yellow teeth. The three children turned around expecting to see Leana in the room; she was not there.

"No, not back there," said the clown, jovially. "She is in the mirror. Some trick, do you not agree?" He honked his nose annoyingly.

"Leana," Marista sobbed as she reached out and touched the mirror. "Are you all right? Where are the others? You look awful." Turning to the clown she said, "Let her out; she is scared and hungry. She is only a little girl. How can you be so cruel?"

"Boo hoo—cry me a river. I told that little retch how to escape the mirror. It is up to her now," snarled the clown.

"Tell us," Carter demanded. "What does she have to do to get out?"

The evil, painted creature turned to the mirror and said, "You know what to do. Now, show them, or stay here forever."

Leana approached her side of the mirror, but she did not stand in front of her sister. Instead, she stood in front of Kat. "What is your name?" asked the frightened girl.

"My name is Catherine Hamsted, but you can call me Kat. This is my friend Carter," she said as she glanced at the boy. "We have come a long way to rescue you and your sisters and brother."

Leana put her hand up to the surface of the mirror and held it there. Then she said, "If you wish to help me escape, you must put your hand up to mine."

"Wait, Leana. Why will you not let me help you? I am your sister; that girl is a stranger. Let me put my hand to yours," Marista said as she moved in front of Kat.

Leana quickly pulled her hand away from the mirror and said, "No, it has to be one of the strangers."

Looking a little hurt, Marista stood aside and let Kat put her hand up to the smooth cold surface of the mirror.

Leana stepped up to the surface again. The effect of seeing Leana inside of Kat's reflection was very eerie. The trapped girl raised her hand slowly toward Kat's, and just before she touched the surface opposite Kat's hand, Leana said, "I am sorry." And then she made contact. As soon as their hands met, something unexpected happened. The two girls exchanged places. The switch was so fast that at first no one realized what had happened. Everyone was watching Leana inside of Kat's reflection so when the switch took place, the onlookers (except for the clown) did not realize that they were now looking at Kat inside of Leana's reflection. It was only when Leana turned to her sister and fell into her arms, sobbing, that they understood what had happened.

Carter shook his head to clear it of his disorientation. Then, realizing what had just happened, he yelled, "Kat!"

For a moment, Kat suffered her own feeling of disorientation. "What happened? I feel strange. I feel like I've been turned inside out."

"Kat, you're inside the mirror. When Leana put her hand up to yours, you switched places with her. She is out here with us, and now you're in the mirror!" Carter was getting angry, and he turned toward Leana and exclaimed, "What have you done? You knew what would happen if you touched hands on the mirror. You saved yourself, and let Kat take your place!"

Still clinging to her sister, the girl cried deep sobs of sorrow and guilt. "I am sorry. I was so lonely in there. There is nothing to do. You do not eat or drink; you just exist. And *they* come—dark creatures come up through the floor and out of the walls. They bring feelings of horror and deep sorrow. Then they pass over you, and you cannot breathe. I could not stand it any longer!" Leana let go of her sister, walked to the mirror, and stood in front of Kat. "I do not know which is worse, the guilt I feel or living with the horrors of the mirror."

Carter jumped in and said, "You should feel guilty for what you've done."

"Carter, don't be too hard on her. She is young, and I don't know that I might do the same thing if given the opportunity," said Kat sadly.

"Okay then," Carter said as he put his hand on the mirror in front of his partner. "Change places with me. I'll stay in the mirror; you save the orphans."

"Oh, that is so sweet. The brave young warrior is willing to sacrifice himself for his friend," said the clown. He pulled a large, green silk scarf out of his sleeve and pretended to wipe tears from his eyes. Then he held the scarf to his face and blew his nose loudly.

"Come on, Hamsted; put your hand up here, and switch with me," Carter ordered.

"No. I'm staying, and you are going to save the orphans. And to make sure that I never get to the point where I let temptation overcome me so that I take advantage of someone else, I'm going to apply the people rule." Kat turned around and looked at the night table next to the bed.

"Wait a minute, Kat. What are you doing?" Carter was getting scared as it dawned on him what she was planning.

"Since I would want someone to spare me the tortures of this mirror, I will spare all who may enter this room by shattering the mirror so that no one else will ever be trapped here." Kat walked over to the night table, picked it up, and brought it to her side of the mirror surface.

All at once, Marista, Leana, and Carter began talking at the same time, begging her not to do anything she would regret. They wanted her to think about it, wait and see if they could work something out. The clown was the only one who was quiet and strangely somber.

Kat stood looking at her best friend for a long time, and then she said, "Goodbye, Carter." With all her strength, she slammed the night table into the mirror surface. Large cracks appeared and spread over the surface. The cracks kept growing and multiplying so that more and more of the mirror's surface cracked, and eventually it became impossible to see into it. Finally, the surface of the mirror fell into a pile of shining glass dust. Where there was once a "magical mirror," there was only the mirror frame and Kat standing in front of the wall. "Kat—you did it! Who knew that just breaking the mirror would set you free?" Carter said excitedly.

The clown raised his hand and said, "I did. That was a secret way out. Only a person who was willing to use the people rule would be able to escape the mirror without using someone to exchange places.

"That is two for two, now. You used the people rule to beat the dunking machine and now the mirror trap. That is most unusual and most disturbing. I am getting tired of your annoying tendency to ruin my fun. I am through playing around with you. I am going to take you to the last two orphans so you can all be together for one final contest where only the winners will be set free." The clown abruptly lifted his right hand, snapped his fingers, and the lights went out.

A FAMILY REUNION

After a brief moment of dizziness, the darkness cleared a bit. The room they had been in was dark, but now they found themselves in a place that was even darker. A lone torch outside of their cell provided the only light they had. "Carter, we are in some kind of a jail cell," Kat observed. Looking out iron bars, the partners saw that all four orphans were together in a similar cell directly across from them.

"How do you like your new accommodations?" the clown asked as he stepped into view. "I apologize that there are no beds or facilities of any kind, but then, you will not need them. You partners are in cell 00 at the far end of the fortress dungeon. All four of the orphan children are across from you in an identical cell: number 0000.

"I love the dungeon; it is my favorite part of the castle. Here is where I have the most fun with my guests, and I have prepared something very special for you."

The partners could hear the two youngest, Rebee and Shawnter, crying. It was clear that being separated from their siblings and suffering torments from the Adversary had traumatized the little ones.

"You know something?" Carter growled. "That stupid clown

costume isn't fooling anybody. Why don't you show yourself in your true form, Adversary?"

In a flash, Carter saw the clown's cruel eyes fill with white-hot rage. "So you knew who I was all along, clever boy. But this is not my true form either," he said as his appearance changed from the evil clown to the image of the Adversary with which they were familiar.

"Since you were foolish enough to ask me to show you my true appearance, I will." The Adversary began to change color. His white robe, hair, and skin turned fiery red. Then his whole body began to grow larger and morph into a monstrous, red, scaly dragon. As the dragon continued to change and shift its form, it grew seven heads. Out of each head, a sharp curved horn appeared. Since the monster had a huge tail and a massive body that was too large to fit into the space, the whole dungeon expanded to accommodate the beast. The heads were rounded with short snouts, and rows of pointed teeth lined very wide mouths. The eyes, in each face, rested under heavy hooded brows and had the same look of hate and cruelty that was present in the human form of the Adversary. Once the transformation was complete, the Adversary lifted all seven of his heads, and he roared with pride in his display of power and might.

The partners were overwhelmed with fear. They felt their knees weaken and their stomachs clinch. The four orphan children crouched down in a back corner of their cell and screamed hysterically. "Please, you are terrifying the little ones. Change back to your human form," Carter pleaded.

All seven heads lowered and peered into the partners' cell. Since the heads were very large, and the cell was rather small, the seven heads more than filled the area directly in front of the bars. The heads stared at the frightened partners, and they flashed their sharp teeth and snapped their jaws at them.

The partners ran to the back of their cell in a useless attempt to move away from the monstrous heads. The cell bars began to bend and stretch inward toward the partners as the heads moved toward them. Carter and Kat found themselves trapped between the back wall of the cell and the bars that were only an inch from their faces.

The dragon's heads were up against the bars. Forked tongues darted out of the large toothy mouths to brush the partners' faces. Some of the heads snorted and sprayed them with dragon mucus.

The hot breath that came from the mouths was so foul that it caused the partners to gag and retch. The dragon's heads remained directly in front of the children's faces for a long time as they squirmed and tried to turn away from the nightmare that had them pinned to the wall.

"Okay, we get it. You're big, nasty, and you like tormenting little children; you're evil and bad to the bone. Now, will you please, resume your human form?" Carter tried to sound brave but failed.

The Adversary returned to his human form in the twinkling of an eye, and the expanded area returned to normal size as well. "What? You do not think I am beautiful?" he asked and then laughed. Glancing over at the orphans' cell—the children were still huddled in a corner crying uncontrollably—he said, "I see I have made quite an impression on the little brats." Then he laughed again.

"If you think that was scary, wait until I tell you what comes next. On second thought, I am not going to tell you about it just yet. I will wait until the orphan brats calm down. They need to be focused when I reveal the final challenge. I will be back when they stop blubbering," he said, and then vanished.

"Carter," said Kat, trembling, "I don't understand. I thought when we got the four children together that our mission would be over. Why are we still here?"

"I don't know. We just have to wait and see what comes next. The children are reunited now, so I guess the only thing left to do is help them escape."

"Help them escape? How are we going to do that? We are locked in a cell with iron bars and no doors. We don't have anything but a flashlight and our bare hands." Kat was starting to sound hysterical as she continued. "We're just two kids ourselves, facing a monster. What possible help can we be to anyone?"

"I know. I know, Kat," said Carter in a calm voice. "We have made it this far using the people rule, a spirit of self sacrifice, and help from the Guardian. We just have to keep our wits about us and trust what we have learned. We need to trust what has worked for us. A few minutes ago, you were willing to trap yourself in a mirror for eternity. Why is your nerve failing you now?"

Kat shrugged and said, "I guess when I was in the mirror, I acted without thinking about what I was in for, but now it's all crashing in on me. Seeing the Adversary's true form was almost more than I could handle. Carter, if we fail now, what will become of us?"

"We are not going to fail. The Adversary is making every effort to impress us because he has failed to deter us from reaching our intended final destination. That's why he left us alone. He's hoping that we will lose our nerve. The waiting and uncertainty are worse than facing what's to come. We need to get a hold of ourselves and try to calm the kids. Just stop for a minute, close your eyes, take a deep breath, and remember how you felt when Guard touched you after Stewborn was killed."

Kat nodded, closed her eyes, took a deep breath, and let it out slowly. After a moment, Carter saw a little smile appear on his best friend's face. Kat opened her eyes and nodded.

"Better?"

"Yes. Thank you, Carter." Kat stepped to the front of the cell and took hold of the bars. She looked across the walkway toward the orphans' cell. She was unable to see them because they were still huddled in the back corner. Their wailing had calmed a bit.

"Carter, let me use the flashlight." Carter handed her the light, and she pointed it into the orphans' cell. Immediately, the children began to scream and cry in fear of the light. Kat quickly turned it off and said, "I'm sorry. That was just me. It won't hurt you. Marista, it's okay. Everything is going to be okay."

The partners could hear Marista trying to clam the younger children. "That was really a stupid move," Kat chided herself. "Marista, I'm sorry about the light. Will you come to the front of your cell and talk to me?"

After several unsuccessful attempts to calm her youngest siblings, Marista said to Leana, "Stay with Shawnter and Rebee."

Marista finally appeared at the bars. "They are terrified, and so am I! What is going to happen to us? I thought you said that you came here to help us. How can you help us when you are just as trapped as we are?"

Kat could hear the fear and disappointment in the girl's voice. "It's true, Marista; we came here to help all of you to get back to Harfet. You have to trust us; we didn't come here alone. A powerful being called the Guardian sent us. He knows our situation, and he has assured us that if we get you all together that we will be able to escape. You are all together now, so there has to be a way out. We just have to be calm and trust that an opportunity will present itself. When it does, we all have to be ready for it. Do you think you can control the little ones?" Kat was not able to see the girl's face clearly in the dim light, but she thought she saw doubt in her gaze. "It's really important, Marista, that you trust us. Can you do that?"

"I will try," is all she said.

"Good. Now you must get the others to calm down and be ready."

As Marista disappeared back into the shadows, Carter said, "I hope she can do it. They have to be ready to do what's needed when it's time to act. Anyway, while we have some time, why don't we search the cell and see if there is a weakness or a secret that we might discover."

"That's a good idea," said Kat. "You take the flashlight and check the walls, and I'll check the bars."

"Yes, ma'am," Carter said with a little salute.

As the partners searched the cell, it appeared that the bars, walls, floor, and ceiling were all made of solid iron. Carter was just about to give up and declare that he had found nothing helpful when he saw a vertical hole in the back wall. It was small, about a half-inch long and a quarter-inch wide. "Kat, come here and see what you make of this."

Kat said, "It looks like a keyhole."

"Maybe, but I cannot make out a door or anything that might open."

Kat ran her hand over the wall. "I'm not sure," she said. "But I think I feel a hair-thin line that could be a door. It may be my imagination, wishful thinking, or a door so snugly fit into the wall that the gap between the door and wall is almost undetectable."

Carter ran his hand over the same area and said, "I don't feel anything." The boy sighed and then looked over at the other cell and said, "I wonder if they have the same type of hole in the back of their cell."

"I'll try and get Marista to check. It could be important." Kat stepped up to the bars and called out, "Marista, we need you to feel the wall in the back of your cell and see if there is a little hole that feels like a keyhole. It should be about a third of the way up from the floor and about a third of the way over from the right wall as you face the rear."

The partners heard a weak, "Very well." After a few moments, the girl reported, "I think I found it. What is it? Is it important?"

Carter called back, "We're not sure. It might be a keyhole of some sort. There is one over here too. Can you stick a little piece of cloth in it to make it easier to locate?"

"Yes. I can tear a piece of my robe off to put in it."

"Good. Now Marista, do you think you can search around your cell and see if you can locate anything else that might be helpful?" Carter asked.

"I will try. It is dark in here. I cannot see much," the girl said sounding doubtful and discouraged.

"I know, Marista, but it's important. Feel around with your hands. Maybe if you can get the others to help you, it will take their minds off our situation and calm them down," Carter suggested.

At first, it did not look like Marista was going to be able to convince the others to leave the meager comfort of their dark corner. But with a little coaxing and a suggestion that maybe they could find a secret way out, they all decided to try. The youngest almost immediately said, "I found something."

"What is it?" Carter asked.

"Shawnter found two poles. They are long, sturdy, and the same size," answered Marista.

"Good work. Keep looking; you might find something else. Anything you find could be important," Carter encouraged.

"Do not waste your time looking for anything else," the Adversary said as he stepped into view and stood between the two cells. "You have everything you need for the final challenge—except for this." The Adversary held up a key. "This key will open both back doors of your cells. I wonder if any of you have noticed the *X* here on the floor," said the Adversary as he put the key down on a red *X* painted on the floor. "This is exactly in the middle between your two cells. The two sticks that the brats found are all you need for one group to get the key. If either group gets the key, use it to open the rear door of your cell. The partners' door opens up to the Dead Forest. The orphans' door opens up to the Adobe Orphanage. The key will only work once, and then it will disappear.

"Now, I realize that this is an easy puzzle for children as clever as Toby and Catherine to figure out, so I have decided to make it more interesting. There will be a time limit and serious consequences for the group that does not escape. Ah, do you hear that?" the Adversary asked as he cupped his ear and leaned slightly toward the dark hallway.

At first, the children heard nothing, but then Kat said, "I hear a humming sound."

"I hear it too," Carter said. "It sounds like a bee swarm."

"Close, Toby, but no cigar." The Adversary sneered.

The three youngest children asked almost at once, "Marista, what is that sound?"

"I do not know, but you have to be brave. Remember, we are going to be okay."

"Perhaps you will be okay, and perhaps not. It depends on how quick you are in solving the challenge. If you do not solve it in time, both groups will die instead of just one. That sound you hear comes from a swarm of fire wasps. They get their name from their venom that makes their stings burn like fire.

I would wish you good luck, but I am counting on none of you getting out in time." The Adversary snapped his fingers. "The wasps are on their way," he said, and then he vanished.

A STICK-KEY SITUATION

"What should we do?" Marista nearly screamed across to the partners.

"Quick! Use a stick, and move the key toward your cell," said Kat.

"I don't think that's going to work," Carter said. "That really would be too easy."

Marista reached out of the bars of her cell with one of the poles. With grunts and straining gasps, she squeaked out, "I cannot do it! I am touching the key, but I cannot get the stick on top or over it to slide it to me."

"Carter," Kat said. "The humming is getting louder; we have to think fast."

"I have it figured out; I know the solution to the puzzle," Carter said. "Marista, I know how we can help you to get the key. You have to toss the other stick over to us."

"But your arms are longer than mine. If I give you a stick, you will get the key and leave us here," the girl said accusingly. The younger children were urging her to keep trying to reach the key.

"Marista, you have to trust us," Kat said pleadingly. "We came here to rescue you, and that's what we intend to do."

408

"You have to hurry; the wasps will be here any minute," Carter urged. "If you throw me a stick, I will use it to push the key closer to you so you can reach it with your stick. I may only be able to push it about an inch closer. It will still be difficult for you to get the key, so you need to hurry, and make sure you have enough time to get it, open the door, and escape."

"I do not believe you. Why would you throw away your lives to help us escape? That makes no sense."

Carter was starting to lose his composure. He called back, "Marista, what choice do you have? You can't reach the key anyway. Didn't I save you from the dunking game?"

"Yes," the girl said weakly.

"Wasn't Kat willing to trap herself in the mirror so that no one else would get trapped there?"

"Yes."

"We have proven ourselves to be worthy of your trust. Now hurry! The wasps are closing in on us. We may only have about two minutes left; you must hurry!"

"Very well, I will throw you the stick, but please do not leave us here," she said pathetically.

"Okay, but be careful, and throw it hard enough to reach us, but not so hard that it hits the bars and bounces off. It could land out of my reach, and then we'll all be done for."

Marista's brother and sisters were pulling on her arm and screaming, "No! No! Do not throw the stick to them. They will leave us here!" Finally, she yelled at them to stop and get back. They moved away, but they were still crying and pleading with her. With a trembling hand, the girl tossed a stick toward the partners' cell. It landed about four feet from the bars and rolled another foot and a half diagonally. This put it well over two feet from the bars.

Carter quickly stooped down and reached out to grab the stick, but his reach was a bit short. Strain as he would, he was not able to touch the stick. "That's great. I cannot reach the stick," he said as he continued to strain.

"Use the flashlight. It should be long enough for you to roll the stick a bit closer," said Kat.

"Yes, that should do it," Carter said as he grabbed the light. "That's got it," Carter said triumphantly. He rolled the stick closer and then grabbed it. He immediately pointed the stick at the key and shoved it another two inches closer to the orphans. Then, he shoved the stick at the key, letting go of it, and it knocked the key another six inches closer to the other cell.

Quickly, Marista moved the key within her reach. The little ones were screaming at her to hurry. The buzzing of the wasps was so loud and ominous that it was causing panic to well up in the girl. "I cannot do it!" she screamed. "There is not enough time; I cannot do it!"

"Yes, you can!" Kat yelled. "You have to focus; the wasps aren't here yet. Go to the keyhole, pull out the cloth you used to mark it, and open the door. You're almost home. Get your brother and sisters to safety; do it *now*!"

"I will try. Oh please, please, I do not want to die!" she said, crying, on the verge of hysteria.

All three of the younger children were screaming and crying as Marista went to the back wall. "I cannot find the keyhole! Where is it? Oh we are going to die; we are all going to die!" the girl shrieked as she frantically tried to locate the keyhole in the dark.

"Stop it! Marista, stop it!" Kat yelled. "We will shine the flashlight over at your cell to help you see."

Carter turned the light on the orphan's cell, and it was bright enough that even the partners could see the bit of cloth on the back wall. Marista quickly pulled the cloth out and with trembling hands tried to insert the key, but she dropped it.

"It's okay, Marista. Just pick it up and calm yourself." Kat almost had to yell to be heard over the intense buzzing of the swarm. It was so close now that the partners could see the dark cloud of pestilence and agonizing death moving toward them. "You can do it. Just close out everything but my voice and concentrate."

The young girl could not help sobbing, but her hand seemed to calm a bit as she finally got the key in the hole. She attempted to turn it one way and then the other, nothing happened. "I cannot get the key to turn!" she said frantically.

The wasp swarm was close enough now that the partners could make out individual forms of the larger fire wasps. It was clear that if Marista did not get the door open in the next fifteen seconds, it would be too late. "Take the key out, turn it over, and try again," Carter suggested.

Marista grabbed the key with both hands to make sure she did not drop it again. She pulled it out, turned it over, and reinserted it. This time when she turned the key, there was a click, the key vanished, and a large section of the back wall disappeared. There was a clear view of the Adobe Orphanage through the doorway. The four children quickly ran out of the cell.

To the partner's surprise, Marista stopped and looked back. For the briefest of moments, they saw in the girl's face wonder and gratitude. Then the section of wall that had disappeared, reappeared. Immediately after, there was a terrible roar of passionate fury and defeat—the worst they had heard yet. The entire dungeon shook with it.

The partners, alone now, faced the swarm as it began to fill their cell. Instinctively, they ran to a back corner. Carter tried to shield Kat with his body as she stood pressed to the corner covering her face with her hands.

The wasps were filling the cell. The smallest wasps were buzzing around the partners' heads and ears while the larger ones attached themselves to Carter's back. The cell was so full of the buzzing mass that it sounded like the hum of a powerful electric generator. Try as he might, Carter could not shield his friend from the swarm. Every inch of body surface, where a wasp could land, was covered. The weight of the creatures on the boy's back, legs, head, face, and arms forced Carter to drop to his knees, leaving Kat fully exposed. Eventually, she too dropped to the ground. They had to keep their eyes closed because gnat-sized wasps covered their eyelids. Even though the wasps covered them, they did not sting. Carter wanted to say something to Kat, but he was afraid that if he opened his mouth that wasps would fly into it. Still, the creatures did not block their breathing.

Suddenly, an unexpected thing happened: the wasps fell into an eerie silence. It was like the calm before a storm. Then they heard the Adversary say, "I have stayed the wasps because I want to savor this moment. You and that stupid Goodman have started a chain reaction that will undo many long years of work. Dearth was my most successful effort in creating an environment of spiritual suffering and want. This was a place where human kindness was the rare exception not the rule. Now you have exposed Dearth to the people rule and selflessness. You have planted the seeds of life in the hearts of hungry souls, and it will spread like wildfire.

"Though it will provide little satisfaction, I will vent my rage upon you. I will personally direct the individual wasps when to sting, so it could take days for you to die. I will play them like keys on a piano, and each sting will raise a piercing scream. Let me see, who will feel a fiery sting first? Yes, the girl will be first because I know that hurting her will pain you, Toby, even more than the stings of the wasps. Shall we begin?" The partners could not see the Adversary as he stood outside their cell and raised his arms like a conductor ready to direct an orchestra. "For our first number, we shall hear *She'll be Screaming Round the Dungeon.*"

Carter was beside himself with panic. The Adversary was correct in saying that the worst pain he could imagine was to hear Kat scream in agony and be helpless to stop it. He could not understand why Guard had not intervened. *He promised that if we succeeded we would meet him in the Dead Forest,* Carter raged inside his head.

The Adversary called out, "Let us begin: and a one...and a two...and a three...Then he brought his right arm down for the downbeat.

THE BATTLE RAGES ON

The weight vanished, and the warmth of the sun fell on Carter's face. He opened his eyes and found himself in the Dead Forest. He sat up and saw Kat sitting next to him.

"Well done! Yes indeed. That was well done," they heard the Guardian say from behind them. Turning around, they realized that they were at the campfire site where they first met Guard. The partners stood up and sat on the same log they sat on that first night, across from Guard. "I am very proud of you. You finished your adventure. You triumphed over the powers of evil that sought to destroy you and keep you from fulfilling the prophecy. The lessons you have learned will serve you well in your life here on Earth, as they did on Dearth. And as I said, before you began your adventure, others will learn from your story."

"Is it true?" Kat asked. "Are we really home?"

"Once you leave the Dead Forest, you will be back in your realm. This place will vanish."

"What about you?" Carter asked. "Will we ever see you again?"

"Perhaps some day we will meet again. You have proven yourselves powerful warriors in the fight against evil. The battle rages in your realm; you must fight the good fight where you live. It is true that there may come a day when a special mission will require your service. If that day comes, we will meet again." The Guardian noticed a look of doubt on Carter's face. "What is it, Carter? What is troubling you?"

"Did we really make a difference?" Carter asked. "I mean, we did learn and grow as people, and we rescued four children. You make it sound like we impacted a world."

"My dear boy, you two children have set in motion something that will completely change Dearth. You brought down the witch of the Valley of the Gods. She was one of the Adversary's favorite servants. You helped break the link between Ev and her sister. This duo accomplished unthinkable atrocities among their people. You discovered the people rule and exposed all those you met to its powerful truth. You made possible a friendship between Houtdec and Casbar in Omagora that, even now, is bearing fruit. But most important, you planted the seeds of selfless love in the hearts of four little orphans who will grow up to be great spiritual champions on the level of Goodman."

"Guard?" Kat asked with a hint of urgency. "What is to keep the Adversary from seeking to destroy the orphans or steal them away again?"

"The Adversary must play by the same rules I do. He cannot force anyone to do anything against his or her will. He will try, as he did with you, to lead them down a path of destruction, but they will have me to guard them as you did. No, I have faith that the prophecy will be fulfilled, and Dearth will want no more." Guard beamed and added, "The impact of what you have done has already started to reshape the land. It is starting to rain in the Plane of the Dark Earth! Glimmers of sunshine are breaking through the cloud cover over the Doom Marsh. I do not have to tell you that light is death to the marsh."

"And what about Dark Beard? Did he survive the witch?"

The Guardian chuckled and said, "Ah yes, whatever happened to Dark Beard? You do not have to worry about him. He is headed for the northern kingdoms on his own quest."

Before the Guardian could say more, the Adversary stepped out from behind a tree and raged, "There you are! I thought I might find you here."

The Guardian stood up and confronted the Adversary. "What are you doing here? You have been bested, and now it is time for you to go away."

"*No!* Those who have destroyed my work must pay!" he shouted as he began to morph into his true form of the seven-headed dragon.

The Guardian began to change into a beautiful being glowing with golden light, and powerful wings growing out of his back. A fiery, two-edged sword appeared in his right hand. He turned to the partners and said, "Run! Return to your homes. The battle rages on. I will fight on my plane of existence as you fight on yours. Now go, and do not look back until you are out of the Dead Forest!"

The last thing that the partners saw before they ran for their lives was the Adversary swooping toward them and the Guardian rising to block him. Sounds of battle filled their ears as they ran. They heard the Adversary roaring as he did in the stronghold's dungeon. There were sounds of thunder and shouts of battle.

When the partners' feet touched ground that was not part of the Dead Forest, they heard a huge explosion and saw a flash of light that, even though they were still running and looking away from the battle, momentarily blinded them. After that, all was quiet.

The children looked over their shoulders and saw that the Dead Forest was gone. Nothing about the landscape even hinted that the Dead Forest had ever existed. In the days that followed, the partners tried to find the Dead Forest just because they were curious to see if they could; nevertheless, it was gone.

When the two arrived home, it was just as the Guardian had promised. Even though several days had passed for the partners, to their parents they had only been gone a couple of hours. Because of this time difference, the show of emotion their children lavished upon them was a bit confusing to the parents. Carter's mother commented, "My goodness, Toby, you would think you had been gone a month the way you are acting. What has gotten into you anyway?"

Carter's response was, "I'm just glad to see you guys. What's for dinner, Mom? I'm starving."

When Kat saw her mother, she tried to hide her tears of joy as she hugged her. Her mother responded with, "What is it, honey? Did something happen when you were out?"

Kat sniffed and said, "It's nothing, Mom. I just got something in my eye, that's all."

LIVE

---

listen|imagine|view|experience

AUDIO BOOK DOWNLOAD INCLUDED WITH THIS BOOK!

In your hands you hold a complete digital entertainment package. Besides purchasing the paper version of this book, this book includes a free download of the audio version of this book. Simply use the code listed below when visiting our website. Once downloaded to your computer, you can listen to the book through your computer's speakers, burn it to an audio CD or save the file to your portable music device (such as Apple's popular iPod) and listen on the go!

How to get your free audio book digital download:

1. Visit www.tatepublishing.com and click on the e|LIVE logo on the home page.
2. Enter the following coupon code:
   a14e-dc6a-0e6a-c0a1-deaa-b34a-5d4f-51c7
3. Download the audio book from your e|LIVE digital locker and begin enjoying your new digital entertainment package today!

CPSIA information can be obtained
at www.ICGtesting.com
Printed in the USA
FSOW01n0341080716
22474FS

9 781615 664368